P9-ASI-767

4/07   Wells

HIDE

**Center Point
Large Print**

**This Large Print Book carries the
Seal of Approval of N.A.V.H.**

HIDE

Lisa Gardner

CENTER POINT PUBLISHING
THORNDIKE, MAINE

This Center Point Large Print edition
is published in the year 2007 by arrangement with
The Bantam Dell Publishing Group,
a division of Random House, Inc.

Copyright © 2007 by Lisa Gardner, Inc.

All rights reserved.

The text of this Large Print edition is unabridged. In other
aspects, this book may vary from the original edition.
Printed in the United States of America.
Set in 16-point Times New Roman type.

ISBN-10: 1-58547-924-1
ISBN-13: 978-1-58547-924-5

Library of Congress Cataloging-in-Publication Data

Gardner, Lisa.
    Hide / Lisa Gardner.--Center Point large print ed.
       p. cm.
    ISBN-13: 978-1-58547-924-5 (lib. bdg. : alk. paper)
    1. Young women--Massachusetts--Boston--Fiction. 2. Police--Massachusetts--
Boston--Fiction. 3. Large type books. I. Title.

PS3557.A7132H53 2007b
813'.54--dc22

2006031071

HIDE

1

MY FATHER EXPLAINED it to me the first time when I was seven years old: The world is a system. School is a system. Neighborhoods are a system. Towns, governments, any large group of people. For that matter, the human body is a system, enabled by smaller, biological subsystems.

Criminal justice, definitely a system. The Catholic Church—don't get him started. Then there's organized sports, the United Nations, and of course, the Miss America Pageant.

"You don't have to like the system," he lectured me. "You don't have to believe in it or agree with it. But you must understand it. If you can understand the system, you will survive."

A family is a system.

I'd come home from school that afternoon to discover both of my parents standing in our front room. My father, a professor of mathematics at MIT, was rarely home before seven. Now, however, he stood next to my mother's prized floral sofa, with five suitcases stacked neatly by his feet. My mother was crying. When I opened the front door, she turned away as if to shield her face, but I could still see her shoulders shaking.

Both of my parents were wearing heavy wool coats, which seemed odd, given the relatively warm October afternoon.

My father spoke first: "You need to go into your room. Pick two things. Any two things you want. But hurry, Annabelle; we don't have much time."

My mother's shoulders shook harder. I set down my backpack. I retreated to my room, where I stared at my little pink-and-green painted space.

Of all the moments in my past, this is the one I would most like to have back. Three minutes in the bedroom of my youth. Fingers skimming over my sticker-plastered desk, skipping over framed photos of my grandparents, hopscotching past my engraved silver-plated brush and oversize hand mirror. I bypassed my books. Didn't even consider my marble collection or stash of kindergarten art. I remember making a positively agonizing choice between my favorite stuffed dog and my newest treasure, a bridal-dressed Barbie. I went with my dog, Boomer, then grabbed my cherished baby blankie, dark pink flannel with a light pink satin trim.

Not my diary. Not my stash of silly, doodle-covered notes from my best friend, Dori Petracelli. Not even my baby album, which would've at least given me photos of my mother for all the years to come. I was a young, frightened child, and I behaved childishly.

I think my father knew what I would choose. I think he saw it all coming, even back then.

I returned to our family room. My father was out-side, loading the car. My mom had her hands wrapped around the pillar that divided the family room from the eat-in kitchen. For a minute, I didn't think she'd

8

let go. She would take a stand, demand that my father stop this foolishness.

Instead, she reached out and stroked my long dark hair. "I love you so much." She grabbed me, hugging me fiercely, cheeks wet against the top of my head. The next moment, she pushed me away, wiping briskly at her face.

"Outside, honey. Your father's right—we have to be quick."

I followed my mother to the car, Boomer under my arm, blankie clutched in both hands. We took our usual places—my father in the driver's seat, my mother riding shotgun, me in the back.

My father backed our little Honda out of the drive. Yellow and orange leaves swirled down from the beech tree, dancing outside the car window. I spread my fingers against the glass as if I could touch them.

"Wave at the neighbors," my father instructed. "Pretend everything is normal."

That's the last we ever saw of our little oak-dotted cul-de-sac.

A family is a system.

We drove to Tampa. My mother had always wanted to see Florida, my father explained. Wouldn't it be nice to live amid palm trees and white sandy beaches after so many New England winters? Since my mother had chosen our location, my father had picked our names. I would now be called Sally. My father was Anthony and my mother Claire. Isn't this fun? A new town and a new name. What a grand adventure.

I had nightmares in the beginning. Terrible, terrible dreams where I would wake up screaming, "I saw something, I saw something!"

"It's only a dream," my father would attempt to soothe me, stroking my back.

"But I'm scared!"

"Hush. You're too young to know what scared is. That's what daddies are for."

We didn't live amid palm trees and white sandy beaches. My parents never spoke of it, but as an adult looking back, I realize now that a Ph.D. in mathematics couldn't very well pick up where he left off, especially under an assumed identity. Instead, my father got a job driving taxis. I loved his new job. It meant he was home most of the day, and it seemed glamorous to be picked up from school in my own personal cab.

The new school was bigger than my old one. Tougher. I think I made friends, though I don't remember many specifics about our Florida days. I have more a general sense of a surreal time and place, where my afternoons were spent being drilled in self-defense for first-graders and even my parents seemed foreign to me.

My father, constantly buzzing around our one-bedroom apartment. "What'd you say, Sally? Let's decorate a palm tree for Christmas! Yes, sir, we're having fun now!" My mother, humming absently as she painted our family room a bright shade of coral, giggling as she bought a swimsuit in November, seeming genuinely intrigued as she learned to cook different kinds of flaky white fish.

I think my parents were happy in Florida. Or at least determined. My mother decorated our apartment. My father resumed his hobby of sketching. On the nights he didn't work, my mother would pose for him beside the window, and I would lie on the couch, content to watch my father's deft strokes as he captured my mother's teasing smile in a small charcoal sketch.

Until the day I came home from school to find suitcases packed, faces grim. No need to ask this time. I went into my room on my own. Grabbed Boomer. Found my blankie. Then retreated to the car and climbed in the back.

It was a long time before anyone said a word.

A family is a system.

To this day, I don't know how many cities we lived in. Or how many names I assumed. My childhood became a blur of new faces, new towns, and the same old suitcases. We would arrive, find the cheapest one-bedroom apartment. My father would set out the next day, always coming home with some kind of job—photo developer, McDonald's manager, salesclerk. My mother would unpack our meager belongings. I would be shuffled off to school.

I know I stopped talking as much. I know my mom did, too.

Only my father remained relentlessly cheerful. "Phoenix! I've always wanted to experience the desert. Cincinnati! Now, this is my kind of town. St. Louis! This will be the place for us!"

I don't remember suffering any more nightmares. They simply went away or were pushed aside by more pressing concerns. The afternoons I came home and found my mother passed out on the sofa. The crash courses in cooking because she could no longer stand up. Brewing coffee and forcing it down her throat. Raiding her purse for money so I could buy groceries before my father returned from work.

I want to believe he had to know, but to this day I'm not sure. It seemed for my mother and me at least, the more we took on other names, the more we gave away of ourselves. Until we became silent, ethereal shadows following in my father's blustery wake.

She made it until I was fourteen. Kansas City. We'd lasted nine months. My father had risen to manager in the automotive department of Sears. I was thinking of going to my first dance.

I came home. My mother—Stella, she was called then—was facedown on the sofa. This time no amount of shaking woke her up. I have a vague memory of racing across the hall. Of banging on our neighbor's door.

"My mother, my mother, my mother!" I screamed. And poor Mrs. Torres, who'd never been granted a smile or wave from any of us, threw open her door, bustled across the hall, and hands flying to her suddenly wet eyes, declared my mother dead.

Cops came. EMTs. I watched them remove her

body. Saw the empty orange prescription bottle slip out of her pocket. One of the officers picked it up. He gave me a pitying look.

"Someone we should call?"

"My father will be home soon."

He left me with Mrs. Torres. We sat in her apartment, with its rich smells of jalapeño peppers and corn tamales. I admired the brightly striped curtains she had hanging on her windows and the bold floral pillows covering her worn brown sofa. I wondered what it would be like to have a real home again.

My father arrived. Thanked Mrs. Torres profusely. Ushered me away.

"You understand we can't tell them anything?" he kept saying over and over again, once we were safely tucked back inside our apartment. "You understand we have to be very careful? I don't want you saying a word, Cindy. Not one word. This is all very, very tricky."

When the cops returned, he did the talking. I heated up chicken noodle soup in the tiny kitchenette. I wasn't really hungry. I just wanted our apartment to smell like Mrs. Torres's apartment. I wanted my mom to be back home.

I found my father crying later. Curled up on the sofa, holding my mother's tattered pink robe. He couldn't stop. He sobbed and sobbed and sobbed.

That was the first night my father slept in my bed. I know what you're thinking, but it wasn't like that.

A family is a system.

13

We waited three months for my mother's body. The state wanted an autopsy. I never did understand it all. But one day we had my mom back. We accompanied her from the morgue's office to the funeral home. She was put in a box labeled with someone else's name, then sent into the fire.

My father purchased two small glass vials that dangled from chains. One for him. One for me.

"This way," he said, "she can always be close to our hearts."

Leslie Ann Granger. That was my mother's real name. Leslie Ann Granger. My father filled the vials with ashes, and we put them around our necks. The rest of her, we turned loose into the wind.

Why buy a tombstone that would only cement a lie?

We returned to the apartment, and this time my father didn't have to ask; I had packed our suitcases three months earlier. No Boomer and blankie this time. I had placed them in my mother's wooden box and sent them with her into the flames.

Once your mother is dead, it is time to be done with childish things.

I chose the name Sienna. My father would be Billy Bob, but I would allow him to use B.B. He rolled his eyes but played along. Since I'd done the honors with the names, he chose the city. We headed for Seattle; my father had always wanted to see the West Coast.

We did better in Seattle, each in our own way. My

father returned to Sears and, without ever disclosing that he'd worked at one before, was taken to be a complete natural who flew up the managerial ranks. I enrolled in yet another overcrowded, underfunded public school, where I disappeared into the nameless, faceless B-average masses.

I also committed my first act of rebellion: I joined a church.

The small Congregational church existed one block from our home. I walked by it every day to and from school. One day, I poked my head in. The second day, I took a seat. The third day, I found myself talking to the reverend.

Will God let you into Heaven, I wanted to know, if you were buried under the wrong name?

I talked to the reverend for a long time that afternoon. He had bottle-thick glasses. Sparse gray hair. A kind smile. When I got home, it was after six, my father was waiting, and there was no food on the table.

"Where were you?" he demanded.

"I got held late—"

"Do you know how worried I've been?"

"I missed the bus. I was talking to a teacher about a homework assignment. I'm . . . I had to walk all the way home. I didn't want to bother you at work." I was babbling, my cheeks flushed, not sounding anything like myself.

My father frowned at me for a long time. "You can always call me," he said abruptly. "We're in this together, kiddo."

He ruffled my hair.

I missed my mother.

Then I walked into the kitchen and started the tuna casserole.

Lying, I've discovered, is as addictive as any drug. Next thing I knew, I'd told my father I'd joined the debate team. This, of course, gave me any number of afternoons I could spend at the church, listening to the choir practice, talking to the reverend, simply absorbing the space.

I'd always had long dark hair. My mother used to braid it for me when I was a child. As an adolescent, however, I had relegated it to an impenetrable curtain I let hang over my face. One day, I decided my hair was blocking the true beauty of the stained glass, so I walked to the corner barbershop and had it chopped off.

My father didn't speak to me for a week.

And I discovered, sitting in my church, watching my neighbors come and go, that my oversize sweatshirts were too drab, my baggy jeans ill-fitting. I liked people in bright colors. I liked the way it brought attention to their faces and made you notice their smiles. These people looked happy. Normal. Loving. I bet there wasn't a three-second delay every time someone asked them their name.

So I bought new clothes. For the debate team. And I started spending every Monday night at the soup kitchen—school requirement, I told my father. Everyone's got to fulfill so many hours of community service. There happened to be a nice young man who also volunteered there. Brown hair. Brown eyes. Matt Fisher.

Matt took me to the movies. I don't remember what was playing. I was aware of his hand on my shoulder, the sweaty feel of my own palms, the hitch to my breath. After the movies, we went for ice cream. It was raining. He held his coat over my head.

And then, tucked inside his cologne-scented jacket, he gave me my first kiss.

I floated home. Arms wrapped around my waist. Dreamy smile upon my face.

My father greeted me at the front door. Five suitcases loomed behind him.

"I know what you've been doing!" he declared.

"Shhhh," I said, and put a finger to his lips. "Shhhh."

I danced past my stunned father. I drifted into my tiny, windowless room. And for eight hours I lay on my bed and let myself be happy.

I still wonder about Matt Fisher sometimes. Is he married now? Has two-point-two kids? Does he ever tell stories about the craziest girl he ever knew? Kissed her one night. Never saw her again.

My father was gone when I got up in the morning. He returned around twelve, slapping the fake ID into my hand.

"And I don't want to hear it about the names," he said as I arched a brow at my new identity as Tanya Nelson, daughter of Michael. "Trying to get paperwork at a moment's notice already set me back two grand."

"But you picked the names."

"They were all the guy could give me."

"But you brought home the names," I insisted.

"Fine, fine, whatever."

He already had a suitcase in each hand. I stood firm, arms crossed, face implacable. "You picked the names, I pick the city."

"Once we're in the car."

"Boston," I said.

His eyes went wide. I could tell he wanted to argue. But rules are rules.

A family is a system.

When you have spent your life running from the Bad Thing, you have to wonder what it will feel like one day when it finally catches you. I guess my father never had to know.

The cops said he stepped off the curb and the speeding taxi killed him instantly. Sent his body soaring twenty feet through the air. His forehead connected with a metal lamppost, caving in his face.

I was twenty-two. Finally done slogging through an endless procession of schools. I worked at Starbucks. I walked a lot. I saved up money for a sewing machine. I started my own business, making custom-designed window treatments and matching throw pillows.

I liked Boston. Returning to the city of my youth

had not left me paralyzed with fear. Quite the opposite, in fact. I felt safe amid the constantly moving masses. I enjoyed strolling through the Public Garden, window-shopping on Newbury Street. I even liked the return of fall, where the days became oak-scented and the nights cool. I found an impossibly small apartment in the North End where I could walk to Mike's and eat fresh cannolis any time I wanted. I hung curtains. I got a dog. I even learned to cook corn tamales. While at night I stood at my barred fifth-story window, cradling my mother's ashes in the palm of my hand and watching the nameless strangers pass below.

I told myself I was an adult now. I told myself I had nothing left to fear. My father had directed my past. But I owned my future and I would not spend it running anymore. I had picked Boston for a reason, and I was here to stay.

Then one day it all came together. I picked up the *Boston Herald* and read it on the front page: Twenty-five years later, I'd finally been found dead.

2

PHONE RINGING.

He rolled over. Grabbed a pillow. Stuffed it over his ear.

Phone ringing.

He threw down the pillow, yanked up the covers instead.

Phone ringing.

Groan. He grudgingly peeled open one eye. Two thirty-two a.m. "Frickin', frickin', frickin . . ." He slapped out a hand, fumbled with the receiver, and dragged the phone to his ear. "What?"

"Cheerful as always, I see."

Bobby Dodge, Massachusetts's newest state police detective, groaned louder. "It's only my second day. You can't tell me I'm being called out my second day. Hey." His brain cells belatedly kicked to life. "Wait a sec—"

"Know the former mental hospital in Mattapan?" Boston Detective D.D. Warren asked over the line.

"Why?"

"Got a scene."

"You mean *BPD* has a scene. Good for you. I'm going back to sleep."

"Be here in thirty."

"D.D. . . ." Bobby dragged himself to sitting, awake now in spite of himself and not feeling amused. He and D.D. went way back, but two-thirty in the morning was two-thirty in the morning. "You and your friends want to harass a rookie, pick on your own department. I'm too old for this shit."

"You need to see this," she said simply.

"See what?"

"Thirty minutes, Bobby. Don't turn on the radio. Don't listen to the scanner. I need you to view it clean slate." There was a pause. More quietly, she added, "Bobby, keep it tight. This one's gonna be ugly." And then she was gone.

• • •

Bobby Dodge was no stranger to being called out of bed. He'd served nearly eight years as a police sniper with the Massachusetts State Police Special Tactics and Operations Team, on call twenty-four/seven, and inevitably activated most weekends and major holidays. Hadn't bothered him at the time. He'd enjoyed the challenge, thrived on being part of an elite team.

Two years ago, however, his career had derailed. Bobby hadn't just been called out to a scene; he'd shot a man. The department ultimately declared it justifiable use of deadly force, but nothing had felt the same. Six months ago, when he submitted his resignation from the STOP team, no one had argued. And more recently, when he'd passed the detectives' exam, everyone had been in agreement: Bobby's career could use a fresh start.

So here he was, a two-day-old Homicide detective, already assigned half a dozen active but not urgent cases, just enough to get his feet wet. Once he proved he wasn't a complete and utter moron, they might actually let him lead an investigation. Or he could always hope to catch a case, be the lucky on-call suit who was roused out of bed for a major incident. Detectives liked to joke that homicides only occurred at 3:05 a.m. or 4:50 p.m. You know, just in time for the day shift to start early and last all night.

Midnight phone calls were definitely part of the job. Except those phone calls should be coming from another state police officer, not a Boston detective.

21

Bobby frowned again, trying to puzzle this one out. As a general rule, Boston detectives loathed inviting state suits to their parties. Furthermore, if a BPD detective honestly did think she might need state expertise, her commanding officer would contact Bobby's commanding officer, with everyone operating with all the openness and trust you would expect from such an arranged marriage.

But D.D. had called him directly. Which led Bobby to theorize, as he dragged on his pants, struggled into a long-sleeved shirt, and splashed water on his face, that D.D. wasn't looking for state help. She was looking for *his* help.

And that made Bobby suspicious.

Last stop in front of his dresser now, operating by the glow of the night-light. He found his detective's shield, his pager, his Glock .40, and—the weapon prized most highly by the working detective—his Sony mini-recorder. Bobby glanced at his watch.

D.D. had wanted him there in thirty. He'd make it in twenty-five. Which gave him five extra minutes to figure out what the hell was going on.

Mattapan was a straight shot down I-93 from Bobby's triple-decker in South Boston. Three to five a.m. were probably the only two hours a day 93 wasn't a bloated snake of vehicles, so Bobby made good time.

He took the Granite Avenue exit and headed left down Gallivan Boulevard, merging onto Morton Street. He pulled up next to an old Chevy at a stoplight. The two occupants, young black males, gave his Crown Vic a knowing look. They pinned him with their best dead-man's stare. Bobby responded with a cheery wave of his own. The instant the light turned green, the kids made a hard right and sped away in disgust.

Just another glorious moment in community policing.

Strip malls gave way to housing. Bobby passed side streets choked with rows of triple-deckers, each building looking more tired and dilapidated than the last. Huge sections of Boston had been revitalized in the past few years, housing projects giving way to luxury condos on the waterfront. Abandoned wharfs becoming convention centers. The whole city being strategically and cosmetically rearranged to fit the vagaries of the Big Dig.

Some neighborhoods had won. Mattapan obviously had not.

Another light. Bobby slowed, glanced at his watch. Eight minutes to ETA. He swung his car left, looping around Mt. Hope Cemetery. From this angle, he could peer out his side window as the enormous no-man's-land that was Boston State Mental Hospital finally came into view.

At one hundred and seventy acres of lushly wooded inner-city green space, the Boston State Mental Hos-pital was currently the most hotly contested develop-ment site in the state. It was also, as former home to a century-old lunatic asylum, one of the spookiest damn places around.

Two dilapidated brick buildings perched on top of the hill, winking down at the population with windows gone crazy with shattered glass. Huge overgrown oaks and beeches clawed at the night sky, bare limbs forming silhouettes of gnarled hands.

Story went that the hospital was built in the middle of forested grounds to provide a "serene" setting for the patients. Several decades of overcrowded buildings, strange midnight screams, and two violent murders later, the locals still talked of lights that randomly came on the middle of the ruins, of spine-tingling moans that whispered from beneath the crumbling piles of brick, of flickering silhouettes spotted among the trees.

So far, none of the tales had frightened off the developers. The Audubon Society had secured one corner of the property, turning it into a popular nature preserve. Major construction was currently under way on a brand-new lab for UMass, while Mattapan buzzed with rumors of public housing, or maybe a new high school.

Progress happened. Even to haunted mental institutions.

Bobby turned around the far corner of the cemetery and finally spotted the party. There, in the left-hand corner of the site: Giant beams of light burst through the skeletal beech trees, pushing against the dense, moonless night. More lights, tiny pinpricks of red and blue, zigzagging through the trees as additional police cars sped up the winding road toward one corner of the property. He waited to see the outline of the former hospital, a relatively small, three-story ruin, come into view, but the patrol cars veered away, heading deeper into the woods instead.

D.D. hadn't been lying. BPD had a scene, and judging by the traffic, it was a big one.

Bobby finished his loop of the cemetery. One minute to ETA, he passed through the yawning black gate and headed for the ruins on the hill.

He came to the first patrol officer almost immediately. The BPD cop was standing in the middle of the road, wearing an orange safety vest and armed with a high-beam flashlight. Kid looked barely old enough to shave. He arranged his face into a fine scowl, however, as he scrutinized Bobby's shield, then grunted suspiciously when he realized Bobby was with the state police.

"Sure you got the right place?" Kid asked.

"Dunno. I plugged 'crime scene' into MapQuest and this is what it spit out."

Kid regarded him blankly. Bobby sighed. "Got a personal invite from Detective Warren. If you got a problem, take it up with her."

"You mean Sergeant Warren?"

"Sergeant? Well, well, well."

Kid slapped Bobby's creds back into his hand. Bobby headed up the hill.

The first abandoned building appeared on his left, multipaned windows winking back twin reflections of his headlights. The brick structure sagged on its foundation, front doors padlocked shut, roof disintegrated from the inside out.

Bobby took a right, passing a second structure, which was smaller, and in even greater disrepair. Cars were stacking up roadside now, parked bumper-to-bumper as detectives' vehicles, ME's van, and crime-scene technicians all vied for space.

The spotlights beckoned farther out, however. A distant glow in the shrouded woods. Bobby could just hear the hum of the generator, brought in on the crime-scene van to power the party. Apparently, he had a hike ahead of him.

He parked in an overgrown field next to three patrol cars. Grabbed a flashlight, paper, and pen. Then, on second thought, a warmer jacket.

The November night was cool, down in the forties, and frosted with a light mist. No one was around, but the beam of his flashlight illuminated the trampled path blazed by the death investigators who'd come before him. His boots made heavy tromping sounds as he went.

He could still hear the generator, but no voices yet. He ducked beneath some bushes, feeling the earth grow marshy beneath his feet before firming up again. He passed a small clearing, noticed a refuse pile—rotting wood, bricks, some plastic buckets. Illegal dumping had been a problem on the ground for years, but most of that was by the fence line. This was too deep in. Probably leftovers from the asylum itself, or maybe one of the recent building projects. Old, new, he couldn't tell in this kind of light.

Noise grew louder, the hum of the generator building to a dull roar. He ducked his head into the collar of his jacket, shielding his ears. As a ten-year veteran patrol officer, Bobby had attended his fair share of crime scenes. He knew the noise. He knew the smell.

But this was his first scene as a bona fide detective. He thought that's why it felt so different. Then he cleared another line of trees and came to an abrupt halt.

Guys. Everywhere. Most in suits, probably fifteen, eighteen detectives and easily a dozen uniforms. Then there were the men with the graying hair in the thick woolen overcoats. Senior officers, most of whom Bobby recognized from various retirement parties for other big guns. He spotted a photographer, four crime-scene techs. Finally a lone female—if memory served she was an ADA, Assistant District Attorney.

A lot of people, particularly given Boston's long-standing policy of demanding a written report from anyone who entered a crime scene. That had a tendency to keep gawking patrol officers out and, even more important, the brass away.

But everyone was here tonight, pacing small circles in the glow of the blazing spotlights, stomping their feet for warmth. Ground zero appeared to be the blue awning erected toward the back of the clearing. But from this angle Bobby still couldn't see any signs of remains or evidence of a crime scene even beneath the protective cover of the tarp.

He saw a field, a tent, and a lot of very quiet death investigators.

It made the hairs rise up on the back of his neck.

A rustling sound came from his left. Bobby turned to see two people entering the clearing from a second path. At front was a middle-aged woman in full Tyvek, followed by a younger man, her assistant. Bobby recognized the woman immediately. Christie Callahan from the OCME—Office of the Chief Medical Examiner. Callahan was the designated forensic anthropologist.

"Ah shit."

More movement. D.D. had magically emerged from beneath the blue awning. Bobby's gaze went from her pale, carefully composed features to her Tyvek-covered clothes to the inky darkness behind her.

"Ah shit," he muttered again, but it was too late.

D.D. headed straight for him.

"Thanks for coming," she said. They shared an awkward moment, both of them trying to figure out if they should shake hands, peck cheeks, something. D.D. finally stuck her hands behind her and that settled matters. They would be professional acquaintances.

"Wouldn't want to disappoint a sergeant," Bobby drawled.

D.D. flashed a tight smile at the acknowledgment of her new title, but didn't comment; now was not the time nor place.

28

"Photographer's already done the first round of shooting," she said briskly. "We're waiting for the videographer to wrap up, then you can go down."

"Down?"

"Scene is subterranean, entrance beneath the awning. Don't worry; we got a ladder in place, so it's not hard to access."

Bobby took a moment to let that sink in. "How big?"

"Chamber is approximately six by ten. We're holding it to three people max, or you can't move around."

"Who found it?"

"Kids. Discovered it last night, I guess, while engaged in some recreational drinking and/or other hobbies. Thought it was cool enough to return tonight with a flashlight. They won't do that again."

"Are they still around?"

"Nah. EMTs gave them sedatives and took them away. It's for the best. They were useless to us."

"Lot of suits," Bobby commented, eyeing the area around them.

"Yeah."

"Lead detective?"

Her chin came up. "I'm the lucky duck."

"Sorry, D.D."

She grimaced, her face bleaker now that it was just the two of them. "Yeah, no shit."

The sound of a throat clearing came from behind them. "Sergeant?"

The videographer had emerged from beneath the

tarp and was waiting for D.D.'s acknowledgment.

"We'll shoot again in intervals," D.D. told the videographer, turning back toward the assembled masses. "Around once an hour to keep things up-to-date. You can grab a cup of coffee if you'd like, there's a thermos in the van. But keep close, Gino. Just in case."

The officer nodded, then headed for the van where the generator thundered away.

"All right, Bobby. We're up."

She started walking without waiting to see if he'd follow.

Beneath the blue awning, Bobby found a pile of Tyvek coveralls plus shoe booties and hairnets. He pulled the papery material over the top of his clothes, while D.D. exchanged her soiled booties for a fresh pair. There were two eye-and-snout masks lying next to the coveralls. D.D. didn't take one, so neither did he.

"I'll go first," D.D. said. "I'll yell 'Clear' when I hit the bottom, then it's your turn."

She gestured toward the back and Bobby caught the faint glow coming from a roughly two-by-two-foot opening in the ground. The top of a metal ladder pro-truded above the earthen lip. It gave him a strange feeling of déjà vu, as if he should know exactly what he was seeing.

And then, in the next instant, he got it; he knew why D.D. had called him. And he knew what he would see when he went down into the pit.

D.D. brushed his shoulder with her fingertips. The touch shocked him. He flinched; she immediately pulled away. Her blue eyes were somber, too large in her pale face.

"See you in five, Bobby," she said quietly.

She disappeared down the ladder.

Two seconds later, he heard her voice again: "All clear."

Bobby descended into the abyss.

3

IT WASN'T DARK. Spotlights had been placed in the corner, moveable light strips hung from the ceiling; crime-scene technicians needed bright lights for their laborious work.

Bobby kept his gaze focused in front of him, breathing shallowly through his mouth and processing the scene in small bits.

The chamber was deep, at least six feet tall; it easily cleared the top of his head. Wide enough for three people to stand shoulder to shoulder, it loomed ahead of him for nearly two full body lengths. Not a random sinkhole, he thought immediately, but something intentionally and painstakingly made.

The temperature was cool, but not cold. It reminded him of caves he'd once visited in Virginia; the air a constant fifty-five degrees, like a walk-in refrigerator.

Smell, not as bad as he had feared. Earthy, laced with the faintest odor of decay. Whatever had happened here, it was almost done now, hence the presence of the forensic anthropologist.

He touched one earthen wall with his gloved hand. It felt hard-packed, lightly ridged. Not bumpy enough to have been dug with a shovel; space was probably too big for that kind of labor anyway. He would guess the cavern had originally been dug with a backhoe. Maybe a culvert that had been ingeniously reengineered with another purpose in mind.

He moved ahead two feet, came to the first support beam, an old, splintering two-by-four. It formed part of a crude buttress arching over the room. A second buttress appeared three feet after the first.

He explored the ceiling with his fingertips. Not dirt, but plywood.

D.D. caught his motion. "Whole ceiling's wood," she supplied. "Topped with dirt and debris except for the opening, where he left an exposed wooden panel he could plop on and off. When we first got here, it looked like random construction debris lying in the middle of an overgrown field. You'd never guess . . . You'd never know . . ." She sighed, looked down, then seemed to try to shake herself out of it.

Bobby nodded curtly. The space was fairly clean, spartanly furnished: an old five-gallon bucket placed next to the ladder, lettering so faded with age, only dim shadows remained; a folded-up metal chair, corners laced with rust, propped against the left-hand wall; a metal shelving unit, spanning the length of the far wall, covered in bamboo blinds on the verge of disintegration.

"Original ladder?" he asked.

"Metal chain link," D.D. answered. "We've already bagged it as evidence."

"Plywood cover obscuring the opening, you said? Find any good sticks around?"

"One approximately three feet in length and an inch and a half thick. Bark worn off. Props up the plywood cover about as you'd expect."

"And the shelves?" He took a step toward them.

"Not yet," D.D. spoke up sharply.

He concealed his surprise with a shrug, then turned to face her; it was her party after all.

"I don't see many evidence placards," he said at last.

"It's that clean. It's like the subject closed it up. He used it. For a while, I'm willing to bet, then one day he simply moved on."

Bobby studied her intently, but she didn't elaborate.

"Feels old," he commented.

"Abandoned," D.D. specified.

"Got a date?"

"Nothing scientific. We'll have to wait for Christie's report."

He waited again, but once more she refused to provide additional information.

"Yeah, okay," he said after a moment. "It looks like his work. You and I only have secondhand details, though. Have you contacted the detectives who worked the original scene?"

She shook her head. "I've been here since midnight; haven't had a chance to check the old case file yet.

That's a lot of years back, though. Whichever officers handled it, they're bound to be retired by now."

"November eighteen, 1980," Bobby provided softly.

D.D. got a tight look around her mouth. "Knew you'd remember," she murmured grimly. She straightened her shoulders. "What else?"

"That pit was smaller, four by six. I don't recall any mention of support beams in the police report. I think it's safe to say it was less sophisticated than this one. Jesus. Reading about it still isn't the same as seeing it. Jesus."

He touched the wall again, feeling the hard-packed earth. Twelve-year-old Catherine Gagnon had spent nearly a month in that first earthen prison, living in a timeless black void interrupted only by visits from her captor, Richard Umbrio, who had held her as his own personal sex slave. Hunters had found her by accident shortly before Thanksgiving, when they had tapped on the plywood cover and been startled to hear faint cries below. Catherine had been saved; Umbrio sent to prison.

The story should've ended there, but it didn't.

"I don't remember any mention of other victims at Umbrio's trial," D.D. was saying now.

"No."

"Doesn't mean he hadn't done it before, though."

"No."

"She could've been his seventh victim, eighth, ninth, tenth. He wasn't the type to talk, so anything's possible."

"Sure. Anything's possible." He understood what

34

D.D. left unsaid. *And it's not like they could ask.* Umbrio had died two years ago, shot by Catherine Gagnon, under circumstances that had been the true death knell to Bobby's STOP career. Funny how some crimes just went on and on and on, even decades later.

Bobby's gaze returned to the covered shelves, which he noticed D.D. was still avoiding. D.D. hadn't called him at two in the morning to look at a subterranean chamber. BPD hadn't issued red-ball deployment for a nearly empty pit.

"D.D.?" he asked quietly.

She finally nodded. "Might as well see it for yourself. These are the ones, Bobby, who didn't get saved. These are the ones who remained down in the dark."

Bobby handled the blinds carefully. The cords felt old, rotting in his hands. Some of the tiny interwoven pieces of bamboo were splintering, snagging on the strings, making the shade difficult to roll. He could smell the taint stronger here. Sweet, almost vinegary. His hands shook in spite of himself and he had to work to steady his heartbeat.

Be in the moment, but outside the moment. Detached. Composed. Focused.

The first blind rolled up. Then the second.

What helped him the most, in the end, was sheer incomprehension.

Bags. Clear plastic garbage bags. Six of them. Three on the top shelf, three on the bottom, positioned side by side, tied neatly at the top.

Bags. Six of them. Clear plastic.

He staggered back.

There were no words. He could feel his mouth open, but nothing was happening, nothing coming out. He just looked. And looked and looked, because such a thing couldn't exist, such a thing couldn't be. His mind saw it, rejected it, then saw the image and fought with it all over again. He couldn't . . . It couldn't . . .

His back hit the ladder. He reached behind, grabbing the cool metal rungs so hard he could feel the edges bite into the flesh of his hands. He focused on that sensation, the sharp pain. It grounded him. Kept him from having to scream.

D.D. pointed up to the ceiling, where one of the light strips had been hung.

"We didn't add those two hooks," D.D. said quietly. "They were already there. We didn't find any lanterns left behind, but I would assume . . ."

"Yeah," Bobby said roughly, still breathing through his mouth. "Yeah."

"And the chair, of course."

"Yeah, yeah. And the fucking chair."

"It's, uh, it's wet mummification," D.D. said, her own voice sounding shaky, working at control. "That's what Christie called it. He bound the bodies, put each in a garbage bag, then tied the top. When decomp started . . . well, there was no place for the fluids to go. Basically, the bodies pickled in their own juices."

"Son of a bitch."

"I hate my job, Bobby," D.D. whispered suddenly, starkly. "Oh God, I never wanted to see anything like this." She covered her mouth with her hand. For a moment, he thought she might break down, but she caught herself, soldiered through. She turned away from the metal shelves, however. Even for a veteran cop, some things asked too much.

Bobby had to work to abandon his grip on the metal ladder rungs.

"We should go up," D.D. said briskly. "Christie's probably waiting. She just needed to fetch body bags."

"Okay." But he didn't turn toward the ladder. Instead, he walked back to the exposed metal shelves, to a sight his mind couldn't accept but already would never forget.

The bodies had turned the color of mahogany with time. They were not the dried, empty husks he'd seen on shows of Egyptian mummies. They were robust, almost leathery in appearance, each feature still distinct. He could follow the long ropy lines of impossibly thin arms wrapped around gently rounded legs, bent at the knees. He could count ten fingers, clasped at the ankles. He could make out each of the faces, the hollows of their cheeks, the pointy tips of their chins resting upon their knees. Their eyes were closed. Their mouths pursed. Hair matted against their skulls, long lank strands covering their shoulders.

They were small. They were naked. They were female. Children, mere children, crouched inside clear garbage bags from which they would never escape.

He understood now why the detectives above weren't saying a word.

He reached out a gloved hand, lightly touched the first bag. He didn't know why. Nothing he could say, nothing he could do.

His fingers fell upon a thin, metal chain. He plucked it from the pleated folds at the top of the bag, to discover a small silver locket. It bore a single name: *Annabelle M. Granger.*

"He tagged them?" Bobby swore viciously.

"More like trophies." D.D. had come to stand behind him. She reached behind a second bag with her gloved hands and carefully revealed a small tattered bear hanging from a string. "I think . . . Hell, I don't know, but each bag has an object. Something that meant something to him. Or something that meant something to her."

"God."

D.D.'s hand was on his shoulder now. He hadn't realized how hard his jaw was clenched until she touched him. "We have to go up, Bobby."

"Yeah."

"Christie needs to get to work."

"Yeah."

"Bobby . . ."

He yanked his hand away. Looked at them one last time, feeling the pressure, the need, to imprint each image into his brain. As if it would bring them comfort to know they would not be forgotten. As if it mattered to them anymore to know they were not alone in the dark.

He headed back for the ladder. His throat burned. He couldn't speak.

Three deep breaths and he burst up through the opening, under the light blue tarp.

Back into the cool misty night. Back to the glow of spotlights. Back to the noise of news choppers who'd finally caught whiff of the story and were now whirling in the sky overhead.

Bobby didn't go home. He could've. He'd come as a favor to D.D. He'd confirmed what she'd suspected. No one would've questioned his departure.

He poured a cup of hot coffee from the crime-scene van. Leaned against the side of the vehicle for a while, buffered by the white noise of the roaring generator. He never drank the coffee. Just twisted the cup around and around with shaky fingers.

Six a.m. arrived, sun starting to peek over the horizon. Christie and her assistant brought up the bodies, encased now in black body bags. The remains fit three to a gurney, making for two trips to the ME's van. First stop would be to the BPD's lab, in order for the plastic garbage bags that encased each body to be fumigated for prints. Then the remains would journey on to the OCME lab, where postmortem would finally begin.

As Christie departed, so did most of the detectives. These kinds of scenes were run by the forensic anthropologist, so with Callahan gone, there wasn't much left to do.

Bobby dumped out his cold coffee, tossed the cup in the garbage.

He was waiting in the passenger's seat of D.D.'s car when she finally walked out of the woods. And then, because they had loved each other once, even been friends after that, he cradled her head against his shoulder and held her while she cried.

4

MY FATHER LOVED old sayings. Among his favorites, Chance favors the prepared mind. Preparedness, in my father's eyes, was everything. And he started to prepare me the minute we fled Massachusetts.

We started with Safety 101 for a seven-year-old. Never accept candy from a stranger. Never leave school with anyone, not even someone I know, unless he or she provides the correct password. Never get close to an approaching car. If the driver wants directions, send him to an adult. Looking for a lost puppy? Send him to the police.

Stranger appears in my room in the middle of the night? Yell, scream, bang on the walls. Sometimes, my father explained, when a child is deeply terrified, she finds it impossible to operate her vocal cords; hence, kick over furniture, throw a lamp, break small objects, blow on my red emergency whistle, do anything to make noise. I could destroy the entire house, my father promised me, and in that situation my parents would not be mad.

Fight, my father told me. Kick at kneecaps, gouge at eyes, bite at throat. Fight, fight, fight.

With age, my lessons grew more involved. Karate for skill. Track team for speed. Advanced safety tips. I learned to always lock the front door, even when at home in broad daylight. I learned to never answer the door without first looking through the peephole and to never acknowledge someone I didn't know.

Walk with your head up, steps brisk. Make eye contact, but do not maintain. Enough for the other party to know you're attuned to your surroundings, without calling undue attention to yourself. If I ever felt uncomfortable, I should catch up to the nearest group of people in front of me and follow in their wake.

If I was ever threatened in a public bathroom, yell "Fire;" people will respond to the threat of a fire before they'll respond to cries of rape. If I was ever uncomfortable in a mall, run to the nearest female; women are more likely to take action than men, who often feel uncomfortable getting involved. If I was ever confronted by someone pointing a gun, make a run for it; even the most skilled sharpshooter had difficulty hitting a moving target.

Never leave the shelter of your home or workplace without having your car key in hand. Walk to your vehicle with the key protruding from between your curled fingers like a shank. Do not unlock the door if a stranger is standing behind you. Do not climb into the car without first checking the backseat. Once inside, keep the doors locked at all times; if you need air, a window may be cracked one inch.

My father did not believe in weapons; he had read that women were more likely to lose possession of their firearm and have it used against them. That's why until the age of fourteen I wore a whistle around my neck for use in case of emergency and always carried mace.

That year, however, I knocked out my first opponent in a juniors sparring contest at the local gym. I had given up karate in favor of kickboxing, and it turned out I was quite good at it. The assembled crowd was horrified. The mother of the boy I flattened called me a monster.

My father took me out for ice cream and told me I'd done good. "Not that I'm condoning violence, mind you. But if you're ever threatened, Cindy, don't hold back. You're strong, you're fast, you have a fighter's instinct. Hit first, question later. You can never be too prepared."

My father entered me in more tournaments. Where I honed my skills, learned to focus my rage. I am fast. I am strong. I do have a fighter's instinct. It all went well until I started winning too much, which of course garnered unwanted attention.

No more tournaments. No more life.

Eventually, I would throw the words back in my father's face: "Prepared? What's the use of being so prepared when all we ever do is run away!"

"Yes, sweetheart," my father would explain tirelessly. "But we can run because we are so prepared."

I headed for the Boston Police Department straight from my morning shift at Starbucks. Departing Faneuil Hall, I had only a one block walk to the T, where I could catch the Orange Line to Ruggles Street. I had done my homework the night before and dressed accordingly: low-slung, broken-down jeans, frayed cuffs dragging against the pavement. A thin chocolate-colored tank top layered over a black, tight-fitting long-sleeve cotton top. A multicolored scarf of chocolate, black, white, pink, and blue tied around my waist. An oversize blue-flowered April Cornell bag slung over my shoulder.

I left my hair down, dark strands falling halfway to my waist, while giant silver hoops swung from my ears. I could, and had on occasion, pass as Hispanic. I thought that look might be safer for where I would be spending my afternoon.

State Street was hopping as usual. I tossed my token into the slot, breezed my way down the stairs to the wonderful, rich, urinal smell that accompanied any subway station. The crowd was typical Boston—black, Asian, Hispanic, white, rich, old, poor, professional, working-class, gangbanger, all milling about in a colorful urban tableau. Liberals loved this crap. Most of us simply wished we could win the lottery and buy ourselves a car.

I identified an elderly lady, moving slowly with a teenage granddaughter in tow. I stood next to them, just far enough away not to intrude, but close enough to seem part of the group. We all regarded the far wall studiously, everyone careful to avoid one another's eyes.

When the subway car finally arrived, we pressed forward as one cohesive mass, squeezing into the metal tube. Then the doors shut with a *whoosh* and the car hurtled into the tunnels.

For this leg of the trip, there weren't enough seats. I stood, holding a metal pole. A black kid wearing a red headband, oversize sweatshirt, and baggy jeans gave up his seat for the elderly woman. She told him thank you. He said nothing at all.

I shifted from side to side, eyes on the color-coded transit map above the door, while I did my subtle best to appraise the space.

Older Asian man, working-class, to my far right. Sitting, head down, shoulders slumped. Someone just trying to get through the day. The elderly woman had been given the seat next to him, her granddaughter standing guard. Then came four black male teens, wearing the official gangbangers' uniform. Their shoulders swayed in rhythm with the subway car, as they sat, eyes on the floor, not saying a word.

Behind me a woman with two small kids. Woman appeared Hispanic, the six- and eight-year-old kids white. Probably a nanny, taking her young charges to the park.

Two teenage girls next to her, both decked out in urban chic, hair in braids, oversize diamond studs winking from their ears. I didn't turn but pegged them

44

as worth keeping on radar. Girls are more unpre-
dictable than boys, thus more dangerous. Males pos-
ture; females have a tendency to get straight in your
face, then when you don't back down, start slashing
away with concealed knives.

I wasn't too worried about the girls, though; they
were the known unknowns. It's the unknown
unknowns that can knock you on your ass.

The Ruggles Street stop arrived without incident.
Doors opened, I departed. No one spared me a second
glance.

I hefted my bag over my shoulder and headed for the
stairs.

I'd never been to the new police headquarters in
Roxbury. I'd only heard the stories of midnight shootings in the parking lot, of people being mugged outside the front doors. Apparently, the new location had
been some political bid to gentrify Roxbury, or at least
make it safer at night. From what I'd read online, it
didn't seem to be working.

I kept my bag tucked tight to my side and walked on
the balls of my feet, ready for any sudden movement.
The Ruggles Street station was large, crowded, and
dank. I wove my way swiftly through the mass of
humanity. Appear purposeful and focused. Just
because you're lost is no reason to look that way.

Outside the station, down a steep flight of stairs, I
spotted the towering radio antennae to my right and
took the hint. Just as I headed down the sidewalk,
however, a sneering voice yelled from behind me,

45

"Looking good, Taco! Wanna try a burrito with real meat?"

I turned, spotted a trio of African American boys, and flipped them off. They just laughed. The leader, who looked about thirteen, grabbed his crotch. Now it was my turn to laugh.

That took some of the thunder out of them. I twisted back around and headed up the street, footsteps calm and even. I clenched my hands into fists so they wouldn't tremble.

BPD headquarters was hard to miss. For one thing, it was a vast, glass-and-metal structure plopped down in the middle of crumbling brown housing projects. For another, concrete barricades were positioned all around the front entrance, as if the building were actually located in downtown Baghdad. Homeland security, brought to every government building near you.

My footsteps faltered for the first time. Since I'd decided what I was going to do last night, I hadn't allowed myself to think about it. I'd planned. I'd acted. Now here I was.

I put my bag down. Drew out a corduroy blazer the color of milk chocolate and put it on, the best I could do to dress myself up. Not that it mattered. I had no proof. The detectives would simply believe me or not.

Inside, there was a line in front of the metal detector. The officer in charge demanded to see my driver's license. He inspected my oversize bag. Then he looked me up and down in a manner that was supposed to inspire me to say, Yes, I'm secretly smuggling guns/bombs/drugs into police headquarters. I had nothing to say, so he let me through.

At the front desk, I drew out the newspaper article, checking once more for the detective's name, though in all honesty, I knew it by heart.

"Is she expecting you?" the uniformed officer asked me with a stern frown. He was a hefty guy with a thick mustache. Immediately, I thought of Dennis Franz.

"No."

Another up-and-down look. "You know, she's busy these days."

"Just tell her Annabelle Granger is here. She'll want to know that."

The officer must not follow the news much. He shrugged, picked up the phone, told someone my message. A few seconds passed. The officer's look never changed. He merely shrugged again, set down the phone, and told me to wait.

Other people were in line, so I took my bag and drifted to the middle of the long, vaulted lobby. Someone had erected a special display documenting the history of the police department. I studied each photo, read the captions, walked up and down the exhibit.

Minute passed into minutes. My hands grew shakier. I thought I should run while I still had the chance. Then I thought maybe I'd feel better if I could just throw up.

Footsteps finally rang out.

A woman appeared, walked straight toward me.

Slim-fitting jeans, tall stiletto boots, a tight-fitting, white-collared, button-up shirt, and a really big gun, holstered at her waist. Her face was framed by a wild mass of blonde curls. She looked like she ought to be a cover girl. Until you saw her eyes. Flat, direct, unamused.

That blue gaze homed in on me, and for one moment, something flickered across her face. She looked as if she might have seen a ghost. Then she closed the space.

I took a deep breath.

My father had been wrong. There are some things in life for which you cannot be prepared. Like the loss of your mother when you are still a child. Or the passing of your father before you had a chance to stop hating him.

"What the hell?" Sergeant Detective D.D. Warren demanded to know.

"My name is Annabelle Mary Granger," I said. "I believe you're looking for me."

5

THE OFFICES OF the Boston Homicide unit looked like they belonged to an insurance company. Bright, expansive windows, twelve-foot-high drop ceilings, pretty blue-gray carpet. The beige cubicles were modern and sleek, breaking the sunlit space into smaller desk areas, where black filing cabinets and gray overhead bins were decorated with plants, family photos, a child's latest grade-school art project.

I found the whole setup disappointing. So much for all the years I'd dedicated to *NYPD Blue.*

The receptionist gave Sergeant Warren a friendly smile as we walked in. Her gaze flickered to me, open, unassuming. I looked away, fingers fidgeting with my bag. Did I look like a perpetrator? A key informant? Or maybe the family of a victim? I tried to see myself through the receptionist's eyes but came up empty.

Sergeant Warren led me to a small, windowless room. A rectangular table filled most of the tiny space, barely leaving room for chairs. I searched the walls for signs of a two-way mirror, anything to fit in with my TV-prepped expectations. The walls were blank, painted a clean bone-white. I still couldn't relax.

"Coffee?" she asked briskly.

"No, thank you."

"Water, soda, tea?"

"No, thank you."

"Suit yourself. I'll be right back."

She left me in the room. I decided that must mean I didn't look too guilty. I set down my bag, surveyed the space. Nothing to look at, though. Nothing to do.

The room was too small, the furniture too big. Abruptly, I hated it.

The door opened again. Warren was back, this time bearing a tape recorder. Immediately, I shook my head.

"No."

She appraised me coolly. "I thought you were here to make a statement."

"No tape."

"Why not?"

"Because you just declared me dead, and I plan on keeping it that way."

She set the recorder down but didn't turn it on. For the longest time, she stared at me. For the longest time, I stared right back.

We were equal height, five foot four. About equal weight. I could tell from the expanse of her shoulders, the slight bulge of her crossed arms, she also trained with weights. She had the gun on her side. But guns had to be drawn, aimed, fired. I didn't have any of those constraints.

The thought gave me my first measure of comfort. My arms uncrossed. I took a seat. After a moment, she did, too.

Door opened again. A man walked in, wearing tan pants and a long-sleeve dark blue dress shirt, credentials clipped at his waist. A fellow homicide detective, I presumed. He wasn't huge, maybe five ten, five eleven, but he had a lean, sinewy build to go with a lean, hard-edged face. The moment he saw me, he also did a little double-take, then quickly caught himself and blanked his expression.

He stuck out a hand. "Detective Robert Dodge, Massachusetts State Police."

I returned the handshake less certainly. His fingers were callused, his grip firm. He held the handshake longer than necessary, and I knew he was appraising me, trying to get a read. He had cool gray eyes, the kind used to sizing up game.

"Want some water? Something to drink?"

"She already played Martha Stewart." I jerked my head toward Sergeant Warren. "With all due respect, I'd just like to get this done."

The two detectives exchanged glances. Dodge took a seat, the one closest to the door. The space seemed overcrowded, closing in on me. I placed my hands on my lap, trying not to fidget.

"My name is Annabelle Mary Granger," I began. Dodge's hand reached for the recorder. Warren stopped him with a single touch.

"We're off the record," she told him. "At least for the moment."

Dodge nodded, and I took another deep breath, trying to rein in my scattered thoughts. I'd spent the past forty-eight hours rehearsing the story in my head. Obsessively reading all the front-page stories of the "grave" found in Mattapan, of the six remains that had been collected from the site. Details had been sparse—the forensic anthropologist could confirm only that the remains were female, the police spokes-woman had added that the grave was possibly decades old. They had released one name, my own; the other identities remained a mystery.

In the absence of real information, and with round-the-clock coverage to fill, the TV personalities had begun speculating madly. The site was an old Mafia dumping ground, possibly a legacy from Whitey Bulger, the mobster whose murderous work was still being dug up around the state. Or maybe it was a former cemetery for the mental hospital. Or perhaps the hideous hobby of one of its homicidal patients. A satanic cult was operating in Mattapan. The bones were actually from victims of the Salem Witch Trial.

Everyone had a theory. Except, I guess, me. I honestly didn't know what had happened in Mattapan. And I was here right now not because of the help I could give the police, but because of the help I was hoping they could give me.

"My family fled for the first time when I was seven years old," I told the two detectives, and then with gathering speed ran through my story. The parade of moves, the endless procession of fake identities. My mother's death. Then my father's. I kept the details sketchy.

Detective Dodge took a few notes. D.D. Warren mostly watched me.

I exhausted the story more quickly than I'd expected. No grand finale. Just The End. My throat felt parched now. I wished I'd had that glass of water after all. I lapsed awkwardly into silence, keenly aware that both detectives were still studying me.

"What year did you leave?" Detective Dodge, pencil posed.

"October, '82."

"And how long did you stay in Florida?"

I did my best to run through the list again. Cities, dates, aliases. Time had dulled the specifics more than I'd realized. What month had we moved to St. Louis? Was I ten or eleven when we hit Phoenix? And the names . . . In Kansas City, had we been Jones, Jenkins, Johnson? Something like that.

I started sounding less and less certain and more and more defensive, and they hadn't even gotten to the hard questions yet.

"Why?" Detective Warren asked bluntly when I had wrapped up the geography lesson. She spread out her hands. "It's an interesting story except you never said why your family was running."

"I don't know."

"You don't know?"

"My father never gave me the details. He considered it his job to worry, my job to be a child."

She arched a brow. I couldn't blame her. By the time I was sixteen, I'd become skeptical of that platitude myself.

"Birth certificate?" she asked crisply.

"For my real name? I don't have one."

"Driver's license, Social Security card? Your parents' wedding license? A family photo? You must have something."

"No."

"No?"

"Original documentation can be found and used against you." I sounded like a parrot. I suppose for most of my life I had been one.

Sergeant Warren leaned forward. This close I could see the shadows under her eyes, the fine lines and pale cheeks of someone who was operating on little sleep and even less patience. "Why the hell did you come here, Annabelle? You've told us nothing, you've given us nothing. Are you looking to get on the news? Is that what this is about? You're going to claim the identity of some poor dead girl in order to snag your fifteen minutes of fame?"

"It's not like that—"

"Bullshit."

"I told you already, I had only minutes to pack and I didn't think to grab my scrapbook."

"How convenient."

"Hey!" My own temper was starting to rise. "You want some evidence? Go get it. You're the goddamn police after all. My father worked at MIT. Russell Walt Granger. Look it up, they'll have a record. My family lived on 282 Oak Street in Arlington. Look it up, there'll be a record. For that matter, dig in your own damn case files. My whole family disappeared in the middle of the night. I'm pretty fucking sure you got a record."

"If you know that much," she replied evenly, "why haven't you followed up?"

"Because I can't ask any questions," I exploded. "I don't know who I'm afraid of!"

I pushed back from the table abruptly, disgusted by my own outburst. Sergeant Warren straightened more slowly. She and the other detective exchanged another glance, probably just to piss me off.

Warren got up. Left the room. I stared at the far wall resolutely, not wanting to give Detective Dodge the satisfaction of breaking the silence first.

"Water?" he asked.

I shook my head.

"Must've been hard to lose both of your parents like that," he murmured.

"Oh, shut up. Good cop, bad cop. You think I haven't seen the movies?"

We sat in silence until the door opened again. Warren returned holding a large paper sack.

She'd put on a pair of latex gloves. Now she set the bag down, unrolled the top, and pulled an object from its depths. It wasn't big. A delicate silver chain bearing a small oval locket. Child-size. She held it out on her gloved palm. Showed me the front, engraved with a filigree of swirls. Then she opened it, revealing two hollow ovals inside. Finally, she flipped it over. A single name was engraved on the back: Annabelle M. Granger.

"What can you tell me about this locket?"

I stared at the locket for a long while. I felt as if I were sifting through a deep fog, searching carefully in the mist of my mind.

"It was a gift," I murmured at last. I unconsciously fingered my throat, as if feeling the locket still hanging there, silver oval cool against my skin. "He told me I couldn't keep it."

"Who told you?"

"My father. He was angry." I blinked, trying to recall more. "I don't . . . I don't know why he was so mad. I'm not sure I knew. I liked the locket. I remember thinking it was very pretty. But when my father saw it, he made me take it off. Told me I had to throw it away."

"Did you?"

Slowly, I shook my head. I looked up at them, and suddenly, I was afraid. "I went outside to the garbage," I whispered. "But I couldn't bring myself to throw it in the trash. It was so pretty. . . . I thought maybe if I just waited, he'd get over it. Let me wear it again. My best friend came out to see what I was doing."

Both detectives leaned forward; I could feel their sudden tension. And I knew that they now understood where this was going.

"Dori Petracelli. I handed the locket to Dori. Told her she could borrow it. I figured I would get it back later, maybe wear it when my father wasn't around. Except there was no later. In a matter of weeks, we packed our bags. I haven't seen Dori since."

"Annabelle," Detective Dodge asked quietly, "who gave you the locket?"

"I don't know." My fingers were on my temples, rubbing. "A gift. On the front porch. Wrapped in the *Peanuts* comic strip. Just for me. But without a tag. I liked it. But my father . . . he was mad. I don't know . . . I don't remember. There had been other items, small, inconsequential. But nothing made my father as angry as the locket."

Another pause, then Detective Dodge again: "Does the name Richard Umbrio mean anything to you?"

"No."

"What about Mr. Bosu?"

"No."

"Catherine Gagnon?"

Warren flashed him a sudden, hostile glance. But the significance was lost on me. I didn't know that name either.

"Did you . . . Did you find this locket on a body? Is that why you thought it was me?"

"We can't comment on an active investigation," Sergeant Warren said crisply.

I ignored her, my gaze going to Detective Dodge. "Is it Dori? Is that who you found? Did something happen to her? Please . . ."

"We don't know," he said gently. Warren frowned again, but then she shrugged.

"It will take weeks to identify the bodies," she volunteered abruptly. "We don't know much of anything at this point."

"So it's possible."

"It's possible."

I tried to absorb this news. It left me feeling cold and shaky. I squeezed my left hand into a fist and pressed it into my stomach. "Can you look her up?" I said. "Run her name. You'll see if she has an address, a driver's license. The bodies are children, right, that's what the news says. So if she has a driver's license . . ."

"You can be sure we'll look into it," Sergeant Warren said.

I didn't like that answer. My gaze went to Detective Dodge again. I knew I was pleading, but I couldn't help myself.

"Why don't you give us your number," he said. "We'll be in touch."

"Don't call me, I'll call you," I murmured.

"Not at all. You're welcome to contact us at any time."

"And if you remember anything more about the locket . . ." Sergeant Warren prodded.

"I'll sell my story to the cable news."

She gave me a look, but I waved it away. "They wouldn't believe me any more than you do, and I can't afford to come back from the dead."

I rose, grabbed my bag, then provided my home phone number when it became clear that some form of contact information was mandatory.

At the last minute, standing in the door, I hesitated. "Can you tell me what happened to them? To the girls?"

"We're still waiting for that report." Sergeant Warren, sounding as official as always.

"But it's murder, right? Six bodies, all in one grave . . ."

"You ever been to the Boston State Mental Hospital?" Detective Dodge interjected evenly. "What about your father?"

I shook my head. All I knew about the site were the development wars I'd been hearing on the local news. If I'd ever known the lunatic asylum as a child, it didn't mean anything to me now.

Sergeant Warren escorted me back downstairs. We walked in silence, the heels of our boots making sharp staccato beats that rang up the stairwell.

At the bottom, she held open the heavy metal door to the lobby, extending her business card with her other hand.

"We'll be in touch."

"Sure," I said without a trace of conviction.

She looked at me sharply. "And Annabelle—"

I shook my head immediately. "Tanya. I go by Tanya Nelson; it's safer."

Another raised brow. "And *Tanya,* if you remember anything more about the locket, or the days before you left town . . ."

I had to smile again. "Don't worry," I told her. "I learned how to run away with the best of them."

I exited the glass doors into the brisk fall air and started my journey home.

6

BOBBY WOULD LIKE to believe he'd been asked to help with the Boston State Mental Hospital investigation because of his natural brilliance and solid work ethic. He'd even settle for being welcomed aboard for his good looks and charming smile. But he knew the truth: D.D. needed him. He was the trump card she had tucked away in her back pocket. D.D. had always been good at looking ahead.

Not that he was complaining. Being the only state detective on a city team was awkward at best, filled with daily shots of resentment at worst. But such arrangements had precedent. D.D. declared him a source of "local knowledge" and, voilà, hijacked him for her purposes. The fact that he was new and not embroiled in any major state investigations made the transition swift and relatively painless. One day he'd reported to the state offices, the next he was working out of a teeny tiny interrogation room in Roxbury, Mass. Such was the glamorous life of a detective.

From his perspective, it was a no-brainer: serving on a high-profile task force would add heft to his file. And having entered that underground chamber, having seen those six girls . . . It wasn't the kind of thing a cop walked away from. Better to work it than to just dream about it night after night.

Most of the other detectives seemed to feel the same. The case wasn't lacking for overtime hours. Bobby'd been at the BPD headquarters for nearly two days now. If people disappeared, it was simply to shower and shave. Food consisted of pickup pizza or take-out Chinese, consumed mostly at one's desk, or perhaps in a task-force meeting. Not that real life magically went away. Detectives still had to attend to previously scheduled grand jury hearings, sudden developments in a current case. The arrival of an informant. The murder of a key witness. Other cases didn't stop just because a new and more shocking murder leapt into the fray.

Then there was family life. Last-minute calls to apologize for missing Junior's soccer game. Guys disappearing into interrogation rooms at eight p.m., trying to find a little privacy for the good-night phone call that would have to do in lieu of a kiss. Detective Roger Sinkus had a two-week-old baby. Detective Tony Rock's mother was in the intensive care unit, dying of heart failure.

High-profile homicide investigations were a dance, a complex work flow of officers fading in and out, of attending to critical tasks, of abandoning any others. Of single guys like Bobby staying until three a.m., so a new father like Roger could go home at one. Of everyone trying to push one case forward. Of no one getting what they needed.

And at the top of it all sat D.D. Warren. First big case for the newly minted sergeant. Bobby had a tendency to be cynical about these things, but even he was currently impressed.

For starters, she had managed to keep one of the most sensational crime scenes in Boston history under wraps for nearly forty-eight hours. No leaks from the BPD. No leaks from the OCME's office. No leaks from the DA. It was a miracle.

Second, while operating under the full onslaught of a dozen major TV personalities screaming for more information, ranting about the public's right to know, and alternately accusing the Boston police of covering up a major threat to public safety, she'd still managed to organize and launch a half-decent investigation.

First step in any homicide case, establish a time line. Unfortunately for the task force, a time line was usually generated by the victimology report, which included an estimated time of death. Forensic anthropology wasn't exactly an overnight kind of analysis, however. Plus, in Boston, the forensic anthropologist's position wasn't a full-time one, meaning one half-time expert, Christie Callahan, was now trying to handle six remains. Then you had the mummified condition of such remains, which no doubt demanded a whole slew of painstaking, methodical, and frighteningly expensive tests. All in all, they'd probably have the victimology report about the same time Detective Sinkus's new baby hit college.

D.D. had brought in a botanist from the Audubon Society to help them out. He'd studied the woodland brush, grass, and saplings that had taken root above the subterranean chamber. Best guess—thirty years' worth of overgrowth, give or take a decade. Not the most precise time line in the world, but it got them started.

One three-person detective squad was now creating a list of missing Massachusetts girls, going back to 1965. Since records were only computerized from 1997 on, that meant manually skimming massive printouts of every single missing person from '65 to '97, identifying which of the cases were still unsolved and involved a female minor, then record those case-file numbers to be looked up separately on microfiche. Currently, the squad completed six years of missing persons every twenty-four hours. They were also consuming approximately one gallon of coffee every ninety minutes.

Of course, the Crime Stoppers hotline was also going insane. The public only knew that the remains of six females had been found on the site of the former Boston State Mental Hospital, and the scene appeared to be dated. That was still enough to have the crackpots out in force. Reports of strange nighttime lights coming from the property. Rumors of a satanic cult in Mattapan. Two callers claimed to have been abducted by UFOs and had seen all six girls aboard the ship. (Really, what did they look like? What were they wearing? Did they give you their names?) Those callers had a tendency to hang up quick.

Other calls were more intriguing: girlfriends ratting out ex-boyfriends who had bragged of doing "something awful" at the former hospital site. Others were simply heartbreaking: parents, from all over the country, calling in to ask if the remains might be those of their missing child.

Every call generated a report, every report had to be followed up by a detective, including the monthly call from a woman in California who insisted that her ex-husband was the real Boston Strangler, mostly because she'd never liked him. It was taking five detectives to handle the load.

Which left D.D.'s squad, plus Bobby, with miscellaneous management tasks. Determining a list of "interview subjects" based on the various real estate developers and community projects active at the site. Trying to get a list of patients and administrators from a mental hospital that had shut down thirty years ago.

Entering the crime-scene elements into VICAP, given the uniqueness of the subterranean pit.

Following up the resulting hit—Richard Umbrio—had become Bobby's project. He had pulled the microfiche of the original case file, including a decent collection of photos. He'd also put in a call to the lead detective, Franklin Miers, who'd retired to Fort Lauderdale eight years ago.

Now Bobby was sitting in the tiny interrogation room that served as his temporary office, studying a hand-sketched diagram of the pit that had once held twelve-year-old Catherine Gagnon.

According to Miers's notes, Catherine had been abducted while walking home from school. Umbrio had come upon Catherine when driving around the neighborhood and asked if she would help him look for a lost dog. She took the bait and that was that.

A hulking bear of a man even at the age of nineteen, Umbrio had no problem subduing the slightly built sixth-grader. He whisked her away to an underground chamber he had prepared in the woods, and that's when Catherine's real ordeal began. Nearly thirty days in an underground pit, where her only visitor was a rapist with a penchant for Wonder bread.

If hunters hadn't stumbled upon the pit, most likely Umbrio would've eventually killed her. Instead, Catherine survived, identified her attacker, and testified against him. Umbrio was whisked away to prison. Catherine was left to rebuild her life, the so-called Thanksgiving Miracle whose adult life wasn't so miraculous after all. Being held by a monster had definitely left its mark.

Miers's notes described a case that was shocking, but routine. Catherine was a credible witness, and evidence found in the pit—a metal chain-link ladder, a plastic bucket, the plywood cover—bore out her story.

Umbrio did it. Umbrio went to prison. And two years ago, when Umbrio was mistakenly paroled from prison, he returned to stalking Catherine with the same homicidal zeal he had shown prior to his arrest.

In short, Umbrio was a murderous, monstrous freak of nature, quite capable of killing six girls and interring their bodies on the grounds of an abandoned mental institute.

Except Umbrio was safe behind bars by the end of 1980. And according to Annabelle Granger, she didn't receive the locket found on Unidentified Mummified Remains #1 until 1982. Which meant . . . ?

Forty-eight hours into a critical investigation, Bobby didn't have any answers, but he was developing a fascinating list of questions. D.D. finally returned from escorting Annabelle out of the building. She yanked out a chair and plopped down like a puppet whose strings had just been cut. "Jesus fucking Christ," she said.

"Funny, I was thinking the exact same thing."

She ran a hand through her tangled hair. "I gotta get a cup of coffee. No, wait, I drink any more java, I'm gonna start pissing Colombians. I need something to eat. A sandwich. Rare roast beef on rye. With Swiss cheese and one of those really big, no-messing-around dill pickles. And a bag of potato chips."

"You've given this some thought." Bobby set down the diagram. D.D. might look like a supermodel, but she ate like a trucker. When she and Bobby had been dating—back in their rookie days, ten years and God knows how many major career moves ago—Bobby had learned quickly that D.D.'s idea of foreplay generally included an all-you-can-eat buffet.

He felt that little pang again, a longing for good old days that had only become good by virtue of distant memory and encroaching loneliness.

"Lunch is the only thing I have to look forward to today," D.D. said.

"Too bad. Your chance of getting a decent roast beef sandwich around here is about one in ten."

"I know. Even lunch is a goddamn pipe dream."

Her shoulders sagged. Bobby let her have a moment. Truth was, he was reeling a bit himself. As of this morning, he'd managed to convince himself that any resemblance between the mental hospital site and Richard Umbrio's work was mere happenstance. Then Annabelle Granger. In D.D.'s words, Jesus fucking Christ.

"Are you going to make me say it?" she asked at last.

"Yep."

"It doesn't make any sense."

"Yep."

"I mean, okay, there's a resemblance. Lots of people look alike. Don't they say every person in the

66

world has an unknown twin?"

Bobby just stared at her.

She exhaled heavily, then sat herself up, leaning into the table, her favorite thinking pose: "Let's go through it from the top."

"I'm game."

"Richard Umbrio used an underground pit; our subject used an underground pit," D.D. started off.

"Umbrio's pit was four by six, and by all appearances, a manually enlarged sinkhole," Bobby supplied, gesturing to the diagram decorating the top of the table. "Our subject used a six-by-ten chamber, complete with wooden reinforcements."

"So, same but different."

"Same but different," Bobby concurred.

"Except for the 'supplies'—the ladder, plywood cover, plastic five-gallon bucket."

"Exactly the same," Bobby agreed.

She puffed out a breath, swishing up her bangs. "Maybe the logical provisions for an underground chamber?"

"Possible."

"Now, the metal folding chair and shelves . . ."

"Different."

"More sophisticated," D.D. amended out loud. "Bigger chamber, more furniture."

"Which brings us to the next key difference . . ."

"Richard Umbrio kidnapped one known victim, twelve-year-old Catherine Gagnon. Our subject kidnapped six victims, all young females."

"Need more information for proper analysis," Bobby said immediately. "One, we don't know if the six victims were abducted at once—which is somewhat doubtful—or individually over a span of time. Are the girls related? Family members, religious affiliation, daddies all worked for the Mafia? Did their time in the chamber overlap? Or were they even kept alive down there? That's an assumption we're making based on the Catherine Gagnon case. But maybe the space only operated as a burial chamber. A place where the subject could come . . . be with them. A viewing gallery. We don't know yet what floated this guy's boat. We can guess, but we don't *know*."

D.D. nodded slowly. "Except, then you have Annabelle Granger."

"Yeah, well, except."

"My God, she looks exactly like her. I'm not crazy, right? Annabelle could be Catherine Gagnon's twin."

"She could be Catherine's twin."

"And what are the chances of that? Two women who look so much alike, growing up in the same city, both becoming targets of madmen who favor kidnapping young girls and sticking them in underground pits."

"This is where we make the left turn into the Twilight Zone," Bobby agreed.

D.D. sat back. Her stomach growled. She rubbed it absently. "What do you think of her story?"

Bobby sighed, sat back himself, clasping his hands behind his head. His favorite thinking pose. "Can't decide."

"Seems pretty far-fetched."

"But richly detailed."

D.D. snorted. "She flubbed half the details."

"All the more realistic," Bobby countered. "You wouldn't expect a perfect list of dates and names from someone who'd been just a kid."

"Think the father knew something?"

"You mean, did he sense his daughter had been targeted somehow and that's why they fled?" Bobby shrugged. "Don't know, but this is where life gets tricky: If something was going on in Arlington in the fall of '82, it definitely *wasn't* Richard Umbrio. He was arrested without bail at the end of '80, tried in '81, and began his stint at Walpole by January '82. Meaning the threat would have to be from elsewhere."

"Troubling. Any chance Catherine was wrong about Umbrio? It was someone else who grabbed her? I mean, yeah, she ID'd him, but she was only a twelve-year-old kid."

"Subsequent events would appear to rule that out, let alone the corresponding pile of physical evidence."

"Bummer."

Bobby shook his head, equally frustrated. "It's hard without the father to interview," he said abruptly. "Annabelle just can't—or won't—tell us enough."

"Rather convenient that both parents are dead," D.D. muttered darkly. She slanted him a look. "'Course, we could ask Umbrio, but conveniently enough, he's dead, too."

Bobby knew better than to take that bait. "I'm sure

Annabelle Granger doesn't find it so convenient that her parents are deceased. Sounded to me as if she wouldn't mind questioning her father some more herself."

"You got the list of cities and aliases?" D.D. asked abruptly. "Look 'em up. See what you can find. It's a good detective exercise."

"Gee, thanks, Teach."

D.D. rose out of her chair, their little conference apparently over. At the doorway, however, she paused.

"Have you heard from her yet?"

No need to define who. "No."

"Think she'll call?"

"As long as we keep calling the scene a grave, probably not. But the minute the media finally figures out it was an underground chamber . . ."

D.D. nodded. "You'll let me know."

"Maybe, maybe not."

"Robert Dodge—"

"You want an official phone call with Catherine Gagnon, you pick up the phone. I'm not your lackey."

His tone was level, but his gaze was hard. D.D. took the rebuke about as gracefully as he'd expected. She stiffened in the doorway, features frosting over.

"I never had a problem with the shooting, Bobby," she said curtly. "Myself, a lot of officers out there, we respected that you did your job, and we understood that sometimes this job really sucks. It's not the shooting, Bobby. It's your attitude since then."

Her knuckles rapped the doorjamb. "Police work is

about trust. You're either in or out. Think about that, Bobby."

She gave him one last pointed look, then she was gone.

7

I FELL IN love with a coffee mug when I was nine years old. It was sold in the little convenience store next to my elementary school where I sometimes used my milk money to buy candy after class. The mug was pink, hand-painted with flowers, butterflies, and a little orange-striped kitten. It came in a variety of names. I wanted Annabelle.

The mug cost $3.99, roughly two weeks' worth of chocolate/milk money. I never questioned the sacrifice.

I had to wait another agonizing week, until a Thursday when my mother announced she had errands to run and might be late picking me up. I spent the day jittery, barely able to focus, a warrior about to launch her first mission.

Two thirty-five the school bell rang. Kids who didn't ride the bus congregated at the front of the brick building, like clusters of flowers. I'd been at this school six months. I didn't belong to any of the groups, so no one cared when I slipped away. Those were the days before you had to sign kids in and out. Before parent volunteers stood guard after hours. Before Amber Alerts. In those days, only my father seemed obsessed with all the things that could happen to a little girl.

In the store, I picked out the mug carefully. Carried it all the way to the register using two hands. I counted out $3.99 in quarters, fingers fumbling the coins with my urgency.

The clerk, an older woman, asked me if my name was Annabelle.

For a moment, I couldn't speak. I almost ran out of the store. I could not be Annabelle. It was very important I not be Annabelle. My father had told me this over and over again.

"For a friend," I finally managed to whisper.

The woman smiled at me kindly and wrapped my prize in layers of protective tissue.

Outside the store, I tucked the mug in my backpack next to my schoolbooks, then returned to school grounds. A minute later, my mother arrived in our new used station wagon, back loaded with groceries, fingers tapping absently on the steering wheel.

I felt an agonizing wave of guilt. I was sure her gaze saw right through the blue vinyl of my backpack. She was staring at my mug. She knew exactly what I had done.

Instead, my mother asked about my day. I said, "Fine," and climbed into the front bench seat beside her. She never looked in my bag. Never asked about the mug. She simply drove us home.

I kept the pink mug hidden behind a pile of outgrown clothing on the top shelf of my closet. I would bring it down at night, when my parents thought I was sleeping. I would take it into bed, hiding under the covers and admiring the pink, pearlescent sheen under the glow of a flashlight. I would run my fingertips over the raised brushstrokes of flowers, butterflies, kitten. But mostly I traced the name, over and over again.

Annabelle. My name is Annabelle.

About six weeks later, my mother found it. It was a Saturday. My father was working. I think I was watching cartoons in the family room. My mother decided to clean up a little, taking down the pile of clothes to trade in at the secondhand store where we purchased most of our things.

She didn't scream. Didn't yell. In fact, I think what finally alerted me was the silence, the total utter silence, compared to the usual white noise of my mother puttering around the tiny apartment, folding laundry, banging pans, opening and shutting cupboard doors.

I had just climbed up off the gold shag carpeting when she appeared in the doorway, holding my treasure in her hand. She looked stunned but composed.

"Did someone give this to you?" she asked me quietly.

Wordlessly, heart thumping in my chest, I shook my head.

"Then how did you get it?"

I couldn't look her in the eye and tell my story. Instead, I scuffed my toes against the carpet. "I saw it. I . . . I thought it was pretty."

73

"Did you steal it?"

Another quick head shake. "I saved my milk money."

"Oh, Annabelle . . ." Her hand flew to her mouth. To show me she was appalled, even horrified? Or to cover the unforgivable sin of saying my name?

I wasn't sure. But then she held out her arms, and I ran to her and held on to her waist very hard, and started crying myself because it felt so nice to hear my mother say my real name. I had missed hearing it from her lips.

My father came home. Caught us huddled like coconspirators in the family room, mug still clutched in my mother's hand. His response was immediate and thunderous.

He grabbed the pink ceramic cup from my mother and shook it in the air.

"What the *hell* is this?" he roared.

"I didn't mean—"

"Did a stranger give this to you?"

"N-n-no—"

"Did she give this to you?" Finger pointed at my mother, as if somehow she was even worse than a stranger.

"No—"

"What the hell are you doing? Do you think this is a game? Do you think I gave up my post at MIT, that we are living in this shitty little dump of an apartment because of some game? What were you thinking?"

I couldn't speak anymore. I just stared at him,

cheeks flushed, eyes wild, knowing I was trapped, wishing desperately for some means of escape.

He turned on my mother. "You knew about this?"

"I just found out myself," she said calmly. She put a hand on his arm as if to soothe him. "Russ—"

"Hal, the name is *Hal!*" He shook her hand away. "Christ, you're nearly as bad as she is. Well, I know how to put a stop to this."

He pounded into the kitchen, yanked open the drawer under the phone, pulled out a hammer.

"Sophia," he said pointedly, staring at me. "Come here."

He sat me at the kitchen table. He placed the mug in front of me. He handed me the hammer.

"Do it."

I shook my head.

"Do it!"

I shook my head again.

"Russ . . ." My mother, sounding plaintive.

"Goddammit, Sophia, you will break that mug or you are *not* getting up from that table. I don't care if it takes all night. You will pick up that hammer!"

It didn't take all night. Just until three a.m. When I finally did the deed, I didn't cry. I picked up the hammer with both hands. I studied my target. Then I delivered the killing blow with such force, I broke off a chunk of the table.

My father's and my problem was never that we were so different, but that, even back then, we were too much alike.

• • •

When you are a child, you need your parent to be omnipotent, the mighty figurehead who will always keep you safe. Then, when you are a teenager, you need your parent to be flawed, because it seems the only way to build yourself up, to break away. I am thirty-two years old now, and mostly I need my father to be insane.

The thought started with my father's untimely death. After his constant vigilance against would-be pedophiles, rapists, serial killers, it seemed notable that no monster got him in the end. Instead, it was an overworked, English-challenged taxi driver who never stood trial after threatening to countersue the city for improperly marking the construction detour for the Big Dig, thus setting the stage for the shocking accident and, of course, causing the driver debilitating back pain that meant he'd never work again.

I began to wonder if, all his life, my father had feared the wrong things. And then it was only a hop, skip, and jump to wonder if he had had anything to fear at all.

What if there had never been any monster hiding in the closet? No homicidal sexual deviant waiting to snatch little Annabelle Granger off the streets?

Academics are notorious for their brilliant, brittle minds. And mathematicians in particular. What if it had all been in my father's head?

Truth is, looking back on all of our days on the road, I never noticed anything out of the ordinary. I never felt unknown eyes watching me. I never saw a car slow down so the driver could catch a second glance. I never, ever felt threatened, and I thought about it, believe me, I thought about it every time I came home and found our five suitcases packed and stacked next to the front door. What had gone wrong this time? What sin had I committed? I never got an answer.

My father had fought a war. Wholeheartedly, manically, obsessively.

My mother and I simply had gone along for the ride.

I wonder about it again, as I traverse yet another crowded subway train, filled with potential danger, and yet emerge safely at my destination. As I climb up the stairs into the rapidly darkening night. As I make a left and head once more to my tiny North End apartment.

My footsteps are brisk and sure, my chin up, my shoulders square. But I'm not simply telegraphing my capabilities to potential muggers. I'm honestly happy to be going home. I'm looking forward to seeing my dog, Bella, and I know that after spending all day cooped up alone, she is looking forward to seeing me.

We will probably go for a jog along the waterfront, even though it's after dark and in a crime-infested city. We'll run very fast. I'll bring a Taser. But we'll go, because Bella and I both like to run, and what else can you do?

I am alive. And I am young, and I am helpless not to look ahead. I want to expand my business someday, maybe have two or three assistants and rent a real office space. More than sewing, I have a flair for color and space. I've been thinking about taking classes in interior design, of building my own little Martha Stewart empire.

Sometimes I think of meeting someone special. I attend the small community church just around the corner. I have made some passing acquaintances. Every now and then, I try to date. Maybe I will fall in love, get married. Maybe, someday, I'll have a baby. We will move to the suburbs. I will plant dozens of roses and paint murals in every room. I will never allow my husband to buy luggage; he will think it's a charming eccentricity.

I will have a daughter; in my dreams it's always a daughter, never a son. I will name her Leslie Ann and I will buy her dozens of personalized ceramic mugs.

I think of these things as I reach my apartment building, as I look left, then right, note no strangers lurking in the shadows, then slip the outer-door key from between my clenched fingers and unlock the old, solid wood door. Bright lights fire up the little antechamber, left-hand side covered with a row of slender brass mailboxes. I close the exterior door, making sure it latches behind me.

I get my mail: some bills, some junk mail—good news, a client's check. Then I peer through the glass window of the inner door to make certain the lobby is clear. No one is about.

I enter the lobby, I start climbing up five flights of narrow, creaky stairs. I can already hear Bella above, having caught a whiff of my approach, whining excitedly at the door.

There is only one problem with my fantasies, I think now. In my dreams, no one is ever calling me Tanya. In my dreams, the man I love calls me Annabelle.

8

IT PLAYED OUT like this: The police weren't going to help me. Paranoid or not, my father had been right: Law enforcement is a system. It exists to aid victims, to catch perpetrators, and to advance key officers' careers. Witnesses, sources—we were fodder along the way, disposable objects inevitably ground up by the huge, bureaucratic machine. I could sit by my phone all day, waiting for a call that would never come. Or I could find Dori Petracelli myself.

My desk was covered in a jumbled pile of fabric scraps, window-treatment sketchings, and client proposals, not an unusual state of affairs for an apartment that offered more ambience than square footage. I gathered the whole mess into my arms and shifted it to the alarmingly large pile tilting dangerously on the coffee table. Now I could see my target: my laptop computer. I booted it up and got to work.

First stop, the website for the National Center for Missing and Exploited Children. I was greeted with photos of three small children who had been declared missing in the past week. One boy, two girls. One was from Seattle, one from Chicago, the other from St. Louis. All cities where I used to live.

I wonder sometimes if this is what got my mother in the end. That no matter how much we ran, we still ended up running again. If you want to get technical about things, there's no safe place to raise a child. Crime is universal, registered sex offenders live everywhere. I know; I check the databases.

The National Center for Missing and Exploited Children hosts its own search engine. I entered *female, Massachusetts,* and *missing within 25 years.* I clicked on the arrows to launch the search, then sat back and chewed on my thumbnail.

Bella came out from the tiny kitchenette, having just scarfed down her dinner. Now she regarded me reproachfully. *Run,* her gaze said. *Outside. Get a leash. Fun.*

Bella was a seven-year-old purebred Australian shepherd, her leggy, athletic body a mottled mix of white splashed with patches of brown and blue. Like a lot of Australian shepherds, she had one blue eye, one brown. It gave her a perpetually quizzical look she liked to use to her advantage.

"One moment," I told her.

She whined at me and, when that still didn't work, flopped onto the floor in full doggy snit. I had received Bella in lieu of payment from a client four years ago. Bella had just destroyed the woman's favorite pair of Jimmy Choo heels, and the woman had had enough of the dog's high-strung behavior. Truthfully, Australian sheepdogs aren't good apartment dogs. If you don't keep them occupied, they do get in trouble.

But Bella and I did all right. Mostly because I liked to run and, even entering the middle-aged phase of a dog's life, Bella thought nothing of whipping out a quick six miles.

I would have to take her out soon, or risk losing one of my favorite throw pillows or perhaps a beloved bolt of fabric. Bella always knew how to make her point.

The search was done. My computer screen filled with a scrolling column of bright, happy faces. School photos, close-ups from the family album. Photos of missing children always showed them happy. The whole point was to make you hurt worse. Search results: fifteen.

I reached for the mouse and slowly worked my way down the column: *Anna, Gisela, Jennifer, Janeeka, Sandy, Katherine, Katie . . .*

It was hard for me to look at the pictures. Even with my doubts about my father, I always wondered if I might have become one of them. If we hadn't moved, if he hadn't been so obsessed.

I thought again about the locket. Where had it come from? And why, oh why, had I given it to Dori?

Her name did not appear on the list. I allowed myself to exhale. Bella perked up, sensing the release in tension, the possibility of beginning our normal nightly routine.

But then I noticed the dates. None of these cases were older than '97. Despite the open search parameters for time, the database must not go back that far. I chewed on my thumbnail again, debating options.

I could call the hotline, but that might raise too many questions. I preferred the anonymity of Internet searches. Well, at least the appearance of anonymity, since God knows the proliferation of spyware probably meant Big Brother, or at least a marketing megamachine, was following my every move.

I knew another site to try. I didn't go there as much. It made me sad.

I typed into my Internet search engine: www.doenetwork.org. And in two seconds, I was there.

The Doe Network deals primarily with old missing-persons cases, trying to match skeletalized remains found in one location with a missing-persons report that might have been filed in another jurisdiction. Its motto: "There is no time limit to solving a mystery."

The thought gave me a chill as I sat, one hand now clasping the vial of my mother's ashes, the other hand typing in the search parameter: *Massachusetts*.

The very first hit sent me reeling. Three photos of the same boy, starting when he was ten, then age-progressed to twenty, then to thirty-five. He had gone missing in 1965 and was presumed dead. One minute he'd been playing in the yard, the next he was gone. A pedophile doing time in Connecticut claimed to have raped and murdered the child, but couldn't remember where he'd buried the body. So the case remained open, the parents working as feverishly now to find their son's remains as they must have once worked, forty years ago, to find their child.

I wondered what it was like for the parents to have to look at these age-progressed photos. To get that glimpse of who their son might have been, had the mom not gone inside to answer the phone or the father not rolled under the car to change the oil. . . .

Fight, my father always told me. Seventy-four percent of abducted children who are murdered are killed within the first three hours. Survive those three hours. Don't give the bastard a chance.

I was crying, I don't know why. I never knew this little boy. Most likely, he died over forty years ago. But I could understand his terror. I felt it every time my father started one of his lectures or training exercises. Fight? When you are a fifty-pound child against a two-hundred-pound male, whatever in the world can you do that will honestly make a difference? My father may have had his illusions, but I have always been a realist.

If you are a child and someone wants to hurt you, chances are, you'll wind up dead.

I moved to the next case: 1967. I looked at just the dates now; I didn't want to see the pictures. It took me five more clicks. Then, November 12, 1982.

I was staring at Dori Petracelli. I was looking at her photo, age-progressed to thirty. I was reading the case study of what had happened to my best friend.

Then I went into the bathroom and vomited until I dry-heaved.

Later, twenty, forty, fifty minutes, I didn't know

anymore, I had the leash in one hand, the Taser in the other. Bella danced around my feet, practically tripping me in her haste to get downstairs.

I clipped the leash to her collar. And we ran. We ran and we ran and we ran.

By the time we returned home, a good hour and a half later, I thought I had composed myself. I felt cold, even clinical. I still had my family's luggage. I would start packing immediately.

But then I turned on the news.

Bobby arrived home shortly after nine p.m., a man on a mission: He had approximately forty minutes to shower, eat, chug a Coke, then return to Roxbury. Unfortunately, South Boston parking had other ideas. He worked an eight-block radius around his tripledecker before getting pissed off and parking up on the curb. A Boston cop would take great personal delight in ticketing a state trooper, so he was living dangerously.

A pleasant surprise: One of his tenants, Mrs. Higgins, had left him a plate of cookies. "Saw the news. Keep up your strength," her note said.

Bobby couldn't argue with that, so he started his dinner by eating a lemon square. Then three more as he sorted through the pile of mail scattered on his floor, picking out key envelopes bearing bills, rent checks, leaving the rest.

One more lemon square for the road, chewing without even tasting anymore, he headed down the long narrow hallway to his bedroom at the back of the unit. He unbuttoned his shirt with one hand, emptied his pants pockets with the other. Then shrugged out of his shirt, kicked off his pants, and hit the tiny blue-tiled bathroom in beige dress socks and tighty whities. He got the shower going to full roar. One of the best things he still remembered from his tactical team days—coming home to a long, hot shower.

He stood under the scalding spray for endless minutes. Inhaling the steam, letting it sink into his pores, wishing, as he always did, that it would wash the horror away.

His brain was a spin cycle of overactive images. Those six little girls, mummified faces pressed against clear plastic garbage bags. Old photographs of twelve-year-old Catherine, her pale face hollowed out by hunger, her eyes giant black pupils from spending a month alone in the dark.

And, of course, the other image he was forced to see, would probably be seeing for the rest of his life: the look on Catherine's husband's face, Jimmy Gagnon's face, right before the bullet from Bobby's rifle shattered his skull.

Two years later, Bobby still dreamed about the shooting four or five nights a week. He figured someday it would become three times a week. Then twice a week. Then maybe, if he was lucky, he would get down to three or four times a month.

He'd done counseling, of course. Still met with his old LT, who served as his mentor. Even attended a meeting or two of other officers who'd been involved in critical incidents. But from what he could tell, none of that made much difference. Taking a man's life changed you, plain and simple.

You still had to get up each morning and put on your pants one leg at a time like everyone else.

And some days were good, and some days were bad, and then there were a whole lotta other days in between that really weren't anything at all. Just existence. Just getting the job done. Maybe D.D. was right. Maybe there were two Bobby Dodges: the one who lived before the shooting and the one who lived after. Maybe, inevitably, that's how these things worked.

Bobby ran the shower till the water turned cold. Toweling off, he glanced at his watch. He had a whole minute left for dinner. Microwave chicken, it was.

He stuck two Tyson chicken breasts into the microwave, then retreated to the steamy bathroom and attacked his face with a razor.

Now officially five minutes late, he threw on fresh clothes, popped open a Coke, stuck two piping-hot chicken breasts onto a paper plate, and made his first critical mistake: He sat down.

Three minutes later, he was asleep on his sofa, chicken falling to the floor, paper plate crumpled on his lap. Four hours of sleep in the past fifty-six will do that to a man.

He jerked awake, dazed and disoriented, sometime

later. His hands lashed out. He was looking for his rifle. Jesus Christ, he needed his rifle! Jimmy Gagnon was coming, clawing at him with skeletal hands.

Bobby sprang off his sofa before the last of the image swept from his mind. He found himself standing in the middle of his own apartment, pointing a greasy paper plate at his TV as if he were packing heat. His heart thundering in his chest.

Anxiety dream.

He counted forward to ten, then slowly back down to one. He repeated the ritual three times until his pulse eased to normal. He set down the crumpled plate. Retrieved the two chicken breasts from the floor. His stomach growled. Thirty-second rule, he decided, and ate with his bare hands.

First time Bobby had met Catherine Gagnon, he'd been a sniper called out to the scene of a domestic barricade—report of an armed husband, holding his wife and child at gunpoint. Bobby had taken up position across from the Gagnon residence, surveying the situation through his rifle scope, when he'd spotted Jimmy, standing at the foot of the bed, waving a handgun, and yelling so forcefully that Bobby could see the tendons roping the man's neck. Then Catherine came into view, clutching her four-year-old son against her chest. She'd had her hands clasped over Nathan's ears, his face turned into her, as if trying to shield him from the worst.

The situation went from bad to worse. Jimmy had grabbed his child from Catherine's arms. Had pushed the boy across the room, away from what was going to happen next. Then he had leveled the gun at his wife's head.

Bobby had read Catherine's lips in the magnified world of his Leupold scope.

"What now, Jimmy? What's left?"

Jimmy suddenly smiled, and in that smile, Bobby had known exactly what was going to happen next.

Jimmy Gagnon's finger tightened on the trigger. And fifty yards away, in the darkened bedroom of a neighbor's townhouse, Bobby Dodge had blown him away.

In the shooting's aftermath, there was no doubt that Bobby made some mistakes. He'd started drinking, for one. Then he'd met Catherine in person, at a local museum. That had probably been his most self-destructive act. Catherine Gagnon was beautiful, she was sexy, she was the grateful widow of the abusive husband Bobby had just sent to an early grave.

He'd gotten involved with her. Not physically, like D.D. and most others assumed. But emotionally, which was perhaps even worse, and the reason Bobby never bothered to correct anyone's assumptions. He had crossed the line. He'd cared about Cat, and as the people around her had started dying horrific deaths, he'd feared for her life.

Turned out, for good reason.

To this day, D.D. contended that Catherine Gagnon was one of the most dangerous females ever to live in Boston, a woman who had most likely (though they lacked solid evidence) set up her own husband to be killed. And to this day, whenever Bobby thought of her, he mostly saw a desperate mother trying to protect her small child.

A person could be both noble and callous. Self-sacrificing and self-absorbed. Genuinely caring. And a stone-cold killer.

D.D. had the luxury of hating Catherine. Bobby understood her too well.

Now Bobby threw away the paper plate, crumpled the Coke can, tossed it in the recycling bin. He was just gathering up his car keys, mentally steeling himself for what would probably be a very expensive parking ticket, when his phone rang.

He glanced at caller ID, then at the clock. Eleven-fifteen p.m. He understood what had happened before he ever picked up the receiver.

"Catherine," he said calmly.

"Why the hell didn't you tell me?" she exploded hysterically.

Which was how Bobby learned that the media had finally discovered the truth.

9

"ALL RIGHT, PEOPLE," D.D. Warren said crisply, passing around the latest reports. "We have approximately"—she glanced at her watch—"seven hours, twenty-seven minutes for damage control. The big guys upstairs are in agreement that at oh-eight-hundred, we're giving our first press conference. So, for God's sake, give me some progress to report or we're all going to look like assholes."

Bobby, who was trying to slip discreetly into the conference room, caught the tail end of her statement, just as D.D.'s gaze swung up and spotted his late entrance. She scowled at him, looking even more exhausted and ragged than the last time he'd seen her. If he'd caught six hours of sleep in the past two and a half days, D.D. had snagged about three. She also appeared nervous. He scanned the room, then spotted the deputy superintendent, head honcho of Homicide, sitting in the corner. That would do it.

"Nice of you to join us, Detective Dodge," D.D. drawled for the room's benefit. "I thought you were grabbing dinner, not six hours at a spa."

He gave the best apology a cop could make. "I brought lemon squares."

He placed the last of Mrs. Higgins's homemade treasures in the middle of the table. The other detectives pounced. Eating baked goods trumped needling the state guy any day of the week.

"So, as I was saying," D.D. continued, slapping away hands until she could snag a cookie for herself, "we need news. Jerry?"

Sergeant McGahagin, head of the three-man squad in charge of compiling the list of missing girls, looked up from the table. Rather hastily, he brushed powdered sugar off his report, fingers shaking so hard from his two-day caffeine binge, he actually missed the single sheet of paper the first three times. McGa-hagin settled for reading the executive summary where it lay on the table.

"We got twelve names of missing females under the age of eighteen unsolved from '65 to '83; six names from '97 to '05; and, of course, fourteen years to go in between," he spat out as one rapid-fire sentence, eyes blinking furiously. "I could use two more bodies to help scan lists if anyone finds himself with free time. 'Course we also need the forensic anthropologist's report for cross-reference. And then you gotta wonder if the bodies are all from Mass. or do we need to broaden out to the greater New England area—Rhode Island, Connecticut, New Hampshire, Vermont, Maine. Really hard to do, you know, without a victim profile; I don't even know if we're barking up the right tree, that's all I have to report."

D.D. stared at him. "Jesus, Jerry. Lay off the coffee for an hour, will you? You're gonna need a blood transfusion the rate you're going."

"Can't," he said, twitching. "Will get a headache."

"Can you even hear through the ringing in your ears?"

"Huh?"

"Oh boy." D.D. sighed, stared out at the wider table. "Well, Jerry has a point. Hard to know how good any of our research is going without the victimology report. I spoke with Christie Callahan two hours ago. Bad news is, we probably get to wait at least two weeks."

The detectives groaned. D.D. held up her hand. "I know, I know. You guys think you're overloaded? She's even more screwed than we are. She's got six mummified remains that all have to be processed properly, and not even a brilliant—and might I add charming—task force to assist. Of course, she's also doing this by the book. Which means the remains first had to be fumigated for prints. Then they had to be sent to Mass General for X-rays, and are just now returning to her lab.

"Apparently, wet mummification is its own peculiar thing. It occurs naturally in the peat bogs of Europe, and there've been a few cases in Florida. But this is a first for New England, meaning Christie is learning as she goes. She's guessing three or four days to process each mummy. Given six mummies, you do the math."

"Can she give us results one at a time, as she gets each corpse processed?" Detective Sinkus asked. He was the one with the new baby, which probably explained the state of his clothing.

"She's considering it. There's archaeological protocol, or some shit like that, which argues for treating the remains as a group. Individually, we may not see what is implied by the group as a whole."

"What?" Detective Sinkus asked.

"I'll work on her," D.D. said. She switched gears to Detective Rock, who was handling the Crime Stoppers reports. "Tell us the truth: Anyone confess yet?"

"Only about three dozen. Bad news, most of 'em have recently gone off their meds." Rock picked up an impressive stack of papers and started passing it around. Rock had been on the Boston PD roughly forever. Even Bobby had heard stories of the veteran detective's legendary abilities to zoom straight from hideous crime A to random bit of evidence B to evil perpetrator C. Tonight, however, the detective's hearty boom carried a forced undercurrent. His buzz-cut black hair seemed to have picked up extra highlights of gray, while shadows had gathered beneath his eyes. Given his mother's rapidly deteriorating health, working a massive investigation had to be difficult. Still, he was getting things done.

"You only have to pay attention to the top sheet," Rock was explaining. "The detailed logs are just for those of you with time to kill."

That elicited a few tired chuckles.

"So, we're averaging a call every few minutes, and that's before the media went ballistic tonight. Kind of sad about the leak." He looked at D.D. as if she might comment.

She merely shook her head. "Don't know how it happened, Tony. Don't have time or energy to care. Frankly, I'm impressed we made it as long as we did."

Rock shrugged philosophically at that. Fifty-six hours under the radar had been a minor miracle. "Well, before the leak, we had a pretty easy time eliminating the whackos. We'd just ask if they buried the remains together or separately. Once they went into elaborate descriptions of the grave site, we could merrily cross them off our list. So yeah, there's been a lot of calls, but it's been pretty smooth sailing. Don't know if you'll find me saying that tomorrow."

"Any good leads?" D.D. pressed.

"Couple. Got a call from a man who claimed to be an attendant nurse at Boston State Mental in the mid-seventies. Said one of the patients at that time was the son of a very wealthy family in Boston. They didn't want anyone to know the kid was there, never paid him a visit. Rumor mill was that the son had done something 'inappropriate' with his little sister. This was the family's way of dealing with it. Patient's name was Christopher Eola. We're running it now, but can't find a current address or driver's license for him. We're working on tracking down the family."

D.D. raised a brow. "Better than I expected," she said. "Gives us at least one person to dangle in front of the press."

"Given the location," Rock said dryly, "I thought we'd have a longer list of crazies to track down. Then again, the night's young."

He took a deep breath, scrubbed at his gray-stubbled cheeks. "And, as you'd expect with these types of cases, we've had some outreach from families with missing kids. I have a list." He held it up for Sergeant McGahagin. "Some of these folks are outta state, so I guess we're getting started on that wider survey you were talking about. And"—he skimmed down the names McGahagin had reported—"I see three matches already: Atkins, Gomez, Petracelli."

D.D.'s expression didn't change. Bobby thought it

interesting she hadn't volunteered any details from her conversation with Annabelle Granger yet, including the mention of Dori Petracelli. Then again, D.D. always liked to play things close to the vest.

He'd done some follow-up digging on Dori Petracelli himself, so inclusion of her name on the list of missing girls didn't surprise him. It was the date—November 12, 1982—that continued to stump him.

Detective Rock sat down. Detective Sinkus took the floor.

"So, uh, I thought I should have a handout. But when I looked at everything I had to share, it was fifty pages of names, and I thought, hell, no one here has time to read fifty pages of names, so I didn't bother."

"Thank God," someone said.

"Appreciate it," another detective commented.

The deputy superintendent cleared his throat in the corner. They immediately shut up.

Sinkus shrugged. "Look, my job's to assemble a preliminary list of interview subjects. We're talking contractors, neighbors, former lunatic-asylum workers, and known offenders in the area, going back thirty years. List? It's a goddamn phone book. Not saying we can't work it"—he glanced hastily at the deputy superintendent—"I'm just saying we'd have to quadruple the Boston police force to make a dent in this sucker. Basically, without more information to narrow down the suspect pool, like, say, a definitive time line, I don't think the current task is manageable. Honest to God, this is one area where we need the victimology report."

"Well, we don't have it," D.D. said flatly, "so try again."

"Knew you'd say that," Sinkus mumbled with a sigh. He stuck his hands in his pockets. "Okay, so I had an idea."

"Spit it out."

"I got an appointment tomorrow to interview George Robbards, former clerk at the Mattapan station. He processed all the incident reports from '72 to '98. I figure if there's anyone who might have a bead on the area—and probably a good recollection of what activities, or what people, cops were talking about, even if they didn't have enough to file on—it would be him."

D.D. was actually stunned into silence. "Well, hell, Roger, that's a brilliant idea."

He smiled sheepishly, hands still in his pockets. "Honestly, it was my wife's. Good news about having a newborn, my wife's always awake now when I go home, so what the hell, we talk. She remembered me saying once that the clerks are the real brains of any police station. We all come and go. The clerks stay forever."

That was true. A cop spent maybe three or four years at a single station. The police clerks, on the other hand, might serve for decades.

"Okay," D.D. said briskly. "I like it. Those are the kinds of ideas we need. In fact, I'll even forgive your lack of paperwork right now, as long as you deliver a transcript of tomorrow's interview the second it's completed. I've heard good things about Robbards. And given that six bodies in one location implies a subject who operated in the area for years, yeah, I'd like to hear Robbards's thoughts. Interesting."

D.D. picked up her copies of the reports. Pounded them into a neat pile.

"Okay, people. So this is where we're at: We're manning a machine-gun investigation, spraying the area with bullets and hoping like hell we'll hit something. I know it's tiring, it's messy, it's painful, but this is why we get paid the big bucks. Now, we have"— she glanced at her watch again—"seven hours and counting. So go forth, discover something brilliant, and report back by oh-seven-hundred. First person who tells me something we can use in the press briefing gets to go home to sleep."

She started to push back from the table, half rising out of her chair. But then, at the last moment, she paused, regarded them more gravely.

"We all saw those girls," she said gruffly. "What happened to them . . ." She shook her head, unable to continue, and around the table, guys looked away uncomfortably. Homicide detectives saw a lot of shit, but the cases that involved children always touched a nerve.

D.D. cleared her throat. "I want to send them home. It's been thirty years. That's too long. That's . . . too sad for all of us. So let's do this, okay? I know everyone's tired, everyone's stressed. But we gotta push ahead. We're gonna make this happen. We're gonna get these girls home to their families. And then we're gonna stalk the son of a bitch who did this to the bitter ends of the earth, and nail his ass to the floor. Sound like a plan? I thought as much."

D.D. pushed away from the table, strode for the door.

A full minute passed in silence. Then one by one the detectives headed back to work.

10

BOBBY CAUGHT D.D. in her office. She was hunched over her computer screen, skimming a list of names with a pencil clenched in her fist. She was flying down the list so fast, Bobby wasn't sure she could honestly be reading anything. Maybe she just wanted to look busy, in case someone, such as him, wandered by.

"What?" she asked presently.

"Got a call."

She stopped reading, straightened, looked at him. "Thought you weren't my lackey."

"Thought you were my friend."

"Oh Bobby. You're such a jerk."

The insult made him smile. "I never realized until now just how much I missed you. Can I come in yet, or am I supposed to be bearing roses?"

"Fuck roses," she said. "I still want a decent roast beef sandwich." But her voice had lost its edge. She waved to the empty desk chair across from her. He took that as an invitation, plopping down in the high-backed executive chair. D.D. pushed away from the computer. She really did look like hell, purple bags under her eyes, fingernails bitten down to the nubs. Minute she saw herself on TV, she was gonna be pissed.

"Catherine send her regards?" D.D. asked dryly.

"Not in so many words, but I'm sure she was thinking of her love for the Boston police the entire time we talked."

"So what'd she say?"

"In a minute."

An arched brow. "In a minute?"

"I have other news to report first. Come on, D.D., give a guy a break. Working these hours, I could use some foreplay."

The corner of her mouth twitched up in an unexpected smile. For a moment, Bobby found himself thinking about the good old days again—in particular, the area they had gotten right. . . . He caught himself, straightening quickly, flipping through his spiral notebook.

"I, um . . . looked up Russell Granger. Started checking on Annabelle's story."

D.D.'s smile disappeared. She sighed, leaning forward to rest her elbows on her knees. They were back to business. "Am I going to like this report? More important, can I use it for the press conference?"

"Possibly. So: Russell Granger filed a police report in August of '82, one of three reports he would file leading up to October. First report was trespassing.

Brooke County Library
945 Main Street
Wellsburg, WV 26070

Granger heard someone in his yard in the middle of the night. Went out himself, swore he heard someone running away. When he checked again in the morning, he found muddy footprints all around the perimeter. Couple of uniforms went out, jotted down his story, but not much to do: no real crime, no description of the subject. Report got filed, 'Call us again if you have any trouble, Mr. Granger,' yada, yada, yada.

"Second report was a Peeping Tom, filed September eight. Also called in by Mr. Granger, but on behalf of his elderly neighbor, Geraldine Watts, who swore she saw a young man 'skulking' around the Granger residence and peering into one of the windows. Two uniformed officers were dispatched once again, Stan Jezukawicz and Dan Davis, known more affectionately as Stan-n-Dan. They interviewed Mrs. Watts, who provided a description of a white male, between five nine and six two, dark hair, 'disheveled' in appearance, wearing a gray T-shirt and jeans. She never got a look at his face. As she was picking up the phone to dial Mr. Granger, the subject took off running down the street."

"Where did Mrs. Watts live?"

"Across the street from the Grangers. Point is, the window where the unidentified subject was 'skulking' belonged to Annabelle, the Grangers' seven-year-old daughter. At this point, according to Stan-n-Dan, Mr. Granger started to get very agitated. Turned out that for the past few months, little 'gifts' had been appearing on his front porch. One had been a plastic horse, one a yellow Super Ball, one a blue marble. You know, kid kind of stuff. Mr. Granger and his wife had assumed that one of the other children on the block had a crush on Annabelle, was a secret admirer."

"Ah shit," D.D. said. "The locket. Wrapped in the *Peanuts* comic strip, isn't that what Annabelle said?"

"Yeah. Stan-n-Dan take the hint and, with Granger in tow, start canvassing all the neighbors. Plenty of kids, none of them have any idea what Mr. Granger is talking about. Mr. Granger gets upset; he's convinced the Peeping Tom *is* the secret admirer, meaning a grown man is stalking his daughter. He demands immediate police protection, all sorts of stuff. Stan-n-Dan talk him down. Again, no crime has been committed, you know? And maybe the secret admirer is actually a classmate from Annabelle's school. They promise to check it out.

"Stan-n-Dan depart, write up their report. It's sent over for a detective's review, but again, what's the crime? Stan-n-Dan, to be fair, are conscientious. They follow up with the school and get the principal to talk to Annabelle's classmates. These 'interviews' don't generate any hits, unfortunately—if the 'secret admirer' is one of Annabelle's schoolmates, the kid is too intimidated to confess.

"This info gets filed away. And the case languishes. What's there to do? There's record of Mr. Granger calling in a few more times, demanding answers, but no one has much to tell him. Keep his eyes out, call again if there's any problems, yada, yada, yada.

"October nineteen, eleven-oh-five p.m., Mr. Granger calls police dispatch requesting immediate assistance. There's an intruder in his house. Dispatch sends four cars to the neighborhood. Stan-n-Dan catch the news on the radio and also go flying over, concerned about the family.

"Guess it's a mob scene when they get there. Granger is out on his front porch, dressed in pajamas, wielding a baseball bat. Man nearly gets himself shot by the first responders before Stan-n-Dan sort it all out. Dan notes in his report that Granger doesn't look too good these days. Ragged, jerky. Sounds like Granger hasn't slept much; since the last incident, he's been up most nights 'keeping watch.'

"Also turns out Mr. Granger told a little white lie. Upon being pressed, no one actually broke into his house. Instead, he once again heard sounds outside. But Granger didn't think the police would take that seriously enough, hence he'd 'expanded' his report. Most of the officers don't take this so well, but again, Stan-n-Dan feel an obligation. They walk around the perimeter, looking for signs of trouble. They notice a few changes to the landscaping—Mr. Granger has ripped out the shrubs near his house, chopped down two trees. Yard is pretty open now, not many places to hide. They both think this is a little paranoid, until they get to Annabelle's window: There are deep gouges in the wood beneath the frame. Fresh tool marks, like the kind made from a crowbar. Someone was trying to break in."

"But Annabelle is fine?" D.D. interjected with a frown.

"Absolutely. She's not sleeping in her room anymore, you see. Mr. Granger and his wife had already made the decision after the Peeping Tom report to move her into their room. In all three incidents, the kid never heard a thing. As for the wife, I don't know. The uniforms never interviewed her. Sounds like Mr. Granger did the talking. Mrs. Granger was always inside the house with Annabelle."

D.D. rolled her eyes. He knew what she was thinking: sloppy police work. Both spouses should have been interviewed, separately, the seven-year-old as well. But twenty-five years later, what could you do?

"Given the tool marks," Bobby continued, "Stan-n-Dan conduct a door-to-door canvass of the neighborhood. When they get to Mrs. Watts's house, the woman who originally reported the Peeping Tom, she appears really agitated. Turns out she hasn't been sleeping well—the mice in the attic are making too much noise."

"The *mice?*"

"That's what Stan-n-Dan think, too. They go flying upstairs. In the attic they discover a 'nest': a used sleeping bag, flashlight, can opener, bottles of water and, get this, a five-gallon empty plastic bucket that's obviously been serving as a latrine."

"Please tell me we have that plastic bucket in evidence."

"We would never be so lucky. They did try to print it, however, so we would have a copy of the prints on file, except that there were no prints."

"Sweet Jesus. Did anything go right with this investigation?"

"No. This thing was FUBAR all the way around. Now, of course, Mrs. Watts is hysterical—looks like someone has been living in her attic. But that's nothing compared to Russell Granger, who pretty much demands the National Guard deploy just to protect him and his family. It gets even worse when the detectives start going through the 'nest' and find a whole stack of Polaroids: of Annabelle walking to school; of Annabelle out at recess; of Annabelle playing hopscotch with her best friend, Dori Petracelli . . ."

D.D. closed her eyes. "All right, cut to the chase."

Bobby shrugged. "There was nothing the police could do. They had no description of the man, and in regard to Annabelle, they didn't have a crime. It's '82, before the anti-stalking laws. They revisit Annabelle's school, interrogating bus drivers, janitors, male teachers, anyone who's come into contact with Annabelle and therefore might have formed an 'attachment' to her. They work the scene in Mrs. Watts's house. Initial examination of evidence doesn't yield prints, doesn't yield much of anything. The detectives spin their wheels searching for a vagrant/pedophile who's partial to stalking little girls and living in old ladies' attics. They visited mental health institutes, soup kitchens, the usual roundup of perverts. It was all local knowledge in those days, and it doesn't get them anywhere.

"In the meantime Mr. Granger goes nuts. Accuses the cops of not caring. Accuses his neighbors of knowingly harboring perverts. Accuses the DA of single-handedly being responsible for the future murder of Granger's seven-year-old daughter. Then one day the cops return to the Granger residence for a follow-up interview, and no one's there. A week later, the DA gets a call from Mr. Granger announcing that since the Commonwealth of Massachusetts refused to protect his daughter, he's moved. Granger hangs up before anyone can ask him any questions, and that's it. The department steps up patrols of the neighborhood for a week or two, but nothing's seen or reported again. And the case dies a natural death, the way these things do."

"Wait a minute. Where's that damn list again? Okay, according to what we learned today, Dori Petracelli went missing November twelve, just weeks after all this happened. Shouldn't that have raised a few brows?"

"Dori didn't disappear from her house. She vanished when she was visiting her grandparents out in Lawrence. Different jurisdiction, different circumstances. Looks like the Lawrence department asked for a copy of the police report for the unknown subject in Geraldine Watts's house, but nothing came of it. Remember—no prints, no detailed physical description in the file. I think Lawrence gave the Granger incidents a cursory glance, and then, realizing there wasn't anything solid there to sink their teeth into, focused their attention on their own case."

D.D. sat back. "Shit. You're thinking Annabelle was the real target, Dori the consolation prize."

"Something like that."

"Where does that leave us?"

"Twenty-five years wiser. Look." Bobby leaned back, tucked his hands behind his head. "I don't want to criticize Stan-n-Dan. I went through their report, and they gave Mr. Granger more time than a lot of officers would. I think what hurt them, however, was that they weren't hunters. They went up in that attic, they saw a nest. Once it got that term, everyone else saw a nest as well, and that, coupled with the description of the guy as 'disheveled,' led all the investigators down a certain path. It's one of the reasons this case didn't seem to connect strongly to Dori Petracelli. According to reports, Dori's abductor was driving a white van. But no one thought of the Peeping Tom on Annabelle's street as owning a vehicle, as having those kinds of resources."

"They were chasing a homeless man, someone mentally ill."

"Exactly. But when I look at the scene in the attic, I don't see a vagrant seeking shelter. From a sniper's perspective, this was a hunting blind. Think of the vantage point—three stories up and directly across the street from the target. Guy's got cover over his head,

106

a sleeping bag for comfort, snacks in case he gets a little hungry, and a bucket for bodily functions. It's perfect. Hunting is about waiting. This guy had come up with the perfect setup to wait a very long time."

"Premeditated," D.D. said softly.

"Calculated," Bobby clarified. "Clever. This guy, the Peeping Tom, he'd done it before."

"Maybe five other times?"

"Yeah." Bobby nodded quietly. "Maybe. My two cents—Annabelle Granger was targeted by a sophisticated pedophile who had probably already abducted at least one other girl by this time. And if Annabelle's father hadn't proved to be such a paranoid little shit, it would be her body down there in that pit, not Dori Petracelli's. Annabelle Granger got away. Dori wasn't so lucky."

D.D. rubbed her face. "We're sure this is 1982? There is absolutely, positively no chance that every single investigator involved got the date wrong?"

"It was 1982."

"And you're sure—absolutely, positively sure—that Richard Umbrio was already incarcerated in Walpole at this time?"

"Yep. Got that date on several reports as well. The Peeping Tom wasn't Umbrio, D.D. It's not even a matter of comparing dates. Look at MO. Umbrio was an opportunistic predator, snatch and grab, Hey, little girl, have you seen my lost dog? This is far more elaborate, almost ritualized. We're talking a totally different breed of whacko."

"But the use of an underground pit!" D.D. exploded. "The close physical match between Annabelle Granger and Catherine Gagnon. You can't tell me it's completely coincidence."

"There are other options. Copycat, for one. By August '82, Umbrio's trial's long finished, the details of the abduction made public. Maybe someone found it 'inspirational.'"

"But victims' pictures, particularly children, aren't made public," D.D. countered. "So, again, how to explain the physical resemblance between Annabelle and Catherine?"

"Pictures aren't made public during the trial phase, but Catherine's description would've been broadcast when she was declared missing. And that search went on for four weeks."

"Huh." D.D. chewed on her lower lip, considered that information.

Bobby unlaced his fingers. "Umbrio wasn't a talker. He never volunteered information to the police on what he did, not even after being found. So you have to consider maybe he had other victims. And/or maybe he had help."

"An accomplice who went unidentified?"

"Yep. Umbrio was barely twenty when he was convicted, nearly a kid himself. Sometimes, two angry juvenile minds . . ."

"Klebold and Harris."

"It happens. Finally, I'm wondering about cellmates or pen pals. Pedophiles seem to have a thing for networking. Just consider all the 'Internet groups' and international 'child sex slave' rings that have been uncovered in recent years. More so than the other homicidal maniacs out there, pedophiles like to chat. Now, Umbrio went to prison with a reputation as a fairly brilliant, if not creative, offender. Maybe someone went looking for him there."

"Well, this just keeps getting better and better." D.D. scowled at him. "I thought you had something for my press briefing. What the hell here can I report to the press?"

Bobby held up a staying hand. "One last thing to consider. It's not scientific, but we can't dismiss it: cop instinct. You felt it the minute you entered the chamber. I did, too. Catherine Gagnon's case is somehow tied in to what happened out in Mattapan. I can't feel it, touch it, or taste it, but I know it's true, and so do you. Which is why Catherine's phone call matters so much."

D.D. suddenly perked up. She appeared almost wild with hope. "Catherine's returning to Massachusetts? She's going to talk to us? She's going to let us finally arrest her for setting up the murder of her husband!"

"Mmm, not quite. Her answer to returning to Mass., as the saying goes, is not anatomically possible. We're going to her."

"Oh yeah, two detectives flying to Arizona. Brass will love that."

"Ahh," Bobby said with a wiggle of his eyebrows, "but they will. Once you explain to the press that you've already had a major break in the case, and will soon be interviewing not one, but two potential witnesses." Bobby rose out of his chair, headed to the door. Now was the time for a clean getaway. Unfortunately, he wasn't quite fast enough.

"What do you mean, two witnesses?" D.D. called after him. "Catherine Gagnon is only one."

"Oh, didn't I mention that? I meant to include Granger. In return for Catherine's cooperation, she is demanding to meet Annabelle."

11

BOBBY GOT LUCKY at the North End apartment complex; one of the residents was walking out as he was walking up. The thirty-something male took in Bobby's olive khakis, collared shirt, blue tweed sports coat, and politely held the door. Bobby jogged up the front stairs, grabbed the heavy outer door, and waved his thanks. Gotta love urban professionals; they automatically trusted anyone who dressed like them.

Bobby skimmed the mailboxes until he found the right name. Top floor of a walk-up. Wouldn't you know it? Then again, hiking up the narrow staircase was probably as close to real exercise as he was going to get. He hit the stairs, thinking about the good old days when he'd been part of an elite tactical unit who knew how to make an entrance. They could crawl through smoke, drop from choppers, belly-slide through swamps. Only thing you saw was the target in front of you. Only thing you heard was the grunt of the teammate beside you.

Around the third floor, the lack of sleep caught up with him. His stride slowed. He started panting. At the fourth floor, he had to wipe his brow. Definitely time to get his sorry ass to a gym.

At the fifth floor, he spotted the apartment door, saving himself the humiliation of passing out. He paused on the last step, catching his breath. When he finally moved down the hallway, he heard a dog whine excitedly from the other side of the door even before he knocked. He went with a light knuckle rap. The dog promptly hurtled itself at the door, growling and scratching furiously.

A woman's voice from inside: "Bella, down! Bella, stop that. Oh, for heaven's sake!"

The door didn't magically open. He didn't think it would. Instead, he listened to the metal covering scrape back from an ancient peephole. The woman's greeting was almost as warm and friendly as the dog's.

"Ah shit!" Annabelle Granger said.

"Detective Bobby Dodge," he answered politely. "I have a few follow-up questions—"

"What the hell are you doing here? I didn't give you my address!"

"Well, I am a detective."

That reply earned him only silence. He finally held up her phone number. "Reverse directory. I put in your number and, voilà, I got a name and address.

Technology is a wonderful thing, yes?"

"I can't believe you didn't tell me about the pit," she called out from the other side of the door. "How could you sit right across from me, relentlessly milking me for information, and still withhold those kinds of details? Particularly once you realized one of those girls might be my best friend."

"I see you've been watching the news."

"Me and all of Boston. Jerk."

Bobby spread his hands. He found it difficult to negotiate with a solid wood door, but he did his best. "Look, we're all on the same page. We want to know what happened to your friend and find the sorry son of a bitch who did it. Given that, do you think I can come in?"

"No."

"Suit yourself." He reached inside his jacket pocket, withdrew his audio mini-recorder, a spiral notepad, his pen. "So—"

"What do you think you're doing?"

"I'm asking my questions."

"In an open stairway? Whatever happened to privacy?"

"Whatever happened to hospitality?" He shrugged. "You set the ground rules, I'm just playing by them."

"Oh, for heaven's sake." Two sharp metal thunks as steel bolt locks drew back. The rasp of a chain being temperamentally released. A third, more resonant thunk from the vicinity of the floor. Annabelle Granger took her home security seriously. He was curious to see how a professional curtain seamstress had managed to reconcile ambience with the iron bars that no doubt guarded her windows.

She flung the door open. There was a flash of white, then a long-legged dog hurtled itself at Bobby's kneecaps, barking shrilly. Annabelle made no move to rein in the animal. Just watched him through narrowly slit eyes, as if this was the ultimate test.

Bobby stuck out a hand. The dog didn't bite it off. Instead, it ran around his legs over and over again. He tried tracking it and immediately grew dizzy.

"Herd dog?"

"Yeah."

"Border collie?"

"They're black and white."

"Australian shepherd."

She nodded.

"Got a name?"

"Bella."

"Will she eventually stop barking?"

A single shoulder shrug. "Are you deaf yet?"

"Almost."

"Then soon."

He stepped gingerly into the apartment. Bella pressed against the backs of his legs, gamely helping him out. When he got in the apartment, Annabelle closed the door. She went back to work on the double bolt lock, chain lock, and floor jam. Bella finally stopped spinning, standing in front of him to bark instead. Pretty dog, he decided. Really long, sharp teeth.

The last steel bolt fired home, and as if a switch had been thrown, Bella shut up. She gave a final huff, then trotted into the tiny sitting area, weaving her way through piles of fabric before plopping down on a half-buried dog bed. At the last moment, she cocked one eye at him, as if to say she was still paying attention, then she sighed, put her head on her paws, and went to sleep.

"Good dog," Bobby murmured, impressed.

"Not really," Annabelle said, "but we suit each other. Neither one of us likes unexpected guests."

"I'm a bit of a loner myself." Bobby walked deeper into the apartment, doing his best to scope out the place while he had the chance. First impressions: small, cramped main room leading to a small, cramped bedroom. Kitchen was about the size of his bedroom closet, strictly utilitarian, with plain white cupboards and cheap Formica countertops. Family room was slightly larger, boasting a plush green love seat, oversize reading chair, and a small wooden table that also doubled as a work space. Walls were painted a rich golden yellow. Two expanses of enormous eight-foot-high windows were trimmed out with scalloped shades made from a sunflower-covered fabric.

As for any other features of the room, they were obscured by piles of fabric. Reds, greens, blues, golds, coorals, stripes, checks, pastels. Silk, cotton, linen, chenille. Bobby didn't know a lot about these things, but he was guessing there was about any fabric you could ever want somewhere in this room.

And cords and trim pieces, too, he figured out, walking past the kitchen counter and discovering the other side adorned with strings of tassels.

"Homey," he commented, then pointed to the windows. "Great lighting, too. Must be helpful for your line of work."

"What do you want?"

"Now that you mention it, a glass of water would be great."

Annabelle thinned her lips, but crossed to the sink, banging on the faucet.

She was dressed casually this morning. Low-rise black sweatpants, a gray long-sleeve top that skimmed to a stop just above her waist. Her dark hair was held back loosely in a ponytail, no makeup adorned her face. Again he was struck by her resemblance to Catherine, and yet he couldn't think of two women who seemed more different.

Catherine was a carefully wrapped package, a woman who consciously honed her sex appeal and wielded it like a weapon. Annabelle, on the other hand, was an advertisement for urban chic. When she slapped the half-full glass of water into his hand, he didn't so much think of sex as he thought she might try to kick his ass. She crossed her arms in front of her chest and he finally got it.

"Boxing," he said.

"What about it?"

"You're a boxer." He tilted his head to the side. "Tony's gym?"

She snorted. "Like I want to work out with a bunch of testosterone-pumped muscle heads. Lee's. He specializes in kickboxing anyway."

"Any good?"

She glanced at her watch. "Tell you what. If you don't have your questions asked in the next fifteen minutes, you can find out."

"You this testy with all cops, or I'm just special?"

She regarded him stony-eyed. He sighed and decided to get on with it. Russell Granger's deep love for law enforcement had apparently been passed on to his daughter. Bobby set down the water, flipped open his notepad.

"So, I learned some things about what happened in the fall of '82." He glanced up expectantly, thinking to find a glimmer of interest in her eyes, a small softening of her stance. Nothing. "Turns out some guy— an unidentified subject, UNSUB, we call him in official police speak—took an interest in you. Started delivering little gifts to the house. Was caught trespassing after dark. Went so far as to try to break into your bedroom.

"The police were called by your father several times. Third time out, they discovered the subject had been hiding in the neighbor's attic across the street, where apparently he had been watching you. They found stacks of Polaroids, notes containing your daily schedule, that sort of thing. Any of this sound familiar?"

"No." She still sounded belligerent, but her arms

116

were down, her expression less certain. "What'd the police do?"

"Nothing. Back in '82, stalking a seven-year-old girl wasn't a crime. Creepy, yes. Criminal, no."

"That's ridiculous!"

"Apparently, your father thought so as well, because within weeks of the final episode, your family disappeared. And weeks after that," his voice grew quieter, "Dori Petracelli was snatched from her grandparents' yard in Lawrence, never to be seen again. You're sure you didn't know?"

"I looked it up online," she said curtly. "Last night. I figured you wouldn't help me. Detectives answer their own questions, not other people's. So I looked it up for myself."

He waited. It didn't take long.

"Have you seen her missing photo, you know, the portrait they posted all over town?"

He shook his head.

"Come here." She crossed the space abruptly, brushing by him, into the family room. He saw a small notebook computer buried under a pile of papers. She swept the papers to the floor, flipped open the lid, and the computer screen came to life. It took only a few clicks of the mouse on the Internet and Dori Petracelli's missing photo filled the screen. He still didn't get it. Annabelle had to point it out to him.

"Look around her neck. It's the locket. She's wearing my necklace."

Bobby squinted, bent closer. The photo was fuzzy,

black and white, but upon closer inspection . . . He sighed. If he'd had any doubts before, this took care of them.

"According to the blurb on the website," Annabelle spoke up quietly, "that photo was taken a week before Dori disappeared. Most recent photo, you know." Her voice changed, grew an edge. "I bet he liked that. I bet it turned him on. Watching all the news stories, flashing her picture, showing that locket, begging for her safe return. *UNSUBs* like to follow their own cases, right? Like to know how clever they have been. Bastard."

She turned away from him, taking several jerky steps across the room.

Bobby straightened more slowly, keeping his gaze on her face. "What do you remember, Annabelle—"

"Don't call me that! You can't use real names. I go by Tanya. Call me Tanya."

"Why? It's been twenty-five years. What do you still have to fear?"

"How the hell am I supposed to know? I've grown comfortable with the fact that my dad was dancing to the tune of a paranoid drummer. You're the one now saying his fears were genuine. What am I supposed to do with that? Some guy stalked me and I never even knew. Then I left and he . . . he snatched my best friend and he . . ."

She broke off, unable to continue. Her hand pressed hard over her mouth, her other arm curling protectively around her waist. From the dog bed, Bella looked up, wagged her tail, and whined.

"Sorry, girl," Annabelle whispered. "Sorry."

Bobby gave her a minute. She pulled it together. Chin coming up, shoulders squaring off. He didn't understand the father yet; he had a lot of questions about the father, actually. But by all appearances, Russell Granger had raised his daughter right. Twenty-five years later, this girl was tough.

Then the buzzer for her apartment sounded and she jumped.

"What the . . ." she started nervously. "I don't get many . . ." She crossed quickly to the bay windows overlooking the street, checking out who was ringing her unit. Bobby already had his hand tucked inside his jacket, fingers resting on the butt of his gun as he fed off her nervousness. Then just as quickly as the episode started, it ended. Annabelle looked out, spotted the UPS truck, and smiled self-consciously as her shoulders sagged in relief.

"Bella," she called, "it's your boyfriend."

Annabelle went to work on the door locks while Bella pawed frantically at the wood.

"Boyfriend?" Bobby asked.

"Ben, the UPS driver. He and Bella have a thing. I order, he delivers, she gets cookies. I know dogs are color-blind, but if Bella could see a rainbow, her favorite color would still be brown."

Annabelle had finally gotten the locks undone. She pushed open the door and nearly got mowed down by her dog.

"Be right back," Annabelle called over her shoulder

119

to Bobby, then disappeared down the stairs in Bella's wake.

The interruption gave Bobby a moment to collect his thoughts. And add to his mental notes. He was getting a pretty good idea of the life Annabelle currently led. Isolated. Security conscious. Insular. Did her shopping by mail-order catalog or Internet. Best friend was her dog. Closest thing to human connection—signing for her daily delivery from the UPS man.

Perhaps her father had done his job a little too well.

Bella returned, panting hard, looking satisfied. Annabelle was a touch slower coming up the stairs. She wiggled through the doorway with a box roughly the size of her desk. Bobby tried to assist, but she waved him off, dropping the box on the kitchen floor.

"Fabric," she volunteered, kicking the large box ruefully. "Occupational hazard, I'm afraid."

"For a client or 'just because'?"

"Both," she admitted. "It always starts as an order for a client, then next thing I know, I've added two bolts of 'just because.' Frankly, it's a good thing I don't live in a bigger space, or Lord only knows."

He nodded, watching as she crossed to the sink and poured her own glass of water. She seemed composed again. Fetching the delivery had allowed her a chance to regroup her defenses. Now or never, he decided.

"Summer of '82," he declared. "You're seven years old, your best friend is Dori Petracelli, and you're living with your mother and father in Arlington. What comes to mind?"

She shrugged. "Nothing. Everything. I was a kid. I remember kid stuff. Going to swim at the Y. Playing hopscotch on the driveway. I don't know. It was summer. Mostly, I remember having fun."

"The gifts?"

"SuperBall. I found it on the front porch, in a little box wrapped in the Sunday comics. The ball was yellow and bounced very high. I loved it."

"Did your father say anything? Take it away?"

"Nope. I lost it under the front porch."

"Other gifts?"

"Marble. Blue. Found a similar way, met a similar fate."

"But the locket . . ."

"The locket made my father angry," she conceded. "I do remember that. But in my mind, I never knew why. I thought my father was being difficult, not protective."

"According to reports, after the second incident, your parents moved you into their bedroom to sleep at night. Does that ring any bells?"

She frowned, looking genuinely perplexed. "There was something wrong with my room," she said shortly, rubbing her forehead. "We needed to paint it? My father was going to fix . . . something? I don't really remember now. Just, something was wrong, needed to be done. So I slept on the floor in their bedroom for a bit. Family camping trip, my father said. He even painted stars on the ceiling. I thought it was really cool."

"Did you ever feel threatened, Annabelle? Like someone was watching you? Or did a stranger come up to you? Offer you gum or candy? Ask you to take a ride in his car? Or maybe the father of one of your school friends made you uncomfortable? A teacher who stood too close . . ."

"No," she said immediately, voice certain. "And I think I would remember that. Of course, that was before my father's version of safety boot camp, so if someone had approached me . . . I don't know. Maybe I would've taken the candy. Maybe I would've gotten in the car. Eighty-two was the good year, you know." She briskly rubbed her forearms, then added more flatly, "The days before it all went to hell."

Bobby watched her for a bit, waited to see if she would say more. She seemed done, though, memories mined out. He couldn't decide if he believed her or not. Kids were surprisingly perceptive. And yet she'd lived in the middle of a major neighborhood drama, uniformed officers called to her house three times in two months, and she never suspected a thing? Again, kudos to her father, who'd gone out of his way to protect his little girl? Or indication of something worse?

He waited until she finally looked up. The next question was the most important. He wanted her full attention.

"Annabelle," he asked shortly. "Why did you leave Florida?"

"I don't know."

"And St. Louis and Nashville and Kansas City?"

"I don't know, I don't know, I don't know." She threw up her hands, once again frustrated. "You think I haven't asked these questions? You think I haven't wondered? Every time we moved, I spent countless nights trying to figure out where I went wrong. What I did that was so bad. Or what threat I didn't see. I never got it. I *never* got it. By the time I was sixteen, in my best judgment, my father was simply paranoid. Some fathers watch too much football. Mine had a penchant for cash transactions and fake IDs."

"You think your father was crazy?"

"You think sane people uproot their families every year and give them new identities?"

He could see her point. He just wasn't sure where that left them. "You're positive you don't have any pictures from your childhood lying around? Photo album, pictures of your old house, neighbors, schoolmates? That would help."

"We left it all in the house. I don't know what happened to it after that."

Bobby frowned, had a thought, made a note. "What about relatives? Grandparents, aunts or uncles? Someone who would have their own copies of your family photos, be happy to hear you're back?"

She shook her head, still not meeting his eyes. "No relatives; that's one of the reasons it was so easy to move away. My father was an orphan, a product of the Milton Hershey School in Pennsylvania. Credited their program, actually, for giving him his academic start. And as for my mother, her parents died shortly after I was born. Car accident, something like that. My mother didn't talk about them much. I think she still missed them.

"You know," she said abruptly, head coming up. "There is someone who would have photos, though. Mrs. Petracelli. Dori and I lived on the same block, went to the same school, attended the same neighborhood barbecues. She might even have photos of my family. I never thought of that. She might have a photo of my mother."

"Good, good idea."

Her voice grew hesitant. "Have . . . have you told them?"

"Who?"

"The Petracellis. Have you notified them about having found Dori? It's horrible news, and yet in the perverse way these things work, I imagine they'll be grateful."

"Yeah," he murmured quietly. "In the perverse way these things work . . . But no, we haven't told them yet. We'll wait until we have evidence to support the ID. Or, more likely, we'll end up approaching them for a DNA sample to use for matching." He contemplated her for a moment, then made a quick judgment call, one D.D. could hang him for later. "You want the inside track? The remains are mummified. Something the news reports haven't managed to learn yet. Given that, it's going to take a bit before we have more information on any of the bodies."

"I want to see it."

"What?"

"The grave. Where you found Dori. I want to go there."

"Oh no," he stated immediately. "Crime scenes are for professionals only. We don't do public tours. Lawyers, judges, *D.D.,* frown on that sort of thing."

She worked that tilt of her chin again. "I'm not just a member of the public, I'm a potential witness."

"Who, by her own admission, never saw anything."

"Maybe I just don't remember. Going to the site might trigger something."

"Annabelle, you don't want to visit a crime scene. Do your friend a favor: Remember her as your happy seven-year-old playmate. That's the best thing you can do." He closed his notebook, tucked it inside his jacket, then finished his water before placing the empty glass in the sink.

"There is one thing," he said suddenly, as if the thought had just occurred to him.

"What?"

"Well, I don't really know. I mean, Dori Petracelli went missing in '82; everyone's sure about the date. What's so puzzling, however, is that her kidnapping bears a resemblance to another case from 1980. A man named Richard Umbrio kidnapped a twelve-year-old girl and, get this, kept her in a pit. Probably would've killed her, too, except hunters stumbled upon the opening and set her free."

"She lived? She's still alive?" Annabelle's voice perked up.

He nodded, tucking his hands in his pants pockets. "Catherine testified against Umbrio, sent him to prison. That's what's so odd, you see—Umbrio was incarcerated by January of '82 and yet . . ."

"The cases seem related," she filled in for him.

"Exactly." He looked her up and down. "You're sure you've never met Catherine?"

"I don't think so."

"For the record, she doesn't think she's met you either. And yet . . ."

"What does she look like?"

"Oh, about your height. Dark hair, dark eyes. Actually, not so dissimilar, come to think of it."

She blinked uncomfortably at that news. He decided it was now or never.

"Say, what would you think of meeting her in person? Face-to-face. Maybe, if we got the two of you in the same room . . . I don't know, it might shake something loose."

He knew the moment she figured out he'd been playing her, because her body went perfectly still. Her face shut down, her eyes becoming hooded. He waited for an outburst, more swearing, possibly even physical violence. Instead, she just stood there, untouchable in her silence.

"You don't have to like a system," she murmured. "You just have to understand it. Then you can always survive." Her dark brown eyes flickered up, held his. "Where does Catherine live?"

"Arizona."

"Are we going there or is she coming here?"

"For several reasons, it would be best if we go there."

"When?"

"How about tomorrow?"

"Good. That will give us plenty of time."

"For?"

"For you to escort me to the crime scene. You scratch my back, I scratch yours. Isn't that how the saying goes, Detective?"

She had him, fair and square. He nodded once, admitting his defeat. It still didn't soften the rigid set of her shoulders, the stubborn tilt of her chin. He realized, belatedly, that his deceit had hurt her. That for a moment there, they had been conversing almost like real people, possibly she had even liked him.

He thought he should say something; couldn't think of what. Policing often involved lying, and there was no sense in apologizing for something he'd do again if he needed to.

He headed for the door. Bella had risen from her dog bed. She licked his hand while Annabelle unlocked the fortress. Door opened. Annabelle gazed at him expectantly.

"Are you afraid?" he asked abruptly, gesturing to the locks.

"Chance favors the prepared mind," she murmured.

"That doesn't answer my question."

She was quiet for a moment. "Sometimes."

"You live in the city. Locks are smart."

She studied him a moment longer. "Why do you keep asking why my family fled so many times?"

"I think you know."

"Because perpetrators don't magically stop. An UNSUB doesn't spend years stalking and abducting six girls, then suddenly decide one day to get a new hobby. You think my father knew something. You think he had a reason to keep us on the run."

"Locks are smart," he said again.

She simply smiled, stoic this time, and for some reason that made him sad. "What time?" she asked.

He considered his watch, the phone call to D.D. he was gonna have to make, the temper tantrum he was about to endure. "Pick you up at two."

She nodded.

He exited, starting back down the stairs, as up above the bolt locks once again fired home.

12

I'D NEVER RIDDEN in a police car before. I didn't really know what to expect. Hard plastic seats? The stench of vomit and urine? Like my experience with the Boston police station, reality was a letdown. The dark blue Crown Vic looked like any other four-door sedan. Inside was just as prosaic. Plain blue cloth seats. Navy blue carpet. The dash had a two-way radio and a few extra toggle switches, but that was it.

The vehicle appeared recently cleaned—floor freshly vacuumed, air scented by Febreze. A small consideration for me? I didn't know if I was supposed to say "Thank you" or not.

I belted myself in the passenger's seat. I was nervous, hands shaking. It took me three times to work the metal clasp. Detective Dodge didn't try to help or make any comment. I appreciated that more than the car's freshened hygiene.

I'd spent the time since the detective's departure trying to complete an elaborate window valance for a client in Back Bay. Mostly, however, I'd held the watered silk fabric beneath the needle of my sewing machine, foot off the pedal, eyes glued to the TV. Coverage of the Mattapan case was easy to find, every major news station giving it round-the-clock attention. Few, unfortunately, had anything new to say.

They had confirmation that six remains had been found in a subterranean chamber, located on the grounds of the former lunatic asylum. The remains were believed to be those of young girls and had possibly been in the chamber for some time. Police were pursuing several avenues of investigation at this time (Is that what I was? An avenue of investigation?). Reports diverted quickly into wild speculation from there. No mention of the locket. No mention of Dori. No mention of Richard Umbrio.

I'd abandoned my sewing and looked up Umbrio on the Internet. I had found the story under "Fatal Shooting in Back Bay," an account of how the survivor of a midnight police shooting, Catherine Gagnon, had endured tragedy once before: As a child, she'd been held captive by convicted pedophile Richard Umbrio until rescued by hunters shortly before Thanksgiving.

Umbrio, however, was merely a sidebar. The big story—how Jimmy Gagnon, Catherine's husband and the only child of a wealthy Boston judge, had been fatally shot by a police sniper during a tense hostage situation. The officer who had made the kill: Robert G. Dodge.

Criminal charges had been filed against Officer Bobby Dodge by the victim's father, Judge Gagnon, who alleged that Officer Dodge had conspired with Catherine Gagnon to murder her husband.

Now, there was a small tidbit neither Detective Dodge nor Sergeant Warren had bothered to mention.

In case that wasn't shocking enough, I then found another story, dated a few days later: *Bloodbath in Penthouse* . . . Three people were declared dead and one critically wounded after a recently paroled inmate, Richard Umbrio, stormed a luxury hotel in downtown Boston. Umbrio murdered two people, one with his bare hands, before being fatally shot by Catherine Gagnon and an assisting Massachusetts State Police officer, Robert G. Dodge.

Interesting and more interesting.

I didn't say anything as I sat beside Detective Dodge now. Instead, I hoarded my little nuggets of truth. Bobby had been exploiting the details of my past. Now I knew some things about him. I stole a glance at him, sitting next to me. He drove with his right hand resting casually on the wheel, left elbow propped against the door. Life as a police officer had obviously made him immune to Boston traffic. He zigged in and out of narrow side streets and triple-parked cars like a NASCAR driver doing a warm-up lap. At this rate, he'd have us to Mattapan in under fifteen minutes.

I didn't know if I would be ready by then.

I turned away, staring out the window. If he could be comfortable in the silence, then so could I.

I didn't know why I wanted to go to the crime scene so badly. I just did. I had read the story of Dori's last days. I'd stared at my locket, worn so proudly around her neck. And then my brain had filled with too many questions, the kind her parents had probably wondered about every night for the past twenty-five years.

Had she screamed for help as she was snatched from the yard in front of her grandparents' house and stuffed into an unmarked van? Had she struggled with her abductor? Had she tried to open the doors, only to discover the true evil of childproof locks?

Did the man speak to her? Did he ask about the locket? Accuse her of stealing it from her friend? Had she begged him to take it back? Had she asked him, once he got started, to please stop and kidnap Annabelle Granger instead?

I honestly hadn't thought of Dori Petracelli in twenty-five years. It was humbling, horrible, to think now that she had died in my place.

The car slowed. I blinked rapidly, ashamed to find my eyes filled with tears. As quickly as I could, I swiped at my face with the back of my hand.

Detective Dodge pulled over. I didn't recognize where we were. I saw a block of old triple-deckers, most in need of new paint and maybe some actual grass in their front yards. The neighborhood looked tired, poor. I didn't understand.

"Here's the deal," Dodge said from the driver's seat, turning toward me. "There are only two entrances onto the site. We, the police, have smartly cordoned them off in order to preserve the crime scene. Unfortunately, the media are camped outside both entrances, desperate for any comment or visual they can stick on the news. I'm guessing you don't want your face on the news."

The notion terrified me so much, I couldn't even speak.

"Yeah, okay, like I thought. So, this isn't exactly glamorous, but it will get the job done." He gestured to the backseat, where I now saw a folded-up blanket, roughly the same hue as the upholstered seats. "You lie down; I'll cover you with the blanket. With any luck, we'll pass through the vicious hordes so fast, no one will be any wiser. Once we're actually on the grounds, you can sit up. The FAA agreed to restrict the airspace, so nobody gets to play in their choppers anymore."

He popped open his door, stepping out. Moving on autopilot, I shifted to the backseat, lying down with my knees curled up, arms tucked tight against my chest. With a sharp *snap,* he unfolded the blanket, then settled it over me. A couple more tugs to cover my feet, obscure the top of my head.

"Okay?" Detective Dodge asked.

I nodded. The back door slammed. I heard him move around, settle back into the driver's seat, put the car in gear.

I couldn't see anymore. Just hear the sound of the asphalt rumbling beneath the tires. Just smell the nauseous mix of exhaust and air freshener.

I squeezed my eyes shut, and in that moment, I got it. I knew exactly how Dori had felt, thrown into an unknown vehicle, tucked away out of sight. I understood how she must have curled up tighter and tighter, closing her eyes, wishing her own body would disappear. I knew she had whispered the Lord's Prayer, because that's what we said at bedtime when I slept over. And I knew she had cried for her mother, who always smelled of lavender when she kissed us good night.

Underneath the blanket, I covered my face with my hands. I cried, never making a sound, for that's how you learn to cry when you spend your life on the run.

The car slowed again. The window came down, I heard Detective Dodge give his name, hand over his badge. Then the larger background rumble of gathered voices crying out for recognition, a question, a comment.

The window came up. The car started to drive again, engine downshifting as the vehicle ground its way up a hill.

"Ready or not," Detective Dodge said.

Beneath the blanket, I once again wiped my face. *For Dori,* I told myself, *for Dori.*

But mostly I was thinking of my father and how much I hated him.

Dodge had to let me out of the backseat. Turns out, back doors in police sedans do have some differences from ordinary cars—they only open from the outside. His face was unreadable as he assisted me, hooded gray eyes peering at a spot just beyond my right shoulder. I followed his gaze to a second car, already parked beneath the skeletal umbrella of a massive oak tree. Sergeant Warren stood beside it, shoulders hunched within her caramel-colored leather jacket, expression as annoyed as I remembered.

"She's lead officer," Detective Dodge murmured low, for my ears only. "Can't very well visit her crime scene without her permission. Don't worry, she's only pissed off at me. You're just an easy target."

Being labeled a target offended me. I straightened up, shoulders squaring, balance shifting. Dodge nodded approvingly, and immediately I wondered if that hadn't been his intention. The thought left me more off balance than Sergeant Warren's perpetually sour look.

Dodge headed over to the sergeant. I followed in his wake, arms hugging my body for warmth. The afternoon was gray and chilly. Leaf-peeping season, easily the most beautiful time to be living in New England, had peaked two weeks ago. Now the brilliant crimsons, bright oranges, and cheerful yellows had succumbed to muddy browns and dreary grays. The air smelled damp and moldy. I sniffed again, caught the faint odor of decay.

I had read about the Boston State Mental Hospital site online. I knew it started as the Boston Lunatic Hospital in 1839, before becoming the Boston State Hospital in 1908. Originally, the compound had housed a few hundred patients and operated more like a self-sustaining farm than a role model for *One Flew Over the Cuckoo's Nest.*

By 1950, however, the patient population had ballooned to over three thousand patients, with the compound adding two maximum-security buildings and an enormous wrought-iron security fence. Not such a tranquil place anymore. When deinstitutionalization finally closed the hospital in 1980, the community was grateful.

I expected to feel an eerie chill as I entered the grounds, maybe goose bumps rippling down my arms as I sensed the presence of a lingering evil. I would gaze upon some spookily Gothic structure, like the abandoned Danvers mental hospital that still towers over I-95, spotting—just for an instant—a pale, haunted face peering from a shattered window.

Actually, from this vantage point, I didn't see the two remaining buildings at all. Instead, I gazed upon a thicket of snarled bushes, capped by an enormous hundred-year-old oak tree. When Sergeant Warren followed a narrow trail through the shrubs, we entered a yawning expanse of drying marsh grass that winked gold and silver in the rippling wind. The view was lovely, more of a nature hike than an impending crime scene.

The ground firmed up. A clearing appeared on our right. I saw what appeared to be some sort of refuse pile. Warren halted abruptly, gestured toward the overgrown heap of debris.

"Botanist started poking through that," she commented to Dodge. "Found the remains of a metal shelving unit similar to what we saw in the chamber. Sounds like the hospital had a lot of those kinds of shelves. I've got an officer combing through archive photos now."

"You think the supplies came from the hospital itself?" Detective Dodge asked sharply.

"Don't know, but the clear plastic bags . . . word is, they were commonly used in government institutions in the seventies."

Sergeant Warren started walking again, Detective Dodge falling in step behind her. I brought up the rear, puzzling through their exchange.

Suddenly, we passed through another copse of trees, burst into a clearing, and a brilliant blue awning rose up before me.

For the first time, I paused. Was it my imagination, or did it seem quieter here? No birds chirping, leaves rustling, or squirrels squawking. I couldn't feel the light wind anymore. Everything seemed frozen, waiting.

Sergeant Warren marched ahead, her movements determined. She didn't want to be here, I realized. And that started to unnerve me. What kind of crime scene scared even the cops?

Underneath the blue awning were two large plastic bins. Warren removed the gray lids, revealing white coveralls made of a thin, papery fabric. I recognized the Tyvek suits from all the true-crime shows on Court TV.

"While technically the scientists have already processed the scene, we want to keep it as clean as possible," she said by way of explanation, handing me a suit, then one to Detective Dodge. "This kind of situation . . . you never know what new experts might step forward with something to offer, so we want to be prepared."

She stepped into her own coveralls briskly. I couldn't figure out what were the arms and what were the legs. Detective Dodge had to help me. They moved on to shoe coverings, then hairnettings. By the time I got it all figured out, they'd been waiting for what felt like hours, and my cheeks burned with embarrassment.

Warren led the way to the back of the awning. She stopped at the edge of a hole in the ground. I couldn't see anything; the depths were pitch-black.

She turned to me, blue gaze cool and assessing.

"You understand you cannot share what you see below," she stated crisply. "Can't talk about it to your neighbor, your coworker, your hairdresser. This is strictly on the QT."

"Yes."

"You may not take any pictures, sketch any diagrams."

"I know."

"Also, by virtue of visiting this scene, you may be called to testify at trial. Your name now appears in the crime-scene logbook, which makes you fair game for questioning by both the prosecution and the defense."

"Okay," I said, though I hadn't really thought of that. A trial? Questioning? I decided to worry about that later.

"And in return for this *tour,* you agree to accompany us to Arizona tomorrow morning. You will meet with Catherine Gagnon. You will answer our questions to the best of your ability."

"Yes, I agree," I stated, sharply now. I was getting impatient—and more nervous—the longer we stood there.

Sergeant Warren pulled out a flashlight. "I'll go first," she said, "flip on the lights. When you see that, you'll know it's your turn to descend."

She gave me a last measuring look. I returned it, though I knew my gaze wasn't as unwavering as hers. I had been wrong about Sergeant Warren. Had we met in a sparring ring, no way would I have dropped her. I might be younger, quicker, physically stronger. But she was tough. Down to the core, willfully-descend-into-a-pitch-black-mass-grave tough.

My father would have loved her.

The top of Warren's head disappeared below. A

second later, the opening burst into a pale glow.

"Last chance," Detective Dodge murmured in my ear.

I reached for the top of the ladder. Then I just didn't let myself think anymore.

13

FIRST THING THAT struck me was the temperature. It felt warmer belowground than above. The earthen walls offered protection from the wind and insulation against the late-fall chill.

Second thought—I could stand up straight. In fact, I could swing my arms, walk forward, sideways, backward. I had expected to be hunched over, claustrophobic. Instead, the chamber was positively roomy, even as Detective Dodge joined us in the gloom.

My eyes adjusted, sorting out the quilt of dark shadows intermingled with bright spotlights. I moved to a wall, touched the lightly grooved side, felt hard-packed dirt.

"I don't understand," I said at last. "There's no way one man hand-dug a space this big. You're talking backhoe, heavy machinery. How can that be going on and no one notice?"

Sergeant Warren surprised me by doing the honors: "We think it started out as part of another construction project. Maybe a culvert for drainage, or just a pit where they harvested fill for another area. In the late forties, early fifties, the facility was racing to erect enough buildings to keep pace with the increasing patient population. You can find half-started foundations, supply dumps, all sorts of stuff all over the property."

"So this pit was once part of something official?"

"Maybe." She shrugged. "Not a lot of people around from those days anymore to ask. You're talking fifty years."

I put my hand up, felt the wooden ceiling, moved forward, touched the support beams. "But he did all this? Converted it, so to speak?"

"That's our guess."

"Must've taken him time."

No one argued.

"Expense," I continued, thinking out loud. "Wood, nails, hammer. Effort. Would one of the mental patients really be that organized, have access to leave and reenter the grounds like that?"

D.D. shrugged again. "Everything here could've been harvested from the construction dumps on the property. So far, I've seen everything from cement dust to tiles to window frames."

I grimaced at that. "No windows down here."

"No, not for what he had in mind."

I repressed a shiver, walked to the far wall. "When do you think he started?"

"Don't know. There was about thirty years of plant growth over the plywood, so that puts us in the seventies. The hospital was dying by then, the property more abandoned than used. That makes some sense."

"And he operated for how long?"

"Don't know."

"But he must have known this area," I persisted. "Been a patient at the hospital or maybe even someone who worked there. I mean, to have found this space, to know where to harvest his supplies. To feel comfortable returning again and again."

"At this stage of the game, anything's possible." D.D.'s voice told me she was skeptical, though. I had the sense she was focused on the grounds being abandoned, which meant anyone could've been running around the hundred-and-seventy-acre site.

The thought took some of the wind out of my sails. I got my chin up, relentlessly pressing on in my role of amateur investigator.

"You said there were supplies?" I prompted.

"Metal shelving, metal chair, plastic bucket."

"No bedding?"

"Not that we found."

"Lanterns, cookstove?"

"No, but two hooks on the ceiling, which may have been used for hanging lights."

"Why do you say that?"

"Because he placed the hooks in front of the metal shelves where he stored the bodies."

I swayed, reached out to brace myself against the cold, earthen wall, then snatched my hand back. "I'm sorry?"

D.D.'s expression had grown hard, her gaze probing. "You tell me. You're the one pretending to be the witness. What do you see down here?"

"Nothing."

"Property, grounds—any of this familiar to you?"

"No." My voice was faint. "I've never been here before. I would think"—my hand returned to the wall, my fingers touching it tentatively—"I would think you don't forget something like this."

"No," she agreed harshly, "I don't think you do."

D.D. came forward, stood beside me. She placed her hand next to mine, her fingers splayed, palm flat against the cold earth as if to prove she could handle this grave better than I could. "Right where we are standing used to be two long metal shelving units. He used them for storage. It's where he placed the bodies. One per garbage bag, three per shelf. Two neat little rows."

My fingers convulsed, nails sinking into the raw earth, feeling the hard, compacted soil dig beneath my fingernails. And at that moment, I swear I could feel it. The deeply embedded evil, a powerful, biting chill. I retreated hastily, my feet moving in rapid little circles, while my gaze scoured the floor, looking for signs of . . . what? Struggle? Blood? The spot where a monster raped my best friend? Or ripped out her fingernails? Or took pliers to her nipples before he slit her throat?

I had read too many articles, spent too much time being prepped by my father. Why read *Goodnight Moon* to your child when you can read her *21st Century Monsters* instead?

I was going to be sick, but I couldn't be. My thoughts ran too hard, too fast. I was remembering my seven-year-old childhood friend. I was picturing every crime-scene photo my father had ever shown me.

"What did he do?" I found myself demanding. "How long were they kept alive? How did he kill them? Did they know of one another? Did they have to stay down here, surrounded by corpses in the dark?

"Turn off the lights!" My voice was growing wild, incoherent. "Dammit, turn off those lights! I want to know what he did to them! I want to know how it *felt!*"

Detective Dodge caught my hands. He pressed my palms together, stilling my jerky motions, tucking my hands back into my chest. He didn't say anything, just stood there, looking at me with those steady gray eyes until, with a brittle snap, I felt something break inside of me. My shoulders sagged, my arms dropped. The hysteria drained from me, and I was left limp, wrung out, thinking of Dori again and that last summer when neither of us had known that we had it so good.

Dori's favorite flavor of Popsicle was grape. Mine was root beer. We would save those flavors from the assorted packs our mothers bought, swapping the two each Saturday.

We used to race down the street to see which one of us could skip the fastest. Once I fell down and skinned my chin. Dori came back to see if I was okay, and when she was bending down, I jumped up and went skipping over the finish line just so I could say I won. She didn't speak to me for a whole day, but I still wouldn't apologize, because even back then winning mattered more to me than the wounded look on her face.

Every Sunday her family went to church. I wanted to go to church with them because Dori always looked so pretty in her white church dress with light blue piping, but my father told me church was for the ignorant. Instead, I would visit Dori's house on Sunday afternoons and she would tell me stories she had heard that morning, such as baby Moses, or Noah and his ark, or Jesus' miraculous birth in a manger. And I would say a little prayer with her, even though it made me feel guilty. I liked the way her face looked when she prayed, the serene smile that would settle across her lips.

I wondered if she had prayed down here. I wondered if she had prayed to live, or if she had prayed for God's mercy to take her away. I wanted to pray. I wanted to fall down on my knees and beg God to take some of this huge pressure out of my chest, because I felt like a fist had reached inside of me and was squeezing my heart, and I did not know how one person could live with so much pain, which merely made me wonder how her parents had ever gotten through all these years.

Is this what life comes down to in the end? Young girls forced to choose between a life spent running from the shadows or a premature death alone in the dark? What kind of monster did such a thing? Why couldn't Dori have escaped?

I was happy in that instant that my parents were dead. That they didn't have to know what had happened to Dori or what my father's decision had meant for his daughter's best friend.

But then in the next moment, I felt uneasy. Another rippling shadow in the recesses of my mind . . .

He knew. I don't know how I knew it, but I did. My father had known what had happened to Dori, and that filled me with a greater sense of unease than even the four closing walls.

I couldn't take it anymore. My hands came up, cradled my forehead.

"We will have to wait for the forensic anthropologist's reports to know more about the victims," Sergeant Warren was saying.

I merely nodded.

"Suffice it to say, we're looking for someone very methodical, extremely intelligent, and depraved."

Another short nod.

"Naturally, anything you might remember about that time—and particularly the UNSUB watching your house—would be most useful."

"I would like to go up now," I said.

No one argued. Detective Dodge led the way. At the top, he offered me his hand. I refused, climbing out on my own. The wind had picked up, rustling loudly through the dying leaves. I tilted my face toward the stinging breeze. Then I curled my fingers into a fist, feeling beneath my fingernails the grim remnants of my best friend's grave.

14

WHEN WE RETURNED to the vehicles, a patrol officer stood waiting for us. He drew Sergeant Warren aside, speaking in a low voice.

"How many times have you seen him?" she asked sharply.

"Three or four."

"Who does he say he is?"

"Says he used to work here. That he knows something. But he'll only speak to the officer in charge."

Warren looked over the officer's head, to where Detective Dodge and I stood. "Got a minute?" she asked, clearly meaning Bobby, not me.

He glanced at me. I shrugged. "I can wait in the car."

That seemed to be the right answer. Warren turned back to the patrol officer. "Bring him up. He wants to talk so bad, let's hear what he has to say."

I returned to the Crown Vic; I didn't mind. I wanted out of the wind, away from the sights and smells. I wasn't thinking of nature hikes anymore. They should bring in bulldozers and raze this place to the ground.

I slumped down in the passenger's seat, obediently removing myself from view. The moment Detective Dodge crossed to Sergeant Warren's side, however, I cracked the window.

The patrol officer returned in a matter of minutes. He brought with him an older gentleman with a thick shock of white hair and a surprisingly brisk step.

"Name's Charles," he boomed, shaking Warren's hand, shaking Dodge's. "Charlie Marvin. Used to work at the hospital during my college days. Thanks for seeing me. You the officer in charge?" He turned expectantly to Detective Dodge, who did a side nudge with his head. Charlie followed the motion to Sergeant Warren. "Oops," the man boomed, but smiled so broadly it was hard not to like him. "Don't mind me," he told Warren. "I'm not sexist; I'm just an old fart."

She laughed. I'd never heard Sergeant Warren laugh before. It made her sound almost human.

"Nice to meet you, Mr. Marvin."

"Charlie, Charlie. 'Mr. Marvin' makes me think of my father, God rest his soul."

"What can we do for you, Charlie?"

"I heard about the graves, the six girls found up here. Gotta say, it shook me right up. I spent nearly a decade up here, first working as an attendant nurse— AN—then offering my ministering services on nights and weekends. Almost got myself killed half a dozen times. But I still think of it as the good old days. Bothers me to think girls could've been dying the same time I was here. Bothers me a lot."

Charlie stared at Warren and Dodge expectantly, but neither said a word. I recognized their strategy by now; they liked to use the silent approach on me as well.

"So," Charlie said briskly, "I might be an old fart who can't remember what he had for breakfast most of the time, but my memories from back in the day are

147

clear as a bell. I took the liberty of making some notes. About some patients and, well"—he cleared his throat, starting to look nervous for a moment—"and about a certain staff member. Don't know if it will help you or not, but I wanted to do something."

Dodge reached into his breast pocket, flipped out a notebook. Charlie took that as a sign of encouragement, and briskly unfolded a piece of notebook paper he had clutched in his hand. His fingers trembled slightly, but his voice remained strong.

"You know much about the hospital workings?" he asked the two detectives.

"No, sir." Detective Dodge spoke up. "At least, not as much as we'd like."

"We had eighteen hundred patients when I first started working," Charlie said. "We served patients age sixteen and up, all races, genders, socio-economic classes. Some were admitted by their families, a lot were brought in by the police. East side of the complex was for chronic care; west side, where we're standing now, for acute. I started out in admitting. A year later, I was promoted to Charge Attendant and moved to the I-Building, working the I-4 unit, which was maximum security for men.

"We were a good facility. Understaffed—lotta nights it was just me and forty patients—but we got the job done. Never used straitjackets, tie downs, or physical abuse. If you got yourself in trouble, you were permitted to use a hammerlock or full nelson to subdue the patient until backup arrived, at which point a fellow AN would most likely administer a sedative.

"Mostly, ANs were in charge of custodial care, keeping the patients calm, clean, healthy. We'd administer medications as prescribed by the doctors. I received some training in IM—intramuscular—injections. You know, jabbing a needle loaded with sodium amytal in a guy's thigh. Definitely, it got hairy at times—I lifted a lotta weights just to survive. But most of the men, even in maximum security, simply needed to be treated as human. You talked to them. You kept your voice calm and reasonable. You acted as if you expected them to be calm and reasonable. You'd be amazed how often that worked."

"But not always," Sergeant Warren prodded.

Charlie shook his head. "No, not always." He held up one finger. "First time I almost lost my life—Paul Nicholas. Nearly two hundred and thirty pounds of paranoid schizophrenic. Most of the time, he was kept in seclusion—special rooms that only had a barred window and a heavy leather mat for sleeping. Rubber rooms, you'd call 'em these days. One night when I came on duty, however, he'd been let out. My supervisor, Alan Woodward, swore Paulie was doing okay.

"First few hours—didn't hear a thing. Gets to be midnight, I've retired to the first-floor office to do a little studying, when suddenly I hear pounding upstairs, like a freight train roaring down the hall. I knock the phone off the hook—sending the signal for help—and race upstairs.

"There's Paulie, smack-dab in the middle of the Day

149

Room, waiting for me. Minute he sees me, he takes a flying leap. I roll to the side, Paul lands on the couch, flattening the sucker right out. Next thing I know, Paul's grabbing chairs and hurtling them at my head. I run behind a Ping-Pong table. He gives chase, and 'round and 'round we go, like an old cartoon of Tom and Jerry. Except Paulie gets tired of this game. He stops running. Starts tearing apart the Ping-Pong table. With his bare hands.

"You think I'm exaggerating; I'm not. Guy was pumped up on rage and testosterone. He started with the metal trim on the table, ripped it back and then went to work on it chunk by chunk. Right about now, I'm realizing I'm dead; Ping-Pong table's only so big, and Paul's making good progress. Lo and behold, I look up to see two of my fellow ANs finally arrive in the doorway.

" 'Get him!' I yell. 'We need sodium amytal!'

"Except they've gone wide-eyed. They're standing in the doorway, watching Paulie go to town, and if you'll pardon the expression, ma'am, they're shitting their pants.

" 'Hey!' I yell again. 'For God's sake, man!'

"One of them makes a choking sound. It's enough for Paulie to turn. Minute he does, I jump across the table, onto his back, and get him in a hammerlock. Paul starts roaring, trying to toss me off. My fellow ANs finally spring to life and help me tackle him. It still took fourteen grains of sodium amytal and two hours to calm Paulie down. Needless to say, he didn't get out of seclusion for a while after that. So there's one name for you. Paulie Nicholas!"

Charlie looked at the two investigators expectantly. Detective Dodge obediently scribbled down the name, but Sergeant Warren was frowning.

"You said this patient, Paul 'Paulie' Nicholas, stayed in seclusion?"

"Yes, ma'am."

"And when not secluded, I'm betting he was fairly heavily medicated."

"Oh yes, ma'am. Guy like him, there was no other way."

"Well, I understand, Charlie, that Nicholas was a threat to you and the rest of the staff. But given how he was regimented, I would think it unlikely he was ever turned loose to wander the grounds."

"Oh no. Paul was maximum security. That meant full lockdown, twenty-four/seven. Those patients didn't 'wander' around alone."

Sergeant Warren nodded. "The person we are looking for, Charlie, would have to have access to the grounds. A lot of access to the grounds. Were any patients allowed out, or by definition, does that mean we should focus on staff?"

Charlie paused, frowned, reviewed his list. "Well, I didn't want to start with it, but there was an incident. . . ."

"Yes?" Warren prodded.

"Nineteen seventy," Charlie said. "See, there was a reason the head nurse, Jill Cochran, liked us college boys. We were strong, sure, that definitely helped. But also . . . we were fresh, optimistic. We didn't just take care of the patients, we genuinely cared about them. Myself, I already knew back then I wanted to be a minister. A mental hospital is a good place to start if you want to reach troubled souls. I got to learn first-hand what a difference the right word at the right time can mean for a person. But I gotta say, it's a place where no one should linger, not even the staff.

"The older guys, the 'experienced' ANs who hung around for decades . . . hell, some of those guys grew loonier than the patients. They got institutionalized themselves, forgot what life was beyond the hospital walls. When I first started in reception, there was a patient with a filthy bandage on his leg. First night, I asked the Charge Attendant what was with the bandage. He had no idea. Hadn't even noticed the patient had a bandage on his leg. So I enter the patient's room, ask him if I can check out his leg. Minute I remove the bandage, a stream of pus shoots across the room. And then, right in front of my eyes, maggots pour out of the wound.

"Turns out, the poor guy got an ulceration on his leg two months before. Doctor bandaged it up. No one ever checked it again. Not a single AN. They'd been looking at the patient for months without ever *seeing* him.

"Well, that was bad enough. Neglectful. But some-times things got a little worse."

Charlie broke off, looking uncomfortable again. Both Warren and Dodge were listening intently now.

From my vantage point, slouched low in Dodge's car, I could tell both investigators were hanging on Charlie's every word. I know I was.

The retired minister took a deep breath. "So, one night I get a call from the nurse at the residence for female patients. Keri Stracke. She asks me if so-and-so is on duty. I say yes. Keri asks me where he is. Well, I do a little walkabout of the I-Building but don't see him. I tell her he's out, maybe gone for dinner. There's a long pause. Keri tells me, in a very peculiar voice, that I need to come over right now.

"Now, I'm the only one around. I can't just leave I-Building. I try to explain this, but she tells me again, in that funny little voice, that I don't have a choice. She means *right now!* What can I do? Now I'm really concerned. I go over. Keri meets me out front and without a word escorts me upstairs. She stops in front of the closed door of a patient's room. I look through the window, and there's my fellow AN, in bed with a patient. She's seventeen years old, real pretty, and catatonic. I've never wanted to hurt a fellow human being so badly in my life."

"What did you do?" Detective Dodge asked quietly.

"I opened the door. Minute Adam heard the noise, he looked up. You could see on his face he knew it was over. He climbed off her, zipped up, walked out of the room. I escorted him back to the I-Building, to the office, where I called our supervisor. Adam was fired on the spot, of course. I don't care what stories you hear about patient abuse, that kind of behavior was never condoned. Adam was done; he knew it, too."

"Adam's last name?" Dodge asked.

"Schmidt," Charlie sighed.

"They file a police report?" Sergeant Warren asked, more sharply.

Charlie shook his head. "No, management wanted to keep things quiet."

Warren raised a brow at that. "You know what happened to Adam?"

"Not really. But . . ." That hesitation again. "I saw him several more times. On the grounds. Twice from a distance, but I was pretty sure it was him. Third time, I caught up to him, asked him what the hell he was doing. He said he'd had to take care of some paperwork. Given it was nearly ten p.m., that didn't make much sense to me. Next day, I followed up with Jill Cochran. She didn't know anything about it. We kept an eye on the female patients for a bit. No one talked about it, but we were on guard. I didn't see Adam again, but this is a big property."

Dodge frowned. "You guys patrol the grounds, make any attempts at better securing the property?"

"We locked the gates at night, staffed the facility twenty-four/seven. But . . . in the odd hours of the morning, ANs like me were hardly wandering the grounds. We had patients to tend, we stayed in our offices." Charlie shrugged. "It's possible someone could've been coming and going, and we wouldn't have seen a thing. It had happened before, you know."

"Before?" Warren asked sharply.

"We had a murder on the grounds, a female nurse in the mid-seventies. I understand one of the ANs looked out a window of the admitting building and spotted the body first thing in the morning. Ingrid, Inga . . . Inge. Inge Lovell, I think it was. She'd been raped and beaten to death. Terrible, terrible tragedy. The police were called, but didn't have any witnesses—none of the other attendants had seen a thing."

Warren was nodding now, Charlie's story apparently having sparked her own memory of the event. "No arrest was ever made," she said.

"Rumor mill was that a patient had done it," Charlie supplied. "In fact, most folks thought Christopher Eola did it. Wouldn't surprise me. Eola was admitted after my days as an AN. I ran into him once or twice, however, when I came in on Sundays. Scary customer, Mr. Eola. The cold side of crazy."

Dodge was flipping through his pages. "Eola, Eola, Eola."

"The hotline," Warren murmured.

Both of them snapped to attention.

"What can you tell us about Eola?" Warren asked Charlie now.

Charlie tilted his head to the side. "You want the straight story or the version with the gossip mingled in?"

"We'd like to hear it all," Warren said.

"Eola came to us a young man. Admitted by his parents, that's what I was told. They dropped him off and hightailed it back to their mansion, never to return. Rumor was, Eola had had an inappropriate relationship with his younger sister. His parents discovered them together, and that was that. Bye-bye, Christopher.

"Eola was a good-looking kid. Light brown hair, bright blue eyes. Not big. Maybe six feet, but slender, refined. Maybe even a tad effeminate, which is why most of the ANs didn't consider him a threat right away.

"He was also smart. Very social. You'd think someone with his privileged upbringing would hold himself apart. Instead, he liked to hang out in the Day Room, playing music for his fellow patients, holding a reading hour. More important, he'd roll cigarettes— I know that's all considered evil now, but back in those days, everyone smoked, the doctors, the nurses, the patients. In fact, one of the best ways to guarantee cooperation from a patient was to give him a cigarette. It's simply how things were done.

"Well, most of the cigarettes were roll-your-own, and some of the patients whose motor skills were impaired by various medications had a hard time getting it done. So Christopher would help them. That's what he was doing the first time I saw him. Sitting in the Sunroom, cheerfully rolling cigarettes for a line of patients. It's funny, but first time he looked up and saw me, I knew I didn't like him. I knew he was trouble. It was his eyes. Shark eyes."

"What did Eola do?" Dodge interrupted. "Why was he considered such a menace?"

156

"He learned the system."

I perked up. I couldn't help myself. Sitting in the nearby car, my ear glued to the cracked open window, I had a sense of déjà vu, of my father talking, of a shadowy man named Christopher Eola taking the same notes I once did. It gave me a chill.

"The system?" Dodge was asking.

"Hours, shift changes, dinner breaks. And, more important, medications. No one put it together until after poor Inge's murder. But as management started asking more questions, it came out that some of the ANs had been falling asleep on their shifts. Except it wasn't just one guy or one time. It was everyone, all the time. Well, this got the head nurse's goat. So one night Jill did a surprise inspection of admitting. She found Eola in the office, mixing something into the AN's brown-bag dinner. He looked up, spotted her, and, quite suddenly, smiled.

"Moment she saw that look, Jill knew she was dead. She grabbed the door and slammed it shut, trapping Eola inside. Eola tried to reason with her. Told her she was overreacting, swore he could explain everything. Jill dug in her heels. Next thing she knew, Eola was throwing himself at the door, snarling like an animal. A large man probably could've busted himself out, but like I said, Eola was all brains, not brawn. Jill kept Eola trapped for fifteen minutes, until another attendant arrived and they'd loaded up some sodium amytal.

"Later, they determined Eola had been stealing thorazine capsules from his fellow patients and mixing the powder into the ANs' food. Furthermore, he would encourage his fellow patients into various disagreements, creating situations upstairs. When the AN rushed up to handle the problem, he'd slip into the office and go to work. Of course, Christopher never admitted to anything. Anytime you asked him a question, he'd just smile."

Warren and Dodge were exchanging looks again. "Sounds like Eola had plenty of opportunities to wander the grounds."

"Guess so."

"And what year was this?"

"Eola was admitted in '74."

"How old?"

"I believe he was twenty at the time."

"And what happened to him?"

"He finally got caught."

"Doing what?"

"Organizing the patients into a revolt. Somewhere along the way, he'd commandeered one of the leather mats from an isolation room. Then he recruited the more 'with it' patients into creating a disturbance. When the AN appeared upstairs, the patients charged him with the mat, knocked him out cold. But Eola had made a slight miscalculation. We had another patient here at the time—Rob George. Former heavyweight champion. He spent his first two years in the hospital catatonic. But just three days earlier, he'd walked all the way to the Day Room by himself. The AN on duty got him back to bed without incident, only to find him sitting up an hour later. Clearly, he was coming 'round.

"Well, the night of Eola's revolt, the whole unit got hopping. And apparently this got our boxing champion outta bed. Rob appeared in the middle of the Day Room. He looked at the AN, unconscious on the ground. Then stared at Christopher, grinning back up at him.

"'Good news, man—' Eola started to say.

"And Mr. George pulled back his fist and knocked Christopher out cold. Good solid left-hand hook. Then he went back to bed. One of the other patients went down to the office at that point and took the phone off the hook. Without Eola, no one knew what to do.

"The ANs arrived, got everything in order. Next morning, Rob woke up and asked for his mother. Six weeks later, he was released. According to him, he never remembered the events of that night. I understand from the doctors, however, that upon emerging from a catatonic state, most patients' first movements are reflexive, a matter of muscle memory. Like sitting up. Or walking. Or, I guess, if you're a former boxing champ, a solid left hook."

"So what happened to Christopher?"

"His fellow patients ratted him out, and given his history, Admin had enough to transfer him to Bridgewater, which handles the criminally insane. I never heard about him again. But Bridgewater is like that. This place here"—Charlie pointed to the ground beneath his feet—"was a treatment facility. Bridge-water . . . once you go in, no one expects to see you again."

Sergeant Warren raised a brow. "Charming."

Charlie shrugged. "Just the way things were."

"But he could've been released," Dodge prodded. "By the late seventies, weren't patient populations shrinking everywhere? Deinstitutionalization didn't just close Boston Mental, it affected everyone."

Charlie was nodding. "True, true. Damn shame, if you ask me." He cocked his head. "You know what kept me here? Working for four years, volunteering for six years after that? I've told you the scary stuff, the stories people *want* to hear about a mental institution. But truth is, this was a good hospital. We had patients like Rob George, who, with proper treatment, emerged from a catatonic state and got to go home to his loved ones. Second guy who almost killed me was a street kid named Benji. He was a good-looking kid, handsome Italian stock, but feral as they came. Police brought him in. First week, Benji stayed in a seclusion room, stark naked. He'd painted the wall and his body with his own feces. All you could see were his white eyeballs glowing in the dark.

"One day, when I was tending him, he sprang onto my back and damn near strangled me before another AN pulled him off. But you know what? He turned out to be a good kid. Regression, the doctors called it. Some kind of trauma had reverted him to a nearly two-year-old state; he wouldn't talk, eat, use the toilet, or dress himself. But once we started treating him like a two-year-old, we all got along great. I'd come in on Sundays, read him children's books, play silly songs. With a little bit of time, treatment, and human kindness, Benji grew up again, right before our eyes. He started wearing clothes, using the toilet, eating with silverware, saying please and thank you. Two years later, he was doing so well, a member of our board got him enrolled in Boston Latin. He went to school during the day—and slept in his room here at night. You'd find him studying in the middle of complete chaos in the Day Room.

"Eventually Benji graduated, got a job, moved out on his own. None of that would've happened without this hospital." Charlie shook his head sadly. "People think it's a sign of accomplishment when a mental institute closes. Three thousand people used to receive treatment here. Do you really think it's all gone away? Mental illness has just moved underground, into the homeless shelters and the city parks. Out of sight, out of mind for the taxpayers. It's a crying shame."

Charlie sighed, shook his head again. Another moment passed. He squared his shoulders, holding out his paper. "I drew a map of the old compound," he told Sergeant Warren. "How it looked before they started tearing down the buildings. Don't know if it helps your investigation or not, but it sounded like the grave is old. That being the case, thought you might like to put the crime scene in the proper context."

Warren took the paper, glancing at its contents.

"This is perfect, Charlie, very helpful. And I appreciate you taking the time to speak with us. You're a true gentleman."

Dodge took the man's contact information. Things seemed to be wrapping up.

At the last minute, as the police officer was escorting Charlie back to the cruiser, the older man happened to look my way. In my eavesdropping mode, I had risen up, until my face was in the window, my ear tilted toward the open slit.

The moment Charlie spotted me, he did a little double-take.

"Excuse me, miss," he called over. "Don't I know you?"

Immediately, Detective Dodge stepped between us. "Just another person assisting with the investigation," he murmured, directing the retired minister back to the police cruiser. Charlie turned away. I slumped down, quickly working the window back up. I didn't recognize Charlie Marvin. So why would he think he knew me?

The police cruiser drove off.

But my heart continued to pound too hard in my chest.

15

THEY WERE BOTH silent on the drive back to the North End: Annabelle staring out the side window, sliding the glass pendant back and forth on her necklace; Bobby staring out the windshield, drumming his fingers on the wheel.

Bobby thought he should say something. He tried out several lines in his head: *Don't worry. Things will seem better in the morning. Life goes on.*

It sounded like the same bullshit people had fed him after the shooting, so he kept his mouth shut. Truth of the matter was, Annabelle's life *did* suck, and he had a feeling things were only going to get worse. Particularly once she came face-to-face with Catherine Gagnon.

He'd first mentioned Annabelle's name to Catherine out of sheer curiosity; Annabelle claimed to not know Catherine, what was Catherine's impression? Catherine, it turned out, was as oblivious to Annabelle's existence as Annabelle was to hers.

Yet both women had been targeted by predators who favored underground chambers. Both women shared a close physical resemblance. And both had resided near Boston in the early eighties.

Bobby continued to believe, had to believe, there was a connection.

Apparently, the higher-ups had agreed, because they'd okayed the Arizona expedition. Theory was, if they could get Catherine and Annabelle together in a room, something was bound to shake loose. The connecting factor. The common denominator. The startling revelation that would break the case wide open, making the BPD look like heroes and allowing everyone to resume sleeping at night.

Earlier, the idea had seemed a slam-dunk winner. Now Bobby was less certain. He had too many questions racing through his mind. Why had Annabelle's family continued to run even after leaving Massachusetts? How had Annabelle become a target in Arlington, if the perpetrator was operating out of Boston State Mental in Mattapan? And why did a former lunatic-asylum volunteer, Charlie Marvin, also seem to recognize Annabelle, when according to her she'd never set foot on Boston State Mental grounds?

Bobby blew out a puff of air, rubbed at the back of his neck. He wondered when he was going to start to develop some answers instead of a longer list of questions. He wondered how he was going to squeeze approximately twelve hours' worth of phone calls into the approximately two hours he had before the next task-force meeting.

He wondered, once again, if he should say something reassuring to the subdued woman sitting beside him.

No answers yet. He kept driving, hands upon the wheel.

Night had descended, end of day prodding the city to life. Route 93 streamed ahead of them, a long ribbon of glowing red brake lights coiling to an island of glittering skyscrapers. People commented that the Boston cityscape was particularly beautiful at night. Bobby'd spent his whole life living in the city and his whole career driving around it. Frankly, he didn't get it. Tall buildings were tall buildings. Mostly, this time of night, he wanted to be home.

"You ever lose someone close?" Annabelle spoke up abruptly. "A family member, friend?"

After the long silence, her question startled him into an honest answer. "My mother and brother. Long time back."

"Oh, I'm sorry . . . I didn't mean . . . That's sad."

"No, no, no, they're still alive. It's not what you think. My mother walked out when I was six or seven. My brother made it about eight more years, then followed suit."

"They just left?"

"My father had a drinking problem."

"Oh."

Bobby shrugged philosophically. "Back in those days, the choices were pretty much flee the scene or dig your own grave. To give my mother and brother credit, they didn't have a death wish."

"But you stayed."

"I was too young," he said matter-of-factly. "Didn't have long enough legs."

She blinked her eyes, looking troubled. "And your father now?"

"Has been sober for nearly ten years. Been a rough road for him, but he's holding course."

"That's great."

"I'm proud of him." He glanced over at her for the first time, making eye contact, holding it for the fraction of an instant driving would allow. He wasn't sure why he said this, but it felt important to get it out: "I'm not so great with booze myself. I understand how hard my father has to fight."

"Oh," she said again.

He nodded at that. *Oh* summarized his life quite nicely these days. He'd killed a man, gotten involved with the victim's widow, realized he was an alcoholic, confronted a serial killer, and derailed his policing career all in the course of two years. *Oh* was pretty much the only summary he had left.

"Do you still miss your family?" Annabelle was asking now. "Do you think about them all the time? I honestly hadn't thought of Dori in twenty-five years. Now I wonder if I'll ever get her out of my head."

"I don't think about them the way I used to. I can go weeks, maybe even a month or two, not thinking of them at all. But then something will happen—you know, like the Red Sox winning the World Series—and I'll find myself wondering, What is George doing right now? Is he cheering in some bar in Florida, going nuts for the home team? Or when he left us, did he leave the Red Sox, too? Maybe he only roots for the Marlins these days. I don't know.

"And then my mind will go nuts for a few days. I'll find myself staring in the mirror, wondering if George has the same wrinkles around his eyes that I'm getting. Or maybe he's a plump insurance salesman with the beer gut and double chin. I haven't seen him since he was eighteen years old. I can't even picture him as a man. That gets to me sometimes. Makes me feel like he's dead."

"Do you call him?"

"I've left messages."

"He doesn't return your calls?" She sounded skeptical.

"Not so far."

"And your mom?"

"Ditto."

"Why? That doesn't make any sense. It's not your fault your father was a drunk. Why do they blame you?"

He had to smile. "You're a kind person."

She scowled back. "I am not."

That just made his smile grow. But then he sighed. It felt strange, but not bad, to be talking about his family. He had been thinking about them more and more since the shooting. And leaving more messages.

"So, I went to this shrink a couple years ago," he said. "Department orders. I'd been involved in a critical incident—"

"You killed Jimmy Gagnon," Annabelle said matter-of-factly.

"I see you've been busy on the Internet."

"Were you sleeping with Catherine Gagnon?"

"I see you've been talking to D.D."

"So you *were* involved with her?" Annabelle sounded genuinely surprised. Apparently she'd just been fishing, and he'd stupidly taken the bait.

"I have never so much as kissed Catherine Gagnon," he said firmly.

"But the lawsuit—"

"Was ultimately dropped."

"Only after the shoot-out in the hotel—"

"Dropped is dropped."

"Sergeant Warren obviously hates her," Annabelle said.

"D.D. will always hate her."

"Are you sleeping with D.D.?"

"So," he said loudly, "I did my job and shot an armed man holding his wife and child at gunpoint. And the department sent me to a shrink. And you know that old saw that shrinks only want to talk about your mother? It's true. All the woman did was ask about my mother."

"All right," Annabelle said, "let's talk about your mother."

"Exactly, one soul-baring moment at a time here. It was interesting. The longer my mother and brother stayed away, the more, on some level, I'd internalized things as being my fault. The shrink, however, raised some good points. My mother, brother, and I shared a pretty traumatic time in our lives. I felt guilty they'd had to run away. Maybe they felt guilty for leaving me behind."

Annabelle nodded, jingled her necklace again. "Makes some sense. So what are you supposed to do?"

"God give me the strength to change the things I can change, the courage to let go of the things I need to let go, and the wisdom to know the difference. My mother and my brother are two of those things I can't change, so I gotta let go." Their exit was coming up. He put on the blinker, worked on getting over.

She frowned at him. "What about the shooting? How are you supposed to handle that?"

"Sleep eight hours a day, eat healthy, drink plenty of

water, and engage in moderate amounts of exercise."

"And that works?"

"Dunno. First night, I went to a bar, drank until I nearly passed out. Let's just say I'm still a work in progress."

She finally smiled. "Me, too," she said softly. "Me, too."

She didn't speak again until he parked in front of her building. When she did, her voice had lost its edge. She simply sounded tired. Her hand went to the door latch.

"When do we leave in the morning?" she asked.

"I'll pick you up at ten."

"All right."

"Pack for one night. We'll handle the arrangements. Oh, and Annabelle—to board the plane you're going to need valid photo ID."

"Not a problem."

He arched a brow but didn't press. "It won't be so bad," he found himself saying. "Don't let the news articles fool you. Catherine's a woman, same as any other. And we're just going to talk."

"Yeah, I guess." Annabelle popped open the door, stepped out onto the curb. At the last moment, however, she turned back toward him.

"In the beginning," she said softly, "when I saw myself declared dead in the paper, I was relieved. Dead meant I could relax. Dead meant I didn't have to worry about some mysterious boogeyman chasing me anymore. Dead left me feeling a little giddy."

She paused, took a deep breath, then looked him in the eye. "But it's not like that, is it? You, Sergeant Warren, and I aren't the only ones who know it wasn't my body in that grave. Dori's killer also knows he abducted my best friend in my place. He knows I'm still alive."

"Annabelle, it's been twenty-five years . . ."

"I'm not a helpless little girl anymore," she filled in.

"No, you're not. Plus, we don't know if the perpetrator is active these days. The chamber was abandoned. Meaning he could've been incarcerated for another crime, or here's a thought, maybe he did the world a favor and dropped dead. We don't know yet. We don't."

"Maybe he didn't stop. Maybe he moved. My family kept running. Maybe it was because someone kept chasing."

Bobby didn't have an answer for that one. At this point, anything was possible.

Annabelle shut the door. He rolled down the window, so he could monitor the situation while she went to work inserting the keys. Maybe he was getting a little paranoid, too, because his gaze kept scouring up and down the street, checking every shadow, making sure nothing moved.

The outer door opened. Annabelle turned, waved, stepped into the brightly lit space. He watched her pull the door shut firmly behind her, then go to work on the inner sanctum. Then that door was also opened and closed and he caught one last glimpse of her back as she headed up the stairs.

16

BOBBY WAS LATE to the task-force meeting again. No baked goods this time, but the other officers were too busy listening to Detective Sinkus to care. As promised, Sinkus had met with George Robbards, the District 3 clerk who'd served in Mattapan from '72 to '98. Apparently, Robbards had a lot to say about their favorite suspect du jour, Christopher Eola.

"The body of the nurse was found gagged with a pillowcase that came from the hospital supply room. Coroner's report indicated that she'd been worked over before death, which was from manual asphyxiation. Originally, the investigation focused on a former boyfriend of Lovell's—they'd recently broken up— and a couple of key staff members who worked at the hospital. Theory was, no way a patient could've been missing that long without someone noticing. Plus, the most logical suspect pool for patients would've been the guys in maximum security, and according to the head administrator, most of them were too drugged up to pull off something this sophisticated.

"Boyfriend got ruled out early on—had an alibi for the time in question. Three male staff members were interviewed, but the only thing they volunteered was the name Christopher Eola. Seems every time a staff member was questioned about the patient population, they ended up saying, 'Oh, our guys couldn't have done something like that, well . . . except for Eola.'

"Lead detective was Moss Williams. He personally interviewed Mr. Eola four times. Later, he told Robbards that within the first five minutes of speaking to Eola, he knew the guy had done it. Didn't know how, didn't know if they could prove it, but said there was no doubt in his mind Eola had murdered Inge Lovell. Williams would stake his badge on it.

"Unfortunately, that plus a quarter would still only fetch you a cup of coffee. They never could build a case. No one saw anything, Eola wasn't admitting anything, and they had no physical evidence. Best Williams could do was advise the staff to keep a much shorter leash on Eola.

"Shortly thereafter, Eola led some kind of patient revolt in the I-Building and finally earned himself a transfer to Bridgewater. Williams didn't hear about it until nearly a year later, and it pissed him off. According to Robbards, Williams believed they could've used the Bridgewater transfer as a bargaining chip. Maybe make some kind of deal with Eola, so at least the Lovell family could have some closure. No dice, however. Boston State Mental, apparently, preferred to handle its problems on its own—and without public knowledge."

Sinkus cleared his throat, setting down his report expectantly. Most of his fellow detectives around the room were frowning at him.

"I don't get it," McGahagin said. He seemed to have laid off the coffee today, his voice having lost its over-caffeinated edge, though his face still had the pallor of someone who was spending too much time under fluorescent lights. "Are we really thinking one of the patients from the hospital did this? I admit, examining the local loonies makes sense. But like you said, the patients with a history of violence were supposedly locked up. And even if one did get out, how'd he get off the grounds to kidnap not one, but six girls? Then get back on the grounds. And prepare a chamber and spend time down there. And no one saw a thing?"

"Maybe he wasn't a patient anymore," Sinkus said. "Robbards had one other interesting thing to report. In the early eighties, he started noticing a disturbing trend: missing pets. Lots and lots of missing pets. Now, in the suburbs when Fluffy and Fido disappear, you wonder about encroaching coyote populations. But no one believes there are any four-legged predators operating in inner-city Mattapan. Not even on a hundred acre site."

"What are you thinking?" D.D. pressed.

Sinkus shrugged. "We all know certain killers start by preying on animals. And it always struck Robbards that the same year the hospital shut its doors for good, local animals suddenly seemed to become prey. It kind of makes you wonder. Where did all those patients who were treated at Boston State Mental go when the hospital closed? And were all of them magically sane?

"More and more, I'm thinking we're looking for a *former* patient of Boston State Mental. And if you're going to look at former patients, then Christopher

Eola has to lead the list. By all accounts, he's shrewd, resourceful, and has already gotten away with murdering Inge Lovell."

"All right," D.D. said, spreading her hands. "You convinced me. So where's Mr. Eola these days?"

"Dunno. Left a message with the hospital superintendent at Bridgewater an hour ago. I'm waiting to hear back."

D.D. considered the matter. "Pay her a personal visit. This isn't the first time I've heard Eola's name today."

D.D. launched into a brief summary of her and Bobby's conversation with Charlie Marvin. She shared the minister's concerns about Eola, as well as about former staff member Adam Schmidt. Then, taking a very deep breath, D.D. mentioned the appearance of Annabelle Granger.

The task force went from stunned silence to full uproar in under ten seconds.

"Whoa! Whoa, whoa, whoa!" McGahagin's rasping voice finally cut through the clatter. "You're telling us we have a witness?"

"Mmm, too strong a word. Bobby?" D.D. turned to him neatly, her gaze perfectly steady, as if she weren't dumping a load of shit in his lap. He gave her a tighter, thanks-a-lot-Teach smile of his own, then scrambled to boil down three days of covert activities into three salient points for the task force's consideration.

One, Annabelle Granger was still alive and the remains found with her engraved locket most likely

174

belonged to her childhood friend, Dori Petracelli.

Two, this narrowed their time line to the fall of '82, where they had evidence an unidentified white male subject was stalking seven-year-old Annabelle, then possibly kidnapped Dori as a substitute after the Granger family fled to Florida.

Three, there was the highly messy, disturbing, niggling little detail that Annabelle Granger happened to be the spitting image of another young girl, Catherine Gagnon, who was kidnapped and held in an underground pit in 1980, two years before Dori Petracelli vanished. Catherine's abductor, Richard Umbrio, had been imprisoned by the beginning of '82, however, meaning he couldn't have been involved in Annabelle's case.

Bobby stopped talking. His fellow officers stared at him.

"Yep," he said briskly. "That's about what I think, as well."

Detective Tony Rock spoke first. "Holy shit," he declared. He looked worse tonight than he had last night. The long hours, or the situation with his mother?

"Another astute observation."

McGahagin turned on D.D. "Were you ever going to tell us about this?"

Score one for McGahagin.

"I thought it was important to verify Annabelle's story first," D.D. replied steadily, "given its rather perplexing impact on our investigation. She herself couldn't provide any supporting documentation. Instead, Detective Dodge has spent the past twenty-four hours substantiating the details. I'm willing to believe her now. Unfortunately, I still don't know what any of this means."

"We can add to the profile of our suspect," Sinkus spoke up. "We're definitely looking for a predator who's methodical and ritualized in his approach. He doesn't just abduct his victims—he stalks them first."

"Who might be in some way connected to Richard Umbrio," another detective thought out loud. "Can we interview Umbrio?"

"Dead," Bobby volunteered, but didn't elaborate.

"But you said he was imprisoned."

"At Walpole."

"So maybe they still have his personal effects. Including correspondence?"

"Worth a try."

"What about Catherine Gagnon? Any connection between her and Annabelle Granger?"

"Not that we've determined," Bobby said. "But we've set up a meeting between the two women for tomorrow afternoon. Perhaps once they see each other in person . . ." He shrugged.

A couple of the task-force members were studying him now. Detectives had a relentless memory for details, such as that two years ago Officer Dodge had been involved in a fatal shooting involving a man named Jimmy Gagnon. Surely the last name wasn't just a coincidence.

But they didn't ask and he didn't tell.

"Charlie Marvin spotted Annabelle at the Boston State Mental site," D.D. was saying now. "Said he thought she looked familiar. I caught up with him after Annabelle left and tried to press him for details. Maybe he'd seen her or someone who looked like her in Mattapan. He was vague, though. Just thought for a moment he recognized her from somewhere, one of those passing things. I don't know if there's something more significant there or not. Annabelle would've been just a child when Boston State Mental closed, so an actual connection between her and the site . . ."

"Not probable," Sinkus filled in for her.

"No, I don't think so."

The task-force room fell silent.

"So where are we?" McGahagin prodded, trying to wrap things up.

"Tracking down Christopher Eola," Detective Sinkus offered.

"Finishing our report on missing girls," D.D. added, with a pointed look back at McGahagin. "And," her voice grew conciliatory, more thoughtful, "honing in on the time line of 1980 through '82. We know the mental hospital closed in 1980. We know, thanks to Detective Sinkus, that animals began disappearing in Mattapan—which is an interesting little sidebar. We also know that at least one perpetrator, Richard Umbrio, had come up with the idea of imprisoning a girl in an underground pit. And we know that by the fall of '82, a man was stalking a girl in Arlington and that her best friend disappeared shortly thereafter twenty-five miles away in Lawrence. We have some reason to believe all these events are related, if only by their proximity in time, so let's get that nailed down.

"Sinkus, you're on Christopher Eola—from the moment he left Boston State Mental, where did he go, what did he do? Where is he now? McGahagin, your team can finish the comprehensive list of missing girls. I want you to focus on all names from the early eighties, summarize the details from each case file, start looking for any connections—and I mean *any*— between the missing girls. How many names do you have?"

"Thirteen."

"All right, start digging. See if you can tie any of those missing girls to Mattapan, Christopher Eola, Richard Umbrio, or Annabelle Granger. I want to know if any of the families remember their daughters receiving anonymous gifts before they disappeared, about any incidents of Peeping Toms in the neighborhood, that sort of thing. Let's assume Annabelle's case gives us an MO, and see if any of the others fit the pattern.

"As for the Catherine Gagnon connection—Bobby and I will be flying to Arizona tomorrow to meet with her in person. Which gives Bobby exactly"—she glanced at her watch—"twelve more hours to uncover all relevant connections between Richard, Catherine, and Annabelle. All right, people, that's a wrap."

D.D. pushed out of her chair. Belatedly, the rest of them followed suit.

Bobby followed D.D. out of the room. He didn't speak until they were in the relative privacy of her office.

"Nice ambush," he commented.

"You handled it okay." D.D. had never been one to apologize. Even now, she mostly appeared impatient. "What?"

"Started thinking about something this evening."

"Good for you. Bobby, I'm tired, I'm hungry, and I would sell my soul for a shower. Instead, I'm five minutes from meeting with the deputy superintendent, where I get to convince him we've made significant progress in an investigation when I think we honestly understand less today than we did yesterday. Don't talk dirty to me. I'm too fucking tired."

He made a motion with his fingers—the world's tiniest violin playing in sympathy.

She sat down heavily and scowled at him. "What?"

"According to Annabelle Granger, her whole family fled in the middle of the afternoon, taking with them only five suitcases. So what happened to the house?"

D.D. blinked at him. "I don't know. What happened to the house?"

"Exactly. I've spent two hours poring over newspaper stories from the end of '82 through '83. Think of it: an entire house, fully furnished, suddenly abandoned in the middle of a neighborhood. You'd think someone would notice. But I can't find any reports in the news or the police files."

"What are you thinking?"

"I'm thinking the house wasn't abandoned. I'm thinking someone, maybe Russell Granger, returned to wrap up loose ends."

D.D. perked up. "For no one to notice, he would've had to do it fairly quickly," she mused.

"Yeah, within a matter of weeks, I'm guessing."

"Meaning right around the time Dori Petracelli disappeared."

"Seems about right."

"You check storage units, real estate records?"

"So far, no storage units or real estate transactions under the name Russell Granger."

"Then who owned Annabelle's house in Arlington?"

"According to property records, Gregory Badington."

"Who's Gregory Badington?"

Bobby shrugged. "Dunno. Name's listed as deceased. I'm working on identifying next of kin."

D.D. scowled. "So Russell didn't own the house. Maybe he rented. But still, you're right. Furniture, clothes, stuff. All of that had to be taken care of somehow by someone." D.D. picked up a pencil, bounced the eraser off the top of her desk. "Do you have a Social Security number for Mr. Granger? What about a license?"

"Am searching DMV records now. Got a call in to his former employer, MIT."

"Keep me apprised."

"One more thing. We'd have to work it from your end. . . ."

"And that is?"

"Sure would be good to know the order of the victims. Like you said, we seem to be narrowing in on a time line. I think we need to place each of those six girls in that time line. I think it makes a great deal of difference whether Dori Petracelli was the beginning—or the end."

D.D. nodded thoughtfully. "I'll call Christie. No guarantees, however. Her limitations are her limitations, and the information you want means by definition she's analyzed all six remains."

"Yeah, got that."

"You'll keep pushing the Russell Granger angle?"

"Yep."

"Anything else we need for tomorrow?"

"Told Annabelle I'd pick her up at ten."

"Ah, a day with Catherine Gagnon," D.D. murmured. "God give me strength."

"You'll leave the brass knuckles at home?" he asked dryly.

She merely gave him a pinched smile. "Now, Bobby, a girl's gotta have *some* fun. . . ."

17

BELLA AND I ran. Down Hanover, exiting right, weaving through a myriad of side streets until we burst through to the main drag of Atlantic Avenue. We picked up pace, thundering into Christopher Columbus Park, bursting up the short flight of stairs, flying beneath the long, dome-shaped trellis before pounding down the other side, across the street, and into Faneuil Hall. My breath grew ragged. Bella's tongue lolled.

But still we ran. As if I could be fast enough to escape the past. As if I could be strong enough to face my fears. As if through sheer force of will I could block Dori's grave from my mind.

We hit Government Center, then looped back to the North End, dodging reckless taxis, passing the clusters of homeless bedded down for the night, then finally returning to Hanover Street. There, we finally slowed, chests heaving, and limped our way back to the apartment. Once inside, Bella drank an entire bowl of water, collapsed on her bed, and closed her eyes with a contented sigh.

I showered for thirty minutes, put on my pajamas, lay on my bed wide-eyed. It would be a long night.

I dreamed of my father for the first time in ages. Not an anxiety dream. Not even an angry dream, where he appeared as some omnipotent giant and I was a tiny little person, yelling at him to leave me alone.

Instead it was a scene from my twenty-first birthday. My father had invited me to dinner at Giacomo's. We arrived promptly at five, because the local favorite seated only a handful and never took reservations; on a Friday or Saturday night, the line for a table would wrap around the block.

But it was a Tuesday, quiet. My father, feeling

expansive, had ordered each of us a glass of Chianti. Neither of us drank much, so we sipped our wine slowly while dipping thick slices of homemade bread into peppered olive oil.

Then my father, out of the blue: "You know, this makes it all worth it. Seeing you looking so beautiful, all grown up. It's all a parent wants for his child, sweetheart. To raise her, to keep her safe, to see the adult he always knew she could become. Your mother would be proud."

I didn't say anything. My throat felt too tight. So I sipped more wine. Dipped more bread. We sat in silence and it was enough.

Eighteen months later, my father would step off the curb into the path of a zigzagging taxi, his face so badly shattered by the impact, I identified his remains based upon the vial of ashes he still wore around his neck.

I honored his wishes by cremating his body and mixing his ashes with my mother's in my pendant. Then I took the urn down to the waterfront late one moonless night and turned the rest of his ashes loose in the wind.

All these years later, my father's entire worldly possessions still fit in five neat suitcases. His only personal item: a small box containing fourteen charcoal sketches of my mother.

I packed up my father's apartment in one afternoon. Canceled the utilities, wrote those last few checks. When I shut his apartment door behind me for the last time, I finally understood. I had my freedom. And the price of it was to always be alone.

Bella crawled into bed with me around three. I think I had been crying. She licked my cheeks, then turned around three times before collapsing in a heap at my side. I curled around her, and slept the rest of the night with my cheek against the top of her head and my fingers curled into her fur.

Six a.m., Bella wanted breakfast, I needed to pee. My thoughts were still scattered, I had dark circles under my eyes. I should finish my current project, send out the invoice, then get packed for Arizona.

I thought instead of the day ahead. The meeting with Catherine Gagnon, who everyone agreed that I didn't know. Yet the cops were willing to fly all the way to Phoenix to see her with me.

The unknown unknowns. My life seemed to be full of them.

And then, brushing my teeth, the gears finally started churning in my brain.

With four hours before departure to Arizona, I knew what I needed to do next.

Mrs. Petracelli opened the door and seemed to step right out of my memory. Twenty-five years later, her figure remained trim, her hair a dark bun pinned conservatively at the nape of her neck. She wore dark wool slacks, a cream-colored cashmere sweater. With

184

her carefully made-up face and red-lacquered nails, she was everything I remembered: the polished Italian wife who took impeccable pride in her home, her family, and her appearance.

As I stood on the opposite side of the screen door, however, she plucked at a loose thread dangling from the hem of her sweater, and I could see her fingers were trembling.

"Come in, come in," she said brightly. "Oh my goodness, Annabelle, I couldn't believe it when you called. It's so nice to see you again. What a fine young woman you have become. Why, you are the spitting image of your mother!"

She waved me inside, hands moving, head bobbing as she gestured me into a butter-colored kitchen, where a round table awaited with steaming mugs of coffee and sliced tea bread. I could feel the forced gaiety behind her words, however, the brittle edge to her smile. I wondered if she could gaze on any of Dori's girlhood friends without seeing what she had lost.

I had looked up Walter and Lana Petracelli this morning, using the phone book listings on the Internet. They had moved from the Arlington neighborhood to a little cape in Waltham. It had cost me a small fortune in cab fare to get here, but I thought it would be worth it.

"Thank you for agreeing to see me on such short notice," I said.

"Nonsense, nonsense. We always have time for old

friends. Cream, sugar? Would you like a slice of banana bread? I made it last night."

I took cream, sugar, and a slice of banana bread. I was glad the Petracellis had moved. Just being around Mrs. Petracelli was giving me a terrible case of déjà vu. If we had been visiting in their old kitchen in their old house, I wouldn't have been able to take it.

"Your parents?" Mrs. Petracelli asked briskly, taking the seat across from me and picking up her own coffee, which she drank black.

"They died," I said softly, adding hastily, "Several years back," as if that made a difference.

"I'm sorry to hear that, Annabelle," Mrs. Petracelli said, and I believed her.

"Mr. Petracelli?"

"Still in bed, actually. Ah, the price of getting old. But we still get out and about quite a bit. In fact, I have a meeting at nine for the Foundation, so I'm afraid I can't linger too long."

"The Foundation?"

"The Dori Petracelli Foundation. We fund DNA tests for missing persons cases, in particular, very old cases where the police departments may not have the resources or the political will to pay for all the tests now available. You'd be amazed at how many skeletal remains are simply tucked away in morgues or whatnot, having been shelved before the advent of DNA testing. These are the cases where the new technology might have the most impact, yet these are precisely the victims who remain overlooked. It's a catch-22—victims often need an advocate to apply pressure to an investigation, and yet without an identity there's no family to advocate for the victim. The Foundation is working to change that."

"That's wonderful."

"I cried for two years after Dori disappeared," Mrs. Petracelli said matter-of-factly. "After that, I grew very, very angry. All in all, I've found the anger to be more useful."

She picked up her mug, took a sip of coffee. After a moment, I did, too.

"I didn't know until recently what had happened to Dori," I said softly. "That she'd been abducted, gone missing. I honestly . . . I had no idea."

"Of course not. You were just a child when it happened, and no doubt had your own worries getting adjusted to your new life."

"You knew about our move?"

"Well, sweetheart, when the moving vans came and loaded up your house, that was certainly a hint. Dori was devastated. I'll be honest—we were very surprised. Certainly as . . . good friends of your family, we thought we'd receive prior notice. But that was a crazy time for your parents. I understand now, better than ever, their desire to keep you safe."

"What did they tell you?"

Mrs. Petracelli cocked her head, seemed to be dredging up memories from the old days. "Your father came over one afternoon. He said that in light of everything that was happening, he'd decided to take the family away for a few days. I understood, of course, and was concerned for how you were doing. He said you were holding up well, but he thought it might be nice to go on a little vacation to take everyone's mind off things.

"I didn't think of it much for the first week. I was too busy keeping Dori entertained—as your absence had put her in a bit of a sulk. Then the phone rang one night and it was your father again, saying we'd never believe it, but he'd gotten a great job offer and he'd decided to take it. So you wouldn't be returning after all. In fact, he was arranging with a moving company to just pack everything up and ship it to your new address. He thought things would be better that way.

"We were devastated. Walter and I enjoyed seeing your parents very much and, of course, you girls were so close. I'll confess my first thought was simply how to break the news to Dori. Later, I grew a little angry. I felt . . . I wished your parents had returned one last time so you two girls could at least say a proper good-bye. And I wasn't an idiot—your father was very vague on the phone, we didn't even know which city you'd moved to. While I respected that privacy was his prerogative, I felt offended. We were friends, after all. Good friends, I'd thought. I don't know . . . it was such a strange, strange autumn."

She looked at me, head tilted to the side, and her next question was surprisingly gentle.

"Annabelle, do you remember what was going on before your family moved? Do you remember the police coming to your home?"

"Some of it. I remember finding little gifts on the porch. I remember they made my father furious."

Mrs. Petracelli nodded. "I didn't know what to think at the time. I'm not even sure I completely believed the initial reports of a Peeping Tom. Why would a grown man want to peek in a little girl's bedroom? We were all so unbelievably innocent back then. Only your father seemed to understand the danger. Of course, once we learned a strange man had been hiding in Mrs. Watts's attic, we were horrified. Such things weren't supposed to happen in our neighborhood.

"Mr. Petracelli and I started talking about moving, especially after your family left. That's what we were doing that week. We'd sent Dori to my parents for the weekend so we could go house hunting. We'd just gotten back from talking to a Realtor when our phone rang. It was my mother. She wanted to know if we knew where Dori was. 'What do you mean?' I said. 'Dori is with you.' Then there was this long, long silence. And then I heard my own mother start to cry."

Mrs. Petracelli set down her coffee mug. She gave me a soft, apologetic smile, brushed self-consciously at the corners of her eyes. "It doesn't get any easier. You tell yourself it will, but it doesn't. There are two moments in my life that will always be with me till the day I die: the moment my daughter was born and the moment I received a phone call telling me she was gone. Sometimes I negotiate with God. I'll give Him all the memories of joy, if He'll just take away the ones filled with pain. Of course, it doesn't work like that. I get to live with the whole kit and caboodle, whether I want to or not. Here"—her voice had gone brisk again—"have another piece of banana bread."

I took another piece. Both of us moved by rote, using the rituals of polite society to keep the horror of our conversation at bay.

"Were there any leads?" I asked. "To Dori?" I dug a walnut out of the bread with my forefinger and thumb, placed it beside my coffee cup on the table.

"One of the neighbors reported seeing an unmarked white van in the area. Best he could remember, a young man with short dark hair and a white T-shirt was at the wheel. The neighbor thought he might be a contractor working in the area. No one ever came forward, however. And in all the years, none of the tips have panned out."

I forced myself to meet her eye. "Mrs. Petracelli, did my father know that Dori had gone missing?"

"I . . . Well, I don't know. I certainly never told him. I never spoke to your father again after that last phone call. Which, come to think of it, does seem strange. But with everything that happened that November, we weren't really thinking about you and your family anymore; we were too busy trying to save ours. Dori's disappearance was on the news, however. For the first few days in particular, when the volunteers were pouring in and the police were launching round-the-clock searches. I don't know if your parents saw the story or not. Why do you ask?"

"I don't know."

"Annabelle?"

I couldn't look at her anymore. I hadn't come to say this. I didn't mean to say this. I was supposed to be doing reconnaissance, mining Mrs. Petracelli for information about Dori's disappearance, preparing myself for the war ahead. But sitting in this cheery yellow kitchen, I couldn't do it anymore. I knew when she looked at me, she saw her daughter, the little girl who'd never gotten to grow up. And I know when I looked at her, I saw my mother, the woman who'd never gotten to grow old. We had both lost too much.

"I gave Dori the locket," I blurted out. "It was one of the gifts. One of the things he left me. My father told me to throw it away. But I couldn't do it. Instead, I gave it to Dori."

Mrs. Petracelli didn't say anything right away. She pushed back her chair, stood up, started clearing the dishes from the table.

"Annabelle, do you think my daughter was killed because of some silly locket?"

"Maybe."

She took my coffee cup, then her own. She set them carefully, as if they were very fragile, in the sink. When she returned, she bent, placed her hand on my shoulder, and enveloped me with the soft scent of lavender.

"You did not kill my daughter, Annabelle. You were her best friend. You brought her immeasurable joy. Truth is, none of us control how much time we have here on earth. We can only control the life we lead while we have it. Dori led a loving, gracious, joyful existence. I think of that every morning when I wake up, and I think of it every night before I go to bed. My daughter had seven years of love. That's a greater gift than some people ever get. And you were part of that gift, Annabelle. I thank you for that."

"I'm sorry," I said.

"Shhhh . . ."

"You are so brave. . . ."

"I'm playing the hand I was dealt," Mrs. Petracelli said. "Bravery has nothing to do with it. Annabelle, I am enjoying speaking with you. It's not often I get to talk to someone who knew Dori. She disappeared so young, and it was so long ago. . . . But it is time, dear. I have my meeting."

"Of course, of course." I belatedly scooted back my chair, let Mrs. Petracelli escort me to the door. Halfway across the family room, I looked up to see Mr. Petracelli coming down the stairs, dressed in dark chinos, a blue-checkered dress shirt, and a deep blue sweater-vest. He took one look at me, did an abrupt about-face, and headed back up the stairs, empty coffee cup dangling from his fingertips.

I glanced at Mrs. Petracelli, saw the strain of her lie regarding her husband stamped in the lines on her face. I didn't say a word, just squeezed her hand.

At the door, however, one last thing occurred to me. "Mrs. Petracelli," I asked, "do you think I could get a picture?"

192

18

THE PHEONIX INTERNATIONAL Airport was a sea of
white Bermuda shorts, broad straw hats, and red-flip-
flop-wearing humanity. We dodged families, business
travelers, and youth groups, trailing our carry-on luggage through an endlessly long terminal. My memory
of Arizona was bright Southwest colors, dancing
green kokopelli dolls, red terra-cotta pots.

Apparently, no one had told the airport designers
that. This terminal, at least, was decorated in morose
shades of gray. Taking the escalator downstairs was
even more depressing. Dark concrete walls gave the
entire space the feeling of a dungeon.

None of it improved my state of mind. *Run,* I kept
thinking. *Run while you still have the chance.*

I'd barely made it back to my apartment from the
Petracelli home when Detective Dodge showed up. I
made him wait downstairs while I frantically tossed
items in my overnight bag. Then I broke the news that
we'd need to drop Bella off at the vet's on the way to
the airport. He didn't seem to mind, taking my bag,
opening the car's back door for my enthusiastic dog.

"Why don't you call me Bobby," he said on the way
to the vet's. We dropped off Bella—who gave me a
last devastated look before the vet's assistant led her
away—then continued on our way.

At the airport, D.D. was waiting at the terminal with
her usual grim expression.

"Annabelle," she acknowledged curtly.

"D.D.," I shot back. She didn't blink an eye at the familiarity.

Apparently, we were one big happy family. Until we boarded the plane. D.D. opened her briefcase, fanned out an assortment of files, and got to work. Bobby wasn't any better. Had his own files, pen, plus a propensity to mutter.

I read *People* cover to cover, then studied the Sky Mall's choices for pet products. Maybe if I bought Bella her very own drinking fountain, she'd forgive me for boarding her.

Mostly, I tried to keep myself busy.

I'd never flown before. My father didn't believe in it. "Too expensive," he'd say. *Too dangerous* is what he really meant. Flying involved buying tickets, and tickets could be traced. Instead, he relied on old clunker automobiles purchased with cash. Whenever we left town, we'd stop at some salvage yard along the way. Bye-bye, family automobile. Hello, new bucket of rust.

Needless to say, some of these cars proved more reliable than others. My father became an expert at repairing brakes, replacing radiators, and duct-taping various windows, doors, bumpers. It amazed me now that I'd never wondered before how an overeducated mathematician became so good with his hands. Necessity is the mother of invention? Or maybe I simply didn't want to know all the things I didn't want to know.

For example, if a moving van had packed up our old house, why had I never seen any of my childhood furniture again?

We'd finally reached the airport exit. Thick, smoked-glass doors parted. We stepped into the enveloping heat. Immediately, a man in a chauffeur's uniform headed toward us, bearing a white placard with Bobby's name.

"What's this?" D.D. demanded to know, blocking the chauffeur's path.

The man stopped. "Detective Dodge? Sergeant Warren? If you would please follow me." He gestured behind him, where a sleek black limo was parked across the way, at the median strip.

"Who arranged this?" D.D. asked in the same clipped tone.

"Mrs. Catherine Gagnon, of course. May I help you with your bag?"

"No. Absolutely not. Not possible." D.D. turned back toward Bobby, stating in a vehement undertone: "Department regs specifically state that officers may not accept free goods or services. This is clearly a service."

"I'm not a police officer," I offered.

"You," she said flatly, "are with us."

D.D. resumed walking. Bobby fell in step behind her. Not knowing what else to do, I gave the perplexed chauffeur a last apologetic shrug, then trailed in their wake.

We had to wait twenty minutes for a taxi. Enough time for the sweat to build up under my armpits and trickle down my spine. Enough time for me to remember that my New England family had only made it nine months in Phoenix before fleeing to a cooler climate.

Once in the taxi, D.D. provided an address in Scottsdale. I started to put the pieces together. Former Back Bay resident, now living in Scottsdale, with a penchant for sending limos. Catherine Gagnon was rich.

I wondered if she needed any window treatments done, then had to cover my mouth with my hand to stifle a hysterical giggle. I wasn't doing very well anymore. Blame it on the heat, the company, the sensory overload of my first plane ride. I could feel tension knotting in my belly. The growing tremors in my hand.

Everyone wanted me to meet this woman, but no one was really telling me why. I'd already said that I'd never heard of Catherine Gagnon. Yet the city of Boston was still willing to pick up the check for two detectives and one civilian to fly five thousand miles round-trip and overnight in Phoenix. What did Bobby and D.D. know that I didn't? And if I was so smart, why did I already feel like a pawn of the BPD?

I pressed my forehead against the warm glass of the window. I wished desperately for a glass of water. When I looked up again, Bobby was watching me with an inscrutable expression. I turned away.

The cab made a left. Weaved in and out of dusty, purple-hued hills. We passed towering saguaros, silver creosote bushes, red-tipped barrel cacti. My mother and I had been so intrigued when we'd first moved here. But we'd never adapted. The landscape always felt like someone else's home. We were too used to snowcapped mountains, dense green woods, and granite gray cliffs. We never knew what to make of this terrible, alien beauty.

The cab came to a long whitewashed stucco wall. Black wrought-iron gates appeared on our right. The cab slowed, turned toward the gates, and found a speaker mounted on the outer wall.

"Say Sergeant D.D. Warren is here," D.D. instructed.

The cabbie did as he was told. The elaborately swirling gates swung open and we entered a shaded green wonderland. I saw an acre of perfectly manicured lawn, lined by broad-leafed trees. We followed the winding road to a circular drive, where a tiled fountain bubbled amidst a carpet of flowers. Which set the stage perfectly for the enormous Spanish Mission–style house that unfolded in front of us.

To the left: towering windows framed in dark mahogany beams, set in thick adobe walls. To the right: more of the same, except this side also included a glass atrium and what I guessed was an indoor pool.

"Holy mother of God," I murmured, and to my deep shame, really was curious if the mysterious Mrs. Gagnon might need any window treatments. The size and scope of the windows here. The challenge. The money . . .

"Back Bay dollars go far in Arizona," Bobby said lightly.

D.D. just took in the whole thing with a tight look on her face.

She paid the driver, asked for a receipt. We trudged up the long, sinuous walk to a pair of massive dark walnut doors. Bobby did the honors of knocking. D.D. and I clustered behind him, clutching our luggage like self-conscious guests.

"What do you think it costs to water this lawn?" I started to babble. "I bet she spends more on her grounds crew each month than I do on rent. Did she ever remarry?"

The right-side door opened. We were confronted by a matronly Hispanic woman with iron gray hair, a short stocky figure, and drab taste in housecoats.

"Sergeant Warren, Detective Dodge, Señorita Nelson? Please, come in. Señora Gagnon will see you in the library."

She took our luggage, asked if we required refreshment after our long trip. We all moved on autopilot, surrendering our belongings, assuring her we were fine, then following her lead from the vaulted foyer into the mansion.

We walked down a broad, creamy white hallway, walls periodically inlaid with quartets of Mexican tile. Dark exposed beams supported a twelve-foot-high ceiling. More thick planks formed the flooring beneath our feet.

We passed an atrium, an indoor pool, a fine collection of antiques. If the outside of the house made the point, the interior added an exclamation point: For Catherine Gagnon, money was no object.

Just as I wondered how long one hallway could be, the housekeeper turned to the left and paused in front of a pair of heavy walnut doors. The library, I presumed.

The housekeeper knocked.

"You may enter," a muffled voice replied.

The doors parted and I caught my first glimpse of the infamous Catherine Gagnon.

19

CATHERINE STOOD IN front of a sun-drenched expanse of windows. The bright backlight obscured her features, revealing only a slender silhouette with long dark hair. I noted thin arms, crossed at her stomach. Jutting hip bones, protruding beneath the panels of a long peasant skirt. Rounded shoulders displayed by a sleeveless, chocolate-brown wrapped shirt, tied at her waist.

I glanced at Bobby. He seemed to be looking everywhere but at Catherine. In contrast, she couldn't keep her eyes off him, her fingers caressing her bare forearm as if she could already feel her fingers splayed across his chest. The tension in the room was palpable and no one had said a word.

"Catherine," Bobby acknowledged finally, coming to a halt well back. "Thanks for seeing us."

"A promise is a promise." Her gaze flickered briefly

to me, but didn't linger. "I trust you had a good flight."

"No complaints. How is Nathan?"

"Excellent, thank you. Attending a very fine private school. I have many hopes for him." She was smiling now, a knowing look on her face as Bobby continued to hang back and she continued to stroke her arm. She finally turned to D.D.

"Sergeant Warren." Her voice chilled ten degrees.

"Long time no see," D.D. commented.

"And yet, not long enough."

Her gaze returned to me, if only to make a point of dismissing D.D. This time, she regarded me thoughtfully, eyes going from the top of my head to the bottom of my feet and back again. I held up under the scrutiny, but I was acutely aware of my cheap cotton top, my fraying jeans, my ratty shoulder bag. I worked two jobs to cover my rent as it was. Haircuts, manicures, fancy clothes. Those were luxuries meant for a woman of leisure like her, not for a working stiff like me.

I still couldn't read her face, but caught a faint tremor down her spine. I realized suddenly this meeting was costing her as much as it was costing me.

She turned briskly to the dark wooden table that dominated the room. "Shall we?" She gestured to the leather chairs, then to an older, gray-haired gentleman I'd just now realized was sitting in the room. "Detective Dodge, Sergeant Warren, please meet my lawyer, Andrew Carson, whom I've asked to join us."

"Feeling guilty?" D.D. asked lightly.

Catherine smiled. "Just Catholic."

She took a seat. I chose the one across from her. Something about the way she tossed her hair, slightly defiantly, right before she sat down, gave me a flicker of déjà vu. And then in that instant, I got it. She honestly did look like me.

Bobby took out a recorder, placed it in the middle of the table. Catherine glanced at her lawyer, but he didn't protest, so neither did she. D.D. was also getting herself in order, arranging piles of paper around her like a small fortress. The only people who did nothing were Catherine and me. We simply sat, guests of honor for this strange little party.

Bobby started up the recorder. Announced the date, the location, and the names of those present. He paused on my name, started to say "Annabelle," then caught himself in time to switch it to "Tanya Nelson." I appreciated his discretion.

They began with the preliminaries. Catherine Gagnon confirmed she had once lived in Boston at such and such address. In 1980, she had been walking home from school. A vehicle had pulled up beside her, a man calling out from the window, *"Hey, honey. Can you help me for a sec? I'm looking for a lost dog."*

She described her subsequent abduction, rescue, and finally the trial of her kidnapper, Richard Umbrio, in May of 1981. Her voice was toneless, almost bored, as she ran swiftly through the chain of events; a woman who has told her story many times.

"And after the conclusion of the trial in '81, did you have occasion to see Mr. Umbrio again?" D.D. asked.

The lawyer, Carson, immediately raised a hand. "Don't answer."

"Mr. Carson—"

"Mrs. Gagnon graciously agreed to answer questions related to her abduction in October through November of 1980," the attorney clarified. "Whether she saw Mr. Umbrio after 1980, therefore, does not fall under the scope of your interview."

D.D. appeared highly annoyed. Catherine merely smiled.

"When you were with Mr. Umbrio, *in October and November 1980,*" D.D. added for emphasis, "did he ever talk to you about other crimes, abductions, or assaults on other victims?"

Catherine shook her head, then added belatedly, for the sake of the tape recorder, "No."

"Have you ever visited Boston State Mental Hospital?"

Carson held up his hand again. "Mrs. Gagnon, did you ever visit the Boston State Mental Hospital *in the fall of 1980?*"

"I've never even heard of the Boston State Mental Hospital, before or after 1980," Catherine conceded graciously.

"What about Mr. Umbrio?" D.D. persisted.

"If he had, he obviously didn't mention it to me, or I would have heard about it, wouldn't I?"

"What about friends, confidantes? Umbrio ever mention anyone he was close to, or perhaps bring a 'guest' to the pit?"

"Please, Richard Umbrio was a teenage version of Lurch. He was too big, too cold, and just plain too freaky even at the age of nineteen. Friends? He had no friends. Why do you think he kept me alive so long?"

This elicited slightly shocked expressions. Catherine simply spread her hands, regarding the rest of us as if we were idiots. "What? You think I never figured out that he was going to kill me? I can tell you for a fact, he tried to kill me every other day. He'd wrap his big sweaty fingers around my neck and squeeze like he was wringing a chicken. Liked to look me right in the eye as he did it, too. But then, at the last second, he'd let me go. Kindness? Compassion? I don't think so. Not from Richard.

"He just wasn't ready for me to die yet. I was the perfect playmate. Never argued, always did as I was told. Like he was going to get that lucky in real life."

She shrugged, the very flatness of her voice making her words that much more cutting.

"He'd strangle you?" D.D. pressed. "With his bare hands? You're sure of that?"

"Very."

"Never brought a knife, used a ligature, played around with a garrote?"

"No."

"You said he tied you up. Rope, handcuffs, other?"

"Rope."

"One kind of rope, different kinds of ropes? Favorite knots?"

"I don't know. Rope. He had a whole coil of it. It

203

was thick, maybe half an inch. White. Dirty. Strong. He would pound stakes into the wooden ground, then tie my limbs to the stakes. I will confess that at the time I didn't notice the knots." Her voice remained remote.

"Did he ever bring trash bags to the scene?"

"Trash bags? What do you mean? Like a Hefty bag?"

"Like any kind of trash bag."

Catherine shook her head. "Richard favored plastic grocery bags. He'd have supplies and/or food in them. You'd be proud of Richard, he was a conscientious camper, carried in, carried out. A regular Boy Scout, that one."

"Mrs. Gagnon, do you know why Mr. Umbrio kidnapped you?"

"Yes."

D.D. momentarily faltered, as if not expecting this answer, though she was the one who asked the question. "You do?"

"Yes. I was wearing a corduroy skirt with knee-high socks. Turns out, Richard had a fetish for Catholic schoolgirls. Took one look, decided I was it. No one else was around, so lucky me."

D.D. and Bobby exchanged glances. Bobby had been taking furious notes while D.D. asked the questions. Cataloging the details of Catherine's attack to compare to the victims found at Boston State Mental, I would suspect. But this bothered them. Now both stared at Catherine.

"Catherine," D.D. asked quietly, "had you met Richard before that afternoon?"

"No."

"Had he by any chance noticed you? Mentioned following you home from school before or watching you on the school playground, that sort of thing?"

"No."

"So, that afternoon, when his car turned down the street. That's the first time you and Richard met?"

"Like I said, lucky me."

D.D.'s frown deepened. "After you got into his car, what happened?"

"The door was jammed, locked, I don't know. It wouldn't open."

"Did you scream, did you struggle?"

"I don't remember."

"You don't remember?"

"No. I remember getting into his car. I remember growing . . . confused, uneasy. I think I tried the door handle and then . . . I don't remember. Police and therapists have asked me for years. I still don't remember. I would guess I screamed. I would guess I fought. But maybe I did nothing. Maybe my lack of memory is my cover for shame." Her lips curved slightly, but the self-conscious smile never reached her eyes.

"What *do* you remember?" D.D.'s voice was gentler now. It seemed to put the steel back in Catherine's spine.

"Waking up in the dark."

"Was he there?"

"Ready to rock and roll."

"In the pit?"

"Yep."

"So he'd already prepared the pit, before he'd spotted you and decided to make his move?"

Bobby and D.D. exchanged that look again.

Bobby spoke up this time. "According to what you said earlier, Umbrio grabbed you on impulse, based on your outfit. So how could he have known to be so prepared?"

Catherine looked at him. "The pit wasn't new. He'd found it one day exploring in the woods. Turned it into a sort of secret hideaway for himself, where he could stash his weenie-whacking magazines and get away from his parents. And, of course, maintain his own personal sex slave." She shrugged again.

"But do *I* think he grabbed me on impulse? No. He *said* that, but I never believed him. He had rope, material for gagging my mouth, covering my eyes. What normal kind of person has that kind of stuff lying around in his car? Richard was a bondage freak. Every single fucking porn magazine he had was pretty much *Bind That Bitch* or *Smack Her Ass*. You're the experts, you tell me, but I would guess the idea of his own little rape kitten had been growing in his mind for some time. He had the physical size to do as he pleased. And he had the perfect location. All he lacked was the unwilling subject. So one afternoon in October, he went shopping."

"Shopping—your word or his?" D.D. asked sharply.

"Does it matter?"

"Yes."

Catherine arched a brow. "I don't remember."

"Catherine"—Bobby spoke up, earning an annoyed frown from D.D., who clearly planned on running the show—"how *experienced* do you think Umbrio was when he abducted you? Were you number one, number three, number twelve?"

"That's asking for speculation," Carson interjected.

"I understand."

Bobby kept staring at Catherine. She had placed her hands on the table. Now she flexed and curled her fingers as she considered his words.

"You mean sexually? Was he a virgin?"

"Yes."

For a moment, she didn't answer. "I was twelve," she said at last. "Not experienced enough myself to be any judge of those things. However . . ."

"However," Bobby prompted when she didn't continue.

"As a woman looking back? He was overeager in the beginning. Climaxed before he ever penetrated, then grew flustered and beat the shit out of me to cover his own embarrassment. That happened frequently those first few days. He would arrive with elaborate plans for what he wanted to do, but be so overexcited he'd ejaculate before we ever got going. With time, however, he settled down. Grew less eager, but more imaginative." Her lips twisted. "He learned to be cruel.

"So, if you ask, as a woman looking back, I would

guess that he was *inexperienced* in the beginning. Certainly, his fantasies grew more complex and demanding with time, if that is any indication."

Her gaze suddenly pounced on me. "Did you know him?"

"Who?" I asked, slightly bewildered to have all eyes on me.

"Richard. What did you think of him?"

"I didn't . . . I haven't . . . I don't know him."

She frowned, turning once more to Bobby. "I thought you said she was a survivor."

"She is. She survived being stalked by an unknown white subject in the early eighties. Who that subject was—e.g., was he Umbrio—is what we're trying to determine now."

She frowned at me again, clearly skeptical. "And you're basing this on what, the fact you believe she looks like me? Honestly, I don't think we bear *that* much of a resemblance." She flipped back her glossy black mane, managing to jut out her breasts in the same motion. I thought that made it clear just what she considered our key differences to be.

"Have you seen her before?" D.D. prodded Catherine, trying to get us back on track. "Does Tanya look familiar to you?"

"Of course not."

D.D. stared at me. "I haven't seen her before either," I confirmed. "But do the math. In the fall of 1980, I was five. What are the chances of me remembering a twelve-year-old girl?"

I turned back to Catherine on my own. "Did you live in Arlington?"

"Waltham."

"Go to church?"

"Hardly," she said.

"Visit any friends or family members in Arlington?"

"Not that stands out in my mind."

"What about your parents, what did they do?"

"My mother was a homemaker. My father worked as an appliance repairman for Maytag," she provided.

"So he traveled."

"Not into the city. His territory was the outlying suburbs. Yours?"

"My father was a mathematician, MIT," I offered.

"Different." Catherine frowned, more speculatively now. "Suffice it to say, in 1980, I doubt our paths crossed, at least not in any memorable kind of way."

"What about other relatives?" Bobby spoke up. "Given the, uh, family resemblance."

Catherine merely shrugged. "You and D.D. are reading too much into this. We both simply look Italian. There must be hundreds of other women in Boston who could say the same."

Everyone looked at me. I had nothing more to add. Frankly, I agreed with Catherine. I didn't think we looked all that much alike. She was much too skinny, for one. And I had better legs.

The interview was petering out. D.D. had a perplexed scowl on her face. Bobby was staring hard at the tape recorder. Whatever they had been looking for, they weren't getting it. MO, I thought. They were trying to compare Richard Umbrio to my stalker; except, according to Catherine, Umbrio had snatched her as a crime of opportunity, whereas the person who had left little gifts for me . . .

The victims may look alike. But the crimes themselves were different.

When no new questions materialized, Catherine planted her hands on the table as if to push back.

"One moment," Bobby said sharply.

"What?"

"Think very hard. Catherine, how sure are you that the man who abducted you was Richard Umbrio?"

"I beg your pardon!"

"You were young, ambushed, traumatized, and most of the time you were with him, you were trapped down in the dark—"

"Mrs. Gagnon," the lawyer started to say nervously, but Catherine didn't need his help.

"Twenty-eight days, Bobby. Twenty-eight days Richard was the only person who occupied my world. If I ate, it was because he brought me food. If I drank, it was because he deigned to give me water. He sat beside me, he laid on top of me. He fucked me holding my head between his massive hands and screaming at me not to turn away.

"To this day, I can picture his face as he stared out the car window. I can see him haloed by the light each time he appeared at the opening of my prison and I knew I'd finally get fed. I remember how he looked by the glow of the lantern light, sleeping just like a baby, my wrist tied to his so I couldn't escape.

"There is no doubt in my mind that Richard Umbrio kidnapped me twenty-seven years ago. And there is no doubt in my mind that each and every day I'm thankful that I stuck the barrel of the gun inside his mouth and blew out his brains."

Carson, the attorney, grew wide-eyed at the end of his client's statement. Bobby, however, merely nodded. He reached across the table, snapped off the recorder.

"All right, Cat," he said quietly. "Then you tell us: If Richard Umbrio went to prison in '81, then who was left to build an even larger underground pit at the site of an old lunatic asylum? Who kidnapped six more girls and stuck them beneath the earth?"

"I don't know. And honestly, I'm a little offended that you think I do."

"We have to ask you, Cat. You're as close to Umbrio as we're going to get."

That clearly pissed her off. This time she did push away from the table, rising to her feet. "I believe we're done here."

"You were alone with him in the hallway," Bobby continued relentlessly. "He talked to you in the hotel suite. Did he mention a friend? A pen pal? Someone he met while in prison?"

"He mentioned exactly how he was going to kill me!"

"What about Nathan? Richard kidnapped him first, maybe while they were alone—"

"You leave my son out of this!"

"Six dead girls, Catherine. Six girls who didn't make it up out of the dark."

"Goddamn you!"

"We need to know. You have to tell us. If Richard had a friend, an accomplice, a mentor, we have to know."

Catherine was breathing hard now, her eyes locked on Bobby's. For an instant, I wasn't sure what she was going to do. Scream? Slap him across the face?

She placed her hands on the edge of the table. She leaned forward until she and Bobby were nearly nose to nose.

"Richard Umbrio had *nothing* to do with your crime scene. He was in prison. And while he was a homicidal son of a bitch, he was also, blessedly for your purposes, a loner. He had no friends. No accomplices. Once and for all, we are done here. Any other questions you have can be delivered to my attorney. Carson."

Carson obediently whipped out business cards.

Catherine straightened. "Now, if you'll excuse us, Annabelle—or Tanya, or whatever her name is—and I have business to attend to."

"We do?" I spoke up rather stupidly.

"Wait a minute—" Bobby started.

"Absolutely not," D.D. echoed, rising from the table.

It was the very vehemence of their response, its implied possessiveness, that made me follow Catherine.

"Don't worry, darlings," our hostess tossed over her shoulder at Bobby and D.D. "I'll have her back before midnight." She shut the library doors behind us and headed down the hall.

"Where are we going?" I asked, having to hustle to keep up.

"Oh honey . . . Obviously, I'm taking you shopping."

20

CATHERINE'S RETAIL-THERAPY location of choice was Nordstrom. Her limo driver dropped us off out front. Catherine breezily informed the chauffeur she'd call him again when needed. He drove off to do whatever it is limo drivers do in between being summoned by their mistresses. I followed Catherine into the store.

She started off by suggesting that we eat. Since my stomach was growling audibly, I didn't protest.

It was after six, and Nordstrom's café was growing crowded. I waited in line for grilled chicken and pesto on focaccia. Catherine ordered a cup of tea.

She glanced at my enormous sandwich, the side of Terra sweet potato chips. She arched a brow, then returned to sipping her green tea. I ate the entire sandwich, the bag of chips, then went back for a piece of carrot cake, simply out of spite.

"So what do you think of Detective Dodge?" she asked, when I was halfway through the cake and presumably so blissed-out on sugar I wouldn't notice the fine hint of longing that had entered her voice.

I shrugged. "As a cop or what?"

She smiled. "Or what."

"If I found him naked in my bed, I wouldn't kick him out."

"Have you?"

"That's not exactly the nature of our relationship." Though the image of Bobby, naked, was taking longer than I would've thought to clear from my head. "Now, him and D.D., on the other hand . . ."

"Never happen," Catherine said immediately. "Sex, maybe, but a relationship? She's far too ambitious for him. I doubt she'll settle for anything less than a politically minded DA, or perhaps a crime boss. Now, *that* would be interesting."

"You two don't like each other very much."

Her turn to shrug. "I have that effect on women. Perhaps it's because I sleep with their husbands. Then again, if the husbands weren't sleeping with me, they would simply be fucking their secretaries, and if you were going to be jilted, wouldn't you rather be jilted for someone who looks like me than for a peroxide blonde with cheap taste in shoes?"

"I never thought of it that way before."

"Few do." Catherine put down her tea. She traced a random pattern on the tabletop with her red-lacquered nail. When she spoke again, her voice was low, with a trace of vulnerability again.

"Once upon a time," she said quietly, "I invited Bobby to move to Arizona with me. Offered him everything, my body, my home, a glamorous life of leisure. He turned me down. Did you know that?"

"Was this before or after he shot your husband?" I asked.

She smiled, seemed amused that I knew that minor detail. "After. You've been listening to D.D., haven't you? She's obsessed with the notion I set up Bobby to kill my husband. I think she's read one too many suspense novels. Ever heard of Occam's razor—the simplest explanation is the best one?"

I shook my head.

"Well, simply put, Jimmy beat the shit out of me, Bobby made the right choice that night, and I'm now living happily ever after, can't you tell?"

Her voice hit a brittle edge on the last word. She seemed to hear it, picked up her tea, and took another sip. I said nothing for a while, just absorbed this woman in front of me, who packaged herself as a walking advertisement for sex, when I was pretty sure now she hadn't felt a thing in nearly twenty-seven years.

Is this the fate I had narrowly avoided when my father decided to flee? And if so, then why didn't I feel more relieved? Because mostly I felt sad. A deep down achy kind of sad. The world was cruel. Grown men preyed on little kids. People betrayed the ones they loved. What was done could never be undone again. That's just the way things worked.

As if reading my mind, Catherine's head came up. She looked me in the eye: "Why are you here, Annabelle?"

"I don't know."

"Richard isn't your stalker. By the time you were seven, he was already sentenced to life in prison. Besides, Richard's fantasies involved physical intimidation and domination. He wasn't subtle enough for stalking."

"You were only twelve; it wasn't your fault."

She actually smiled at me. "You think I don't know that?"

"And you survived."

Now she laughed, a full throaty sound that caused several of the other diners to glance our way. "You think I survived? Oh Annabelle, you are simply *precious*. Come now, as a seven-year-old target yourself, surely you learned something."

"I happen to be an expert kickboxer," I heard myself say stiffly. "My father took my safety very seriously— taught me self-defense, criminology one-oh-one, when to run, when to fight, and how to know the difference. I grew up with over a dozen different aliases, living in a dozen different cities. Trust me, I know how serious this is."

"Your father taught you?" Arched brow again.

"Yes."

"The academic from MIT?"

"The same."

"And how did your father know so much about criminology or self-defense?"

I shrugged. "Necessity is the mother of invention. Isn't that what they say?"

Catherine stared at me in bemusement. "Wait, wait," she said, when she could tell I was getting pissy again, "I'm not trying to mock you. I want to understand. When this all happened, your father . . ."

"He moved my family away. We packed our suitcases in the middle of the afternoon, loaded up the car, and disappeared."

"No!"

"Yes."

"With fake names and everything?"

"Absolutely. There is no other way to be safe. Which reminds me, you're supposed to be calling me Tanya."

She waved away my alias, clearly unconcerned. "And did your father get another job with a university in Florida?"

"Couldn't. Not without a curriculum vitae, and fake driver's licenses rarely come with those kinds of attachments. He drove a taxi."

"*Really?* And your mother?"

I shrugged. "Once a homemaker, always a homemaker, I guess."

"But she didn't protest? She didn't try to stop him? Both of your parents did this for you?"

I was growing puzzled now. "Well, of course. What else was there to do?"

Catherine sat back. She picked up her tea. Her hand had started to shake, causing the liquid to slosh. She set the china cup back down.

"My parents never spoke of what happened," she

said abruptly. "One day, I vanished. Another day, I returned home. We never spoke of the time in between. It was like the twenty-eight days had been some minor blip in the space-time continuum, best left forgotten. We stayed in the same house. I returned to the same school. And my parents resumed their same old lives.

"I never forgave them for that. I never forgave them for being able to still live, still function, still breathe, when every part of me hurt so much I wanted to tear the house apart board by board. I wanted to gouge out my own eyeballs. I wanted to yell and scream so badly, I couldn't make a single sound.

"I hated that house, Annabelle. I hated my parents for not saving me. I hated the block I lived on. And I hated every single child in my school who had walked home safely on October twenty-second without trying to help a stranger find a lost dog.

"And they whispered, you know. They told stories about me on the playground, shared winks and nudges in the locker room. And I never said a word because everything they whispered was true. Being a victim is a one-way ticket, Annabelle. This is who you are now, and no one will ever let you go back."

"That's not true," I protested. "Look at you—you are not weak or defenseless. When Umbrio got out of prison, you didn't just curl up in a ball. You shot him, for God's sake, and more power to you. You met the challenge. You won, Catherine.

"Not like me. I'm all training and no trial. I've spent

my entire life running and I don't even know who it is I'm supposed to fear. 'Can't trust anyone,' was my father's favorite motto. 'Just because you're paranoid doesn't mean they're not out to get you.' I don't know. Maybe my father had a point. Seems like it's always the handsome, charming husband who brutally murders his wife, the mild-mannered Boy Scout leader who's secretly a serial killer, the quiet coworker who one day opens up with an AK-47. Hell, I'm suspicious of the mailman."

"Oh, me, too," Catherine said immediately. "And utility workers, maintenance workers, and customer-service representatives. The amount of information they have at their fingertips is positively scary."

"Exactly!"

"I formed a shell company," she said matter-of-factly. "Put everything in the company's name and— badda bing, badda boom—ceased to exist on paper. It's the only way to be safe. I can have Carson look into it for you."

"Thanks, but I don't exactly have those kinds of assets. . . ."

"Nonsense, it's about security, not money. Trust me on this one. I'll have Carson set you up. You need to think about the future, Annabelle. The real trick to security is keeping one step ahead."

I nodded, but that quickly her words took the wind out of my sails. One step ahead? Of what? What did the future really hold for someone like me? I'd been trained for twenty-five years to live out of suitcases.

To lie. To distrust. To commit to no one. Even in Boston, I had only a passing acquaintance with my Starbucks coworkers, and barely registered one step above a maid with most of my wealthy clients. I attended church, but I always sat in the back. I never wanted to be asked too many questions; I didn't want to lie to a man of God.

And as for my business, what would happen if it did take off, if I tried to hire employees? Would my fake ID hold up under the intense scrutiny of business-licensing boards, referral services? I kept telling myself I was optimistic. I kept telling myself I was in control, had a dream. I would not be my father's pawn! But truth was, week after week, I slogged through the same under-the-radar routine. My business did not grow. I did not make friends or date seriously.

I would never fall in love. I would never have a family. Twenty-five years after I started running, my parents were dead, I was all alone, and I was still terrified.

And then I understood Catherine Gagnon. She was right. She had never escaped from that pit in the ground. Just as I had never stopped living like a target.

"I need to go to the bathroom," I mumbled.

"I'm done, too."

"Please, I think I just need a minute."

She shrugged. "I'll powder my nose."

She followed me to the ladies' lounge, taking up position in front of a gilded mirror. I went into one of the stalls, where I pressed my forehead against the cool metal door and worked on regaining my composure, finding focus.

What was it my father had always said? I was strong, I was fast, and I did have a fighter's instinct.

What did my father know? For all his scheming, he hadn't been able to dodge a lost taxi.

I squeezed my eyes shut, thought of my mother instead. The way she had stroked my hair. The look on her face that fall afternoon in Arlington, when she had told me that she loved me, that she would always love me.

From my pocket, I took out the picture Mrs. Petracelli had given me. Taken at a barbecue in the Petracellis' backyard. I was sitting on the picnic table next to Dori. We were grinning at the camera, each holding a Popsicle. My mom stood to the side, toasting the camera with a margarita, smiling at us indulgently. My father was toward the back, working the grill. He had also noticed the camera, maybe heard Mrs. Petracelli say "Cheese," and had turned with a large, beaming smile.

The smell of searing hamburgers, freshly cut grass, and roasting corn on the cob. The sound of neighbors' sprinklers and other small children playing next door.

I could feel the nostalgia welling in my throat, the tears burning my eyes. And I understood why I never made it forward. Because mostly I wanted to go back. To the last days of summer. To those final weeks when the world still felt safe.

I wiped my eyes. Flushed the toilet. Pulled myself together, because what else was there to do?

I made it to the sink, setting the photograph carefully to the side so it wouldn't get wet while I washed my hands. Catherine wandered over, regarded my reflection in the mirror. She had retouched her lipstick, brushed out her long black hair.

Side by side, we did look like sisters. Except she was the glamorous one, destined for a life amid the stars, while I was clearly going to become the crazy cat lady who lived alone down the street.

Her gaze drifted down, spotted the photo. "Your family?"

I nodded, then felt, more than saw, her stiffen.

"I thought you said your father was a mathematician," she said sharply.

"He was."

"Don't lie to me, Annabelle. I met him. Twice, in fact. Really, you could've just said he was with the FBI."

21

WE VIOLATED CURFEW. Catherine didn't get me back to the hotel Bobby and D.D. had booked until 12:23 a.m. I took a staggering step out of the limo, waved goodbye to my newfound best friend, and worked my way resolutely to the lobby. I figured either Bobby or D.D. would be keeping watch. It was Bobby.

He took one look at my disheveled appearance and

stated the obvious. "You're drunk."

"It was just one glass of champagne," I protested. "We were toasting."

"To what?"

"Oh, you had to be there." We'd been toasting lies, and the men who told them, and that hadn't taken us one glass of champagne, but three.

I was totally shit-faced, going-to-hate-myself-in-the-morning drunk. Catherine had simply mellowed enough to show me photos of her son and smile happily. She had a beautiful son. I wanted a son one day. And a daughter, a precious little girl who I would keep very, very safe.

And I wanted sex. Apparently, champagne made me horny.

"Do you like to barbecue?" I asked Bobby. Then found myself humming, *"If you like piña coladas, or getting caught in the rain . . ."*

Bobby's eyes widened. "We should never have left you alone with her!"

I did a little dance around the lobby. It was tricky, trying to get my feet to move in conjunction with my brain. I thought I did pretty well, though. In the ring, I'd always been admired for my footwork. Maybe I'd take up ballroom dancing. It was all the rage these days. Maybe that would do me good. Practice something beautiful and flowing and flirtatious. You know, instead of hanging out in gyms where sweaty men pummeled one another to death.

Yep, in the morning, I was turning over a new leaf.

I was reclaiming my name. Annabelle Granger was going to shake hands with the first stranger she met. Hell, I'd post my Social Security number online and include all my personal banking information. What was the worst that could happen?

Bobby had a nice set of shoulders on him. Not over-pumped; I never like that on a guy. Bobby's shoulders were compact, well-defined. He wore a loose-fitting polo shirt, and it was fun to watch the way his pectorals rippled beneath the cotton expanse. I liked the way he moved, coiled, lithe. Like a panther.

"You," he said, "need water and aspirin."

"Gonna take care of me, Detective?" I sidled over. He sidled away.

"Ah Jesus Christ," he muttered.

I smiled up at him. "Does the hotel have a pool? Let's go skinny-dipping!"

I thought he actually squeaked.

"I'm calling D.D.," he declared, and made a beeline for the lobby phone.

"Ah, don't spoil my fun now," I called after him. "Besides, you'll want to hear my news."

That stalled him. "What news?"

"Secrets," I murmured. "Deep, dark family secrets."

But I didn't get a chance to tell them. Just then, all those thousands of tiny little champagne bubbles finally penetrated my brain, and I passed out cold.

D.D. didn't have a sense of humor. I had suspected that before. Now I knew it. Bobby half carried, half dragged my sorry ass up to D.D.'s room. No romantic tucking in of precious little Annabelle. Detective Dodge dumped me onto D.D.'s sofa. The sergeant doused me with a glass of ice water.

I bolted upright, sputtering wildly, then racing for the toilet to vomit.

When I came back out, footsteps still unsteady, D.D. greeted me with a fistful of aspirin and a can of spicy V8.

"Don't puke this up," she warned me. "It's from the minibar and it's costing the department a fortune."

Expensive V8 did not taste any better than normal V8. I tried not to be ill.

"Sit. Talk." D.D. still sounded pissed.

I managed to register now that she remained fully clothed, though we were passing one a.m. Her laptop was powered up on the desk, and her cell phone was winking madly that it had new messages.

Apparently, D.D. wasn't getting her beauty rest these days, and that made her one cranky bitch.

I tried to sit. It made the nausea worse. I went with pacing.

Later, when I thought about it, I was very sorry I had the champagne. Not because it made me sick, but because it lowered my defenses. It made me talk when a sober Annabelle would've known better.

"My father was an undercover FBI agent," I blurted out.

D.D. frowned, blinked her eyes, frowned at me again. "What the hell are you talking about?"

"My father. He was with the FBI. Catherine knew him. Hey, stop doing that!"

"Stop doing what?" Bobby asked.

"Exchanging glances. It's very annoying. Not nearly as cool as you two seem to think."

This earned me a pair of arched brows instead.

"Catherine has met your father?" Bobby asked skeptically.

"He went to her hospital room where she was recovering after being rescued." My chest practically swelled with pride. Or gas. "He visited her twice!"

"Your father questioned Catherine?"

"Yes. I'm telling you, he was an FBI agent. And that's what FBI agents do, they question victims of crime."

D.D. sighed, rubbed her forehead, sighed again. "I'm going to brew coffee," she said abruptly. "Annabelle, you've got a lot of sobering up to do."

"I am not lying! Ask Catherine! She will tell you. He came to her room twice."

"In the hospital," Bobby said.

I nodded, an ill-considered motion that almost made me puke again. "He said he was a special agent, FBI, and asked her all sorts of questions about her attack."

Halfway across the room, D.D. stilled, caught the pause, got herself moving again. "All sorts of questions?" she asked. "What kind of questions?"

"Well, you know, FBI questions. Who grabbed her, what did he look like, what kind of car did he drive. Where did the perp take her."

226

"The perp?"

"Oh yeah, the perp. Plus all the stuff you asked. Where, what kind of supplies, how long was she underground. What did Umbrio say, were there any other victims, how did she get away, blah, blah, blah."

The coffee was percolating now, the rich, caffeinated scent permeating the air.

"He visited Catherine twice?" Bobby asked.

"That's what she said."

"Did he show ID?"

"I don't know."

"Was anyone else with him? Another member of law enforcement? A partner?"

"She never mentioned anyone with him." I placed my hand on his muscled arm. "But I think partners are just a TV myth," I told him kindly. "The real FBI doesn't do that sort of thing."

"But they have secret undercover agents," he drawled.

"Oh yes."

"Who still live at home with their families?"

Across the room, D.D. was making frantic ixnay motions with her hand. That, more than anything, caught my attention. All at once, I heard how ridiculous my words sounded. All at once, the true implication of Catherine's words hit me, and I felt my stomach plummet, the floor drop out from underneath me. Except I couldn't be sick anymore. I couldn't pass out cold. I had already played my best denial cards under the influence of alcohol. I had no tricks left.

"They do have undercover agents, don't they?" I heard myself ask. "I mean, they could. . . ."

My hand was still on Bobby's arm. He took it now, led me back to the sofa. I sat down hard. Didn't move.

He took a seat across from me, on the edge of the bed. D.D. brought me a mug of coffee.

"Did your father ever tell you he was an FBI agent?" Bobby asked quietly.

I sipped scalding black coffee, shook my head.

"Did you ever hear him tell anyone else he was an FBI agent?"

Another negative, another bitter sip.

"Of course, we'll call the Boston field office and ask," Bobby said gently.

"But . . ."

"It's the FBI, Annabelle, not the CIA. Besides, no FBI agent worth his salt would call nine-one-one over something as stupid as a Peeping Tom. First, he'd deal with it himself. Second, if he did feel there was a threat to himself or his family, he'd call his buddies to cover his back. Your father was interviewed three times by local officers and never once mentioned being an agent. It's just too important a piece of the puzzle for him *not* to mention it. It . . . it doesn't make any sense."

"But why would he tell Catherine he was with the FBI?" I stopped talking. Finally saw the logical answer they'd seen from the very beginning. Because my father had wanted information on Catherine's abduction. Personal, firsthand information, which was important enough for him to pose as a federal agent not once, but twice.

In November of 1980, my father was already obsessed with violence toward young girls. Except, in theory at least, no one had started stalking me yet.

Coffee spilled out of my mug, burning my hand. I used it as an excuse to retreat once more to the bathroom, where I ran cold water and stared at my reflection in the mirror. My features were ashen. Sweat beaded my brow.

I wanted to be sick again. I wasn't going to be that lucky.

I washed my face with cold water. Again and again.

When I went back out to the main room, I rebuilt my face into a façade none of us were stupid enough to believe.

"I'm going to go to my room now," I said quietly.

"I'll walk you there," said Bobby.

"I'd like to be on my own."

Bobby and D.D. exchanged uneasy glances. Did they think I would bolt? And then it occurred to me: Of course they did. That was my MO, right? The mistress of multiple identities, a girl born to run.

Except that honestly hadn't been me. It had been my father.

Liar, liar, pants on fire.

Every time we moved, my mother and I made so many mistakes. Used the wrong names, referenced the wrong cities, forgot key details. But my father never did. My father was always smooth, fluid, and controlled. How could I never wonder how he learned to lie so well? How he learned to live on the run? How he learned to adapt and reconfigure himself so easily?

My father always said to trust no one. Maybe that also applied to himself.

Bobby and D.D. still hadn't said a word. I couldn't wait anymore. I turned on my heels and headed for the door.

They didn't stop me, not even as the door closed behind me and left me alone in the hall.

For just one moment I thought about it.

Run. It's not so hard. Just put one foot in front of the other and *go*.

But I didn't run. I walked. Slowly, very carefully, step by step, to my assigned room.

Then I lay down fully clothed on top of the cheap hotel bed. I stared at the whitewashed ceiling. And I counted down the hours to dawn, holding on to the vial of my parents' ashes and praying desperately to find strength for the days ahead.

22

BOBBY'S ALARM WENT off at five a.m. He thought that was mean, so he hit Snooze. That bought him two more minutes, then his phone rang. D.D., of course.

"Are you sleeping at all?" he asked.

"What are you, my fucking mother?"

"Now, see, this is why you need rest."

"Bobby, we have three hours before we have to

leave for the airport. Get your ass up here."

As words went, he didn't find them inspirational. So he showered, shaved, packed, and poured himself a steaming mug of black coffee. By the time he reached D.D.'s room, she looked about thirty seconds from full boil.

He thought she'd launch into another tirade. At the last moment, however, she seemed to realize the error of her ways, and held open the door instead.

Her hotel room looked like it had been hit by a hurricane. Papers strewn, coffee spilled, discarded food decorating a room-service tray. Whatever she'd been doing since Bobby had seen her last, it hadn't involved any rest.

"I already spoke to the hotel manager," she started off curtly. "He promised to alert us immediately if Annabelle tries to check out."

Bobby looked at her. "Because if Annabelle decides to bolt, naturally she'll have the consideration to formally check out of her room first."

"Oh my God—"

"D.D., sit down. Take a breath. For God's sake, you're one step away from the Looney Tunes conga line." He shook his head in exasperation. She merely scowled.

D.D. was wearing the same clothes from the night before, now covered in wrinkles and smelling of day-old sweat. Her skin was sallow; her blonde hair, frizzed; her blue eyes, bloodshot.

"D.D.," he tried again, "you can't go on like this.

One glance, and the deputy will yank your command and send you packing. It's not enough to manage staff burnout. You gotta manage your own."

"Do not take that tone of voice with me—"

"Look in the mirror, D.D."

"I will not be patronized for doing my job—"

"Look in the mirror, D.D."

"I will have you know, I'm one of those people who don't need much sleep."

He took her shoulders and firmly turned her toward the wall mirror.

"Holy crap!" she said.

"Exactly."

She reached up, fingered her wild mane of hair. "It's the humidity."

"We're in Arizona."

"New hair product?"

"D.D., you need sleep. Not to mention a shower and a two-week vacation to Tahiti. For now, however, try a bath."

Her nose crinkled. She finally sighed, her shoulders slumping forward.

"There are just so many pieces of this puzzle," she said tiredly. "And none of them fit."

"I know."

"Christopher Eola, Richard Umbrio, Annabelle's father. My head is spinning."

Bobby pulled out the desk chair, took a seat, lacing his hands behind his head. "Okay, so let's talk it through. November 1980 . . ."

"Umbrio abducts a young girl and stashes her in an underground chamber he's conveniently found in the woods." D.D. plopped down on the edge of the bed, leaning forward and planting her elbows on her knees.

"We believe this is his first act, done independently," stated Bobby.

"Fits his profile as a loner with subpar social skills."

"His victim is selected at random, a crime of opportunity."

"Because she has the right taste in clothes," D.D. amended.

"But also because she's alone and falls for his lure. Point is, no premeditation. So one key difference between Umbrio and the UNSUB who pursued Annabelle Granger."

"Catherine was adamant that Umbrio preferred his bare hands." D.D. hesitated. "I can't be sure, but it looked to me like there was something around the victims' necks, inside the plastic bags. Some form of ligature."

"He tied them up awfully fancy," Bobby agreed.

"So another difference."

"We assume."

"Umbrio only kidnapped one victim," D.D. stated.

"Boston State Mental subject took six. But maybe one at a time, so we're still uncertain there."

"Yeah." D.D. was nodding slowly. She seemed to have recovered from her earlier fugue, was getting it together now. "Then, of course, we have the little gem regarding Annabelle's father."

"Oh yeah. Then there's that."

"Annabelle's father brings us back to our first theory—that someone was inspired by Umbrio's crime and thought to replicate it at Boston State Mental. We'd made the assumption that this 'apprentice' would've reached out to Umbrio in prison, maybe in person or by mail. But masquerading as an FBI agent and grilling Catherine in the hospital does the trick just as well."

"Yes, it does," Bobby concurred grimly.

"How goes the search for background info on Russell Granger?"

Bobby made a face. "Still can't find a driver's license or a Social Security number. Have tried multiple databases, multiple spellings. Have tried Leslie Ann Granger, Annabelle's mother. I got zero, zip, nada."

"In other words, Russell Granger is an alias."

"Your guess is as good as mine. I managed to reach a personnel director with MIT right before we left town. According to her, there's no record of a Russell Granger in the HR files. She's working on tracking down the former head of mathematics in the eighties to verify. Hopefully, I can talk to him the minute we're back in town."

"What about life on the road?" D.D. quizzed. "Every time Annabelle and family got the hell out of Dodge, there must have been a reason. Have you tracked the cities, checked with local law enforcement?"

Bobby gave her a look. "Sure, boss, those are exactly the type of calls I can make in my free time. You know, between two and four a.m."

"Hey, if this job is getting too tough for you—"

"Oh, shut up, D.D."

She smiled at him. Not too many people felt like they could tell D.D. to shut up these days. He supposed it was part of his charm.

Now, however, her expression returned to being serious. "Bobby, what was the alias Annabelle's father was using in Boston again?"

He looked at her in bewilderment. "Russell Granger. I thought that was the whole point of this conversation."

"Not in 1982, Bobby. Later, when he and Annabelle returned to Boston. If she became Tanya Nelson, then he became . . ."

"Mr. Nelson?" Bobby quipped. He flipped through his spiral notepad. First time they'd questioned Annabelle at BPD headquarters, she'd provided a rough overview of cities, aliases, and dates. He found the page in his notes, skimmed through, repeated the process two more times. "I don't . . . I don't have Boston listed. Annabelle didn't discuss their return."

D.D. arched a brow. "Interesting omission, don't you think?"

"There are a lot of cities and akas," he countered, holding up the page for her inspection. "Come on, we just figured out we'd overlooked that information ourselves."

D.D. continued to appear skeptical. "Get the Boston alias, Detective. Run it. Maybe Russell Granger stayed off the radar screen in the early eighties, but when he returned for his second time around . . ."

"Yeah, okay. Sometime, someplace, someone knew this guy."

"Exactly. One last thing—don't tell Annabelle."

"I haven't."

"I don't want to overplay our cards. If Russell Granger is the key to all of this, our only link to him is Annabelle. Meaning, we're going to need her cooperation if we're going to get anywhere." D.D. paused. "And we need to talk to Catherine again."

"You mean, *I* gotta talk to Catherine again," he amended. "Nothing personal, but as you mentioned, clock's ticking here, and it would take you and her half a day just to work out your aggressions. We have"—he glanced at his watch—"approximately two hours, which means I win Catherine, while you get to babysit Annabelle." He glanced around her room. "Maybe you can put her to work cleaning."

"Very funny."

"Promise me you're going to shower."

"Funnier still."

"Put on clean clothes?"

He was rising out of his chair. She smacked his arm. It hurt like hell, so he knew she was feeling better.

"Meet you at the airport," he called over his shoulder.

"I can hardly wait."

• • •

It took Bobby ten minutes to grab his luggage, square away his room, and hail a cab. The sun was just coming up, tingeing the sky an unnatural shade of pink, streaked with smoky purple. Traffic would hardly be a problem.

He doubted Catherine would be up at this hour. Which might work to his advantage, or might not. He wondered if she still had nightmares, and if so, were her dreams haunted by Richard Umbrio? Or her dead husband?

It took two tries before a voice answered the box outside the elaborate front gates. The taxi driver's eyes widened as he entered the estate, but he didn't say a word.

"Can you wait for me?" Bobby asked the driver, flashing his badge.

If anything, he made the hunch-shouldered Hispanic man more nervous.

"It's okay, you can leave the meter running," Bobby assured him. "Moment this meeting is done, I gotta hustle to the airport. Be good to have a cab already waiting."

The driver reluctantly agreed and Bobby nodded in satisfaction. He wanted the cab visible from the house. A subtle reminder that Bobby was just passing through.

The housekeeper opened the door. She registered no surprise at his appearance. Simply told him the señora would be with him shortly. Would he like something to drink?

Bobby declined, then followed her to the atrium, where she showed him to a small patio table beautifully inset with a peacock mosaic and bearing a silver coffee service.

He took a seat, poured himself a cup of coffee, and tried not to glance at his watch. He wondered how long Catherine would make him wait. Anticipation or punishment? With her, it was always hard to know.

The answer was fifteen minutes.

When she finally did appear, she wore a royal blue satin robe, belted at the waist. The long, sinuous fabric moved with her as she walked toward him, the rich color setting off her glossy black hair. A smile toyed with the corners of her mouth. He recognized her look instantly.

First time Bobby had met Catherine after the shooting, it had been at the Isabella Stewart Gardner Museum. She'd been standing in front of a Whistler painting, *Lapis Lazuli*, which featured a nude woman lounging against a rich sea of blue oriental fabric. Catherine had remarked on the sensual lines of the painting, the erotic nature of the pose.

She had picked that painting to befuddle him then, just as she had picked this robe to befuddle him now.

And even knowing better, he could feel his stomach tighten in response.

She drew toward him, pausing in front of the table. She didn't take a seat.

"Miss me, Detective?"

"Heard the coffee was good."

Her smile broadened. "Still playing hard to get."

"And still as astute as always," he acknowledged. "How's Nathan this morning?"

A shadow flickered across her eyes. "Rough night. I don't think he'll be going to school today."

"Nightmares?"

"It happens. He's seeing a good therapist now. Plus, he has his dog. Who knew Richard's own puppy could make such a difference? But the dog calms him, often better than I can. I think he's making progress."

"And you?"

She gave him a playful look. "I'm much too old to tell a complete stranger how I really feel." She finally pulled out a chair, gracefully taking a seat. He poured her a cup of coffee in paper-thin china. She accepted it wordlessly.

For a few minutes, both of them sipped their coffee and let the silence be enough.

"You're here about Annabelle," Catherine said at last. "Because I recognized her father."

"Came as a bit of a shock," he acknowledged. "Can you tell me about it?"

"What's there to tell? I was in the hospital. He came to my room. Asked me some questions."

"Did he give you a name?"

"No, just said he was a special agent, FBI."

Bobby arched a brow, but she put down her coffee cup, dead serious now.

"I only remember him because he kept arguing with me. I was in the hospital, happy to finally have everyone

239

gone, not asking me all sorts of ridiculous questions. *How do you feel, Catherine? What do you need? Can we get you anything?* Really, I was starving, dehydrated, and raped out of my fucking mind. What I needed was for everyone to leave me alone.

"And then this man walked in, dressed in a dark suit and tie. Not a big man, but quite handsome. He flashed his badge and announced, 'Special Agent, FBI.' Just like that. With authority. I remember feeling impressed. His tone was firm, strict. Like what you would expect from an FBI agent."

"What did he do, Catherine?"

She shrugged. "He asked questions. Police questions. What did I remember about the vehicle—color, make, model, plates, interior? Please describe the man who was driving. Height, weight, coloring, age, ethnicity. What did he say, what did he do? Where did he take me, how did we get there, and on and on and on. Then he showed me a sketch."

"A sketch?"

"Yes, a pencil drawing. Black and white. Nicely detailed, like what I imagined a police artist would do. I was hopeful, because no one had made an attempt to identify my attacker yet. But the drawing wasn't of Richard."

Bobby blinked a few times. "The sketch *wasn't* Richard Umbrio?"

"No, the man pictured was smaller, more refined around the jawline. When I told Mr. Special Agent that, he didn't take it so well."

"What do you mean?"

"I mean he started arguing with me. Maybe I didn't remember quite right, it was dark, I was underground. Honestly, the agent started to piss me off. But then the door opened, a nurse appeared, and he left."

"Mr. Special Agent left, just like that?"

"Yes. Closed up his notebook, exited stage right."

"Did the nurse say anything?"

"Not that I remember."

Bobby frowned, trying to put these pieces together. "Did Mr. Special Agent provide a name, contact information, a business card?"

"No."

"Did you mention his appearance to anyone else? The police, your parents?"

Catherine shook her head. "Everyone was asking me questions. What was one more suit in the room?"

"But he came a second time?"

"The day I was going to be discharged. A nurse was in the room this time, taking my blood pressure. The door opened, he appeared. He looked the same as before. Dark suit, white shirt, dark tie. Maybe the same suit, now that I think about it.

"This time, he flashed his credentials toward the nurse and said we needed a minute alone. She hustled out. He came over to my bed, got out his notebook. He went over all the questions again. His voice was gentler this time, but I liked him less. Everyone was asking me everything and telling me nothing. Then, of course, he produced the sketch again."

"Same sketch?"

"Exact same sketch. Except this time, as I watched, he altered it. Thickened the hair, added shadowing to the cheeks. 'What about now,' he'd ask. I'd shake my head and he'd tinker with another element."

"Wait a minute," Bobby interrupted. "You're telling me the original sketch was something he'd done himself? Not an official police sketch?"

"I'd originally *assumed* it was a police artist's rendering, but to watch Mr. Special Agent go to town, I guess not. His revisions blended into the first picture perfectly. Who knew FBI agents had such skills?" Catherine shrugged.

"So as you watched, he altered the drawing."

"Sure, but it didn't change anything. The man in the sketch was not Richard, and no amount of tinkering with hairstyles was going to change that. Which I told Mr. Special Agent. He didn't take it so well. Insisted I was wrong. Maybe the person in the sketch had gained weight, wore a wig."

Catherine curled one corner of her mouth with disdain. "Really, I was twelve. What the hell did I know of disguises? Mr. Special Agent had asked me a question, I gave him my answer. The minute he started arguing with me, he pissed me off."

"So what happened?" Bobby prodded.

"I told him to leave."

"Did he?"

Catherine hesitated, picking up her coffee cup, holding it in front of her lips. "For a moment . . . For a moment, I wasn't sure he would. And I remember, just for an instant, starting to feel uneasy. But then the orderly showed up and Mr. Special Agent bolted from the room. As the saying goes, good-bye and good riddance." Catherine blew the steam off her coffee and finally took a sip.

"Did you see him again?"

"No."

"Ever mention his visits to anyone?"

"A few weeks later, when the police finally showed me a photo array. I spotted Richard's photo immediately, tapped on it, and said, 'At last you people are listening to me.' The police didn't seem to know what I was talking about. But that didn't surprise me. Even a twelve-year-old can realize that law enforcement types don't play well with one another."

Bobby grunted at that. "What about anyone else from the FBI? Ever get interviewed by any other FBI agents?"

"Nope."

"And that didn't strike you as odd?"

Another shrug. "Why? I wasn't lacking for officers taking an interest in my case. Every goddamn man in uniform wanted to hear all the sordid details. Is it interesting for you guys? Do you get a secret thrill? Stay alone in the office, whacking off while reading your notes from the rape interviews?"

Bobby didn't respond. Catherine had a reason for her rage. Nothing he could do about it all these years later. Not much she could do about it either.

After a moment, Catherine's gaze relented. She went back to sipping her coffee.

"Was he an imposter?" she asked abruptly.

"Annabelle's father?"

"Is that why you're here now? Because he lied?"

"That's what I'd like to figure out."

"He took her away. That should mean something. When his daughter was threatened, he kept her safe. Sounds like more than a mathematician to me."

"Could be."

Bobby didn't fool her for a minute. "If he wasn't actually with the FBI, why come to my hospital room, why ask me so many damn questions?" she exploded. "Why keep showing me the drawing?"

"I don't know."

"You don't know, or you won't tell me?" She sounded bitter, then sighed, and seemed simply depressed.

"You have a beautiful house," he said at last. "Arizona seems to suit you."

"Ah, money."

"I'm happy to hear things are going well with Nathan."

"He is the love of my life," she said fiercely, and Bobby believed her. He knew better than anyone just how far she'd been willing to go to protect her child. It was the reason their relationship would always be only business.

"Thank you for the coffee," he said.

"Leaving so soon?" Her smile was wistful, but he could tell she wasn't surprised.

"Taxi's waiting."

He thought she'd fight him a little, at least protest. Instead, she rose from the table without a murmur, walking with him to the front door. He was tempted to feel insulted, but it wouldn't be fair to either of them.

At the last minute, in the foyer, broad walnut doors looming, she touched his arm, shocking him with the feel of her fingertips grazing his bare skin. "Are you going to help her?"

"Annabelle?" he asked in confusion. "That's my job."

"She's beautiful," Catherine whispered.

He didn't say anything.

"I mean that, Bobby, she's really beautiful. When she smiles, it reaches her eyes. When she talks about fabric, of all things, she gets giddy. I wonder . . ."

Catherine stopped talking. They both knew what she meant. She wondered what her life might have been like if a blue Chevy had not turned down the street, if a young man had not asked her to help find a lost dog, if a twelve-year-old girl had not gotten lost in an endlessly dark pit.

Bobby took her hand, pressed her fingers with his own.

"You're beautiful to me," he told her softly.

He kissed her once, on the cheek. Then he was gone.

23

ANNABELLE WAS AT the airport. She sat four chairs down from D.D., eyes staring out the window at the activity on the tarmac, arms around her knees. She glanced up briefly when Bobby appeared, then returned to her intent study of anyone who wasn't a detective investigating her case. He took that as a hint, and let her be.

D.D. acknowledged him with a wave. Her blonde curls were damp, her clothes fresh. He took that as a good sign while she talked animatedly on her cell phone, unleashing such a long torrent of profanity that a mother traveling with a small child got up and pointedly moved away.

Bobby hit Starbucks. His stomach couldn't stand the thought of more coffee. He purchased three bottles of water, plus yogurt, then returned to the fold. D.D., still on the phone, wrinkled her nose at the yogurt—she'd probably been hoping for a bear claw—but gestured for him to leave the snack on her seat. He then crossed to Annabelle, who, if anything, curled up tighter in her chair.

He held out the treats. She accepted them grudgingly, so he took the seat next to her, digging out two white plastic spoons from the bag.

"How are you feeling?"

She made a face.

"Need more aspirin?"

"Need a new head."

"Yeah, I've been there."

"Oh, shut up," she told him, but she leaned a little closer, going to work on the foil lid of the yogurt. The pendant she always wore dangled down. He eyed the vial until she finally looked up, flushing as she noticed the direction of his gaze. Her fingers folded around the glass self-consciously, tucking it back inside her shirt.

"Whose?" he asked quietly, having finally figured out that the contents resembled ash.

"My mother's and father's," she mumbled, clearly not wanting to talk about it.

So of course he pursued the subject. "What did you do with the rest of their remains?"

"Scattered them. No point in burying them under fake names. Seems too disrespectful to the other dead people."

"What was your mother's name when she died, Annabelle?"

She regarded him uncertainly. "Why?"

"Because I bet of all her names over all those years, there are two you remember. The one from Arlington, and the one from the day she died."

Slowly, Annabelle nodded. "My mother lived as Leslie Ann Granger, but died Stella L. Carter. I remember those names. Always."

"And your father?"

"Lived as Russell Walt Granger. Died Michael W. Nelson."

"I like the pendant," he said quietly.

"It's morbid."

"It's sentimental."

She sighed. "Good cop today, Detective? That must mean D.D.'s really going to work me over on the flight."

He grinned. "You know we're all on the same team here, Annabelle. We're all just trying to find out the truth. I would think you of all people would like to know the truth."

"Don't patronize me, Bobby. For you, this is an analytical exercise. For me, it's my life."

"What are you so afraid of, Annabelle?"

"Everything," she replied flatly. She took her yogurt, twisted away, and resumed her study of the planes.

"Father's last known alias was Michael W. Nelson," Bobby reported three minutes later, upon returning to D.D.'s side.

D.D. peered around him to Annabelle, who was looking away from them both, oblivious to the conversation.

"Excellent work, Detective."

"Got a gift," Bobby said, and pretended he didn't feel like a total heel.

Their flight hit cruising altitude. Across the aisle, Annabelle reclined her seat, fell asleep. While sitting next to Bobby, D.D. turned to him with bright eyes.

"We found Christopher Eola," she said excitedly. "Or rather, we've confirmed that he's lost. Get this, Bridgewater released him in '78."

"Huh?"

"Yeah, some Einstein never actually filed the charges against Eola for leading a patient revolt while in Boston State Mental. So while his patient records contained notes on the alleged 'incidents,' and the local PD listed him as a 'person of interest' in a young woman's murder, technically speaking, he had no criminal record. Bridgewater got overcrowded and guess who they offered the door?"

"Ahhh God."

"According to his patient file, he was a regular choirboy at Bridgewater, so they never thought to follow up with his former institute. In fact, Bridgewater is quite proud of Eola. Considers him to be a real success story."

Bobby laughed, only because it was that or hit something. Misfiled paperwork, incompetent bureaucracies. The public held the police accountable for the rising crime rate. Little did they know, they should go after the pencil pushers in the world. "All right," he said, pulling it together. "So in '78, Eola rejoins the land of the living. Then what?"

"He disappears."

"Seriously?"

"Never checks into the halfway house, never applies for his benefits, never keeps his follow-up appointment. One day he exists, the next he's gone."

"Flew the coop, or disappeared into the black hole of the homeless shelters?"

"Your guess is as good as mine. I'm thinking, given his reported level of intelligence, that he assimilated into society under an assumed identity. Think about it—he came from a life of privilege. What rich kid is going to settle for hanging out on the streets? Plus, even in the homeless circuit, people get known. They attend the same soup kitchens, sleep at the same shelters, hang out at the same street corner day after day. Sooner or later, someone like Charlie Marvin, someone who works with both the mentally ill and the homeless, would be bound to recognize him. No one really disappears anymore, not even in the mean streets of Boston."

"Yes and no. Last I heard, officials listed the city's homeless at six thousand. Given that even a large shelter such as the Pine Street Inn serves only about seven hundred, there's a lot of people whose faces aren't being seen."

"Yeah, but you're talking about someone who's managed to fly under the radar for almost thirty years. That's a long time to be invisible. Which also raises the possibility that Eola's simply dead." D.D. pursed her lips, mulled it over. "We'd never be so lucky. The true sickos always live forever. Have you noticed that, or is it just me?"

"I've noticed that, too." Bobby frowned. "Has Sinkus managed to locate Eola's family?"

"Paid them a visit yesterday afternoon—at their

Back Bay residence," she added meaningfully. "They wouldn't even let him in the door, that's how excited they were to hear about long-lost Christopher."

"Have you ever noticed that the richest families are always the most fucked up, or is that just me?"

"I've noticed that, too. See, there are some advantages of our pitiful wages; we'll never be rich enough for our families to be that fucked up."

"Exactly."

"Wonder of wonders, the Eolas have already lawyered up. They're not answering questions about their son without a subpoena in hand and their lawyer in the room. So Sinkus is pushing the paperwork through now. I'll bet you a buck, he'll have the fine folks, and their overpaid suit, in our offices this afternoon. Couple cups of burnt coffee and they should start talking, if only to preserve their taste buds."

She paused. "I'm guessing they don't know where Eola is. Sinkus said it was clear they had nothing but distaste for their son. I'd like to learn a lot more about the incident that got him sent to Boston State Mental, though. Would be good to develop a more robust profile on Mr. Eola, see how his childhood MO matches up with other things we know."

D.D. nodded to herself, already flipping through her stack of files, cheeks flushed, energy crackling. Nothing like two viable suspects to make the sergeant as giddy as a schoolgirl.

"So," she asked briskly, "how'd it go with Catherine?"

Bobby recapped the highlights: "Catherine claims to have spoken with Russell Granger twice. He introduced himself as Special Agent, FBI—no name—and his questions were consistent with what the other officers were asking her. Most interesting tidbit—he brought a pencil sketch of her alleged attacker."

"Really?" D.D.'s eyes widened.

"According to Catherine, the sketch didn't match Richard Umbrio. Granger's drawing showed a much smaller man. When she tried to tell Granger that, he argued with her. Maybe she didn't get a good enough look at her attacker. Or maybe, if the man in the sketch was wearing a disguise, had gained some weight, he would match her description. That sort of thing."

D.D. remained wide-eyed. "Huh?"

Bobby sighed, tried to fold his arms behind his head, and promptly whacked his elbow on the window well. He remembered why he hated the tiny confines of airplane seating, and he wasn't even that large a man.

"Catherine implied that Granger's main focus was on who attacked her," Bobby thought out loud. "He wanted a physical description, voice intonations, any distinguishing marks. Then he showed her the sketch. Now, this *could've* been a cover. Lull her defenses by pretending to have a suspect, when really he was mining her for all the nitty-gritty details of how she was abducted and what Umbrio had done. If that was his strategy, it worked, because she never caught on to anything."

"He gets her focused on one aspect of the interview," D.D. filled in, "the sketch, when, in fact, ninety percent of his questions have been about her assault. An interview version of sleight of hand."

Bobby smiled. "Gotta give the guy some credit. The strategy sounds like something we would do."

"Great, just what we needed, a smart psychopathic son of a bitch." D.D. rubbed her temples. Sighed. Rubbed her temples again. "Any chance Catherine is making this all up? I mean, she's supplying a great deal of detail for a random FBI agent she only met twice twenty-seven years ago."

"True," Bobby conceded. "I think Mr. Special Agent made a strong impression on her, however. That he brought a sketch of a suspect, then became so adamant that the man in the drawing had to be the person who'd abducted her, even after she told him no. His response was unexpected, thus memorable. Besides, why would she yank our chains?"

"Got you back to her house, didn't it? Plus, it gives her a stake in an ongoing investigation. She has reason to call you, and an excuse to torment me. That sounds like her style."

Bobby shrugged. All good possibilities, except . . . "I think she honestly likes Annabelle."

"Oh please! Catherine doesn't have friends. Lovers, maybe, but not friends."

"I'm a friend," he countered.

D.D.'s raised eyebrow let him know what she thought of that. The disagreement was old and intractable; he returned to matters at hand.

"I think she was telling the truth. The realization that the man she remembered as a pushy FBI agent was actually Annabelle's father seemed to shock and confuse her. Yesterday afternoon, she'd been convinced there wasn't any connection between her case and Annabelle's. This morning, on the other hand . . ."

They both fell silent, considering and reconsidering.

Bobby spoke up at last. "We have two possibilities. One, Granger was playing Catherine. Set her up just so he could learn details about her abduction without anyone being the wiser. Or two, Granger honestly had a suspect in mind. He produced a sketch of the man he had reason to believe was her rapist."

D.D. went along: "Say he had a suspect in mind— why not call the police with the name?"

"Dunno."

"Also, this is 1980, right? Two years *before* Granger's daughter allegedly starts receiving gifts. So why was Granger so obsessed with criminal activity?"

"Concerned citizen?"

"Who thought the best way of serving justice was to masquerade as the FBI? Please. Honest people don't disguise themselves as police officers."

"Honest people generally have records with the DMV, and Social Security numbers," Bobby pointed out.

"Meaning . . ."

"Russell Granger's not very honest."

"And could very well have been researching criminal activity to inspire his own set of crimes. Sinkus is chasing Eola," D.D. declared crisply. "I want you in charge of Granger. Hunt down the neighbors, locate this former head of mathematics at MIT. Let's see what kind of life Annabelle's father led in Arlington. Then get serious about their life on the run. You have cities, you have dates. I want to know—did Annabelle's family run because of something Russell Granger *feared* or because of something Russell Granger *did.* You get me?"

Bobby nodded. "We should follow up with Walpole," he said. "Catherine's convictions aside, we need to check Umbrio's prisoner file for records of previous correspondence, the visitors' log, that sort of thing. Make sure he continued to be the antisocial fuckup she knew so well."

"Agreed."

"I . . . uh, I'm pretty busy covering the Granger angle. . . ."

"Yeah, yeah, yeah, I'll sic someone else on it."

"Okeydokey," Bobby said.

"Okeydokey," D.D. agreed.

Satisfied, she zipped up her files, snuggled deeper into her seat.

"Good night, Bobby," she murmured. Thirty seconds later, she was out cold.

Bobby glanced across the aisle to where Annabelle still slept, seat reclined, long dark hair obscuring her face. Then he glanced back to D.D., whose head was already lolling against his shoulder.

Complicated case, he thought, and tried to get some rest.

24

WE FOUND THE note on D.D.'s car on the third floor of the parking garage at Logan Airport, positioned under the right windshield wiper.

None of us had spoken since we'd disembarked from the plane, trudging through the terminal, the yawning pedestrian skywalk, the labyrinth of walled-off construction sidewalks that tunneled through Central Parking. Outside, it was cold and raining. The weather matched our moods. I was preoccupied with thoughts of my father, questions about my past, and—oh yes—the need to pick up Bella from the vet's, which was always complicated when using public transportation. D.D. and Bobby were no doubt thinking high-level police thoughts, such as who had once kidnapped and murdered six girls, had the subject done such a thing before, and—oh yes—how could they blame my dead father for this entire mess?

Then we saw the note. Plain white paper. Thick black ink. Handwritten scrawl.

D.D. moved immediately to block my view. The first two lines, however, were already seared into my brain.

Return the locket or
Another girl dies.

There was more text. Smaller letters, lots of words

following the opening threat. I couldn't read them, however. Details, would be my guess. How exactly the police should return the locket. Or how exactly another girl would die. Maybe both.

"Shit," D.D. said. "My car. How did he know . . . ?"

She conducted a quick twirl of the vast cement space. Looking for the messenger? I saw her gaze dart to the corners and realized she was checking for security cameras, trying to see how lucky they might get. I glanced around for security cameras myself. They weren't that lucky.

Bobby was already leaning over the front hood of the car, scrutinizing the sheet of paper, careful to touch nothing.

"Gotta treat it as a crime scene," he said in a clipped, tight voice.

"No shit."

"We've been away, what? Thirty, thirty-one hours? Pretty big window for delivery."

"I know," D.D. singsonged, her tone as curt as his.

She shot me a glance over her shoulder, her expression all pissy again.

"Hey, can't blame my father for this one," I said.

She glowered. "Annabelle, now would be a good time to catch a cab."

"Perfect. Wonder how many reporters I can find along the way? I'm sure they'd love to hear about this."

"You wouldn't dare—"

"Gonna return the locket?"

"One, this is police business. Two, this is police business—"

"Who wrote it? Did he sign a name? Mention me? I want to read the note."

"Annabelle, catch a cab!"

"Can't!"

"Why not?"

"Because this is my life!"

D.D. thinned her lips. She pointedly returned to the note, still untouched on the windshield of her car. She wasn't going to let me see it. She wasn't going to share. Law enforcement was a system. One that didn't care about a person like me.

Moment stretched into moment. D.D. read. Bobby studied her face, his own look impenetrable. They were in the zone. I was outside, looking in.

Even I have my limits. I gave up, turned away.

"Wait!" D.D. glanced at Bobby. "Go with her."

"Hey, I don't need a babysitter."

D.D. ignored me, still speaking to Bobby. "I got this covered. You stay with her."

"We need to talk about this—" he stated levelly.

"We will."

"I don't want you doing anything rash."

"Bobby—"

"I mean it, D.D. You may be the sergeant, but I'm the former tac-team guy." He stabbed his finger at the note. "I know about this. This is bullshit. You will not do what this says."

D.D. jerked her head toward me. "Later," she murmured. "Get her settled. I'll assemble the task force. We'll discuss."

He scowled, gaze clearly skeptical. "Later," he grudgingly agreed, peeling away from her unmarked Crown Vic, heading toward me. I used the opportunity to try to catch a glimpse of the rest of the note. I simply saw the same two lines: *Return the locket or . . . Another girl dies.*

Bobby put his hand on my arm, pulling me away. I let him, but only until we were out of earshot of D.D.

"What does it say?" I demanded.

"Nothing. Probably just a publicity stunt."

"The general public doesn't know about the locket. It never made the news."

Apparently not even the fine detective had connected that dot yet. His footsteps faltered. He caught himself. Soldiered on. We had reached the elevator. He punched the down button with more force than necessary.

"Bobby . . ."

"Get into the elevator, Annabelle."

"I deserve to know. This involves me."

"No, Annabelle, it doesn't."

"Bullshit—"

"Annabelle." The elevator doors were closing behind us. "The note doesn't even mention you. The author wants D.D."

He drove me in silence to the vet's. There, Bella greeted me with ecstatic frenzy. She twirled, she jumped, she smothered my face in kisses. I held her longer than I intended, burying my face in the thick mane at her neck, grateful for her warmth, her squirming body, her madcap joy.

Then the traitor turned around and jumped on Bobby with equal enthusiasm. There's no loyalty in the world.

Bella settled down once I got her to Bobby's car. She enjoyed a good car ride as well as the next dog, scooting close to the passenger's door so she could decorate the window with nose prints. She'd already left a trail of fine white hair all over the recently cleaned seat. It made me feel better.

Arriving at my apartment building, Bobby parked illegally and came around to the passenger side. I opened my door on my own, a rather pointed statement. He simply diverted his attention to Bella, who of course bounded out of the car and pranced around his legs, oblivious to the rain.

"Always a pleasure to help a lady," he said, patting the top of her head.

I wanted to hit him. Pummel him. Kick and scream at him as if everything were his fault. The violence of my own thoughts startled me. I walked with shaky footsteps to the building, working my keys with fingers that trembled.

Bella dashed up the stairs to the apartment building. I followed at a slower clip, trying to pull myself together as I went through the motions of unlocking doors, checking mail, securing all portals behind me.

I had a rolling feeling in my stomach. A childish urge to stop and cry. Or better yet, pack five suitcases.

My father had masqueraded as an FBI agent, interviewing a young abduction victim two years before I'd ever been stalked. My best friend had been killed in my place. Someone, twenty-five years later, was now demanding the return of my locket.

My head hurt. Or maybe it was my heart.

Once in my apartment, Bobby made the rounds. His fluid movements should have made me feel better. Instead, his need to secure my apartment only upped my anxiety as I realized that, once upon a time, this was exactly what my father would've done.

When Bobby finished, he gave me a curt nod, permission to enter my own home, then took up position against the kitchen counter. He watched as I went through my own homecoming routine, setting down the mail, depositing my suitcase in my room, filling a water bowl for Bella. The digital display on my answering machine read six messages, unusual volume for my quiet little world. Instinctively, I moved away; I would check the messages later, when Bobby was no longer around.

"So," he said.

"So," I countered.

"Plans for the evening?"

"Work."

"Sewing?"

"Starbucks."

He frowned. "Tonight?"

"People like their java twenty-four/seven. Why? Am I under house arrest?"

"Given recent events, a reasonable level of caution is not a bad idea," he replied levelly.

I couldn't take it. I jutted my chin up and cut to the heart of the matter. "My father didn't do it. Whatever you're thinking, my father wasn't like that. And the note proves it. Dead men aren't known for their personal correspondence."

"Note's not your concern, Annabelle. Note is official police business, which may or may not have anything to do with this case."

"So my father posed as an FBI agent and he visited Catherine after her attack. Maybe as a father he wanted to understand firsthand what kind of monster preyed on little girls. Maybe as an academic, he felt it was the best way to do research. I know there's an explanation!" The words sounded defensive, the theories preposterous even as I laid them out. But I couldn't help myself. After a lifetime of warring with my father, of accusing him of being controlling and manipulative, suddenly I was his biggest defender. It was one thing for me to distrust my father. But I would be damned before I'd let anyone else beat him up.

Bobby seemed to be genuinely considering my words. "All right, Annabelle. Give me a reason. Try something on for size. I'm willing to be open-minded. The pitchforks and torches can come out later."

"He wasn't even around when Dori disappeared," I said sharply. "We were already in Florida."

262

"So you believe," he said.

"So I know! My father never left us once we got settled in Florida!" I told the lie effortlessly. I thought, bitterly, that my father would be proud.

Two weeks after we'd been in Florida, me, waking up in the middle of the night. Screaming. Wanting my father, begging for my father. My mother coming to my side instead. *"Shhh, sweetheart. Shhhh. Your father will be home soon. He just had to go tidy up some loose ends. Shhh, sweetheart, everything is all right."*

Liar, liar, pants on fire.

Bobby's even-toned voice returned me relentlessly to the present: "Annabelle, where is your family's furniture? Your whole family disappeared in the middle of the afternoon. What happened to your stuff?"

"A moving van came and got it."

"Pardon?"

"I talked to Mrs. Petracelli—"

"You *what?*"

"I hid in a corner and shut my eyes," I said sharply, anger returning to full boil. "What did you think I was going to do? Wait for you and D.D. to serve up my life on a silver platter? Please. You're the cops. You don't care about me."

He took a step forward. The look on his face was no longer impassive. His eyes had turned a deep, stormy gray. I thought I should be scared. Instead, I felt excited. I wanted to fight, to war, to rage. I wanted to do anything other than continue to feel helpless.

"What did you tell Mrs. Petracelli?" he demanded.

"What, Bobby," I parodied in falsetto, "don't you trust me? Aren't we all on the same *team?*"

"What the hell did you tell Mrs. Petracelli!"

"I told her nothing, you ass! What did you think I'd do? March into the home of a woman I haven't seen in twenty-five years and announce the police had found the body of her long-lost daughter? Please, I'm not that cruel." I took a step forward myself, stabbed his chest with my finger. It made me feel tough, even as his eyes went a darker shade of granite.

"She told me movers came and packed up our house. No doubt my father arranged it by phone, had everything placed in storage. Maybe he imagined the police would figure things out one day. Then we could return home, pick up where we left off. My father was a big believer in planning ahead."

"Annabelle, there are no real estate transactions, no storage bins, no records for a man named Russell Granger."

My turn to be blindsided. "But . . . but . . ."

"But what, Annabelle? Tell me what was going on in the fall of '82. Give me something to believe."

I couldn't do it. I didn't know . . . I didn't understand. . . .

How could there be no record of Russell Granger? Arlington was supposed to be my real life. In Arlington in '82, at least, I had lived.

Bobby wrapped my hands with his own. That's how I realized I had started trembling, swaying on my feet.

From the doggy bed, Bella issued a nervous whine. I couldn't reach out to her, couldn't speak. I was thinking of my father again, of whispers in the middle of the night. Of things I didn't want to know. Of truths that would be too much to bear.

Oh God, what had happened in the fall of '82? Oh Dori, what did we do?

"Annabelle," Bobby ordered gently. "Put your head between your knees. Draw a breath. You're hyperventilating."

I did as he told me, bending at the waist, staring at my scarred wooden floor as I struggled for air. When I stood up, Bobby's arms went around me and I fell into his embrace quite naturally. I smelled his aftershave, verbena and spice tickling my nose. I felt his arms, warm and hard around my shoulders. I heard his heartbeat, steady and rhythmic in my ear. And I clung to him like a child, embarrassed and overwhelmed and knowing I needed to pull myself together, but desperate for the sanctuary of his arms instead.

If Russell Granger never existed, what about Annabelle? And why, oh why had I believed that moving to Florida was the first time my father had ever told a lie?

"Shhhh," Bobby was whispering in my ear. "Shhh . . ." His lips touched the top of my hair—a small, thoughtless kiss. It wasn't enough for me. I tilted up my head and found him.

The first contact was electric. Soft lips, raspy whiskers. The smell of a man, the feel of his lips pressing against mine. Sensations I rarely allowed myself to experience. Needs I rarely allowed myself to feel. Now I opened my mouth, drawing in his tongue, wanting to feel him, touch him, taste him. I needed this. I wanted to believe in this. I wanted to feel anything but the fear that loomed in the back of my mind.

If he could just hold me, then maybe this moment would last, and the rest would fall away and I wouldn't have to be scared and I wouldn't have to feel alone and I wouldn't have to hear the voices now growing in the back of my mind. . . .

"Roger, please don't go. Roger, I'm begging you, please don't do this. . . ."

In the next instant, Bobby was setting me back and I was reeling away. We retreated to separate corners of the tiny kitchenette, both breathing hard and refusing to meet each other's gaze. Bella scrambled up from her dog bed. Now she pressed against me anxiously. I reached down and focused on smoothing the fur around her face.

Minute turned into minute. I used the time to school my features, to find my composure. If Bobby had taken even one step forward, I would've gone to him. Yet, the moment we were done, I would've pulled away. Hid behind the smooth composure I had perfected over the years.

And I realized again that my mother had not been the only casualty of my father's war. He had taken something from me, too, and I didn't know how to get it back.

"What about my mother?" I asked abruptly. "Leslie Ann Granger. Maybe, for some reason, my parents had everything in her name."

"Annabelle, I've searched for both of your parents' names. Nothing."

"We existed," I insisted weakly, stroking Bella's fur, feeling the reassuring weight of her head pressing against my hands. "We played with the neighbors, had a social life, a role in the community. I went to school, my father had a job, my mother was in the PTA. That's all real. I remember it. Arlington was not a figment of my imagination."

"What about before Arlington?"

"I . . . I don't know. I don't remember a before."

"It's something to ask the neighbors," he said.

"Yes, I suppose."

He had straightened again, seemed to be pulling himself together. "I can't promise you where this will go," he said abruptly. "Six bodies are six bodies. We have an obligation to ask every question, to pursue every lead. Already this case has a life of its own."

"I know."

"Maybe, for the near term, you should keep a low profile."

I had to smile, but it came out lopsided. "Bobby, I live under an assumed name. I have no friends, never speak to my neighbors, and belong to no social organizations. The closest thing I've got to a long-term relationship is the UPS man. Frankly, if I fall much lower on the social ladder, I'll be an amoeba."

"I don't like you working at night," Bobby continued as if I hadn't spoken. His eyes narrowed, he looked from me to Bella then back to me. "Or running after dark."

I shook my head. The worst of the shock was wearing off, my defenses shoring up. "I'm a grown woman, Bobby. I'm not hiding anymore."

"Annabelle—"

"I understand you gotta do your job, Bobby. You might as well understand that I'm going to do mine."

Clearly, he was not happy. But to give him credit, he stopped arguing. Bella seemed to sense the lowering tension. She wandered over to Bobby and shamelessly pressed her nose into the palm of his hand.

"I gotta go," Bobby said, but he still wasn't moving. "Task-force meeting about the note."

He refused to take the bait, so finally I followed his lead and let it go. "I need to get ready for work as well," I said, hoping my voice didn't sound as tired as I felt.

"Annabelle . . ."

"Bobby."

"I can't. You and me. There are ethics involved. I can't."

"I'm not asking you to."

He suddenly scowled. "I know, and it's pissing me off."

I smiled, and this time it was softer, honest, a genuine step forward for me. I crossed to him. Placed my hand on his cheek. Felt the rasp of his five o'clock shadow, the strong line of his jaw. We stood just inches apart, so that I could sense the heat of his body, but nothing more.

He felt like promise, and for one moment, I let myself believe that such things were possible. That I did have a future. That the woman Annabelle Granger had grown up to be had a chance at happiness in her life.

"Do you like barbecues?" I whispered.

I could feel his lips curve against the palm of my hand. "Been known to flip a few burgers in my day."

"Ever dream of white picket fences, two-point-two kids, perhaps an incredibly hyper white dog?"

"My dreams generally include a finished basement, pool table, and plasma-screen TV."

"Fair enough." I pulled my hand away, sighing over the loss of contact, the cool reality that settled in the space between us. "You never know," I said lightly.

"You never know," he acknowledged.

He exited down the stairs. Bella took it the hardest, whimpering pathetically as I locked the door behind him.

My phone rang. I picked it up.

And a male voice whispered, "Annabelle."

25

BOBBY WOVE HIS way through Boston traffic, grill lights flashing as he worked his way south to Roxbury. He had spent longer than he'd intended in Annabelle's apartment. Done more than he'd intended in Annabelle's apartment. Hell, came damn close to behaving like a total ass in Annabelle's apartment.

But he was back in his car, in control, and reacquainting himself with cold, hard reality. He was a detective. He was working a major case. And things were sliding from bad to worse.

Someone knew about the locket. According to the note, that person would meet only with Sergeant D.D. Warren, who was supposed to bring the necklace to the deserted grounds of Boston State Mental at 3:33 a.m. tonight.

Failure to comply would result in immediate repercussions. Another young girl would die.

Bobby's reaction to the note had been instinctive and informed by nearly a decade of tactical team training: clusterfuck.

Someone was playing with them. But that did not mean the consequences of disobeying wouldn't be real.

He hit Ruggles Street driving with one hand, working his cell phone with the other. He had a call back from MIT with the contact info for one Paul Schuepp, former head of mathematics. Another call from a rental agency that had handled Annabelle's former home on Oak Street. More people to call here, more leads to chase there. He did the best he could in the ten minutes he had before reaching HQ.

Dusk had descended, the low ceiling of gray clouds making the hour seem later than it was. Commuters trudged along either side of the street, hidden beneath umbrellas or shrouded in dark raincoats. Living so close to police headquarters had made them oblivious to sirens, and not a single person bothered to look up as he passed.

Finally, up ahead, lights blazing; the glass-and-steel monstrosity of police headquarters firing to life for another long night. Bobby punched End on his cell phone and prepared to get serious: Parking in Roxbury was no laughing matter. At first pass, the street-side spaces were filled. Bobby still didn't turn into Central Parking—and not just because the police parking lot was a notorious spot for getting mugged. Like most of the detectives, he wanted to be properly positioned for a quick getaway should something unexpected occur. That meant parking as close to the building as possible.

Third time was the charm. A fellow officer pulled out, and Bobby ducked into the vacated space.

He already had his ID in hand as he trotted for the building. Six-oh-seven p.m. D.D. probably had the rest of the team in place by now, discussing strategy for the 3:33 a.m. rendezvous. Should they bring the original locket? Risk reprisals by producing a substitute?

They would attempt the handoff. Bobby had no doubt about that. It was too good an opportunity to flush their quarry into the open. Plus, D.D. didn't have enough sense to be afraid.

Bobby cruised through security, swiped his ID

through the reader, and hit the stairwell, taking the steps two at a time. He needed the exercise. It allowed him to work off the worst of his adrenaline and the buzz he was still feeling from kissing a woman he never should've kissed.

Don't go there. Have a mission. Stay on task.

He'd just cleared the stairwell door, was debating sprinting down the long corridor toward the Homicide unit in a mad dash against himself, when the door directly across from him opened up and D.D. stuck her head out.

He jumped self-consciously. "The task-force meeting's in there?" he asked in confusion, trying to figure out why they had moved.

D.D., however, was shaking her head. "Team's meeting in thirty minutes. Eola's parents just arrived. Join the party. Don't say a word."

Bobby's brows shot up. He joined the party. He didn't say a word.

Bobby had never been in this central conference room before. Much nicer digs than the glorified walk-in closets the Homicide suite had to offer. One glance, and Bobby understood the upscale room choice. The Eolas hadn't just brought themselves, but their people, and their people's people, to judge from the crowd.

It took him five minutes to sort it out. Across from him to his left sat a gentleman, age anywhere between eighty and a hundred, in a dark gray suit, with a sparse, horseshoe head of hair, parchment-thin skin, and a hooked patrician's nose—Christopher Eola's father, Christopher Senior. To his right sat a frail, liver-spotted female in navy-blue Chanel and golf-ball-size pearls. Christopher Eola's mother, Pauline.

Next to her, another older gentleman in an expensive double-breasted suit, this time with thicker hair and a softer middle, the proverbial fat cat, otherwise known as the Eolas' lawyer, John J. Barron. To his left, a younger, thinner copycat, the up-and-coming partner, Robert Anderson. Then the token female attorney, complete with her no-nonsense Brooks Brothers suit, sharply pulled-back hair, and angular wire-rim glasses, going by the name Helene Niaru. She sat next to the last female in the row, a young, strikingly beautiful woman who took copious notes and was never referred to by any name at all, the secretary.

Lot of billable hours, Bobby thought, for a son the Eolas supposedly hadn't heard from in decades.

"I want the record to show how much I resent this meeting," Eola Sr. was stating now, his voice shaky with age, but still containing the uncompromising note of someone accustomed to having his orders obeyed instantly. "I find it premature, not to mention highly irresponsible, to be pointing fingers at my son."

"No one is pointing anything at anyone," Detective Sinkus soothed. The Eolas had been his assignment, so he was running the show. "I assure you, this is a routine inquiry. Given the discovery in Mattapan, we're naturally trying to learn as much as we can about all of the patients who resided at the Boston

State Mental Hospital, including, but not limited to," he added dryly, "your son."

Eola Sr. quirked a thin gray eyebrow, still suspicious. His hunch-shouldered wife sniffed and dabbed at her eyes. Apparently, just thinking about her son had brought her to tears.

Bobby wondered where their daughter was, the one with whom Christopher had allegedly had an "inappropriate" relationship. Thirty years later, she was a middle-aged adult. Didn't she have an opinion in all this?

The lawyer cleared his throat. "Naturally, my clients intend to cooperate. We're here after all. Of course, the events of thirty years ago remain highly sensitive for everyone involved. I trust you will take that into consideration."

"I will use only my nice voice," Sinkus assured him. "Shall we?"

Grudging nods from the assembled suits. Sinkus started the recorder. They got to it.

"For the record, sir, can you please verify that Christopher Walker Eola is your son, born April sixteen, 1954, with the following Social Security number." Sinkus rattled off the number. Eola Sr. grunted his grudging consent.

"And Christopher Walker Eola resided with you and your wife in your residence on Tremont Street during April of '74?"

Another grumbled yes.

"Also in residence was your daughter, Natalie Jane Eola?"

At the mention of the daughter, hackles rose, nervous glances were exchanged.

"Yes," said Eola Sr. finally, biting off the word and spitting it out.

Sinkus made a note. "Other people in the residence? Relatives, housekeepers, guests?"

Eola Sr. turned to his wife, who was apparently in charge of staff. Pauline stopped dabbing at her eyes long enough to dredge up four names—the cook, the housekeeper, Pauline's personal secretary, and a full-time driver. Her words were whispery and hard to catch. Her chin rested close to her chest, as if her body had caved in on itself. Advanced osteoporosis, Bobby guessed. Not even big money could stave off age.

Sinkus moved the tape recorder closer to Mrs. Eola. Preliminaries established, he got down to business.

"It is our understanding that in 1974, you, Mr. Christopher Eola, and your wife, Mrs. Pauline Eola, admitted your son, Christopher Junior, to the Boston State Mental Hospital."

"Correct," Eola Sr. granted.

"Exact date, please?"

"April nineteen, 1974."

Sinkus looked up. "Three days after Christopher's twentieth birthday?"

"We had had a small party," Mrs. Eola spoke up suddenly. "Nothing fancy. A few close friends. The cook made duck à l'orange, Christopher's favorite. Afterwards, we had trifle. Christopher loved trifle." Her voice sounded wistful and Bobby pegged her as the weak link.

Mr. Eola was resentful—of the police, the interview, the unwanted memory of his son. But Mrs. Eola was mournful. If the stories were true, had she been forced to incarcerate one child to protect another? And even if you thought your child was a monster, did you still miss him, or at least the idea of who he could've been?

Sinkus turned ever so slightly in Mrs. Eola's direction, bringing her more fully into the open line of his body, the encouraging contact of his gaze. "It sounds like a very nice party, Mrs. Eola."

"Oh yes. Christopher had only been back home a few months from his travels. We wanted to do something special, both to mark his birthday and his homecoming. I invited his friends from school, many of our associates. It was a lovely evening."

"His travels, Mrs. Eola?"

"Oh well, he went abroad, of course. He'd taken time off after high school to see the world, sow a few wild oats. Boys. You can't expect them to settle down too quickly. They need to experience a few things first." She smiled weakly, as if she realized how frivolous it sounded now. She picked up more briskly. "But he had returned around Christmas to start working on his college applications. Christopher had an interest in theater. But he didn't think he was quite that talented. He thought maybe he'd pursue a degree in psychology instead."

"After spending over a year on the road? Can you be more precise, Mrs. Eola? What countries did he visit, for how long?"

Mrs. Eola waved her hand in a fluttery, birdlike motion. "Oh, Europe. The usual sort of places. France, London, Vienna, Italy. He had an interest in Asia, but we didn't feel it was safe back then. You know"—she leaned forward to confide—"given the war and all."

Ah yes, the Vietnam conflict, which Christopher had conveniently managed to dodge. Conscientious objector, Daddy's money, his college aspirations? The possibilities were endless.

"Did he travel alone? Or with friends?" Sinkus asked now.

"Oh, a little of both." Another vague flutter of the hand.

Sinkus changed strategy. "Do you have any notes from that time? Maybe postcards Christopher sent you, even a line or two you might have entered in your diary—"

"Objection—" Barron started.

"Not asking for the diary," Sinkus clarified hurriedly. "Just want to get a more detailed picture of Christopher's global adventures. Dates, locations, people. When you get a chance."

Meaning it could provide a list of places where Christopher might have gone to hide after leaving Bridgewater in '78. Why hide out in a seedy hotel in the U.S. if you could run to Paris instead?

Mr. Eola grunted his consent. Sinkus moved on.

"So Christopher finished high school, did some traveling, then returned home to work on his college applications—"

"Target universities?" Bobby spoke up. He got a warning glance from Sinkus, but ignored the look. He had his reasons.

"Oh, the usual." Once again, Mrs. Eola was vague. "Harvard, Yale, Princeton. He wanted to stay on the East Coast, not go too far from home. Though, come to think of it, he also applied at MIT. Funny choice, that one. MIT for fine arts? Well, one never knew with Christopher."

Sinkus resumed the reins of the interview: "Was it nice to have him back?"

"Oh yes," Mrs. Eola gushed. Eola Sr. shot her a look. She clammed up.

"Look," Eola Sr. said impatiently. "I know what you're trying to ask. Why don't we just cut to the chase? We committed our son. We personally drove our only boy to a mental hospital. What kind of parents do such a thing?"

"All right, Mr. Eola. What kind of parents do such a thing?"

Eola Sr. had his chin up, his skin looking as if it had been stretched too thin over his skeletal face. "This account cannot leave this room."

For the first time, Sinkus faltered. "Now, Mr. Eola—"

"I mean it. Turn the recorder off right now, young man, or I won't say another word."

Sinkus darted a look at D.D. Slowly, she nodded. "Turn it off. Let's hear what Mr. Eola has to say."

Sinkus reached forward, snapped off the recorder. As if on cue, the legal secretary set down her pen and folded her hands in her lap.

"You have to understand," Mr. Eola started. "It wasn't entirely his fault. That girl, the Belgian. She ruined him. If we had understood the situation sooner, been quicker to act . . ."

"What situation, sir? How did you fail to act?" Sinkus's voice stayed patient, respectful. Eola was going to give them what they wanted. All in due time.

"An au pair. We hired her when Christopher was nine and Natalie three. We'd had a wonderful woman up until that point, but she left to start a family of her own. We returned to the same agency, and they recommended Gabrielle to us. Given our previous experience, we didn't think twice. Surely one well-trained au pair was as good as another.

"Gabrielle was younger than we had expected. Twenty-one, fresh out of school. She was a different personality—more festive, more . . . giggly." He made a face. Clearly, giggly was not a compliment. "Sometimes, I thought she was too informal with the children. But she was energetic, had a sense of adventure the children seemed to appreciate. Christopher, in particular, was smitten with her.

"When Christopher turned twelve, there was an incident at his school. He was slightly built for his age, more sensitively inclined. Some of the boys started to . . . take exception. They singled Christopher out. Started picking on him. One day, things went a little too far. Blows were exchanged. Christopher didn't come out on the winning side."

Eola Sr.'s lips twisted in distaste. Bobby couldn't decide if the man was appalled by the thought of violence or that his son had been incapable of dealing with it.

Mrs. Eola was back to dabbing her eyes.

"Naturally," Eola Sr. picked up briskly, "the appropriate actions were taken and the offending parties punished. But Christopher . . . He grew withdrawn. Had problems sleeping. Became . . . secretive. Around this time, I happened to catch Gabrielle leaving Christopher's room in the early morning hours. When I asked, she said she heard him crying and had gone to check on him. I confess, I didn't pursue the matter.

"It was the housekeeper who finally spoke to my wife. According to the housekeeper, the bedding in Gabrielle's room went undisturbed for long periods of time. Whereas the sheets in Christopher's room now required frequent changing. The linens were often stained. You can fill in the rest."

Sinkus's eyes had grown a little wide, but he caught himself. "Actually, sir, I'm going to need you to fill in the rest."

Eola Sr. sighed heavily. "Fine. Our au pair was engaged in sexual relations with our twelve-year-old son. Are you happy? Is that clear enough now?"

Sinkus let the remark past. "Once you made the discovery, Mr. Eola . . ."

"Oh, we fired her. Then took out a restraining order against her and had her deported. All under advice of legal counsel, of course."

"And Christopher?"

"He was a child," Eola Sr. said impatiently. "He'd been seduced and poorly used by some Belgian twit. Naturally, he was devastated. He yelled at me, raged at his mother, locked himself in his room for days on end. He thought he was Romeo and we had banished his Juliet. He was twelve, for Christ's sake. What did he know?"

"I called a doctor," Mrs. Eola volunteered in her whispery voice. "Our pediatrician. He had me bring Christopher in for an exam. But there was nothing physically wrong with Christopher. Gabrielle hadn't hurt him, she'd just . . ." Mrs. Eola made a helpless little shrug. "Our doctor said time was the best cure. So we took Christopher home and waited."

"And what did Christopher do?"

"He sulked," Eola Sr. said dismissively. "He isolated himself in his room, refused to speak with us, dine with us. It went on for weeks. But then he seemed to come around."

"He resumed going to school," Mrs. Eola said. "He joined us for meals, did his homework. If anything, he seemed to have matured from the experience. He started wearing suits, was unfailingly polite. Our friends said he seemed to have turned into a little man overnight. He was charming really. He brought me flowers, spent endless time with his little sister. Natalie idolized him, you know. When he retreated into his room, I think it hurt her most of all. For a while, the household seemed very . . . smooth."

"For a while," Sinkus repeated.

Mrs. Eola sighed and fell silent again, the mournful expression back on her face. Eola Sr. took up the narrative, his voice brisk, unemotional.

"Our housekeeper started complaining about the condition of Christopher's room. No matter what she did, his bed seemed to stink. Something was wrong in there, she said. Something was wrong with him. She wanted permission to not clean his room.

"Naturally, I denied her. I told her she was being foolish. Three days later, I happened to be home when I heard her scream. I ran into Christopher's room to find her standing next to the upended mattress. She had finally identified the source of the odor—there, between the box spring and the top mattress, were half a dozen dead squirrels. Christopher had . . . skinned them. Disemboweled them. Cut off their heads.

"I confronted him the moment he got home from school. He apologized immediately. He had only been 'practicing,' he told me. His science class was due to dissect a frog at the end of the semester. He was worried he'd be too squeamish, maybe faint at the sight of blood. And he was concerned that if he betrayed weakness in front of his classmates, he might once again become a target for bullies."

Eola Sr. shrugged. "I believed him. His logic, his fears, made sense. My son could be quite convincing. On his own, he retrieved the carcasses from his room and buried them in the garden. I considered the matter closed. Except . . ."

"Except . . . ?"

"Except the household was never quite right again. Maria, our housekeeper, started having little accidents. She'd turn and suddenly there would be a broom across her path, tripping her. Once, after finishing off the last of the bleach, she opened a second bottle, dumped it in, and immediately became overwhelmed by the fumes. She made it out just in time. It turned out someone had dumped out the bleach in the new bottle and replaced it with ammonia. Maria quit shortly thereafter. She insisted our house was haunted. But I heard her mutter under her breath that the ghost was named Christopher."

"She thought he was trying to harm her?"

"She believed he was trying to kill her," Eola Sr. corrected bluntly. "Perhaps he'd learned she was the one who'd betrayed his relationship with Gabrielle. Perhaps he wanted revenge. I don't really know. Christopher was polite. Christopher was cooperative. He went to school. He got good grades. He did everything we asked of him. But even . . ." Eola Sr. took a deep breath. "Not even I liked being around my own son anymore."

"What happened in April of '74?" Sinkus asked gently.

"Christopher went away," Eola Sr. answered softly. "And for almost two years, it was as if a dark cloud had lifted from our home. Our daughter seemed less anxious. The cook whistled in the kitchen. We all walked with a lighter step. And no one said anything, because what could you say? We never saw Christopher doing anything wrong. After the squirrel incident and Maria's departure, there were no more little accidents, or strange smells, or anything the least bit suspicious. But the house was better with Christopher gone. Happier.

"Then he came back."

Eola Sr. paused, his voice drifting off. He had lost his clipped, emotionless tone. A mood had settled over his face. Dark, angry, depressed. Bobby leaned forward. He could feel his stomach muscles tightening, steeling him for what was coming next.

"Natalie changed first," Eola Sr. said, his voice far away. "Became moody, withdrawn. She would sit in silence for long periods of time, then suddenly lash out over the tiniest thing. We thought it was adjustment issues. She was fourteen, a difficult age. Plus, for over a year she'd had the house to herself, been like an only child. Maybe she resented Christopher's return.

"He, if anything, seemed to indulge her tantrums. He brought her flowers, her favorite sweets. He called her silly nicknames, invented outrageous little songs. The more she pushed him away, the more he lavished attention on her, taking her to the movies, showing her off to his friends, volunteering to walk her to school. Christopher had grown into a fine young man while he was away. He'd filled out, settled into himself. I think more than a few of Natalie's friends had a crush on him, which of course he used to his advantage.

Pauline and I, we thought perhaps his travels had done him good. He was finally coming around.

"The day after Christopher's birthday dinner, I received a call from a client in New York. Something had come up, I needed to meet with him. Pauline decided to join me, perhaps we could catch a show. We didn't want to pull Natalie away from school, but that wasn't a problem, Christopher was home. So we left him in charge and went away."

That pause again. A heartbeat's hesitation while Mr. Eola fought with his memories, struggled to find words. When he spoke again, his voice was hoarse and low, hard to hear.

"My emergency meeting turned out to not be such an emergency after all. And Pauline could not get tickets for the show she wanted to see. So we returned. A day early. We didn't think to call.

"It was after eight o'clock at night. Our residence was dark, the help gone for the night. We found them right in the living room. Christopher was sitting in my favorite leather chair. He was buck naked. My daughter . . . Natalie . . . He was forcing her to perform . . . a sex act. She was sobbing. And I heard my son say, in a voice I'd never heard before, 'You stupid fucking cunt, you had better swallow, or next time I'll ram it up your ass.'

"Then he looked up. He saw us standing there. And he just smiled. This cold, cold smile. 'Hey Dad,' he said. 'I owe you my thanks. She's much better than Gabrielle.' "

Eola Sr. broke off again. His eyes found some spot on the burnished wood table, locking in. Beside him his wife had collapsed, her shoulders shaking spasmodically as she rocked back and forth.

D.D. moved first. She retrieved a box of tissues, handing one silently to Mrs. Eola. The older woman took it, tucked it into her folded hands, and resumed her rocking.

"Thank you for talking to us," D.D. said softly. "I know this is terrible for your family. Last few questions, then I think we can wrap things up for the day."

"What?" Eola Sr. asked tiredly.

"Can you give us a description of Gabrielle?"

Whatever he'd been expecting, this wasn't it. Eola Sr. blinked. "I don't . . . I hadn't really thought about her. . . . What do you want?"

"The basics would be fine. Height, weight, eye color. Overall appearance."

"Well . . . she was about five foot six. Dark hair. Dark eyes. Slender, but not that rail-thin you see so much these days. She was . . . robust, vivacious. Like a Catherine Zeta-Jones."

D.D. nodded, while Bobby made the same mental connection she probably had. In other words, Gabrielle's general description could also be applied to Annabelle.

Sinkus cleared his throat, drawing everyone's attention back to him. It was time to wrap things up, but the detective appeared troubled.

"Mr. Eola, Mrs. Eola, if you don't mind . . . after you

caught Christopher, he went with you willingly to Boston State Mental?"

"He didn't have a choice."

"How so?"

"My money is my money, Detective Sinkus. And you can be quite sure after that . . . incident, I wasn't giving Christopher one red cent. Christopher, however, did have his own resources. A trust left to him by his grandparents. By the terms of that trust, he was not eligible to collect until he turned twenty-eight. And even then he would need the cooperation of the trustee. Which would be me."

Bobby got it the same minute D.D. did.

"You threatened to cut him off. Deny him his inheritance."

"Goddamn right," Eola Sr. spat. "I let him live that night, that was generosity enough."

"You hit him," Mrs. Eola whispered. "You ran at him. You leapt on him. You kept hitting and hitting. And Natalie was screaming and you were screaming and it went on and on and on. Christopher just sat there. Wearing that terrible smile, his mouth filling with blood."

Eola Sr. didn't bother with an apology. "I chased his scrawny ass up to his bedroom, where he locked himself inside. And I . . . I tried to think of what to do next. I honestly couldn't bring myself to kill my only son. But at the same time, I could not subject my daughter to the scrutiny of the police. I consulted my attorney"—his gaze flickered to Barron—"who sug-

287

gested a third alternative. He warned me, however, that given Christopher's age, committing him to a mental institute would be difficult. I would need him to stay voluntarily, or I would have to get a court order, meaning that we'd have to go to the police.

"My son is smart. I'll grant him that. And as I said, he has an appreciation for the finer things in life. I can't imagine him living on the streets any more than he could. So in the morning, we made a deal. He would stay at Boston State Mental until his twenty-eighth birthday. At which point, assuming he fulfilled the terms of our deal, I would release his inheritance. Three million dollars is nothing to sneeze at, and Christopher knew it. He went, and we never saw him again."

"You never visited?" Sinkus clarified.

"My son is dead to us."

"Never checked on his progress, not even by phone?"

"My son is dead to us, Detective."

"So, you didn't know your son got himself in a bit of trouble at Boston State Mental. Ended up in Bridge-water."

"When Boston Mental announced it would be closing, I called over. The doctor informed me that Christopher had already been sent to Bridgewater. I found it convenient."

Sinkus frowned. "And on Christopher's twenty-eighth birthday?"

"A note arrived at my attorney's office. 'A deal is

a deal,' it read. I signed off on the funds."

"Wait a minute," D.D. spoke up sharply. "Christopher turned twenty-eight in April of 1982. You're telling me that he came into three million dollars on that day?"

"Actually, he inherited three point five. The funds were well managed."

"And he accessed these funds?"

"He has made periodic withdrawals over the years."

"What?"

Eola Sr. turned to his lawyer. "John, if you would, please."

Barron lifted up a leather briefcase, briskly snapped it open. "This is confidential information, Detectives. We trust you will treat it accordingly."

He passed around copies of a stapled sheaf of papers. Financial records, Bobby realized, quickly skimming the sheets. Detailed financial records of Christopher's trust fund, and the date each time he made a withdrawal.

Bobby's gaze went straight to Barron. "How did he make contact? When Christopher wanted money, what did he do, pick up the phone?"

"Ridiculous," Barron snapped. "It's a trust fund, not an ATM. We required a written request, properly signed and notarized, which we kept as part of the official records. Keep flipping, you'll find a copy of each sheet. You'll see that Christopher was partial to increments of one hundred thousand, roughly two to three times a year."

"He wrote, you cut him a check?" Bobby was still quizzing, rapidly flipping sheets.

"He wrote, we liquidated funds, rebalanced the portfolio, and then cut him a check, yes."

"So these checks were never collected in person? You have a mailing address?" This was too good to be true. Which it was, as he spotted on the last page. "Wait a minute, you wrote the check to a bank in *Switzerland?*"

Barron shrugged one shoulder. "As Mrs. Eola mentioned, Christopher spent some time overseas. Obviously, he set up a bank account while he was there."

Bobby arched a brow. Normal nineteen-year-olds did not open Swiss bank accounts. Not even the spoiled sons of Boston's upper class. It felt like a preemptive strike to him. The act of a man who was already assuming he might need to hide assets sometime soon, perhaps for a life on the run. Made Bobby wonder what all Christopher had been doing during his "grand tour" of Europe.

Things were wrapping up now. Eola Sr. had his arm belatedly around his wife as she blotted at her smeared mascara. He whispered something in her ear. She gave him a tremulous smile.

"How is your daughter, Mrs. Eola?" Bobby asked softly.

The woman surprised him with her flinty answer: "She's a lesbian, Detective. What else would you expect?"

Mrs. Eola rose. Her anger had invigorated her. Eola

Sr. capitalized on the moment, ushering her out the door. The lawyers and secretary filed out behind them, one massively overpriced brigade, heading for the elevators.

In the lull that followed, Sinkus spoke first.

"So," he asked D.D., "does this mean I can go to Switzerland?"

26

THE EMERGENCY TASK-force meeting started late, given the overrun of the Eola interview. The majority of the detectives, however, had arrived as scheduled, meaning that by the time Bobby, D.D., and Sinkus appeared, the pizza boxes were empty, the soda consumed, and not even a breadstick remained.

Bobby eyed the lone survivor—a plastic cup of red pepper flakes. He thought better of it.

"All right, all right," D.D. was saying briskly. "Gather 'round, listen up. For a change, we have developments to discuss, so let's get cracking."

Detective Rock yawned, then tried to cover the motion by fanning his piles of paper. "Heard we got a note," he said. "Real deal or wannabe wacko?"

"Uncertain. We announced Annabelle Granger's name in the beginning, but never released details on the locket or the other personal items. So our anonymous author either has inside information or is the real deal."

That perked them up. D.D.'s next announcement,

however, elicited collective groans. "I have copies of the note to distribute. But not yet. First things first: our nightly debrief. Let's figure out what we know now, then we'll consider how this little community out-reach"—D.D. waved the stack of photocopies—"fits into the puzzle. Sinkus, you go first."

Sinkus didn't mind. As the go-to guy for Christo-pher Eola, he was humming with excitement. He recapped the interview with Eola's parents, what they now knew of Eola's sexual activities and how his former nanny matched a general description of Annabelle Granger, one of the known targeted vic-tims. Even more interesting, Eola had access to vast financial resources. Between his Swiss bank account and multimillion-dollar trust fund, it was highly prob-able that he could maintain a lifestyle on the run, below the radar, etc., etc. In fact, just about anything was possible, so they'd have to open up their way of thinking.

Next steps: Put in a call to the State Department to track Eola's passport; outreach to Interpol in case they either had Eola in their sights or a case involving an UNSUB of similar MO; and finally, determine due process for tracing funds transferred out of a Swiss bank account or, better yet, freeze the assets alto-gether.

"Declare Eola a terrorist," McGahagin stated.

At his comment a few guys laughed.

"I'm not kidding," the sergeant insisted. "Homicide means nothing to the Swiss government—or anyone else, for that matter. On the other hand, write up a report that you have reason to believe Eola buried radioactive material in the middle of a major metro area, and you'll have his assets frozen lickety-split. Aren't bodies radioactive? Who in this room remembers anything from science class?"

They looked at one another blankly. Apparently, none of them watched The Discovery Channel.

"Well," McGahagin said stubbornly, "I think it's true. And I'm telling you, it will work."

Sinkus shrugged, made a note. It wouldn't be the first time they'd finessed a square peg into a round hole. That's why laws were written; so enterprising homicide detectives could figure out a way around them.

Sinkus was also in charge of tracking down Adam Schmidt, the AN from Boston State Mental who'd been fired for sleeping with a patient. He covered Schmidt next.

"Have finally located Jill Cochran, former head nurse," Sinkus reported. "I'm told she has most of the records, etc., from the closed institute. She's cataloging them, archiving them, I don't know. Doing whatever it is you do to insane-asylum paperwork. I'm meeting with her in the morning to follow up on Mr. Schmidt."

"Basic background check on Schmidt?" D.D. inquired.

"Nothing came up. So either Adam's been a very good boy since his Boston State Mental days, or he's been much smarter about not getting caught. My spidey sense is not tingly, however. I like Eola better."

D.D. merely gave him a look.

Sinkus threw up his hands in defense. "I know, I know, a good investigator leaves no stone unturned. I'm turning, I'm turning, I'm turning."

Sinkus, apparently, was a little punchy from lack of sleep. He sat down. Detective Tony Rock took over the hot seat, reporting on the latest activity on the Crime Stoppers hotline.

"What can I tell you?" the gravelly voiced detective rumbled, looking exhausted, sounding exhausted, and no doubt feeling as good as he looked and sounded. "We're averaging thirty-five calls an hour, most of which fall into three basic categories: a little bit crazy, a lot crazy, and too sad for words. The a little and a lot crazy categories are about what you'd expect—aliens did it; men in white suits; if you really want to be safe in this world, you need to wear tin foil on your head.

"The too sad for words, well, they're too sad for words. Parents. Grandparents. Siblings. All with missing family members. We got a woman yesterday who's seventy-five. Her younger sister has been missing since 1942. She heard the remains were skeletal, thought she might get lucky. When I told her we didn't believe the remains were that old, she started to cry. She's spent sixty-five years waiting for her baby sister to come home. Tells me she can't stop now; she made her parents a promise. Life is just plain shitty sometimes."

Rock squeezed the bridge of his nose, blinked, forged on. "So, I got a list of seventeen missing females, all of whom vanished between 1970 and 1990. Some of these girls are local. One's as far away as California. I got as much information from the families as possible for identification purposes. Including jewelry, clothing, dental work, bone fractures, and/or favorite toys—you know, in case we can match anything against the 'personal tokens' attached to each of the remains. I'm passing the info along to Christie Callahan. Otherwise, that's it for me."

He took a seat, the air seeming to leave his body until he collapsed, more than sat, in the folding metal chair. The man did not look good, and they lost a moment, staring at him and wondering who would be the first to say something.

"What?" he barked.

"You sure—" D.D. began.

"Can't fix my mom," Rock shot back. "Might as well find the fucker who murdered six girls."

There wasn't much anyone could add to that, so they moved on.

"All right," D.D. declared briskly, "we got one prime suspect of above-average intelligence and financial resources, one still-worth-looking-at suspect who was a former employee, and a list of seventeen missing girls from the Crime Stoppers hotline. Plus, there may be a link to an abduction two years before any of these six girls disappeared. Who else wants to join the show? Jerry?"

Sergeant McGahagin had been in charge of culling unsolved BPD missing-persons cases involving female minors for the past thirty years. His team had developed a list of twenty-six cases from Massachusetts. They had now started on the broader New England area.

He was skimming the copy of Tony Rock's report from Crime Stoppers, identifying five overlapping names between the two lists.

"What I need next," McGahagin stated heavily, "is a victimology report. If Callahan can give me a physical description of the remains, there's a chance I can make a match with an unsolved case. Then we could go to work on making a positive ID, which in turn would give us a time line for the mass grave. Bada bing, bada boom."

McGahagin stared at D.D. expectantly.

She returned his look levelly. "What the hell do you want me to do, Jerry? Pull six victimology reports out of my ass?"

"Come on, it's been four fucking days, D.D. How can we still know nothing about the six remains?"

"It's called wet mummification," D.D. shot back hotly. "And nobody's ever dealt with it in New England before."

"Then with all due respect to Christie, call someone who has."

"She did."

"What?" McGahagin appeared startled. Investigators made requests for resources, experts, forensic tests all the time. That didn't mean the powers-that-be granted them. "Christie is getting reinforcements?"

"Tomorrow, I'm told. Some hotshot from Ireland who specializes in this shit and is curious to see a 'modern' example. The DA sprung for the dough— apparently the Crime Stoppers hotline isn't the only one going insane. The entire city is flooding the governor's office with hysterical complaints that a serial killer is loose and going to murder their daughters next. Which reminds me, the governor would like us to solve this case, mmm, about five minutes ago."

D.D. rolled her eyes. The rest of the detectives managed a few chuckles.

"Seriously, folks," D.D. resumed speaking. "Christie is trying. We're all trying. She believes she needs one more week. So we can sit on our hands and whine, or, here's a thought, conduct some good old-fashioned police work."

She returned her attention to McGahagin. "You said you had a list of twenty-six missing females from Massachusetts? Twenty-six seems like a lot to me."

"As Tony said, it's a shitty world."

"You graph 'em? Do we have, say, a cluster of activity around certain dates?"

"Seventy-nine to eighty-two was not a good time to be a young female in Boston."

"How bad?"

"Nine cases in four years, all unsolved."

"Age parameters?"

"Zero to eighteen."

D.D. considered him. "And if you narrow the age range to, say, between five years old and fifteen?"

"Drops it to seven."

"Names?"

He did the honors, including Dori Petracelli.

"Locations?"

"All over. Southie, Lawrence, Salem, Waltham, Woburn, Marlborough, Peabody. If we make the assumption same subject was responsible for six of the seven cases . . ."

"By all means, let's assume away."

"You're talking someone with a vehicle, for one," McGahagin considered. "Someone who knows his way around the state, is comfortable blending in in a lot of different places. Maybe a utility worker, a repair person. Someone smart. Organized. Ritualized in his approach."

"Time line fits Eola," Sinkus commented. "Released in '78, doesn't have anything better to do . . ."

"Except," D.D. murmured, "incidents wind down in '82. Eola wouldn't have any reason to stop. Eola could theoretically go on forever. Which, frankly, would be true of any perpetrator. Predators don't magically just wake up one day and repent. Something happened. Other events, influences, must have interceded. Which brings us to"—her gaze shifted, found Bobby—"Russell Granger."

Bobby sighed, tilted back his chair. He'd been so busy since returning to HQ he hadn't had time to piss, let alone prepare notes. He had all eyes on him now, the city guys sizing up the state game. He did the best he could off the top of his head.

"According to police reports, Russell Granger first reported a Peeping Tom at his Arlington home in August of 1982. This set in motion a chain of events that culminated with Russell packing up his family and disappearing two months later, ostensibly to protect his seven-year-old daughter, Annabelle. So at first blush, we have a targeted victim—Annabelle Granger—and her poor, beleaguered father. Except . . ."

"Except," D.D. agreed.

Bobby held up a finger. "One," he said briskly, "Catherine Gagnon, who was abducted in 1980, recognized a photo of Russell Granger. Except Gagnon knew him as an FBI agent who interviewed her twice in the hospital after her rescue. That would be November of 1980, almost two years *before* the Peeping Tom report Russell Granger would file in Arlington."

Rock had appeared to be nodding off at the table. This information, however, brought his head snapping up. "Huh?"

"Our thoughts exactly. Two, during his visits with Catherine, Granger produced a composite sketch for her consideration. Catherine said the black-and-white didn't match her attacker. Granger tried to insist it did, got upset when she stayed firm, said it didn't. So, was the sketch an attempt on the part of Granger to distract Catherine, or did he honestly have a suspect in mind as her rapist? I have my opinion." He jerked his head toward D.D. "The sergeant has hers.

"Which brings us to three: There's no record of Russell Granger. No driver's license. No Social. Not for him, not for Annabelle's mother, Leslie Ann Granger. According to real estate records, the Grangers' home on Oak Street was owned by Gregory Badington of Philadelphia from '75 to '86. I'm guessing the Grangers rented the property, except Gregory passed away three years ago, and his wife, who sounded about one hundred and fifty on the phone, had no idea what I was talking about. So one dead end there.

"Yesterday, I started a routine check on financial records, got nowhere. Started a search for the Granger family furniture, ostensibly put into storage. Nada. It's as if the family itself never existed. Except, of course, for the police reports Granger filed."

"You think Russell Granger targeted his own daughter?" Rock said in confusion. "Made the whole thing up?"

Bobby shrugged. "Me, no. Sergeant Warren, on the other hand . . ."

"It would provide the perfect cover," D.D. said flatly. "Maybe by '82, Russell thought police would start noticing the sudden uptick in missing females. By positioning himself as a victim, he figured he could avoid being viewed as a suspect. Plus, it sets up the perfect cover for his own departure come October. Think about it. Seven missing girls between 1979 and 1982, one of them a known acquaintance of Russell Granger's—his daughter's best friend—yet not a single detective tries to track him down and question him. Why? Because he's already established himself as a protective father. It's perfect."

Sinkus appeared crestfallen. It was clear he liked his man, Eola, for the crime, so the sudden rise of Russell Granger as a viable alternative came as a heartbreak.

"One minor detail," Bobby countered. "Russell Granger is dead. Which means regardless of what he was doing in the early eighties, he's not the one leaving a note on D.D.'s windshield."

"You sure about that?"

"You're not really suggesting—"

"Look at the facts, Detective," D.D. said. "So far, you can't prove Russell Granger existed. Therefore, how can you be so sure he's dead?"

"Oh, for crying out loud—"

"I mean it. Do you have a death certificate? Corroboration? No, you have the sole testimony of Russell Granger's daughter, who claims her father was accidentally killed by a taxi. No other supporting documents or details. Damn convenient, if you ask me."

"So Russell Granger is not only a serial killer, but his daughter is covering for him? Now who's devolved from fact into fiction?"

"I'm just saying, we can't jump to conclusions yet. Two things I want to know." D.D. regarded him stonily. "One, when did Russell Granger first arrive in this state? Two, why did he keep running after leaving Arlington? Give me those answers, then we'll talk."

"One," Bobby said crisply, "just got word from MIT

on the name of Russell's former boss. I hope to meet with Dr. Schuepp first thing in the morning, which should help fill in the background info on Russell Granger, including his Massachusetts time line. Two, I'm trying to research the dates and cities after the family left Arlington, but I've been too busy chasing after you to get anything else done."

D.D. smiled grimly. "On that note"—she held up the stack of photocopies—"let's discuss the night's main event."

27

MY MYSTERY CALLER turned out to be Mr. Petracelli. He was no warmer by phone than he had been in person. He wanted to meet. He didn't want Mrs. Petracelli to know about it. Sooner would be better than later.

The sound of my real name over the phone lines had left me rattled. I didn't want him in my apartment. The fact that he was using the phone number I'd given to Mrs. Petracelli felt invasive enough.

We finally settled on meeting at Faneuil Hall, at the east end of Quincy Market, at eight p.m. Mr. Petracelli grumbled about having to drive into the city, find parking, but grudgingly agreed. I had my own issues—how to strategically plan my shift break to coincide with the proper time—but I thought it could be done.

Mr. Petracelli hung up and I stood alone in my apartment, clutching the phone to my chest and working on finding focus. I was due at work in seventeen minutes. I hadn't fed Bella, changed clothes, or unpacked.

When I finally moved, it was to set down the phone and hit Play on my answering machine. First message was a hang up. Second message the same. Third message was my current client, who, come to think of it, didn't like the valances after all; she'd just seen this great new window treatment at her friend Tiffany's house and maybe we could start over, or if that was too much of a problem for me, she could just give Tiffany's interior decorator a call. *Ciao, ciao!*

I scribbled a small note. Then I listened to three more hang ups.

Mr. Petracelli, reluctant to leave a message? Or someone else, desperate to get ahold of me? Suddenly, after years of isolation, I was a popular girl. Good news or bad? It made me nervous.

I chewed my thumbnail, looking outside at the dark, rainy gloom. Somebody wanted the locket back. Somebody had found Sergeant Warren's car. Was it only a matter of time, then, before that same someone found me?

"Bella," I declared suddenly, "how would you like to go to work with me?"

Bella liked the idea very much. She twirled half a dozen times, trotted to the door, and gazed at me expectantly. The news that I had to change clothes wasn't well received, but gave her a chance to eat dinner. While she scarfed kibble, I donned worn jeans, a basic white shirt, and black Dansko clogs, perfect for a long night on my feet. And, of course, I grabbed my handy-dandy Taser, a girl's best friend, and tucked it into my oversized shoulder bag.

Bella and I hustled out the door, pausing only as I tended to all the locks behind me. At street level I hesitated again, looking left, then right. At this hour, traffic was busy, people making the long haul home from work. Over at Atlantic Avenue, it was probably bumper-to-bumper, especially given the rain.

My little side street was quiet, however, just the glow of streetlamps bouncing off the slick, black pavement.

I gathered Bella's leash in my hand and we headed into the gloom.

Working at a coffeehouse sucked. I spent most of my eight-hour shift trying not to chew out the overcaffeinated customers or my undercaffeinated boss. Tonight was no exception.

Eight o'clock came. Five people remained in a straggly line, wanting nonfat this, tall soy mocha latte that. I cranked out shots of espresso and worried about Bella, tied up just under cover outside the glass doors, and Mr. Petracelli, waiting at the other end of the food-vendor-jammed length of Quincy Market.

"Need a break," I reminded my manager.

"Got customers," he singsonged back.

Eight-fifteen. "Gotta pee."

"Learn to hold it."

Eight-twenty, a family of caffeine addicts swarmed in and my manager showed no sign of relenting. I'd had enough. I whipped off my apron, tossed it on the counter. "I'm going to the bathroom," I said. "If you don't like it, buy me another bladder."

I stormed off, leaving Carl with four wide-eyed customers, including a little girl who demanded loudly, "Is she going to have an *accident?*"

I quickly wiped coffee grounds from my shirt, shoved my way through the heavy glass doors, and made a beeline for Bella. She stood, tongue lolling out, ready to go.

She was a little shocked when instead of going for a run, I simply walked her to the other end of Quincy Market, where I hoped Mr. Petracelli was still waiting for me.

I didn't see him at first, trying to sort through the small crowd that had gathered outside Ned Devine's. The rain had stopped, meaning the barflies had returned. I had just started to panic, when someone tapped me on the shoulder. I whirled around. Bella barked madly.

Mr. Petracelli backed way off. "Whoa, whoa, whoa," he said, hands up, nervous eyes on my dog.

I forced myself to take a deep breath, to calm Bella now that so many people were staring. "Sorry," I muttered. "Bella doesn't like strangers."

Mr. Petracelli nodded skeptically, his eyes never leaving Bella, as she finally settled down, pressing against my leg.

Mr. Petracelli was dressed for the weather. A long tan trench coat, black umbrella at his side, dark brown fedora capping his head. He reminded me of someone from a spy movie, and I wondered if that's how he viewed our meeting, some kind of clandestine operation, carried out between professionals.

I didn't feel very professional at the moment. Mostly, I was grateful for the presence of my dog.

It was Mr. Petracelli's meeting, so I waited for him to speak first.

He cleared his throat. Once, twice, three times. "Sorry about, um, yesterday," he said. "I just . . . When Lana said you were coming over . . . I wasn't ready yet." He paused, then, when I still didn't say anything, expanded in a rush: "Lana has her Foundation, her cause. For me, it's not like that. I don't like to think about those days much. It's easier to pretend we never lived on Oak Street. Arlington, Dori, our neighbors . . . it's almost like a dream. Something very far away. Maybe, if I'm lucky, it only happened in my mind."

"I'm sorry," I offered lamely, mostly because I didn't know what else to say. We had moved around to the other side now, away from the bar crowd, to the other corner of the broad, granite-columned building. Mr. Petracelli still hung back, keeping a wary eye on Bella. I preferred it that way.

"Lana said you gave Dori the locket," he declared suddenly. "Is it true? Did you give her one of your . . . presents? Did that pervert who left them for you kill

306

my daughter?" His voice had risen. I saw something move in the shadows of his eyes then. A light that wasn't quite sane.

"Mr. Petracelli—"

"I told the Lawrence detectives there had to be a connection. I mean, first some Peeping Tom looks in our neighbor's window, then our seven-year-old daughter goes missing. Two different cities, they said. Two different MOs. Mind your own business is what they meant. Let us do our jobs, crazy kook."

He was working himself into a state.

"I tried to call your father, thought if he could at least speak to the police, he could convince them. But I didn't have a phone number. How do you like that? Five years of friendship. Cookouts, New Year's Eve parties, watching our daughters grow up side by side, and one day your family takes off without so much as a by-your-leave.

"I hated your father for leaving. But maybe it's just plain old jealousy. Because he left and he saved his little girl. While I did nothing and I lost mine."

His shrill voice broke off, his bitterness undisguised. I still didn't know what to say.

"I miss Dori," I finally ventured.

"Miss her?" he parroted, and that ugly thing flickered in his eyes again. "I haven't heard from your family in twenty-five years. Pretty funny way to miss someone if you ask me."

More silence. I shifted uncomfortably from side to side. I felt that he had something important to say, the real reason he had dragged himself out on such a dark and rainy night, but he didn't know yet how to put it in words.

"I want you to go to the police," he stated finally, peering up from beneath the brim of his hat. "If you tell them your story, especially about the locket, they'll take a fresh interest in the case. There's no statute of limitations on murder, you know. And if they find some new leads . . ." His voice wobbled. He stiffened, soldiered on.

"I got a heart condition, Annabelle. Quadruple bypass, shunts. Hell, I'm more plastic parts than flesh and blood these days. It's gonna get me in the end. My father didn't live much past fifty-five. My brother neither. I don't mind dying. Some days, frankly, it sounds like a relief. But when I die . . . I want to be buried next to my daughter. I want to know she's by my side. I want to know she finally came home. She was only seven. My little girl. God, I miss her so much."

And then he started crying, giant, heaving sobs that made strangers stop in bewilderment. I put my arms around his shoulders. He grabbed on to me so hard, he almost pulled me to the ground. But I braced myself against his weight, felt the waves of his rough, violent grief.

Bella whined, prancing nervously, pawing at my leg. All I could do was wait.

Eventually he straightened, wiping at his face, tightening the belt of his coat, adjusting the brim of his hat. He wouldn't look at me anymore. I didn't expect him to.

"I'll go to the police," I promised him, an easy pledge, since I'd already done so. "You never know. Forensic science is getting better all the time; maybe they've already made an important discovery."

"Well, there is that pit over in Mattapan," he mumbled. "Six bodies. Who knows, maybe we'll get lucky." His face spasmed. "Lucky! Do you hear me? Christ, this is no way to live."

I didn't comment. I sneaked a quick glance at my watch. I'd been gone twenty minutes. I was probably as good as fired anyway. What were a few minutes more?

"Mr. Petracelli, did you ever see the Peeping Tom?"

He shook his head.

"But you believed the man existed, right? That someone was living in Mrs. Watts's attic, keeping tabs on me?"

He regarded me strangely. "Well, I don't think Mrs. Watts and your father would make up something like that. Besides, the police found the man's camping supplies in Mrs. Watts's home. That seems real enough to me."

"So you never got a look at the guy? Saw him for yourself?"

He shook his head. "Nah, but two days after the discovery of the stuff in Mrs. Watts's attic, we had a neighborhood meeting. Your father circulated a description of the Peeping Tom, along with a list of 'presents' you had received and when they had arrived. He told us there wasn't much the police could do; until something criminal actually happened, their hands were tied. Of course, we were all infuriated, especially those of us with kids. We voted to establish a Neighborhood Watch program. We'd just had our first meeting, in fact, when your dad announced that your family was taking a little vacation. None of us realized we'd never see you again."

"Do you happen to have those handouts? The description of the Peeping Tom my father circulated? I mean, I know it's been a long time, but . . ."

Mr. Petracelli smiled softly. "Annabelle, honey, I have a whole fat manila folder containing every single piece of documentation. I've brought it with me to every meeting we've had with the police since my little girl vanished, and at every meeting they've politely set it aside. But I've kept everything. In my heart of hearts, I've always known there was a connection between Dori's disappearance and yours. I just never could get anyone else to believe it."

"May I have a copy?" I was already reaching into my bag, fumbling for one of my business cards.

"I'll do my best."

"Mr. Petracelli, you said you knew my father for five years. Were you the one who was new to the neighborhood, or were we?"

"Your family arrived in '77. Lana and I'd been there since she was pregnant with Dori. We'd heard a rumor that a family was moving in with a daughter Dori's age. Lana had just gotten the cookies out of the oven when the U-Haul showed up. She marched right over

310

with snickerdoodles in hand and Dori in tow. You girls became inseparable from that very afternoon. We had your parents over for dinner the second night, and that sealed the deal."

I smiled at him to encourage further reminiscences. "Oh, really? I honestly don't remember. Guess I was too young."

"You were, what, eighteen months, two years old? Had that great toddler waddle. You and Dori used to chase each other around our house, screaming at the top of your lungs. Lana would shake her head, saying it was a wonder you didn't trip over your own feet." Mr. Petracelli was smiling. No wonder he was so tormented. In spite of his earlier statement, he remembered the past vividly, as if it were an old photograph he viewed often.

"Where did my family move from? Do you know?"

"Philly. Your dad had been with the University of Pennsylvania, or something like that. I never understood Russell's job much. Though for a professor type, I have to say, he had great taste in beer. Plus, he liked the Celtics, which was good enough for me."

"I never understood my father's job much either," I murmured. "Teaching math always sounded so boring to me. I remember I used to pretend he was with the FBI."

Mr. Petracelli laughed. "Russell? Not likely. I've never met a man so squeamish about firearms. At that Neighborhood Watch meeting, a bunch of us discussed buying guns for protection. Your dad wouldn't hear of it. 'It's bad enough some man has brought fear to my house,' he insisted. 'I'll be damned if I'll let him bring violence, too.' Nah, your dad was a liberal academic to the core. Can't we talk this out, give peace a chance, and all that crap."

"Did you buy a gun?"

"I did. Little did I know, I should have sent it with Dori to Lawrence." Mr. Petracelli's face twisted again, the bitterness getting the best of him. His breathing had grown shallower, strained. I wondered about his heart.

"Lana said your parents died," he said abruptly.

"Yes, sir."

"When?"

I considered his question, where he was going with this. "Does it matter?"

"Maybe."

"Why?"

His lips thinned. "Where did you go, Annabelle?" he said brusquely, ignoring my question. "When your family went on vacation, how far away did you go?"

"All the way to Florida."

"And your father really got a job there? That's why you stayed?"

"He drove a taxi. Not the same as being a professor, but I believe he thought the trade-off was worthwhile."

The news seemed to surprise Mr. Petracelli. That my father had been willing to surrender his academic career, or that my father hadn't lied about getting a job? I wasn't sure. He blinked. "Sorry," he said after a moment, "guess I'm just getting paranoid in my old age. It's easy to do, considering I wake up screaming most nights."

The rain had started to spatter down again. Mr. Petracelli was already turning to go. I stopped him by putting my hand on his arm. "Why did you ask about my father, Mr. Petracelli? What do you need to know?"

"It's just . . . after Dori disappeared, a neighbor reported seeing a man driving an unmarked white van in the area, even gave the police a description of the guy. Lana never agreed with me, of course, but my first thought?"

"Yes?"

"Short dark hair, tanned face, real good-looking guy. Come on, Annabelle." Mr. Petracelli's face suddenly changed again, that crafty gleam returning to his eyes. "Tell me who that is."

For a moment, I didn't get it. Then, as his innuendo struck, I tried to snatch my hand away. He grabbed my fingers, held on tight. "Don't be absurd!" I said sharply.

"Yeah, Annabelle, the man who took my Dori, he sounds exactly like your dear old dad."

He flung my arm back at me. I fell to the wet sidewalk, bruised fingers tucked protectively against my chest while Bella went into a paroxysm of barking. I grabbed her, trying to steady her, steady me.

When I looked up again, Mr. Petracelli was gone, and only the ugliness of his accusation lingered in the wet, dark air.

28

CARL FIRED ME. I took the news well, considering I needed the job to cover such luxuries as rent. Mostly, it was a relief to leave the loud, chaotic space of Quincy Market, where Mr. Petracelli's ugly words still tainted the night. Even Bella was subdued, walking obediently beside me as we left Faneuil Hall, crossing into the familiar territory of Columbus Park.

The harborside park was small compared to other Boston green spaces. But it offered a water fountain that kept the kids giggling and wet during the summer, while the adults lounged in the grass or beneath the shade of the long wooden trellis. There was a playground, a rose garden, and a small reflecting fountain, where the homeless kept vigil.

Sometimes, before my Starbucks shift, I'd bring Bella here to run around with her North End neighbors, an informal puppy playgroup. I'd stand to the side of the gathered humans, while the dogs frolicked.

Too cold and wet for children now. Too late for dogs or community gatherings. The homeless slept on the benches. The barflies passed briskly through, mindful of the misty weather as they exchanged Faneuil Hall haunts for North End eateries. Other than that, the park was quiet.

I found myself thinking of the note again. *Return the locket, or another girl will die.*

Was there a young child in bed right now, maybe

tucked in with her favorite stuffed dog and pink fleecy blanket? Did she trust her parents to keep her safe? Believe nothing could happen to her inside her own home?

He would walk across her lawn, heavy metal crowbar slapping against his thigh. He would tuck himself somewhere out of sight, maybe a tree or bush. Then he would inch along the side of the house until he came to her window.

Lifting the crowbar, going to work on the window sash . . .

I pressed the heels of my hands against my eyeballs, as if that would make the images go away. I felt dipped in ugliness, suffocated by violence. Twenty-five years later, I still couldn't escape.

I didn't want to think about Mr. Petracelli's words. I didn't want to think about the threat left on the windshield of D.D.'s car. The past was the past. I was a grown adult. I'd lived in the city for over ten years. Why would the boogeyman suddenly return now, demanding my old locket, threatening new victims? It didn't make any sense.

Mr. Petracelli was insane. A bitter, crazy man who'd never gotten over the terrible loss of his daughter. Of course he blamed my father. Saved him all sorts of parental guilt.

As for Bobby and D.D.'s allegations . . .

They had never met my dad. They didn't know him the way I did. How he could sink his teeth into a problem like a pit bull, refusing to let go. Obviously,

Catherine had information he wanted. In that case, it would've made sense to my father to pass himself off as an FBI agent. Normal fathers probably did not do such things, but they probably didn't move their families to Florida just because the police wouldn't call in the National Guard to look for a Peeping Tom.

And as for my father's brief disappearance shortly after we moved to Florida . . . No doubt there were loose ends to tidy up. Closing out bank accounts, putting things into storage. Except, of course, he could've closed out the bank accounts before we left. And apparently he'd arranged for the moving company by phone. . . .

I didn't want to go there. My father was obsessive, paranoid, and systematic.

That still did not mean he was a killer.

Except maybe he wasn't even Russell Granger?

My temples started to throb again, the beginnings of a first-class headache that had started twenty-five years ago and now threatened to go on without end. I didn't know what to do. I just wanted . . . I just wished . . .

"Hello."

The voice startled me so badly, I squeaked, twirled, and nearly fell. A strong hand grabbed my arm, held me upright.

Bella barked excitedly as I belatedly turned around to discover the old man from Boston State Mental standing beside me. Charlie Marvin. Bella barked louder. Far from being concerned, Charlie simply bent down and held out his hand.

"Beautiful dog," he murmured, waiting until Bella gave up barking long enough to sniff his hand. Another tentative sniff, then she stepped toward him, wagging her tail.

Charlie, apparently, was a dog person. "Oh, there's a good girl. Aren't you beautiful? Look at those markings. You must be an Australian shepherd. Not a lot of sheep around here for herding, I'm afraid. Would you settle for taxis? What do you think? You look like a fast girl. I bet you catch a lot of taxis."

Bella seemed to think this was a fine idea. She pressed herself against Charlie, while eyeing me for approval. The man had totally and completely won over my dog.

He finally straightened from his squat, smiling ruefully as his knees creaked, and he had to grab my arm for support.

"Sorry," he said cheerfully. "It's one thing to get down. Quite another to get up."

"What are you doing here?" I asked, voice sharp, making no apologies.

His blue eyes crinkled at the corners. He seemed to find my concern amusing. He held up both hands in a gesture of mea culpa. "Remember how I said you looked familiar?"

I nodded grudgingly.

"I kept thinking about it, remembered from where. This park. You run through here with your dog. Generally a bit earlier than this, but I've spotted you quite a few times. I never forget a face, particularly a pretty one." He glanced down, tickled Bella under the chin. "Of course I'm talking about you, sweetheart," he crooned.

I couldn't help myself, I finally smiled. Then hastily pulled it together. "And why are you in the park so often?"

He jerked his head toward the corner of Atlantic Avenue. "Working with the homeless. Just because you don't have a roof over your head doesn't mean you should be denied the word of God."

I couldn't think of an argument for that.

"Anyhooo," he drawled, rocking back on his heels, cramming his hands into his pockets, "I'll confess, I've been looking for you."

I didn't say anything, but felt my pulse quicken as I went on high alert.

"You're not with the police," he stated.

No answer.

"But they took you to the crime scene." He cocked his head, regarding me steadily. "So I figure maybe you're another kind of expert. Botanist, bone person. I don't really know anything, I just watch Court TV. But I am a good judge of people and I don't think you're a scientist any more than you're a cop. Which means . . . I'm thinking relative. Of one of those poor girls. But you're too young to be a mother. So maybe a sister? That's my theory, at least. You knew one of the girls whose body has been discovered, and for that I am very sad."

Very slowly, I nodded. Sister. That seemed close enough.

Charlie smiled. "Phew!" He made an exaggerated motion of wiping his brow. "I really am blowing things out my arse, you know. Then again, more often than not, I'm right. The Lord has given me a gift. For now, I am using it for His work. Minute this gig is done, however, that's it. I'm hitting the poker tables. In my old age, I'm gonna get myself a Cadillac!"

His smile was too infectious. I found myself smiling back, while Bella pranced around us, clearly infatuated with her newfound friend.

"All right," I said. "So I'm a relative. What's your interest?"

Charlie sobered up instantly, shaking his head mournfully. "I can't sleep. I know that might sound crazy. I'm a minister. If I don't know the true evil man is capable of, then who does? But I'm an idealist. The times I've been around genuine evil, I knew it. I could feel it, touch it, smell it. Christopher Eola reeked of it.

"But during all my years at Boston State Mental, I never suspected anything as terrible as a mass grave. I never walked the streets of Mattapan and imagined young girls were being stolen from their homes. Never walked through the woods of the property and thought for a second that I heard a young girl scream. And I used to walk those woods with great frequency. Lots of us did. It's one of the finest nature sanctuaries in the state; we would've been fools not to enjoy God's bounty. And that's what I felt when I walked through those fields, skirting the marshes, retreating into the forest—I felt honestly, genuinely, closer to God."

His voice caught. He looked up, pinning me with somber blue eyes. "It's shaken me to my very soul, young lady. If I could not feel the evil on those grounds, then what kind of minister am I? How can I be God's messenger when I was so blind?"

I didn't know what to say. I had never before had a minister come to me with a matter of faith. In the next moment, however, it became clear that Charlie Marvin was not looking for my opinion. He had already formed his own.

"It has become my obsession," he stated. "This grave at Boston State Mental, the souls of those poor girls. Where I have failed once, it is my duty not to fail again. I would like to outreach to the families, but they have not been identified yet. Except for you. So here I am."

I frowned, still uncertain. "I don't understand. What do you want?"

"I'm not here to demand, sweet child. I'm here for you to talk. About anything and everything you'd like. Come, have a seat. It's cold, it's late, you've come to the park instead of finding your warm, cozy bed. Clearly, you have something on your mind."

Charlie gestured to a waiting bench, then headed toward it. I followed reluctantly, not one for talking, and yet, oddly, hating for this meeting to end. Bella was happy. And I'd felt something unfurl inside of me in the presence of such a warm, easygoing man. Charlie Marvin did know the worst about humanity. If he could still find a reason to smile, then maybe so could I.

"All right," he said briskly, when he arrived at the bench and discovered I hadn't bolted yet. "Let's start with the basics." He thrust out his hand. "Good evening, my name is Charlie Marvin, I'm a minister, and it's a pleasure to meet you."

I played along. "Good evening. My name is Annabelle, I do custom window treatments, and it's a pleasure to meet you, too."

We shook. I noted that Charlie showed no reaction to my name, and why should he? But I felt giddy at having spoken my real name in public after twenty-five years.

Charlie took a seat. I followed suit. The hour was late, the park wet and deserted, so I unhooked Bella from her leash. She leapt up with grateful kisses, then was off racing along the trellis.

"So, if you don't mind me saying," Charlie was commenting, "you don't exactly sound as if you're from Boston."

"My family moved a lot when I was growing up. But I consider Boston home. Yourself?"

"Grew up in Worcester. Still can't say my R's."

That made me laugh. "So you're a local boy. Wife, kids, dogs?"

"Had a wife. Tried for kids. Wasn't in God's plans. Then my wife got ovarian cancer. She passed away . . . oh, it's been a good twelve years now. We had a small house up in Rockport. I sold it, returned to the city. Saves me the commute—it's possible that I'm no longer the best guy behind a wheel of a car. My brain is fine. My hands, however, are a little slow to do what they're told."

"And you work with the homeless?"

"Yes, ma'am. I volunteer my time over at Pine Street. Help out with the shelter and the soup kitchen. Plus, I believe strongly in fieldwork. The homeless can't always find it in them to come to you, you gotta go to them."

I was genuinely curious. "So you come to places like this and, what? Preach? Buy soup? Hand out pamphlets?"

"Mostly, I listen."

"Really?"

"Really." He nodded vigorously. "You think the homeless don't get lonely? Sure they do. Even the mentally disadvantaged, the economically forsaken have a basic need for human connection. So I sit with them. I let them tell me about their lives. Or sometimes we don't say anything at all. And that can be just as nice."

"Does it work? Have you 'saved' anyone?"

"I've saved myself, Annabelle. Isn't that good enough?"

"I'm sorry, I meant—"

He waved away my embarrassment. "I know what you meant, dear. I'm just yanking your chain."

I blushed. It seemed to amuse him more. But then he leaned forward, his tone growing serious.

"No, I can't say that I've magically turned someone's life around. Which is a damn shame, given that the average age of a homeless person is twenty-four." He saw my surprised look, and nodded. "Yes, it's sobering to think about, isn't it? And nearly half of all the homeless are mentally ill. To be honest, these folks aren't the kind who are going to turn their lives around after getting a free shower and a cup of soup. They need help, they need guidance, and most, in my humble opinion, would benefit from at least a brief stint in a therapeutic environment. None of which is going to happen to them any time soon."

"You're a nice man, Charlie Marvin."

He playfully clutched at his chest. "Oh, be still, my beating heart. I'm too old to be receiving such high praise from a pretty face. Be careful, or my wife's spirit will come back to chastise us both. She always was a hellion."

That made me laugh, which seemed to make him happy. Bella returned to check on our progress. Seeing we had accomplished nothing, she flopped down at my feet, sighed heavily, and put her head down. For a while, the three of us sat there, gazing at the moon, listening to the water, feeling the peace of the silence.

Of course, I was the one who broke it first.

"Do you know who did it?" I asked, no reason to define "it."

Charlie took his time with his answer. "I'm afraid I know who did this terrible thing," he said at last. "Meaning, when the police figure it all out, the name will be someone I knew from the hospital."

"You mentioned a couple of likely suspects. This Adam Schmidt. Christopher Eola."

"So you *were* eavesdropping."

"I have an interest," I said levelly.

He winked at me. "I'm not criticizing, child. In your shoes, I would've eavesdropped, too."

"Between the two, who do you think is most likely?"

"Not knowing any details of the crime?"

"None of us know many details of the crime," I said, in answer to his underlying question.

"Christopher Eola," he said promptly. "You'd have to be depraved but calculating to kidnap and murder six girls. Adam was a sleaze, don't get me wrong. But he was too lazy for this kind of crime. Christopher, on the other hand . . . He would savor the challenge."

"Do you know where he is now?"

"Well . . ." Charlie started, then stopped.

"Well?" I prodded.

"I got to thinking about it more after talking with Detective Dodge and Sergeant Warren. . . ."

"Yes?"

"Well, the more I thought about Christopher, the more I thought it had to be him. So I called a buddy of mine at Bridgewater. He'd never even heard Eola's name—bad sign right there, if you know what I mean. But he did some digging, and sure enough, Eola was released in '78. Meaning Christopher's had all sorts of time on his hands, yet none of us have heard from him. Makes me nervous."

"You don't think he magically got a job, assimilated into society, became a model citizen?"

Charlie contemplated my question. "Do you consider Ted Bundy was a model citizen? Because if you do, then maybe Christopher has a chance."

"That bad?"

"Man had no morals. No empathy with his fellow human beings. For a guy like that, the whole world is a system meant to be played. And what Christopher Eola enjoyed playing most was outwitting others in order to indulge his very private, very violent fantasies."

I considered Charlie's words. "If that's the case, how do you think he's made it nearly thirty years without coming to police attention?"

"I don't know."

"But you must have some ideas."

Charlie stroked Bella's head, considering. "Eola came from money, so maybe he's tapped into those resources. A little bit of money can cover a lot of messy tracks."

"True."

"And he's smart, which helps. Mostly, however, I think he relies on his appearance."

"You described him to the detectives as effeminate."

"Yes, ma'am. He's strong, though—all muscle and sinew, that one. But he appears—appeared, I guess, when I knew him—quite aristocratic. For some reason, no one ever suspects the cultured academic."

"Academic?" I heard myself say.

"It's not like he actually had a degree or anything. But it was an image he cultivated. Several of our female nurses actually thought he was a Ph.D. until we broke the news he'd never even gone to college."

"What kind of degree did he pretend to have?"

Charlie pursed his lips. "Oooh, that's a long time ago. A degree in history? Master of fine arts? Maybe it was literature. I don't remember now. Just that he led some people to believe he taught courses at MIT. I don't know why. I would've guessed him a Harvard man myself."

Charlie flashed his friendly grin, but I was no longer smiling. Something niggled at me. Too many coincidences.

"Do you have a picture of Christopher?" I asked.

"No, ma'am."

"But there should be something on file. A yearbook? A mug shot? Something."

"I'm not sure, to tell you the truth. Maybe Bridgewater took a photo."

I nodded slowly. Foot starting to tap in agitation. If Eola was loose in '78 . . . Still exiled from his family, with no place to go . . .

Would someone like that drift out to Arlington? Maybe make himself at home in the attic of a little old lady? And given that he had money, if the target of his interest disappeared, would he be inclined to run, too? Maybe the Boston police had never known about Christopher Eola for the same reason they didn't get to know about me. Because we both vanished and spent the next twenty-five years on the road.

The hour was growing late. Lost in my own

thoughts, I hadn't realized that Charlie was already standing, ready to go. Belatedly, I rose, then dug in my purse until I found one of my cards.

"If you think of anything else," I told him, "I would appreciate any help you have to give."

"Oh, not a problem. Pleasure's all mine." He glanced at my card, frowned, and asked, "Tanya?"

"My middle name. I use it for business. You know, a girl can never be too careful."

We shook hands one last time. Charlie headed off toward Faneuil Hall. Bella and I headed for the North End.

Right at the edge of the park, as I was set to cross Atlantic Avenue, something made me turn around. I spotted Charlie, under the trellis now, studying Bella and me intently. An aging gentleman making sure I made it home okay. Or something else?

He saw me staring, raised a hand in acknowledgment, smiled softly, then turned on his heel.

I started running with Bella then, under the streetlights, on the main streets, with my Taser in my hand and my demons chasing me once more.

29

BOBBY SAT THIRTY feet off the ground, cradled in the bare branches of an enormous oak tree. He wore black BDUs, topped with soft body armor. A pair of night-vision goggles rested on his forehead. A Sig Sauer 3000 rifle, outfitted with a Leupold 3-9X 50mm variable scope and loaded with Federal Match Grade .308 Remington 168 grain slugs, was in his arms.

He should be thinking of the good old days. When he'd been able to run faster than a speeding bullet and leap tall buildings in a single bound. When he'd been the best of the best, the baddest of the bad. When he'd had a mission, a team, and a sense of purpose.

Mostly, he wanted to wring D.D.'s neck.

The note on D.D.'s car had contained explicit instructions. At 3:33 a.m., the locket should be delivered to the former site of Boston State Mental, outside the ruins of the admin building. D.D. was to bring the locket herself. She should wear it around her neck. She should come alone.

Bobby might be a rookie detective, but he'd served on a tactical unit for seven years. He understood strategy, was comfortable with special ops.

D.D. read the note and saw an opportunity. He read the note and saw *bait.*

Why D.D.? Why alone? Why, if the whole point was to return the necklace, should she be wearing the locket around her neck?

Then there was the site itself. One hundred and seventy acres of woods. Two crumbling ruins, one construction site, and one subterranean crime scene. There weren't enough SWAT teams in New England to secure that much real estate, particularly in such a tight time frame.

D.D. had countered that there were only two access roads onto the property, not hard to monitor. Bobby had pointed out that while there were only two *legal* entrances/exits to the site, the locals had been digging under the fences, cutting holes, and running amok across the grounds for decades. The site was Swiss cheese, boundaries compromised and fencing worthless.

They needed tactical units. His former team, for one, which would bring thirty-two men to the party. He'd even consider working with the city's SWAT team, as long as they promised not to touch his gun. Bodies were bodies, training was training, and truthfully, the Boston guys were pretty good, even if the state guys didn't like to say such things out loud.

He'd also like choppers, dogs, and night-vision security cameras deployed at strategic intervals.

D.D., of course, had decided to deploy one man onsite: him. The rest would form a discreet perimeter, ready to close in around the subject the moment he appeared. Too many bodies might scare the subject away. Ditto with air support. Security cameras weren't a bad idea, but they didn't have the time to get something that sophisticated in place.

Instead, she'd gone with the basics: Bomb-sniffing dogs had made the rounds three hours ago while two dozen officers combed the woods in the immediate vicinity. Then tech support had hastily installed sensors that shot infrared beams of light from point to point, forming a perimeter around the designated meeting area. First time a beam was broken, the signal would be sent to Central Command, providing Bobby and D.D. with advance warning of the subject's approach.

D.D. was wired beneath her boron-plated Kevlar vest. She wore an earpiece to receive, with the transmitter built into her vest. This enabled her to communicate with him as well as with Command Central, deployed in a van across the street at the cemetery.

D.D. was a fool. A stubborn, pigheaded, tunnel-visioned sergeant who honestly thought she could save the world in a single evening.

Bobby didn't think it was a matter of ambition. He thought, more frighteningly, that D.D. was curious.

She believed the subject would show. And when he did, she hoped to determine if the man was Christopher Eola or Annabelle's long-lost father. Then she would keep the child killer so occupied with her dazzling beauty and witty repartee, he wouldn't think to abduct another little girl. In fact, he'd tell D.D. everything she needed to know, right before the task force descended and led him away in metal bracelets.

D.D. was a fool. A stubborn, pigheaded, tunnel-visioned . . .

Bobby leaned down. Adjusted his Leupold scope. Did his best to block out the sound of the wind, rustling through the skeletal trees.

His hands didn't shake. He was grateful for that much.

After the shooting, in that moment when he was still seeing Jimmy Gagnon's head snap back, blood and brain exploding from the skull, Bobby hadn't been sure he'd ever be comfortable with guns again. Hadn't been sure he'd *want* to be comfortable with guns again.

He'd never been a gun guy. Hadn't fired his first rifle until he'd attended the police academy. There, he'd made the discovery that he was quite good. With a bit of training, he scored expert. With a bit of nudging, he became a sniper. But it had never been true love. The rifle was not an extension of his arm, a calling of his soul. It was a tool he happened to be extremely skilled at using.

Three days after shooting Jimmy Gagnon, he'd gone to an indoor firing range and picked up a handgun. The first clip had been terrible. The second clip, not so bad. He told himself he was a plumber, reacquainting himself with his trade. As long as he kept that perspective, he was good to go.

The wind blew again, carrying a spray of wet drizzle. Made the tree branches shift around him. He thought he heard another low-pitched whine. Reminded himself again that he did not believe in ghosts, not even at the site of a former mental institute.

Goddamn D.D.

His watch glowed 3:21 a.m. Twelve minutes and counting. He lowered the NVGs over his eyes and located his headstrong friend. D.D. paced in front of the crumbling brick ruins of the old building. Her normally slender silhouette appeared bulky and misshapen—the effects of the Kevlar vest. Given the weather, she wore a bright yellow rain jacket over her usual crisp white shirt. No hat, which would limit visibility. No umbrella, which would tie up her hands.

Now she turned, walking back toward him, and Bobby spotted the old silver locket winking in the hollow of her throat. And just for a moment, he could see the black-and-white missing-person's photo of Dori Petracelli, the same locket gleaming around her neck.

The subject was playing them. He didn't care about the locket. And if he wanted to abduct another girl, he was going to abduct another girl. That's what these perverts did.

But maybe D.D. was right, too. Through her rash actions, she was buying them another night. The subject's instructions had been explicit and personal. Obviously, the man had formed some kind of attachment to D.D. Enough that he wanted to see a former trophy from one of his victims, worn around the investigating sergeant's throat.

Maybe he was already here now, perched up in another old tree, or even tucked inside the decaying brick building. Maybe he was peering down, peering out, watching D.D. pace, admiring her long, strong legs, her natural athletic grace.

She hit the crumbling edge of the building. Pivoted on her heel, started pacing the opposite way. Three thirty-one a.m.

Why 3:33 a.m. anyway? Why so precise? Did the subject like the symmetry of 333? Or was it one more way to yank their chains?

Lieutenant Trenton from Central Command suddenly sounded in Bobby's ear. *"We got activity. Perimeter breached, due west."*

D.D. still walking steadily, though she must have heard the news.

Bobby surveyed the scene to his left. Looking for signs of life.

A dark shape, suddenly exploding from beneath the underbrush—

Just as Lieutenant Trenton sounded once more in his ear: *"More movement. North. Activity. East. No, south. No, wait. Jesus Christ. All four sides breached. Perimeter fully breached. Bobby, do you read?"*

Bobby heard. Bobby saw. Bobby moved.

Rifle, swinging around. Sighting, aiming, pulling the trigger. An aborted growl, then a dark shape tumbling down. While three more enraged forms burst from the woods.

D.D. started to scream, then everything was happening at once.

Bobby turned, tried to sight, realized the attack dogs were moving so fast, they were now too close for the set range of his scope. He swore, jerked his head up, and did things the old-fashioned way. Quick squeeze. An eerie, rumbling scream, then the second dog tumbled down.

Gunshots from below. Bobby spotted D.D. sixty yards away. Racing for his tree, firing wildly over her shoulder. She was moving at a good clip.

But she wasn't going to make it.

He was breathing too hard, too fast. Get centered. Inside the moment, but outside the moment. Find the target. Focus on the target. Large black dog with tan markings, converging with another hundred-pound black dog, joining forces to chase down their prey.

Tree branch blocking. Then another. Now, as they passed through a narrow slice between the branches.

He squeezed the trigger. Third dog dropped. As the fourth leapt into the air and landed on D.D.'s back.

She went down as the dog closed its massive jaws around her shoulder and shredded her yellow vinyl jacket.

"Officer down, officer down!" Bobby screamed. "Assistance needed, *now, now, now.*"

Then he was fighting his way through the tree branches, trying to drop thirty feet to the ground, his rifle tangling him up, while the dog went after the back of D.D.'s neck, making a terrible wet, growling sound.

Bobby cleared the branches, jumping the remaining fifteen feet, rolling through the pain that rocketed up his ankles. Rifle was useless; force of the slug would pass through the dog into D.D. Instead, he reached behind his back for his Glock as he tore through the woods.

D.D. was still moving. He could see her arms and legs flailing as she fought to get the massive weight off her, punched feebly behind her at the dog's head.

The dog was fighting with her Kevlar vest. Trying to chew and claw through it. Trying to sink its teeth into soft, white flesh.

Bobby ran. The Rottweiler never looked up. As Bobby placed the muzzle of his gun against the animal's ear. As Bobby pulled the trigger. As the massive animal dropped, and finally there was silence in the woods.

It took them ten minutes to pry the animal's jaws from D.D.'s left shoulder. They rolled her onto her side while they worked, Bobby talking to her constantly. She had a death grip on his hand, wouldn't let go, which was okay, because he wouldn't let her.

Blood. A little bit on her cheek, her neck. Not as bad as they feared. Her vest had protected her from the dog's claws upon her back. When she'd pitched forward, the Kevlar had ridden up, protecting her neck from its fangs. She'd lost a chunk of skin along her jaw, a few clumps of hair on the back of her head. Given the possibilities, she wasn't complaining.

The officers finally wrestled the Rottweiler's body free and it fell limply to the ground beside her.

D.D. braced herself against Bobby and he pulled her upright. "Where did the dogs come from?" she wanted to know. An EMT had arrived, was trying to take her blood pressure. The raincoat was too thick. She shrugged it off, wincing at the movement.

"Woods," Sinkus reported breathlessly, having just caught up with them. "No sign of a human intruder yet, but we found four wire cages about two hundred yards back, covered in bushes and set up with timers. Hour hit 3:33, electronic current shut off, and the doors swung open, releasing the dogs."

Bobby glanced up. "And all four dogs ran to the exact same target?"

"Each cage contains, um, unmentionables," Sinkus said.

"Unmentionables?" D.D. demanded. She touched her jaw gingerly, felt out the bloody tear.

"Yeah. Underwear. One pair in each cage. I'm going out on a limb here, but I'm betting the thongs are yours."

"What?" D.D. turned sharply. The EMT ordered her to stay still. She nailed him with such a glance, he fell back.

It was good to know that D.D. was feeling better, even if it did mean her fingers were now crushing Bobby's hand.

"Have you noticed anything disturbed at home?" Sinkus asked. "Like someone rifling through your drawers or, more probably, going through your dirty laundry? The system works best if the item bears your scent."

"I haven't been home enough in the past four days to check my drawers! Or," she snarled, then sighed, "do any of my laundry."

"Well, there you go. Guy helped himself to a few scent markers. Any well-trained attack dog would take it from there."

D.D. definitely didn't like that thought. She turned, regarding the body of the dog on the ground. Big, black, powerfully muscled. She touched its flank. The

336

look on her face was not so much rage as regret.

"My uncle used to have a Rotty. Her name was Meadow. Biggest, sweetest dog you can imagine. She used to let me ride on her back." D.D.'s hand moved, found the twisted wire around the dog's neck, the kind of collar favored by drug dealers and dog fighters. "Asshole," she suddenly growled. "Dog was probably trained from birth. Never had a chance."

Bobby couldn't look at her anymore. After all, he was the one who had taken out the four dogs that attacked her. And while he couldn't feel bad about it, given the circumstances, he couldn't feel good about it either.

"I don't get it," D.D. muttered. "Making me wear the locket made a crazy kind of sense. Gave the guy a cheap thrill. But why go through all that for this kind of setup? It's like attacking via remote. Except I don't think our subject is a remote kind of guy. I think he's up close and personal."

"It's sophisticated," Sinkus commented. "Allows him to show off his intelligence. Something Eola would do."

D.D. didn't comment. Neither did Bobby. He was thinking of what she'd said. The note had been personal, left on the windshield of D.D.'s car. The choice of trophies for each body they'd found had been personal, too, same with the MO of stalking Annabelle by leaving gifts. The setup here had involved stealing D.D.'s underwear—no doubt, the subject had enjoyed that—so why not stick around for the show? D.D. was right. The subject had invested heavily in foreplay, then denied himself the main event.

That didn't feel right. It wasn't the way this sicko worked.

"Keep searching the grounds," D.D. was saying now. "In addition to a trespasser, have the techies look for signs of video equipment, listening devices. Maybe our subject decided to stage the show, something he could record and watch from the safety of his home. Wanted a little action or a clip he could share on the Internet."

"We'll keep looking," Sinkus assured her.

"We need choppers," D.D. continued crossly, impatiently waving away the hovering EMT. "And dogs. Hell, let's call in the National Guard. Fucking nearly two hundred acres. Fucking loony bin. He could hide out for days without us seeing a thing."

Sinkus was nodding, making notes, preparing to blow the department's annual budget for a one-night search.

Bobby was still not liking it.

Why so elaborate? They were looking for a pedophile, a man accustomed to preying on small children. Now, suddenly, he had his sights set on a grown woman? A female police sergeant who was bound to be smart, armed, and prepared?

Did pedophiles change their preferences so easily? Transition from small children to authority figures?

Unless . . .

It came to him all at once. Unless the man had never

changed focus. Unless the man still had his eyes set on the same target. A target who since recently resurfacing had spent the past two days surrounded by police protection. Until tonight, when by virtue of this operation . . .

Bobby whirled back toward his fellow detectives. "Annabelle!"

30

I WOKE UP hard, hands fisting my sheet, muscles tense. For a second, I felt wild-eyed with alarm. Run, fight, scream. But my thoughts were sluggish, dream-soaked. I couldn't fill in the blanks.

I forced myself to sit up, dragging in ragged gulps of air. Bedside clock glowed 2:32 a.m. Bad dream, I thought. Rough night.

I climbed out of bed, wearing a pair of men's cotton boxer shorts and a faded black tank top. Bella lifted her head, considering the matter. She was used to my restless ways by now. She put her head back down; one of us might as well get some sleep. I padded alone into the kitchen, where I banged on the faucet and poured myself a glass of city water. If that didn't wake me up, nothing would.

I was standing there, staring at the faint line of hallway light glowing beneath my chained and bolted door, when the front ringer buzzed noisily. I jolted, water spilling down my shirt, while Bella came bounding out of the bedroom, scrabbling across the kitchen and barking madly at the door.

I didn't think anymore, I moved. Tossed the plastic cup in the sink. Ran back into the bedroom. Flipped over my pillow, grabbed the Taser I kept tucked beneath it. Go, go, go.

Back in the kitchen now. Bella barking. My heart thudding. Did I hear the creak of the downstairs door? Footsteps on the stairs?

I finally grabbed Bella by the collar and forced her onto the floor. "Shhhh, shhh, shhh," I murmured, but my own tense state kept her agitated. She growled low in her throat as I stared at the sliver of light beneath my apartment door, waiting for the dark shadows of footsteps to appear, the enemy to come into sight.

And . . .

Nothing.

Minute slid into minute. My breathing slowed. My composure transitioned from fight-or-flight to just plain bewildered. Belatedly I thought to move over to the bay windows, peer down at the street. No strange cars were parked below. No person loitered in the shadows.

I collapsed in the window seat, Taser still clutched to my chest. I was overreacting but couldn't give up my vigil. Bella was more practical about things. With a huff, she left her post in favor of the living room dog bed. In a matter of seconds, she was curled up and back asleep, doggy nose tucked on doggy paws. I remained an over-hyped sentinel, trying to talk myself down.

Buzzers go off in the middle of the night, I tried reminding myself. It had happened before. Would happen again. Drunks wander by or even invited guests of another tenant who get the unit numbers confused. My fellow renters were security-conscious. None of us randomly opened doors for unknown buzzers. Which probably only increased the odds that the outside person was going to keep punching buttons until he got results.

In other words, there were a million and a half logical explanations for a doorbell to sound in the middle of the night. And none of them were working for me.

I got off the window seat. Returned to my front door. Pressed my ear against its painted surface and listened for sounds coming from the stairs.

The problem is, there's no soundtrack for real life. In the movies, you know when something bad is going to happen, because the heavy bass tells you so. There isn't a person alive whose heart doesn't race upon hearing the theme song from *Jaws,* and frankly, that's a comforting thing. We like our markers. It gives the world a sense of order. Bad things may happen, but only after the background picks up with *da-dah, da-dah, da-dah-da-dah-da-dah.*

The real world isn't like that. A young girl comes home on a sunny afternoon, climbs the same old stairs, listens to the same old hum of ancient air conditioners, only to enter the apartment and find her mother dead on the sofa.

A man goes out for a walk in the city. Listens to the

rush of cars, the honk of horns, the bustle of his fellow pedestrians chatting away on their cell phones. Steps off the curb an instant too soon, and next thing you know, his face is a pulpy mess, shattered against a lamppost.

One little girl goes out to play in her grandparents' yard. Birds chirping. Fall leaves crunching. Breeze rustling. And winds up screaming in the back of an unmarked van.

Life changes in an instant, with no soundtrack to be your guide.

Which leaves someone like me, jumping at all noises because I don't know how to tell the difference.

I wanted to be like the rest of my urban neighbors, who, when awakened in the middle of the night by their front buzzer, could heartily declare "Fuck off!" before rolling over and going back to sleep. Now, there was a way to live.

I trudged back to my bedroom, lit by three separate nightlights. I stretched out on my twin-size bed, dancing my fingers across the narrow width.

And I let myself imagine, for a moment, what it might be like if Bobby Dodge wasn't a detective and I wasn't a victim? suspect? witness? Maybe we were two ordinary people, meeting at a church social. I'd brought the three-bean salad. He'd brought that perennial bachelor favorite—a bag of tortilla chips. We could talk kickboxing, dogs, white picket fences. Afterwards, I'd let him walk me home. He would slide his arms around my waist. And instead of going rigid with distrust, I would let myself sink into him. The feel of a hard male body, the plane of his chest flattening out my breasts. The ticklish rasp of his whiskers in the instant before he kissed me.

We could have dinner, go out to the movies, spend entire weekends having sex. On the sofa, in the bedroom, on top of the kitchen counter. He was fit, athletic. I bet he'd be very good at sex.

We could even become boyfriend and girlfriend, the way other people did. And I would be normal and not search for his name or likeness in the sex offenders' database.

Except I wasn't normal. I lived with too many years of fear stamped into my psyche. And he lived with the weight of a man's death hanging around his neck. His job already had him lying and manipulating me. My past had me lying and manipulating him. Both of us thought we were right.

I wondered for the first time how well Bobby slept at night. And if we ever did get together, which one of us would be the first to wake up screaming. The thought should've sobered me. Instead, it made me smile. We were both twisted, he and I. Maybe, if given enough time, we could find out if our twistedness made us fit.

I sighed. Rolled over. Listened to the pitter-patter of Bella returning to the bedroom, taking up position next to my bed. I stroked her ears, told her I loved her. It made us both feel better.

Much to my surprise, I relaxed. My eyes drifted

shut. I might have started to dream.

Then the buzzer came again. Loud, shrill, jolting. Again and again and again. A violent onslaught of sound, ricocheting through my tiny apartment.

I leapt from my bed, ran to the window. Streetlights bombarded the slick black space but gave up nothing. Into the kitchen now, skipping forward on the balls of my feet, muscles bunched, Taser ready, eyes glued to the strip beneath the door.

Spotting a telltale shadow.

I froze. Caught my breath. Stared.

Slowly I got down on my hands and knees. I peered beneath the door, desperately searching the framed view of a tiny slice of hall. Not feet. Not a man.

Something else. Something small, rectangular, and perfectly wrapped in bright colored paper, the Sunday comic strips . . .

I rocked back on my heels. Then I attacked my door, frantically working the half-dozen locks as my heart pounded with fear and my hands shook with rage. Bella was barking as the chain lock fell free. Together, we barreled out into the fifth-floor landing, where I stood, half-naked, wielding my Taser and roaring at the top of my lungs: *"Where are you, motherfucker? Come out and fight like a man. You want a piece of me?"*

I leapt over the wrapped package. Bella thundered downstairs. We careened into the downstairs lobby, fueled by pure adrenaline and ready to take on an entire army.

But the building was empty, the stairs deserted, the lobby vacant. I followed the sound of thumping to the front foyer, where I found the building's outer door open and banging in the wind.

I pushed the door wide. Felt the cold onslaught of rain slashing across my face. The night was storming. It was nothing compared to how I felt inside.

No sign of life out on the street. I secured the outer door, called Bella back up the stairs.

Outside my apartment it was still waiting for me. A flat, rectangular box. Snoopy, perched on his red doghouse, smiled on top.

And suddenly, I couldn't take it anymore. Twenty-five years had not been enough. My father's training had not been enough. The threat was back, but I still didn't know who to fight, how to attack, where to direct my rage.

Which left me with only the fear. Of every shadow in my darkened apartment. Of every sound in this old creaky building. Of every person who might randomly wander down the street.

I left the package on the landing. I grabbed Bella by the collar and dragged her into the bathroom, where I locked the door, climbed into the tub, and prayed for the night to end.

"You're sure you didn't see anything?" Bobby was asking. "A car, a person, the back of a coat disappearing down the street?"

I didn't answer. Just watched him pace back and

forth in the three-foot expanse of my kitchen.

"What about a voice? Did he speak, make any kind of sound coming or going up and down the stairs?"

I still didn't say anything. Bobby had been asking the same questions for hours now. What little I'd had to offer was already on record. Now it was about him burning off steam and trying to come to terms with events I still refused to accept.

For example, twenty-five years later, the unidentified white male subject had found me again.

My phone had rung shortly after four a.m., another sharp and shrill noise that made my blood run cold. But the voice that came through my answering machine was not a taunting lunatic's. Just Bobby, demanding for me to pick up.

His voice grounded me, restored my sense of purpose. For him, I had to leave the tub, open the bathroom door, brave my darkened apartment. For him, I could lift the receiver, cradling the cordless phone against my ear as I grimly snapped on lights and reported the night's events.

Bobby hadn't needed me to say much. Two minutes later he was off the phone and on his way to my apartment.

He had arrived with a bunch of men in rumpled suits. Three detectives—Sinkus, McGahagin, Rock. In their wake came a troop of uniformed officers, quickly put to work canvassing my building. The crime-scene techs arrived next, working the front doors, lobby, stairwell.

My neighbors hadn't been happy to be awakened before dawn, but they were intrigued enough to be out now watching the free show.

Bella had gone insane at the sight of so many strangers overrunning her home. Finally, I'd shut her up in Bobby's car; it was the only way the crime-scene techs were going to be able to get the job done. No one was terribly optimistic. Last night's showers had turned into a gray morning mist. Rain washed away evidence. Even I knew that.

The crime-scene techs had started in the foyer and were now working their way upstairs, black fingerprint powder flying everywhere. They were homing in on ground zero, a small, four-by-six-inch rectangular box, neatly wrapped in the comics, waiting outside my door.

No note. No bow. The package didn't require introductions. I already knew who'd sent it.

My apartment door opened again. This time, D.D. entered. Immediately, activity ground to a halt, all eyes on the sergeant. D.D. appeared pale but moved with her usual grim-faced efficiency. Not bad for a woman with a fat patch of gauze taped to the lower half of her cheek.

"You should not—" Bobby began.

"Oh please!" D.D. rolled her eyes. "What the fuck are you gonna do, handcuff me to the hospital bed?"

According to Bobby, D.D. had nearly been mauled to death by an attack dog merely hours ago. Leave it to her not to let a little thing like almost getting killed slow her down.

"When did the package arrive?" she asked crisply, clearly off the bench and back in the game.

"Around three twenty a.m.," Bobby said.

Her gaze flickered to me. "Same as you remember?"

"Yes," I said quietly. "At least from the outside, the box reminds me of the gifts I received when I was young. He always wrapped them in the comic strips."

"What'd you see?"

"Nothing. I searched the building, the street. By the time I opened my door, he was gone."

D.D. sighed. "Just as well. We sustained enough damage for one night."

Detective Sinkus came over. "We're ready," he announced. He had a stain on his left shoulder. It looked like spit-up.

Bobby hesitated, glancing at me.

"You can leave," he offered. "Wait downstairs while we open it up."

I gave him a look that said enough. He shrugged, so obviously my reaction was expected.

He motioned the crime-scene technician over. The man brought the box into the kitchen and set it on the counter. The four of us clustered around, elbow to elbow, and watched the scientist go to work. He used what looked like a surgical scalpel, carefully easing the tape up from each seam, then unwrapping the paper from the box with the detached precision of an artist.

It took four minutes, then the Sunday comics were off, unfolded to reveal the full *Peanuts* strip—who doesn't love Snoopy and Charlie Brown?—plus the remnants of a few other strips on the front page. Inside the wrappings was a simple glossy white gift box. The top wasn't taped on. The technician eased it off.

White tissue paper. The technician unfolded the right side. Then the left, revealing the treasure.

I saw colors first. Stripes of pink, both dark and light. Then the technician lifted the fabric from the box, letting it unfold like a pink shower, and my breath caught in my throat.

A blanket. Dark pink flannel, with light pink satin trim. I staggered back.

Bobby saw my expression and caught my arm. "What is it?"

I tried to open my mouth. Tried to speak. But the shock was too much. It wasn't mine—it couldn't be—but it looked like mine. And I was horrified and I was terrified, but I also dearly wanted to reach out and touch the baby blanket, see if it would feel as I remembered it once feeling, the soft flannel and cool satin sliding between my fingers, soothing against my cheek.

"It's a blanket," D.D. announced. "Like for a baby. Price tag, receipt? Any markings on the box?"

She was talking to the scientist. He had finished spreading out the blanket, turning it this way and that with his gloved fingers. Now he returned to the box, removing the tissue paper, inspecting it inside and out. He raised his head and shook it.

I finally found my voice. "He knows."

"Knows?" Bobby pressed.

"The blanket. When I lived in Arlington, I had a blankie. Dark pink flannel, light pink satin trim. Just like that."

"This is your baby blanket?" D.D. asked in shock.

"No, not my actual blanket. Mine was a little bigger, much more worn around the edges. But it's close, probably as close as he could find, to replicate the original blanket."

I still wanted to touch it. Somehow, that seemed sacrilegious, like accepting a gift from the devil. I fisted my hands at my sides, digging my nails into my palms. All at once, I felt queasy, lightheaded.

How could this one person know me so well, when I still didn't know anything about him at all? Oh God, how could you fight an evil that seemed so incredibly omnipotent?

"In the original police report," Bobby was saying now, "they found a cache of Polaroids in the attic of the neighbor's house. How much do you want to bet some of those snapshots are of Annabelle carrying her favorite blankie?"

"Son of a bitch," I whispered.

"With a very good memory," D.D. added grimly.

The scientist had gotten out a paper bag. Up top, with a big black Sharpie, he wrote a number and a brief description. A moment later, the imposter blanket became a piece of evidence. Next went the box and tissue paper. Then the Sunday comics.

My kitchen counter returned to bare space. The crime-scene technician exited with his latest treasures. You could almost pretend it had never happened. Almost.

I walked into the living room. I peered out the window, where I counted a dozen sedans, police cruisers, detectives' vehicles, etc., parked along the curb. From this height, I could see the roof of Bobby's Crown Vic. The back windows were cracked open. I could just make out the moist black tip of Bella's nose, poking out.

I wish I had her with me right now. I could use someone to hold.

"And you swear you didn't see anyone outside the building." D.D. crossed back over to me. "Maybe earlier in the evening?"

I shook my head.

"What about at work? Someone standing in line at Starbucks or who showed up later when you left Faneuil Hall?"

"I'm careful," I said. While I'd handed out business cards to both Mr. Petracelli and Charlie Marvin, that only gave them a P.O. box, not my street address. The cards also had my work phone number, which a reverse directory would simply trace back to the P.O. box. Something I should've considered days ago, when I gave out my home number to Bobby, and thus apparently invited over half the Boston PD.

"How many people now know you as Annabelle?" Bobby took up position next to D.D.

Logical question. I was still tart. "You, Sergeant Warren, the detectives unit—"

"Very funny."

"Mr. and Mrs. Petracelli. Catherine Gagnon. Oh, and Charlie Marvin."

"What?"

D.D. didn't sound happy. Come to think of it, she never did.

I related my conversation with Charlie Marvin from the night before. The Cliff's Notes version. At the end of my spiel, Bobby sighed. "Why on earth did you tell Charlie your real name?"

"It's been twenty-five years," I mocked. "What do I have to fear?"

"You know more about basic self-defense than anyone in this room, Annabelle. What was the point of getting the education if you're only going to play stupid?"

That pissed me off. "Hey, don't you have a child killer to catch?"

"Hey, what the hell do you think we're doing here? Annabelle, one week ago you started using your real name for the first time in twenty-five years. Now you got a gift on your doorstep. Do I really need to connect the dots?"

"No, you don't, you big jackass. I'm the one who hid in a bathtub. I know how scared I am."

I hit him. Not hard. Not even personally. But because I was tired and scared and frustrated and didn't have a real target to strike. He accepted the thump without protest. Just stared at me with those steady gray eyes.

Belatedly, I realized the other officers were

watching us. And D.D.'s gaze was ping-ponging between Bobby and me, connecting some dots of her own. I jerked away, desperately needing space.

I was sorry I'd welcomed Bobby. I wanted the cops gone. I wanted the crime-scene techs gone. I wanted to be alone, so I could pull out five suitcases and start packing.

The front buzzer blasted. I jumped, bit my tongue. D.D. and Bobby were already gone, hitting the stairs at a run. At the last minute, my fear shamed me. Dammit, I wasn't going to live like this!

I headed for the door. One of the detectives—Sinkus, I think—tried to grab my arm. I swatted him away. He was softer and slower than Bobby; never stood a chance. I cleared the top landing and careened wildly down the stairs. My neighbors were already scurrying into the relative safety of their apartments, doors slamming, locks clicking.

On the last flight of stairs, I grabbed the wood railing, executing a neat, flying leap over the side. I hit the floor hard, went barreling out the door, only to draw up short.

There stood Ben, my aging UPS man, standing at rigid attention while his eyes nearly bugged out of his head. Bobby and D.D. were already on him.

"Tanya?" Ben squeaked.

And that quickly, I started to laugh. It was the semi-hysterical laughter of a woman who's been reduced to terrifying her delivery man for dropping off her latest order of fabric.

"It's okay," I said, trying to sound calm, hearing the wobble in my voice.

"If you could please hand me that box," Bobby ordered.

Ben handed over the box. "She needs to sign for it," he whispered. "Can I . . . Should I . . . Holy Lord."

Ben shut up. One more minute of Bobby's glare, and the poor man was going to pee his pants.

"Smith and Noble," Bobby verified curtly, reading the return address.

"Curtains," I said. "Custom-made fabric shades, to be exact. It's okay, honestly. I get a package a day, right, Ben?"

This time I stepped forward, positioning myself between Bobby and my delivery man.

"It's okay," I repeated. "There was an incident. In the building. The police are checking things out."

"Bella?" Ben asked. In the four years I've known him, I've figured out that Ben doesn't really care for people. He's sort of an anti-delivery man—not so much into his customers, as into his customers' dogs.

"She's okay."

As if on cue, Bella finally heard my voice and, from the back of Bobby's car, started to bark. Far from reassuring Ben, he followed the noise to an unmarked police car and grew wide-eyed all over again.

"But she's a good dog!" he exploded.

And now I almost did laugh, except again, it just wasn't going to be a happy sort of sound.

"We needed her out of the apartment," I tried to

explain. "Bella's fine. You can go over to her. She'd love to see you."

Ben didn't seem to know what to do. Bobby was still holding the box of fabric, scowling. D.D. appeared just plain disgusted with life.

Executive-decision time. I grabbed Ben's wrist by the cuff of his brown uniform and led him to Bobby's car. Bella had her head half through the cracked-open window, barking joyfully. That seemed to do the trick.

Ben dug in his pockets for cookies and we all resumed life as we knew it.

Bella milked him for four dog bones. By the time we returned to the front of my building, the moment had lost its *Miami Vice* intensity and we all tried again.

Bobby had some questions for Ben. What was his route? How often was he in the neighborhood? What times of day? Ever notice anyone lurking around the building?

Ben, it turned out, was a twenty-year UPS veteran. Knew the streets of Boston like the back of his hand. In particular, liked to cut down my street about half a dozen times a day to avoid the congestion on Atlantic. Hadn't noticed anyone, but then, he really hadn't looked. Why would he?

A UPS man's life wasn't easy, I learned. Lots of boxes, complex delivery schedules, intricate routes mapped for maximum efficiency, only to be blown to hell by last-minute arrivals of priority packages. Stress, stress, stress, and then there was Christmas. But apparently, the gig offered a great retirement package.

The thought of someone lurking outside my unit, perhaps stalking Bella and me, had Ben troubled. He would keep a lookout, he promised Bobby. Could probably even work a way to pass through the street a few more times a day. Yeah, he could do that.

Ben wasn't a spring chicken. I pegged his age in the fifties, and he had the oversize bottle-thick glasses and a graying mustache to go with it. His job kept him active, though; he had a fit, rangy build just starting to go soft in the middle. Bobby twenty years from now. Beneath the rim of his brown UPS-issued baseball cap was the face of a former boxer—the crooked nose that had taken one too many punches, a hairline scar running down the left side of his chin from a rebuilt jaw, which twisted his lower face slightly to the left.

Now Ben squared his shoulders, puffed out his chest. Very solemnly, he shook Bobby's hand.

So I had the entire Boston PD, plus one UPS man, standing guard. I ought to sleep like a baby at night.

Ben departed. Bobby carried my box back into the building. I followed behind and decided that I was just plain depressed.

31

I CAUGHT D.D. and Bobby arguing fifteen minutes later. I was supposed to be sitting on my couch, being a good girl. I was too wired for sitting, however, and still couldn't get used to so many bodies crowding my little space. No one seemed to care what I was doing. So I went downstairs to check on Bella.

Bobby and D.D. were outside, by the curb. No other detectives around. I heard D.D.'s tone first and the anger in it brought me up short.

"What the hell do you think you're doing?" D.D. snarled.

"I don't know what you're talking about." Bobby, pretending to be blasé, but already defensive, so apparently he knew exactly what D.D. had on her mind.

I tucked back inside the foyer, ear pressed against the cracked outer door.

"You're involved with her," D.D. accused.

"Who?"

D.D. whacked his arm. I heard the smack.

"Ow! What the hell? Is it beat up on Bobby day?"

"Don't play cute. We've known each other too long."

Pause. Then, when Bobby still didn't say anything: "Jesus, Bobby, what is it with you? First Catherine, now Annabelle. What do you have, a Messiah complex? Can only fall for the damsel in distress? You're a detective. You're supposed to know better."

"I've done nothing wrong." Bobby, steelier this time.

"I saw the way you looked at her."

"Oh, for Christ's sake—"

"So it's true, isn't it? Come on, if it isn't, look me in the eye."

The silence grew long again. I could tell Bobby wasn't looking D.D. in the eye.

"Goddammit!" D.D. said.

"I've done nothing wrong," he repeated stiffly.

"What, that makes you noble? Bobby . . . You know, I was doing my best to overlook the Catherine thing. So you got involved with her. So you lost all common sense. God knows she has that kind of effect on men. But then to have you turn around and do it again . . . Is this why we broke up, Bobby? Because for you to fall in love, the woman's got to be some kind of a victim?"

Oooh, that really pissed me off. It seemed to get Bobby's goat, too.

"You wanna call the shots, hey, I like a challenge as well as the next guy, D.D. Except we never challenged each other, you and I. We're duplicates, D.D. We live our job, eat our job, breathe our job. And when we dated, we brought our jobs along for the ride. Hell, we've known each other ten years, and I just found out six hours ago that you have an uncle. And like Rottweilers. It never came up, because *we never stopped talking shop.* Even when we were in bed, we were cops."

"Hey, there is more to me than this job!" D.D. shot back, and for a horrible moment, I thought she was going to cry.

"Ah Jesus," Bobby said tiredly.

"Stop it." Another *thwack.* I was guessing he'd tried to touch her. "Don't you *dare* pity me."

"Look, D.D. You wanna get personal? Then call a spade a spade. You were never with me for the long haul. I was a curiosity, an elite sniper who sounded pretty cool when he talked about his gun. We both know you've got much bigger game in your sights."

"Now, that's low."

"Well, we're not exactly standing around exchanging compliments."

A long, hard pause.

"She's trouble, Bobby."

"I'm a big boy."

"You haven't done this kind of major case. You can't get personally involved."

"Thanks for the vote of confidence. Now, do you have something specific you need to tell me, sergeant to detective? Because if not, I'm going back inside."

There was the sound of rustling clothes, then a sudden stop. I think D.D. grabbed his arm. "I went to my house, Bobby. I can't find any sign of an intruder. My doors are locked, my windows intact. But Sinkus was right; the underwear is mine. Someone broke in, stole the underwear out of my hamper, and was very, very clever about it."

"The crime-scene techs—"

"There'll be no evidence, Bobby. Just like they've found nothing here. I think that gives us a pretty clear lay of the land."

"Ah nuts. As soon as we're done here, I'll head over with you, look around."

She must have appeared dubious, because he declared with some exasperation, "Former tac team, D.D. I know a thing or two about breaking and entering."

"Please, you guys ram the door with a giant metal 'key.' Your style and our subject's style . . . very far removed."

"Yeah, yeah, yeah," Bobby muttered, but he sounded troubled. "That's what's bugging me—the stalking MO fits but . . . Twenty-five years ago, when the subject first operated, his target was young females. Seven-year-old Annabelle Granger, her best friend, Dori Petracelli. Now, suddenly, he's into grown women? You, Annabelle . . . I'm not a profiler, but I didn't think that sort of thing happened."

"Maybe our ages aren't relevant to him. Annabelle is the one who got away. Having found her again, he's determined that she doesn't escape. And as for me . . . I'm lead investigator. He wants to yank my chain. But I'm also less personal to him, which is why he didn't mind sending dogs instead of doing the deed himself. She's his life's work. I'm a hobby."

"Encouraging thought."

"Especially for me. Who wants to be killed as an afterthought? Also, Bobby, look at Eola. Most people believe he killed a nurse at Boston State Mental. So if Eola is our man, you're talking about someone with a history of targeting females regardless of age. Wasn't Bundy like that? We think of him as attacking college coeds, but some of his victims were quite young. These guys . . . who the hell knows what really makes 'em tick?"

Bobby didn't say anything right away. Then he said, "You still consider Russell Granger a suspect?"

"I will until you prove otherwise."

"Came back from the dead?" Bobby murmured wryly.

D.D. surprised us both. "Spoke with the ME last night, Bobby. Given the current *demands* on your time, I figured I'd do you a favor and follow up on the circumstances surrounding Annabelle's father's death. According to the file, police contacted Annabelle—Tanya—she made the ID, and that was good enough for the ME. Think about it, Bobby. The face was a mess. The ME's office never ran prints or documented any identifying marks—it was just a hit-and-run, and the guy's daughter identified the body. Meaning that corpse could've been anyone carrying Michael W. Nelson's driver's license. A stranger, a vagrant. Some poor slob he pushed into oncoming traffic . . ."

D.D.'s words seemed to have struck Bobby dumb. Which was good, because I didn't think I could hear above the torrent of blood rushing in my ears. D.D. thought my father was still alive? Theorized he might have killed someone else to fake his own death? Honestly believed he was the evil mastermind behind this homicidal crime spree?

But that was absurd. My father wasn't a killer! Not of little girls, not of Dori Petracelli, not of grown men. He never would've done such a thing.

He wouldn't have left me.

My legs gave out. My shoulder hit the front door, pushing it open. D.D. and Bobby didn't notice. They were too busy analyzing their case, ripping apart my father, turning one of the few truths I knew into a giant lie.

We hadn't left Arlington because my father needed to cover his tracks. We had moved to protect me. We had moved because . . .

"Roger, please don't go. Roger, I'm begging you, please don't do this. . . ."

"*Whoever* it is," Bobby was saying now, still sounding clearly skeptical, "the UNSUB wants attention. And for all his 'cleverness' he's making no attempt at being subtle. He left a note on your car, a gift at Annabelle's front door. Why? If he's that brilliant, why not kill both of you and be done with it? He wants the chase. He wants the opportunity to show off. Which is exactly how we're going to catch him. He's going to reach out again, and when he does, we'll nail his ass."

"Hope you're right," D.D. murmured. "Because I'm pretty sure, a guy like this has something scary planned next."

They turned, headed toward the front steps. Belatedly, I stumbled to my feet, bolting up the stairs. Detectives Sinkus and McGahagin looked at me curiously as I swept into my apartment. I went straight into the bedroom. Closed the door.

Seconds passed. Eventually, I heard a tentative knock.

I didn't say anything. Whoever knocked went away.

I sat on my narrow bed, clutching the vial of ashes around my neck and wondering if even it contained a lie.

• • •

In the end, it was my fault. My phone started ringing. I didn't feel like leaving my room to answer it. So naturally, the answering machine picked up. And naturally, Mr. Petracelli left his message with half of the Boston PD listening in.

"Annabelle, I found the sketch from the Neighborhood Watch meeting, as you requested. Of course, I'd prefer not to mail these materials. I suppose I can make it back into the city if you really want me to. Same time, same place? Give me a buzz." He rattled off a number. I sat on my bed and sighed.

The knock that came on my bedroom door this time was not a request.

I opened the door to find Bobby standing there, a very dark look on his face. "Sketch? Same time? Same place?"

"Hey," I said brightly. "Want to go for a ride?"

Mr. Petracelli was relieved to hear he wouldn't have to make the dreaded drive into the city. Bella also thought heading out was a grand idea. Which just left Bobby and me, sitting up front, careful not to meet each other's eyes.

Traffic was light. Bobby called into Dispatch, requesting a background check on my old neighbors. It intrigued me not to be the only one who was paranoid, for a change. Generally, I ran the name of everyone I met through Google.

"Where's D.D.?" I finally asked.

"Had to attend to other business."

"Eola?" I fished.

He slanted me a look. "And how would you know that name, Annabelle?"

I went with a bald-faced lie. "The Internet."

He arched a brow, clearly not fooled, but didn't ignore my question. "D.D. is in the process of running a crime scene in her own home. The subject may have left a gift at your door, but he broke into D.D.'s home and stole her underwear."

"It's because she's a blonde," I said, which only earned me another droll gaze.

We pulled into the Petracellis' driveway.

The tiny gray cape seemed to blend into the overcast sky. White shutters. Small green yard. The right home for an elderly couple who would never have grand-kids.

"Mr. Petracelli never thought the Lawrence police took his daughter's case seriously enough," I volunteered as we got out of the car. Bella whined. I told her to stay. "If you mention you're looking into a connection between Dori's disappearance and my stalker, I think Mr. Petracelli will open up."

"I talk, you listen," Bobby informed me coldly.

Badass, I mouthed behind his back, but didn't say a word as we headed up the flagstone walk.

Bobby rang the doorbell. Mrs. Petracelli opened the door. She sighed when she saw the two of us. Gave me a look I can only describe as deeply apologetic.

"Walter," she said calmly, "your guests are here."

Mr. Petracelli came bounding down the stairs with far more energy than I remembered from my previous visit. He had an accordion-style file folder tucked under his right arm and a bright, almost surreal gleam in his eyes.

"Come in, come in," he said jovially. He shook Bobby's hand, mine, too, then glanced around as if searching for my attack dog. "I was excited to hear you were coming, Detective. And so soon! I have the information, absolutely, it's all right here. Oh, but wait, look at us, standing in the foyer. How rude of me. Let's make ourselves comfortable in the study. Lana dear—some coffee?"

Lana sighed again, headed for the kitchen. Bobby and I trailed after Mr. Petracelli as he went skipping to the study. Once there, he plopped himself on the edge of a leather wingback chair, eagerly opening up his file folder, spreading out sheets of paper. Compared to his ominous, brooding approach last night, he was practically whistling as he pulled out page after page bearing the grim details of his daughter's abduction.

"So you're with the Boston PD?" he asked Bobby.

"Detective Robert Dodge, sir, Massachusetts State Police."

"Excellent! I always said the state should be involved. The locals just don't have enough resources. Small towns equal small cops equal small minds." Mr. Petracelli seemed to finally have all his paperwork arranged just so. He glanced up, happened to notice that Bobby and I both still lingered in the doorway.

"Sit, sit, please, make yourselves at home. I've been keeping detailed notes for years. We have quite a bit to cover."

I sat on the edge of a green plaid love seat, Bobby wedged beside me. Mrs. Petracelli appeared, depositing coffee cups, cream, sugar. She departed as quickly as possible. I didn't blame her.

"Now, about November twelve, 1982 . . ."

Mr. Petracelli had indeed kept scrupulous notes. Over the years, he'd developed an elaborate time line of the last day of Dori's life. He knew when she got up. What she ate for breakfast. What clothes she selected, what toys she had in the yard. At approximately noon, her grandmother told her it was time for lunch. Dori had wanted a tea party instead, with her collection of stuffed bears on the picnic table. Not seeing the harm, Dori's grandmother had delivered a plate of peanut butter and jelly sandwiches, crusts cut off, plus a sliced apple. Last she had seen, Dori was passing out treats among her plush guests. Dori's grandmother went inside to tidy up the kitchen, then got caught up talking to a neighbor on the phone. When she returned out front twenty minutes later, the bears were still sitting, each with a bite of sandwich and apple in front of its nose. Dori was nowhere to be found.

Mr. Petracelli knew when the first call had been placed to 911. He knew the name of the officer who had responded, what questions were asked, how they were answered. He had notes on the search parties formed, lists of the volunteers who showed up—some of whom he'd asterisked for never giving a satisfactory alibi for what they were doing between 12:15 and 12:35 that afternoon. He knew the dog handlers who volunteered their services. The divers who eventually tended to the nearby ponds. He had seven days' worth of police and local activity distilled into elaborate chronological graphs and comprehensive lists of names.

Then he had the information from my father.

I couldn't tell from Bobby's face what he thought of Mr. Petracelli's presentation. Mr. Petracelli's voice raised and lowered with various stages of intensity, sometimes even spitting words as he hashed out obvious failings in what seemed to be a thorough search for a missing girl. Bobby's expression remained impassive. Mr. Petracelli talked. From time to time, Bobby took notes. But mostly Bobby listened, his face betraying nothing.

Personally, I wanted to see the sketch. I wanted to gaze at the face of the man I believed had targeted me, sentenced my family to a lifetime on the run, then killed my best friend.

The reality was disappointing.

I had expected an angrier-looking man. A black-and-white sketch with dark, shifty eyes, the tattoo of a teardrop topping the right cheek. Instead, the artfully rendered drawing, my father's work most certainly, appeared almost pedantic. The subject was young— early twenties, I would guess. Short dark hair. Dark eyes. Small, almost refined-looking jawline. Not a thug at all. In fact, the picture reminded me of the kid who used to work in the neighborhood pizza parlor.

I studied the drawing for a long time, waiting for it to speak to me, tell me all its secrets. It remained a crude sketch of a young man who, frankly, could be any one of tens of thousands of twenty-year-old, dark-haired males who'd passed through Boston.

I didn't get it. My father had run from this?

Bobby asked Mr. Petracelli if he had a fax machine. In fact, we could both see one standing on the desk behind Mr. Petracelli. Bobby explained it might be faster if he faxed the notes, etc., into the office right away, for the other detectives to get started. Mr. Petracelli was overjoyed to have someone finally take his file seriously.

I watched Bobby punch in the fax number. He included an area code, which wouldn't have been necessary for a Boston exchange. And the only piece of paper he fed into the machine was the sketch.

Bobby sent the rest of the pages through the fax on copy function, helping himself to the duplicates. Mr. Petracelli was rocking back and forth on the edge of his chair, his face unnaturally red, his smile beaming. The excitement of the moment had obviously spiked his blood pressure. I wondered how soon before the next heart attack. I wondered if he'd make his goal of living long enough to see his daughter's body recovered.

We drained our coffee cups, just to be polite. Mr.

Petracelli seemed reluctant for us to depart, shaking our hands again and again.

When we finally made it out to the car, Mr. Petracelli stood on the front porch, waving, waving, waving.

My last glance of him was as we drove down the street. He became a small, hunch-shouldered old man, face too red, smile too bright, still waving determinedly at the police detective he firmly believed would finally bring his daughter home.

"You faxed the sketch to Catherine Gagnon," I said the moment we hit the highway. "Why?"

"Your father showed Catherine a sketch when she was in the hospital," he said abruptly.

"He did?"

"I want to see if it's the same drawing."

"But that's not possible! Catherine was in the hospital in '80, and that sketch wasn't done until two years later."

"How do you know?"

"Because the stalker dude didn't start delivering gifts until August of 1982. And you can't have a sketch of the stalker dude without any stalker."

"There's only one problem with that."

"There is?"

"According to the police reports, no one ever saw the face of the 'stalker dude.' Not your father or mother, not Mrs. Watts, and not any of your neighbors. In theory, therefore, stalker dude could not have served as the basis for that drawing."

Well, that was a stumper. I stewed on it, telling myself there was a logical explanation, while realizing I was using that line a lot lately. My father had known something in 1980, I decided. Something serious enough to drive him to masquerade as an FBI agent and visit Catherine with a sketch in hand. But what?

I tried searching my memory banks. I'd been only five in 1980. Living in Arlington and . . .

I couldn't get anything to come to mind. Not even the memory of a comic-strip-wrapped gift. I was certain those started arriving two years later, when I was seven.

The silence was finally broken by the chirping of the cell phone clipped to Bobby's waist. He retrieved it, exchanged a few terse words, slid a look at me sideways. He flipped it shut, seemed about to speak, then the phone rang again.

This time, his voice was different. Polite, professional. The voice of a detective addressing a stranger. He seemed to be trying to work out a meeting, and it wasn't going his way.

"When do you leave for the conference? I'll be honest, sir, I need to meet with you as soon as possible. It involves one of your former professors. Russell Granger—"

Even I could hear the sudden squawk on the other end of the line. And then, that quickly, Bobby was nodding.

"Where do you live again? Lexington. As a matter

of fact, I happen to be right around the corner."

He glanced at me. I answered with a shrug, grateful that I didn't have to elaborate. Obviously, Bobby was trying to set up an interview with my father's former boss and obviously it needed to happen now.

I didn't mind. Of course, there was no way in hell I was waiting in the car.

32

"TIME TO TAKE Bella for a walk," Bobby announced as he drove through a winding side street just north of the Minuteman Statue in Lexington Center. Paul Schuepp had given his house number as 58. Bobby spotted 26, then 32, so he was moving in the right direction. "Looks like a nice area to stretch your legs."

Annabelle took it about as well as he expected. "Ha ha ha. Very funny."

"I mean it. This is an official police investigation."

"Then you'd better start deputizing me, because I'm going in."

House number 48 . . . There, the white colonial with the red brick façade. "You know, it's not exactly the Wild Wild West anymore."

"Have you read the latest accounts of shootings in the city? Could've fooled me."

Bobby pulled into the driveway. He had a decision to make. Spend ten minutes of the thirty Schuepp had agreed to spare arguing with Annabelle, or let her tag along and receive another lecture on proper policing techniques from D.D. He was still annoyed from his last conversation with the sergeant, which, frankly, didn't work in D.D.'s favor.

Bobby popped his door and didn't say a word as Annabelle followed suit.

"Detective Sinkus tracked down Charlie Marvin," he filled her in as they headed for the front door. "Marvin spent the night at the Pine Street Inn, from midnight to eight a.m. Nine homeless and three staff members vouched for him. So whoever came to your building with that gift, it wasn't him."

Annabelle merely grunted. No doubt Charlie Marvin made a good suspect in her mind. On the one hand, he was an urban cross between a priest and Santa Claus. On the other hand, he wasn't her father.

Bobby would like to say he didn't believe Annabelle's father had returned from the dead either. Except he was growing more and more puzzled by the hour. Mr. Petracelli had been a poignant lesson in the power of obsession. Bobby would have an officer follow up on Mr. Petracelli's whereabouts late last night, though, in all honesty, delivering comic-strip-wrapped presents was probably a shade too subtle for someone who was obviously mad as a hatter.

The sketch was the key, Bobby decided. Who had Russell Granger known, and why had he felt threatened nearly two years before filing that first police report?

It had become clear to Bobby within the first five minutes of meeting Walter Petracelli that Annabelle's former neighbor didn't hold the key to those answers. Perhaps Bobby would get luckier with Russell's former boss, whom Bobby had first buzzed at seven this morning from outside Annabelle's apartment. Seemed lately all he did was work his cell phone. Yet, still the *demands* on his time had D.D. operating behind his back. Reaching out to the ME in a thinly veiled attempt to bolster her own theory of the case . . . just thinking about it pissed him off all over again.

Bobby found the brass knocker, strategically located in the middle of a giant wreath of red berries. Three knocks and half a dozen berry droppings later, the door swung open.

Bobby's first impression of Paul Schuepp: about two inches taller than Yoda and two years younger than dirt. The small, wizened former head of MIT's mathematics department had sparse gray hair, an age-spotted scalp, and rheumy blue eyes that peered out from beneath bushy white eyebrows. Schuepp's face was sinking down with the years, revealing red-rimmed eyelids, shaky jowls, and extra folds of skin flapping around his neck.

Schuepp stuck out a gnarled hand, catching Bobby's arm in an unexpectedly firm grip. "Come in, come in. Good to see you, Detective. And this is . . . ?"

Schuepp suddenly stopped, droopy eyes widening. "I'll be damned. If you're not the spitting image of your mother. Annabelle, isn't it? All grown up. I'll be damned. Please, please, come in. Now, this is an honor. I'm going to fetch us some coffee. Oh hell, it's gotta be noon somewhere. I'm fetching us some scotch!"

Schuepp set off at a brisk shuffle, heading through the arched foyer into the formal living room. There, another arched doorway led into the dining room, where a right-hand turn took him into the kitchen.

Bobby and Annabelle followed the man through his house, Bobby taking in the heavy floral furniture, the delicate crocheted doilies, the eucalyptus swags gracing the tops of floor-length mauve drapes. He was hoping there was a Mrs. Schuepp somewhere, because life was too scary if Mr. Schuepp had done the deco-rating.

The kitchen was country-style, with oak cabinets and a massive oval walnut table. A lazy Susan in the middle of the table boasted sugar, salt, and a small pharmacy of drugs. Schuepp fiddled with the cof-feemaker, then moved on to the pantry, where after much clinking of glass, he withdrew a bottle of Chivas Regal.

"Coffee's probably gonna taste like crap," he announced. "The missus passed away last year. Now, *she* could brew a cup of coffee. Personally," he added, dropping the Chivas in the middle of the table, "I rec-ommend the scotch."

Annabelle was gazing at the man wide-eyed. He produced three glasses. When Annabelle and Bobby begged off, he shrugged, poured himself two fingers, and tossed it down. For a moment, Schuepp's scalp turned bright red. He wheezed and started to cough, and Bobby had images of his interview subject suddenly dropping dead. But then the former professor recovered, thumping his shrunken chest.

"I'm not much of a drinker," Schuepp told them. "Given the occasion, however, I could use a belt."

"Do you know why we're here?" Annabelle inquired softly.

"Let me ask you this, young lady: When did your dear father die?"

"Nearly ten years ago."

"Made it that long? Good for him. Where?"

"Actually, we'd returned to Boston."

"Really? Hmmm, interesting. And if you don't mind me asking, how?"

"Hit by a taxicab while crossing the street."

Schuepp arched a bushy white brow, nodding to himself. "And your mother?"

Annabelle hesitated. "Eighteen years ago. Kansas City."

"How?"

"Overdosed. Booze mixed with painkillers. She, um, she'd developed a drinking problem along the way. I found her when I returned home from school."

Bobby shot her a glance. She'd already volunteered more details for Schuepp than she'd ever given him.

"Collateral damage," Schuepp observed matter-of-factly. "Makes some sense. Shall we?" He gestured toward the table. "Coffee's ready, though I insist you should try the scotch."

He returned to the kitchen, loading the coffeepot,

cups, and creamer on a tray. Bobby took it from him without asking, mostly because he couldn't picture a hundred-pound man lifting a ten-pound tray. Schuepp smiled his appreciation.

They made it to the table, Bobby's mind whirling, Annabelle looking paler by the second.

"You knew my father," she stated.

"I had the honor to serve as head of the department of mathematics for nearly twenty years. Your father was there for five of them. Not nearly long enough, but he left his mark. He was into applied mathematics, you know, not pure mathematics. Had an excellent rapport with students, and a brilliant mind for strategy. I used to tell him he should give up teaching and work for the Department of Defense."

"You were his boss?" Bobby clarified for the record.

"I hired him, based upon the glowing recommendation of my good friend Dr. Gregory Badington, at the University of Pennsylvania. It was the only way it could've been done, given the circumstances."

"Wait a minute." Bobby knew that name. "Gregory Badington from Philadelphia?"

"Yes, sir. Greg headed up Penn's math program from '72 to '89, I believe. Passed away a few years back. Aneurysm. I pray I should be so lucky." Schuepp nodded vigorously, without a trace of sarcasm.

"So Gregory Badington was Russell Granger's former boss," Bobby said slowly. "He recommended Russell for your program and at the same time he allowed Russell to move his family into Gregory's home in Arlington. Now, why would Dr. Badington do that?"

"Greg did his graduate work at Harvard," Schuepp filled in. "Never lost his love for Boston. When it became clear Russell's family needed to leave Philadelphia, Gregory was only too happy to lend a helping hand." The old professor turned to Annabelle. He pressed her palm between his own age-spotted digits. "How much did your father tell you, dear?"

"Nothing. He never wanted me to worry; then it was too late."

"Until they discovered the grave in Mattapan," Schuepp finished for her. "I saw it on the news, even debated calling the police myself once I read your name. I was fairly certain it couldn't be your remains that were recovered. I was guessing it was that other young girl, the one from your street."

"Dori Petracelli."

"Yes, that's right. She went missing a few weeks after you left. Nearly killed your father. For all his planning, Russell never saw that coming. What a terrible burden to bear. After that, I can imagine why he never told you a thing. What kind of father wants his daughter to discover he saved her life by sacrificing her best friend? Such terrible, terrible choices, for such terrible, terrible days."

"Mr. Schuepp—" Annabelle started.

"Mr. Schuepp," Bobby interrupted, fumbling with his pen now, frantic to get it all written down.

The wizened old man smiled. "Guess I'm not going to make my conference," he said. He picked up the scotch, splashed it in his glass, and gulped it down.

And started his story from the beginning.

"Your father—Roger Grayson was how he was known back then—lost his parents when he was twelve. It's not something he liked to talk about. I never heard the details from him, only from Greg, who picked up the tale from scuttlebutt around the department. It was a domestic violence case, I'm afraid. Russell, well, Roger, I guess—"

"Russell, call him Russell," Annabelle spoke up. "That's how I think of him." Her lips twisted, she seemed to be trying out the words. "Roger Grayson. *Roger, please don't go. . . .*" She frowned, grimaced, and stated more emphatically, "Russell."

"Russell it is. So Russell's mother tried to leave Russell's father. The father didn't take the news so well, returning to the house one night with a gun. He shot and killed them both. Russell was in the house that night. His younger brother, too."

"Brother?" Annabelle exclaimed, bewildered.

Bobby's pen paused over his notebook. "Two male Graysons?" He pictured the sketch again, the resemblance to the description they had of Annabelle's father, and suddenly everything started to make sense.

Schuepp nodded. "Brother. You have an uncle, my dear, though I'm sure you've never heard of him."

"No, I haven't."

"It's what your father wanted. For good reason. After the shooting, Russell and his brother—Tommy—were fortunate to be admitted into the Milton Hershey School for disadvantaged children. Even back then, both boys showed great academic promise, and the Hershey boarding-school program was an excellent fit. Academic rigor in a lovely, pastoral setting.

"Your father did exceptionally well. Tommy, seven years your father's junior, did not. From the beginning, there were signs of mental health issues. Rage/impulse control problems. ADHD. Reactive attachment disorder. I have an interest in the field; been working to develop a statistical model to assist evaluators examining young children. But that's neither here nor there."

Schuepp waved away his own conversational tangent with his hand, then continued more briskly. "Your father graduated early and was accepted at Penn. He was an incredibly gifted student, and Gregory took a shine to him. Under his guidance, Russell submatriculated into the master's program and began to think seriously about pursuing his Ph.D. in mathematics. Along the way, he fell in love with a beautiful nursing student and halfway through his doctorate program, Russell married your mother.

"It was about this time that Tommy quit the Hershey school. With no other family, Tommy sought out your father. And not knowing what else to do, your father took him in. Not an ideal situation for a newly married man juggling a young wife and demanding studies, but these are the things families do.

"Tommy took a job as a dishwasher in a local restaurant. He worked as a bouncer at night and engaged in general mayhem during the day. Russell bailed him out of jail three times, for minor infractions involving brawling, drugs, alcohol. It was always the other guy's fault, according to Tommy. The other guy started it.

"Finally, your mother sat Russell down one night and told him that she was scared. Twice she'd caught Tommy peeking into the bedroom when she was changing. And once when she was in the shower, she was pretty sure he'd entered the bathroom. When she called out his name, he'd panicked and run.

"That was enough for your father. He'd pulled himself up by his own bootstraps; Tommy could do the same. So Russell kicked out his younger brother. Just in time, apparently, because a few weeks later, your mother discovered she was pregnant.

"Tommy, unfortunately, never really went away. He'd arrive unannounced at odd hours. Sometimes Russell was there. Often he wasn't. Your mother, Leslie—Lucy, as she was known back then—"

Bobby quickly scribbled down the name, while watching Annabelle's lips form the word. Lucy. Lucy Grayson. He wondered what it was like for her to hear her mother's real name for the first time, after all these years. But Schuepp was still talking, leaving little time for speculation.

". . . became so concerned that she'd keep all the

lights off and the TV volume down so it would seem like no one was home," Schuepp was saying. "Except Tommy persisted in showing up, generally within ten minutes of her returning home from a shift at the hospital. Leslie, your mother, became convinced that he was following her.

"Russell confronted his brother, told him this foolishness had to stop. Tommy wasn't invited into their lives anymore. If he showed up again, Russell was calling the cops.

"Shortly thereafter, dead and mutilated animals appeared outside their apartment building. Skinned cats. Decapitated squirrels. Russell was convinced it was Tommy. He consulted with the police. There wasn't much they could do without proof. Russell installed a home security system, added chain locks, even mounted a high-powered motion-sensitive light outside the front door. Leslie agreed not to walk home alone from work anymore. Instead, Russell walked her each way.

"Gregory remembered one night finding Russell sitting in his office, staring at nothing. When Gregory knocked politely on the door, Russell told him, 'He's going to kill her. My father murdered my mother. Tommy will destroy my wife.'

"Gregory didn't know what to say. Life continued, and a few months later, Leslie gave birth. Tommy had disappeared somewhere; Russell didn't know where and didn't care. He loved being a new father. Was crazy about every aspect of it. He and your mother settled in and had the honeymoon they'd never gotten before. Until—"

"Tommy came back," Annabelle filled in quietly.

"You were eighteen months old," Schuepp supplied. "Later, Russell learned the only reason Tommy had vanished was that he'd served time on assault charges. Minute he was released, he picked up just where he'd left off. Except he no longer cared about Leslie. He wanted you.

"First time, he confronted Russell and Leslie on the street. They were walking home from the park, you were in the stroller. It was broad daylight. The minute he saw Russell and Leslie, Tommy crossed the street and blocked their path. 'How are you, good to see you, is this my new niece? Oh, she's gorgeous.' He snatched you up before Russell could move, cooing and cuddling. Russell tried to get you back. Tommy twisted away. He had a gleam in his eye, Russell said. He was terrified. He wasn't sure if Tommy was going to kiss you or toss you in front of oncoming traffic.

"Naturally, Russell made nice. Leslie, too. Finally, they got you back, placed you in the carriage, resumed walking. But they were both terribly shaken.

"Next day, Russell changed the locks and personally paid for a new security system for the whole building. He went back to the police, where they ran a background on Tommy and learned of his criminal history. There still wasn't anything they could do, though. After all, it's not a crime to visit your niece. They noted Russell's concern, made a record.

"Russell left the police station more frightened than when he'd arrived. He ended up talking to Greg about taking a leave of absence. He didn't want to leave Leslie alone with the baby, not even for an hour. Greg talked him down. Russell had just received his doctorate. To take time off now would be disastrous for his career. Besides, your mother was no longer working, someone had to earn a living.

"So Russell agreed to continue working, while Leslie made arrangements for her parents to visit. Surely there would be safety in numbers."

"Oh no," Annabelle whispered. Her hand had come up, was covering her mouth. Bobby followed her train of thought. The grandparents she'd been told had died in a car accident. Somehow, he had a feeling the truth was going to be more devastating than a tragic fender bender.

Schuepp nodded sadly. "Oh yes. Your mother's parents came. Took you for a walk. Never came home. A uniformed officer found them sitting on a park bench side by side. Both shot through the heart with a small-caliber pistol. You were toddling around the grounds all by yourself, clutching a brand-new teddy bear. Attached to its neck was a gift tag reading 'Love, Uncle Tommy.'

"The police picked up Tommy immediately, questioned him about the shootings, but he denied all involvement. According to him, he'd stopped by the park, given you the bear, and chatted briefly with your grandparents. Everyone was fine when he left. The police searched his apartment but came up empty. Without the pistol, without any witnesses or other evidence, there wasn't anything more the police could do. They suggested your father take out a restraining order. He said his mother had tried that.

"That afternoon, he went to Greg's office and announced that he'd made his decision. He and his family were going to disappear. It was the only way, he said, to be safe.

"Once more Greg tried to be the voice of reason. What did Russell and Leslie know about life on the run? How would they get fake identities, new driver's licenses, jobs? It wasn't as easy as in the movies.

"But Russell was adamant. When he looked at his brother, he saw his father. He had already lost enough to one man's obsessive rage. He wasn't going to lose anything more. And the more he talked, the more he brought Gregory around. It was Gregory's idea that Russell and Leslie move to his home in Arlington. The deed was in Greg's name, utilities, too. Surely it would be difficult for Tommy to trace Russell and Leslie to their new home in Massachusetts.

"Gregory also gave me a buzz, explaining the situation. It just so happened we had an opening in the department, so we worked out the details. Russell and your mother would move to Arlington, I would offer your father a job at MIT. Naturally, I had to enter your father into the payroll department under his real name, Roger Grayson. But I smoothed things over with the right people, and for all intents and purposes, your father became Russell Granger, married to Leslie Ann Granger, parents of an adorable daughter, Annabelle Granger. Only the paychecks and other financial records said otherwise.

"We thought we'd been so clever, but we hadn't been smart enough."

"Tommy found them," Bobby said flatly. Annabelle wasn't talking anymore. She sat shell-shocked, too stunned for words.

"That's what Russell believed. There was a case in the news right as they moved to Arlington, the kidnapping of a young girl who could've been your older sister, Annabelle. Instantly Russell was nervous. He worried that Tommy was in the area, searching for Annabelle."

"Catherine's case," Bobby filled in. "Another guy did it, Richard Umbrio. But the strong physical resemblance between Catherine and Annabelle would've spooked Russell, made him think the worst." He glanced at Annabelle. "Even drive your father to masquerade as an FBI agent, so he could get to Catherine in the hospital, question her."

"Tommy's the one pictured in the sketch," Annabelle murmured. "My father drew a picture of Tommy to see how Catherine would react."

"Probably."

She managed a crooked smile. "Told you there was a logical explanation." But her face remained pale, drawn.

"Umbrio, Umbrio," Schuepp was muttering. "That's

right. The police finally arrested this hulking brute of a man, accused him of the crime. I remember now. Still, Russell refused to lower his guard. He took up karate, read obsessively on stalkers. I don't know what it must have been like—first to lose his parents so young, then to feel that the entire tragic situation was happening again.

"I know he felt very guilty for what your mother was going through. I know the few times I saw them together at functions, your father was hyperattentive, relentlessly cheerful. If he could smile broad enough, boom loud enough, then everything would be okay.

"Your mother loved you, Annabelle," Schuepp said quietly. "When the time came, she never hesitated.

"Russell came to my office at the end of October. Tommy was back, leaving gifts for Annabelle at your home, stalking her. It was all his fault, Russell insisted. He hadn't been thorough enough. Bank accounts, IRS records could be traced. It had only been a matter of time.

"This time Russell had purchased new identities for his family, made arrangements to trade your old car for a new vehicle. Everything else was to be left behind. Fast and light, he told me. That was the key. He wouldn't even tell me where you three would be going.

"When he left, I remember wondering if you would make it. Or if I'd simply catch the end of this story one night on the news. For two weeks, all seemed well. And then that young girl, your friend, disappeared.

Minute I heard the street where she lived, I knew who'd done it. According to your father, Tommy had never taken disappointment well."

"Did my father know? About Dori?" Annabelle asked urgently. "Did he talk to you?"

"He called me three days later," Schuepp supplied. "Said he'd heard on the national news. He didn't know what to do. On the one hand, he was sure it was Tommy. On the other hand, if he returned to talk to the police . . ."

"Tommy would be able to find him again," Bobby filled in. "What about you, sir? Did you contact the police?"

"I left an anonymous tip on the hotline number. Enough for my conscience to feel like I'd done something, and yet . . ."

"Not nearly enough to help Dori Petracelli." Bobby gave the man a look. "You knew a vital piece of information. If you'd come forward—"

"The police would've pursued Russell and Leslie," Schuepp stated matter-of-factly. "They would have dragged them back here to Massachusetts, exposed them to Tommy. The Petracelli girl was likely dead. I focused on the life that could be saved—yours, Annabelle."

Bobby opened his mouth. Before he could argue, however, Annabelle beat him to the punch.

"Explain that to Mr. and Mrs. Petracelli. They were parents, too. They deserved better than to have their daughter written off, just so their neighbors could get on with their lives." She turned away bitterly.

Schuepp poured another shot of scotch, pushed it toward her.

She wouldn't take it, though. Instead, she pulled herself together, setting her face in that resolute look Bobby knew so well.

"One last question, Mr. Schuepp: Can you tell me my real name?"

33

MY NAME IS Amy Marie Grayson. Amy Marie Grayson.

I sat in the passenger's seat of Bobby's Crown Vic, clinging to my parents' ashes, while trying out my real name again and again, waiting to see when it would roll naturally off my tongue. We were already back on Route 2. Driving somewhere. It hardly mattered to me.

Amy. Marie. Grayson. It still felt unnatural, stilted on my lips.

All of my life, I had considered myself two people: Annabelle Granger and Current Alias—whatever name I happened to have at the time. Now, according to Mr. Schuepp, I was actually three people: Amy Grayson, Annabelle Granger, and . . . well, et al.

The notion confused me. I rested my head against the cool glass of my window, and for a moment I saw my father again, sitting across from me at Giacomo's as we celebrated my twenty-first birthday, appearing content.

My father had won. I never understood, because he'd never let me be part of the war he was fighting. But that night, my birthday, must have felt like a victory to him. He had lost his mother. He had lost his wife. But his daughter . . . Me, at least, he had kept safe, though it had cost him so much along the way.

And I was amazed now, humbled in a way that brought tears to my eyes, that he had viewed my life as a victory. He had given up his career for me. He had given up neighbors, his home, his own sense of self. Ultimately, he had given up his wife.

I can picture my father remote. I can picture him relentless, hard, aggressive. But I can't remember him ever being bitter or mean-spirited. He always had his cause, his reason, even if his paranoia drove me crazy.

And knowing the whole story now, all I wanted to do was go back in time to tell him I was sorry, to give him a grateful hug, to tell him I finally understood. Then again, niceness was never what my father had wanted for me. We fought, constantly, incessantly, partly because my father had enjoyed a good battle. He'd raised a fighter. And he liked to test my skills.

Amy Marie Grayson. Amy Marie.

And just for a moment, I could almost hear it. My mother's voice, crooning softly, "There's my little angel . . . Good morning, Amy, bobamey, mamey."

I was crying. I didn't want to. But the enormity of it hit me all at once. My mother's sacrifice. My father's loss. And I was sobbing hard and ugly, only vaguely aware of Bobby's hand upon my shoulder. Then the car was slowing down, pulling over. My seat belt retracted. He pulled me onto his lap, an awkward motion, given the hard intrusion of the steering wheel. But I didn't care. I buried my face against his shoulder. Clung to him like a child. And sobbed because my parents had given everything to save my life and I'd been furious at them for doing so.

"Shhhh," he was saying over and over again.

"Dori is dead because of me."

"Shhhhhhh."

"And my mother and father. And five other girls. And for what? What about me is so damn *special?* I can't even hold down a job and my only friend is a dog."

On cue, Bella whined anxiously from the backseat. I had forgotten about her. Now she bounded over the top of the seat to get to the front. I could feel her pawing at my leg. Bobby didn't push her away. He just murmured more low words of comfort. I could feel the strength of his arms around me. The hard band of his muscles.

It made me a little crazy. That he could feel so real, so strong, when I felt as if everything in my life was disintegrating, torn into shreds and drifting away like confetti. And I was grateful at that moment that we were in a car, parked along a busy freeway, because if we'd been at my apartment, I would've stripped him naked. I would've removed every piece of his clothing, bit by bit, just so I could touch his skin, run my tongue along the ridges of his stomach, taste the salt of my own tears upon his chest, because I needed so badly to outrun my own thoughts, to feel only the intensity of one frantic moment, to feel alive.

Amy Marie Grayson. Amy. Marie. Grayson.

Oh Dori, I am so sorry. Oh Dori.

Bobby kissed me. Tilted up my chin, covered my lips with his own. And it was so gentle, so giving, that it made me cry all over again, until I took his hand and pressed it against my breast, hard, because I didn't want to feel like glass and I didn't want him viewing me as someone who would break.

Amy Marie Grayson. Whose uncle had destroyed her entire family.

And found her again last night.

I pulled away, hitting my elbow on the steering wheel. Bella whined again. I slid from Bobby's lap, back onto the seat, and pulled Bella close.

Bobby didn't try to stop me. Didn't say a word. I could hear him breathing heavily.

I scrubbed at my cheeks. Bella helped with a few enthusiastic licks.

"I should get back to work," I said brusquely.

Bobby regarded me strangely. "Doing what?"

"I have a project due. Back Bay. My client is going to wonder."

Bobby stared at me. "Annabelle . . . Amy? Annabelle."

"Annabelle. I just . . . I'm used . . . Annabelle."

"Annabelle, you need to find a new apartment."

"Why?"

Arched brow. "Well, for starters, a crazy man knows you live there."

"Crazy man isn't exactly a spring chicken. And I'm not easy pickings."

"You're not thinking straight—"

"You are *not* my father!"

"Whoa, back up. Despite my, um, obvious personal interest"—he plucked at his trousers, which had tented nicely—"I'm still a state detective. We get training in these things. For example, when an obsessed stalker homes in on a target, bad things are bound to happen. This Tommy—or whatever he goes by these days—has obviously figured out you're alive and well in the North End. He's spent the past twenty-four hours breaking into a police officer's home, arranging an ambush with four attack dogs, and delivering a token of his affection to your front door. In other words, this is not someone you want to mess with. Give us a day or two. Stay in a hotel, keep your head down. There's a difference between playing safe and running scared."

"A hotel won't let me have Bella," I said stubbornly, and tightened my arms around my dog.

"Oh, for heaven's sake . . . There are dog-friendly establishments. Let me make some calls."

"I gotta work, you know. I can't pay my bills on charm alone."

"Then take your sewing machine."

"I'll also need fabric, my computer, trim pieces, designs—"

"I'll help you load up."

I scowled at him for no good reason, then pressed my head against Bella's fur. "I want it over," I confessed.

His look finally softened. "I know."

"I don't want to be Amy," I murmured. "Being Annabelle is hard enough."

Bobby drove me to my apartment. I got out of the car, just in time to hear a honk. I turned, Bella barked furiously.

Up the street lumbered a giant UPS truck, Ben, my aging knight, aboard his faithful brown steed. He slowed, eyeing me and Bella anxiously. I gave him the thumbs-up, and with a solemn nod he continued on.

"See," I told Bobby. "I could, too, stay in my apartment. With an overnight delivery service on my side, who needs the state police?"

Bobby didn't seem amused.

He walked Bella and me upstairs. Someone, the techs, a detective, I don't know, had made some kind of attempt to restore things to their proper place. My apartment had a rumpled look but was otherwise okay.

"Give me an hour," Bobby said. "Two at the most. I need to follow up on a few inquiries, get a couple of things in order—"

"You need to find Tommy," I said. "And tell D.D. to stop suspecting my poor dead father."

Bobby narrowed his eyes at me but didn't push. "I'll give you a buzz when I'm on my way."

"Aye, aye, Captain."

"Pack for a week, just to be safe. I can always pick up something if you forget."

"Really? Like my favorite lacy black bra? A highly necessary hot pink thong?"

His eyes heated dangerously. "Sweetheart, I'd be happy to rifle your underwear drawer. But bear in mind, it might be a uniformed officer who ends up taking the call."

"Oh." I shrugged. "Guess I can pack my own panties, then."

"Take what you need, Annabelle. We can fill the whole car if you'd like."

"Won't be necessary. I happen to be an expert on traveling light."

My attempt at bravado didn't fool him for a moment. He crossed over, grabbed me before I could protest, kissed me hard.

"Two hours," he repeated. "Tops."

Then he was gone.

Bella cried like a baby at the door. I simply wondered how a grown woman could feel so vulnerable inside her own home.

Bobby started working his cell phone the minute he hit his car. He had names, now he wanted information. He started with D.D. but got her voice mail. Ditto with Sinkus.

After a brief internal war, Bobby made his decision. Boston PD was maxed out and he needed information fast. Well, hell, he worked for the state, didn't he? He called in a favor with one of his old buddies and got the ball rolling.

He needed to know everything there was to know about A, Tommy Grayson; B, Roger Grayson; C, Lucille Grayson; and D, E, and F, almost as afterthoughts, Gregory Badington, Paul Schuepp, and Walter Petracelli. That'd keep the wheels churning for a bit.

If Schuepp's story was correct, the person stalking Annabelle was most likely her uncle, Tommy Grayson. And it made the most sense that the person who was stalking Annabelle was the same person who had murdered Dori Petracelli and buried her remains in Mattapan.

Which meant that Tommy Grayson had made it from Pennsylvania to Massachusetts.

Then what?

Tommy knew Annabelle's family had fled. If he'd followed them from Philly to Arlington, it made sense that he'd follow them again. Unlike Christopher Eola, Tommy wasn't independently wealthy. Which meant if he'd continued stalking Annabelle's family, then he'd faced basic logistical concerns. How to earn money for rent and transportation. How to find a new job in a new city every few years. Probably meant he'd done some form of menial employment. Schuepp had mentioned Tommy working as a bouncer in Philly. That was the type of work easy to pick up on the fly. They needed to distribute Tommy's picture to the law enforcement agencies in each city, with recommendations to distribute it to local bars. Perhaps they could pinpoint Tommy's movements, establish a time line for his travels.

Except how did Tommy find Annabelle's family each time? According to Schuepp, Annabelle's father was smart: He'd learned quickly from his mistakes. Yet, as a general rule, the family moved every eighteen months to two years.

Proactive measures on the part of Annabelle's father? Minute word of a missing kid hit the news, he got spooked and packed up his whole family. Or was Tommy that brilliant?

Bobby wanted to know more about Tommy. And Annabelle's father.

Naturally, the good parking spaces at Boston PD were taken. Bobby looped around four times, finally got lucky as someone pulled out. He tucked in, still deeply lost in his own thoughts as he locked up the Crown Vic and headed inside the building.

First thing he noticed when he made it through the glass doors into Homicide was the silence. The receptionist, Gretchen, was staring blankly at her computer screen. A couple of other guys sat at their desks, moving around paperwork, looking subdued.

He tapped the counter in front of Gretchen. She finally looked up.

"What?" he asked softly.

"Tony Rock's mom," the receptionist whispered back.

"Ah jeez."

"He called in about thirty minutes ago. He didn't sound good at all. Sergeant Warren's been trying to reach him since, but he's not answering his phone."

"Ah no."

"Probably just needs some time."

"Sure. That stinks. When you find out about the memorial service . . ."

"I'll let everyone know," Gretchen promised.

Bobby nodded his thanks and headed straight for D.D.'s office. She was on the phone but held up one finger when she saw him. He leaned against the door-jamb, listening to one side of a conversation that mostly consisted of "Yes, mmmhmmm, that's right." Must be talking to the brass.

Bobby rested his shoulder against the wooden frame. All of sudden, he felt exhausted. The stakeout in the woods. D.D. pinned to the ground, being mauled by a giant Rottweiler. Realizing she was okay, calling Annabelle, only to hear her frightened voice over the phone. Another mad dash across town, wondering what he would find, worrying he would be too late.

Was this how Annabelle's father had felt, once upon a time? As if life was spinning out of his control? As if he could see the train coming but couldn't get off the tracks?

Christ, he needed a good night's sleep.

D.D. finally hung up the phone. "Sorry about that," she said curtly. "Rock's—"

"Already heard."

"Naturally, he'll be out for a few days."

"'Course."

"Meaning . . ."

"Hey, hard work is good for us. Builds character."

"So," she said.

"So Russell Granger's real name is Roger Grayson. He, his wife—Lucille Grayson—and their newborn daughter, Amy Grayson, were stalked by Roger's deranged brother, Tommy Grayson, while living in Philadelphia. Roger believed Tommy went so far as to murder Lucy's parents one afternoon when they took Amy to the park. Shortly thereafter, Roger made arrangements to move his entire family to Arlington and live under the assumed name Granger. Unfortunately, he didn't know how to get fake ID, so all financial records remained under their original identities. According to Paul Schuepp, former head of mathematics at MIT, Roger became convinced in '82 that Tommy had found them. That's when he arranged for the family to run a second time, this time doing the job right."

"Holy crap," D.D. said.

"Got a friend running down Roger's name, Lucille's name, Tommy's name, and a few others. Tommy has a criminal history, so it should be in the system. Million-dollar question is, once Tommy realized Annabelle's family had slipped away from him, did he hang in Massachusetts or hit the road? Oh, and where is he now?"

D.D. rubbed her temples. "Our prime suspect is Tommy Grayson?"

"Yeah. Sorry to disappoint you, but I think Annabelle's father is dead."

"But the whole posing as an FBI agent—"

"Russell made the same connection we did—that Catherine looked remarkably like Annabelle. He worried the attack on Catherine was Tommy's work. Given his desire to remain under the radar, he couldn't go to the police, so he handled the matter himself."

"But Tommy wasn't Catherine's attacker."

"No, Catherine's resemblance to Annabelle is pure coincidence. Umbrio's methodology, however, probably inspired Tommy's use of an underground chamber two years later. So the cases have a relationship, but a distant one."

"And Christopher Eola?"

"Most likely a murderer, just not our murderer."

"Charlie Marvin?"

"An honest-to-goodness retired minister who works at the Pine Street Inn. According to witnesses, he was there last night."

"Adam Schmidt?"

"Haven't the foggiest. You'd have to ask Sinkus."

"He's been looking for you," D.D. supplied. "He spent the afternoon with Jill Cochran from Boston State Mental. You two need to catch up."

Bobby stared at her. "That's it? I nail down the real identity of Annabelle's father, crack the case wide open, and you're on my ass because I haven't magically debriefed with my fellow detectives yet?"

"I'm not on your ass," she retorted crankily. "But I

am thinking all your brilliance has still left us with an obvious hole."

"Which is?"

"Where the hell is Tommy Grayson right now, other than skulking around Annabelle's apartment and leaving trained attack dogs in the woods?"

"Well, next time I'll deliver the suspect on a silver platter."

"Seems to me," D.D. continued as if she hadn't heard him, "that if the rest of the Grayson family adopted new identities, why not Tommy? And our best chance of penetrating this identity and finding the SOB sooner rather than later is to probe the other piece of the puzzle we know."

"Other piece of the puzzle?"

"Boston State Mental."

"Oh," Bobby said rather stupidly. Then, in the next instant, as the light went on: "Okay. Yeah. All right. We're back to our original theory—the killer must have had some kind of association with Boston State Mental to be comfortable burying six bodies on the grounds. Meaning, if our killer is Tommy Grayson—"

"Who according to you has a troubled background—"

"He's a certifiable whacko."

"Then Tommy Grayson probably has a history at Boston State Mental."

"And," Bobby managed to fill in the rest all by himself, "Sinkus has that information."

"You'll make it as a detective yet," D.D. said dryly. "Anything else I need to know?"

"I'm working on finding a hotel for Annabelle."

D.D. arched a brow.

"And I'm thinking, though perhaps I didn't mention it to her, that as long as she's tucked away at said hotel, we could staff her apartment with a decoy."

D.D. pursed her lips. "Expensive."

Bobby shrugged. "Your problem, not mine. I don't think the situation will drag on, though. Given the level of activity in the past twenty-four hours alone, seems to me that Tommy's patience is just about used up."

"I'll float it by the deputy," D.D. said.

"Okeydokey."

Bobby turned to leave. D.D. stopped him one last time.

"Bobby," she said quietly. "Not bad."

34

WHEN I WAS twelve years old, I came down with an extremely aggressive viral infection. I remember complaining of feeling hot and nauseous. Next thing I knew, I woke up in the hospital. Six days had passed. By the looks of it, my mother hadn't slept for any of them.

I was weak and groggy, too exhausted to lift my hand, too confused to sort out the maze of lines and wires attached to my body. My mother had been sitting in a chair beside my hospital bed. When my eyes opened, however, she came flying out of it.

"Oh, thank God!"

"Mommy?" I hadn't called her mommy in years.

"I'm here, love. Everything is okay. I'm with you."

I remember closing my eyes again. The cool feel of her fingers brushing back my hair from my sweaty face. I dozed off gripping her other hand. And in that instant, I did feel safe and I did feel secure, because my mother was by my side, and when you are twelve years old you believe your parents can save you from anything.

Two weeks later, my father announced we were leaving. Even I had seen this one coming. I'd spent an entire week in the hospital, poked and prodded by top medical experts. Anonymous people couldn't afford that kind of attention.

I packed my lone suitcase on my own. It wasn't hard. A few pairs of jeans, shirts, socks, underwear, my one nice dress. Had blankie, had Boomer. The rest I already knew how to leave behind.

My father had departed to take care of miscellaneous errands—settle up with the landlord, gas up the car, quit yet another job. He always left my mother to do the packing. Apparently, condensing your entire adult life into four suitcases was women's work.

I had watched my mother perform this drill countless times. Generally, she hummed a mindless tune, moving on autopilot. Open drawer, fold, pack. Open new drawer, fold, pack. Open closet, fold, pack. Done.

That day, I found her sitting on the edge of the double-size bed in the cramped bedroom, staring at her hands. I crawled onto the bed beside her. Leaned against her, shoulder to shoulder.

My mother had liked Cleveland. The two older women down the hall had taken her under their wing. They had her over on Friday nights to play pinochle and sip Crown Royal. Our apartment was tiny, but nicer than the one in St. Louis. No cockroaches here. No high-pitched scream of the local commuter rail screeching to a stop one block away.

My mother had found a part-time job as a cashier at the local grocery store. She would walk to work in the mornings after seeing me onto the bus. In the afternoons, we'd take long walks through the quiet, tree-lined streets, stopping at a nearby pond to feed the ducks.

We'd lasted a whole eighteen months, even surviving the bitterly cold winter. My mother claimed that the gray slushy snow didn't bother her at all; it simply reminded her of life in New England.

I think my mother could've made it in Cleveland.

"I'm sorry," I whispered to her as we sat side by side on the bed.

"Shhhhh."

"Maybe, if we both said no—"

"Shhhhh."

"Mom—"

"You know what I do on days like this?" my mother asked me.

I shook my head.

"I think about the future."

"Chicago?" I asked in confusion, for that's where my father said we were going next.

"No, silly. The ten-year future. Fifteen, twenty, forty years from now. I picture your graduation. I imagine your wedding. I dream about holding grandbabies."

I made a face. "Ugh. Never happen," I told her.

"Sure it will."

"No, never. I'm not getting married."

Her turn to smile, ruffle my hair, try to pretend we both didn't see her shaking fingers. "That's what all twelve-year-olds think."

"No. I'm serious. No husband, no kids. Children mean having to move too much."

"Oh, sweetheart," she said sadly, and gave me a hard, tight hug.

I think of my mother as I leave my apartment now, Bella in tow. I have my Taser in hand. It feels melodramatic, creeping down the stairs in my own apartment building in broad daylight. Bobby was right: My apartment was no longer safe. As it went in the world of secret agents and double lives, my cover was blown. So I might as well take Bobby's advice and hole up in a hotel for a while.

It's what my father would've done.

But leaving meant packing. Packing meant suitcases. Suitcases were kept in my storage locker; one was assigned to each tenant, in the basement below.

I had retrieved items from my storage space count-less times before. I told myself that today was no dif-ferent.

The stair creaked beneath my foot. Instantly I froze. I was on the third-story landing, right outside apart-ment 3C's door. I stared at it, my heart pounding, waiting to see what would happen next. Then, in the next minute, I pulled it together, scolding myself.

I knew the tenants who lived in 3C. A young profes-sional couple. Had a gray tabby cat named Ashton who liked to hiss at Bella from beneath the door. Ashton's attitude aside, we'd all managed to coexist for the past three years. There was no logical reason to suddenly be afraid of them now.

It was more like, why *not* be afraid of apartment 3C? With no tangible focus for my anxiety, it was easy to look at every dark shadow and see the possible outline of evil Uncle Tommy.

I descended to the second floor, then the first. In the lobby came the hard part. My hands were shaking. I had to work to maintain focus.

I sorted through my ring of keys, finally finding the right one and inserting it in the lock. The side door, old and heavy, groaned inward to reveal a black plunge into the bowels of the centuries-old building. I fumbled overhead until I found the chain for the bare-bulb stairwell light.

The smell was different here. Cold and moldy, like mossy stones or damp earth. Like the smell from Dori's grave.

Bella scrambled down the narrow wooden stairs without a second thought. At least one of us was brave.

At the bottom, the crude plywood storage structures were bolted against the far wall. As the fifth-floor tenant, I had the storage unit at the end, secured by my own metal padlock. It took me two tries to get it undone. In the meantime, Bella worked the basement perimeter, making the happy woofing sounds of a dog discovering hidden treasures.

I got out my parents' luggage. Five pieces, pea green, made of some kind of industrial fabric that had been heavily patched with duct tape over the years. The largest piece squeaked alarmingly as I wheeled it along the floor.

And in that instant, I saw so many snapshots of time. My father, that last afternoon in Arlington. My mother, merrily unpacking the suitcase in our first apartment, giddy over the bright Florida sun. Packing up in Tampa. Checking into Baton Rouge. The brief stint in New Orleans.

We had done it. Fighting, building, correcting, warring, grieving. Losing, hating, winning, weeping. We had been messy and tumultuous and bitter and determined. But we had done it. And never, until this moment, had I missed my parents so much. Until my fingers closed around my necklace and I swore that I could feel them standing beside me in this cold, dank space.

And I realized, in that instant, that I would've done

the same thing if I'd been them. I would've moved heaven and earth to save my child. Given up my job, my identity, my community, even my life. It would've been worth it to me, too. That's what being a parent was all about.

I love you, I love you, I love you, I tried to tell them. I had to believe that they could hear me. If only because without that bit of faith, I'd be no better than Mr. Petracelli, drowning in a sea of bitterness and regret.

Onward and upward, my father had always said. *This will be the best place yet!*

"Onward and upward," I whispered. "All right, Daddy, let's get this done."

I organized the luggage, locked up my storage unit, then whistled for Bella. Given the load, I'd have to make two trips. I started with the largest piece, strapping another piece on top, then hooked one of the smaller bags over my shoulder.

I shuffled my way through the narrow corridor between storage units. Looked up.

And saw Charlie Marvin silhouetted at the top of the stairs, his eyes peering down and finding me in the gloom.

Bobby was heading for Sinkus's cubicle when his cell phone chirped. He checked caller ID, then answered. "You got the fax?"

"Hello to you, too," said Catherine.

"Sorry. Lotsa things happening."

"As I can tell from the fax. Well, then, to answer your question, the drawing *could be* of the same man."

"Could be?"

"Bobby, it's been twenty-seven years."

"You recognized the photo of Annabelle's father easily enough," he countered.

"Annabelle's father interacted with me." Catherine sounded annoyed. "He argued and pushed me until I grew angry with him. That made an impression. The sketch, on the other hand . . . What I remember most is my first thought—the man in the drawing *wasn't* the man who attacked me."

Bobby sighed. What he needed now was something more definitive. "But it's possible this sketch is the same sketch you were shown in the hospital?"

"It's possible," she agreed. Moment's pause. "Who is it?"

"Annabelle's uncle, Tommy Grayson. Turns out he started stalking Annabelle when she was about eighteen months old. Her family fled from Philadelphia to Arlington in an attempt to get away from him. He found them."

"Did Tommy know Richard?"

"Not that we know of. Tommy probably got the idea for using an underground chamber, though, by watching your case on the news."

"Happy to help," Catherine murmured dryly.

Because he knew her better than most, Bobby stopped walking. "It's not your fault."

She didn't say anything.

"And anyway," he continued briskly, "now that we know Tommy's name, the case is almost done. We'll get him, lock him up, and that will be that."

"You'll come to Arizona to celebrate?"

"Catherine . . ."

"I know, Bobby. You'll take Annabelle to dinner to celebrate."

His turn to be silent.

"I like her, Bobby. Honestly. It makes me feel good to know that she will be happy."

"Someday, you'll be happy, too."

"No, Bobby, not me. But maybe I'll be less angry. Good luck with your case, Bobby."

"Thank you."

"And when it's over, feel free for you *and* Annabelle to come visit."

Bobby knew he'd never take Catherine up on that offer, but he thanked her before ending the call.

One detail down, about twelve more to go. He headed for Sinkus's cubicle.

Sinkus was miffed, the boy who'd gone to the stadium then looked away at the last minute and missed the game-winning play. He also smelled of sour milk.

"You mean all along this professor knew the whole story?"

"Guess so."

"Oh man, I spent three hours with Jill Cochran. All I learned is that former mental-ward administrators are tougher than Catholic nuns."

Bobby frowned. "What, she rapped your knuckles with a yardstick?"

"No, she delivered a blistering lecture on how unfair it is to always assume the worst of the mentally ill. That wackos are people, have rights. Most are harmless, just misunderstood. 'Mark my words,' she told me, 'you find who did this, and I guarantee it won't be one of our patients. No, it'll be some fine upstanding member of the community. Someone who goes to church, spoils his kids, and works nine to five. It's always the normal ones who commit the truly vile acts against God.' Woman had a lot of opinions on the subject."

"So, where are the records?" Bobby asked, trying not to sound impatient.

"You're looking at 'em." Sinkus gestured to four cardboard boxes, stacked against the wall. "Not as bad as I feared. Remember, the place closed precomputerization. I thought we might be talking hundreds of boxes. But when the facility shut down, Mrs. Cochran knew they couldn't hang on to piles of patient history. So she condensed down the files to a manageable size. This way, when someone needs information on a former patient, she knows where to start. Plus, I got the impression she was thinking of using her years at the place to write a book. Kind of a tell-all with a heart."

Bobby shrugged. Why not?

He opened the first box. Jill Cochran was an organized kind of gal. She had divvied up the information by decade, then by building, each decade holding multiple building files. Bobby tried to remember what Charlie Marvin had told them about the hospital's organization. Maximum security had been in I-Building, something like that.

He went to the seventies and pulled the file for I-Building. Each patient had been distilled to a single page. It still made an impressive weight in his hand.

He came upon the name Christopher Eola first and skimmed Cochran's notes. Date of admittance, brief family history, a bunch of clinical terms that meant nothing to Bobby, then apparently the head nurse's own impression—"extrem. dangerous, extrem. sneaky, stronger than he looks."

Bobby stuck a yellow sticky tab on the page, for future reference. He was confident that the crime scene at Mattapan was the work of Annabelle's uncle. Having decided that, he was equally confident that somewhere at some time, Christopher Eola had performed his own "vile acts against God." Regardless of the resolution of the Mattapan case, he had a feeling the task force would agree to continue tracking down Mr. Eola.

He skimmed through other patient files, waiting for something to leap out at him. A neon Post-it screaming, *I am the madman*. A doctor's note: *This patient is the most likely to have kidnapped and tortured six girls*.

Many of the patients came with notes documenting a history of violence, as well as extensive criminal activity. At least half, however, had no background at all. "Admitted by police," "Discovered vagrant" were very common phrases. Even before the homeless crisis made headlines in the eighties, it was clear the homeless were in crisis in Boston.

Bobby made it through the whole stack and realized it had become one long, depressing blur. He stopped, backed up, tried again.

"Whatya looking for?" Sinkus asked.

"Don't know."

"That makes it hard."

"What are you doing?"

Sinkus held up his own bulging file. "Staff."

"Ah. Any of them look good?"

"Only Adam Schmidt, the perverted AN."

"Bummer. Track him down yet?"

"Working on it. What about age?"

"What?"

"Age. You're looking for a patient who might be Tommy Grayson, yes? You said he was seven years younger than Russell Granger. Had been in and out of prison and/or hospitals since he was what, sixteen?"

"That Russell knew of."

"So, if he was admitted to Boston State Mental, you're talking a young man. Teens to early twenties."

Bobby considered the logic. "Yeah, good guess."

He started sorting through the patient sheets again, culling down the entire file to fourteen men, including Eola and another case Charlie Marvin had told him about, the street kid named Benji who'd attended

Boston Latin while living in the dying mental institute.

Now what?

Bobby glanced at his watch, winced. He'd already
burned up an hour and a half. Time to find a dog-
friendly hotel and return to Annabelle.

He picked up the fourteen sheets. "Mind if I make
copies of these?"

"Be my guest. Hey, didn't you say Charlie Marvin
worked at Boston State Mental?"

"He was an AN," Bobby supplied. "During his college days. Then volunteered his time as a minister
until it closed down."

"Sure about that?"

"It's what the man said. Why?"

Sinkus finally looked up. "Bobby, I got decades of
payroll ledgers in front of me. Nineteen-fifties till
closing. I'm telling you, no Charlie Marvin ever made
a dime."

35

"Would you like some help?" Charlie called down to
me.

"Oh, ummm, that's okay. I'm coming up." Bella was
already bounding up the stairs. Whereas I found
Charlie's sudden appearance disquieting, she was
overjoyed to see her newest best friend.

She hopped, leapt, and licked. I lugged the three
bags up the stairs, thinking fast. Last I knew, Charlie

didn't have my address. Where in God's name had I put my Taser?

Then I remembered. I'd set it down. On the shelf. Inside my storage unit, while I'd pulled out the suitcases. My locked storage unit. I almost turned away, headed back down the stairs. Almost.

"Sounds like you had quite a morning," Charlie commented cheerfully as Bella and I emerged into the gray light of the building's lobby. I saw now that one of my neighbors had propped open both front doors. Unloading groceries, no doubt. It would make an excellent headline for the *Boston Herald*: "Young Woman Brutally Stabbed to Death While Fellow Tenant Stocks Fridge."

I needed to calm down. I was jumping at shadows again. According to Bobby, Charlie had spent last night at the Pine Street Inn. Meaning he couldn't have delivered my latest gift. At eye level again, I realized that Charlie wasn't really that tall, nor large, nor, at his advanced age, threatening. In fact, as I gingerly set down my luggage so I'd be free for defensive measures, Charlie was kneeling and scratching my dog under the chin.

"Some officer called at the shelter, asking about me," he said matter-of-factly.

"Did he? Sorry about that."

"Gave me a chuckle," Charlie said. "Being a 'person of interest' at my age. Anyhoo, one of the guys who runs the shelter has a police scanner. Naturally, we tuned in after that. Dispatch mentioned this address, and being a busybody and all, I thought I'd stop by and check on you for myself. I can't help thinking some of this is my fault."

"Your fault?"

"I'm being followed," Charlie said bluntly. "Least, I'm pretty sure I am. Started the day I met up with Sergeant Warren and Detective Dodge in Mattapan. Wasn't sure at first. Just kept getting a kind of hinky feeling between my shoulder blades. I think maybe I was being followed again the night I ran into you. And I think the same person who is following me knows something about the mass grave. And maybe something about you."

"Why something about me?"

"Because you're the key to that grave, aren't you, Annabelle? I don't know how, I don't know why, but everything that's going on, it's all about you."

My neighbor picked that moment to jog up the stairs, four plastic grocery bags in hand. He gave us a brief nod—what was there to notice, a young woman, an old man, a blissed-out dog—and headed up the central stairs.

Charlie's eyes tracked the man's movements, though his fingers never stopped caressing Bella's ears.

"You know something about Mattapan," I told Charlie, a statement now, no longer a question.

Very slowly, he nodded.

"Something you haven't told the police."

Another slow, thoughtful nod.

"Why are you here, Mr. Marvin? Why are you stalking me?"

"I want to know," he said quietly. "I want to know everything. Not just about him, but about *you*, Annabelle."

"Tell me," I demanded suddenly, a foolish mistake.

Charlie Marvin smiled. "All right. But seeing as we're now friends, you have to invite me into your apartment."

"And if I say no?"

"You'll say yes, Annabelle. You have to, if you want to learn the truth."

He had me and we both knew it. Curiosity killed the cat, I reminded myself. But the truth was too powerful a lure. Slowly, but surely, I nodded my agreement.

I made him go up the stairs first. Seemed slightly less stupid that way. Kept him in my line of sight. I had the suitcases to carry, I told him. If he followed me, I'd probably whack him with one of them accidentally. He had no idea how clumsy I was, I said.

Charlie accepted my explanation with his cheerful smile. Understanding completely. Not at all challenging.

The long hike up five flights of stairs—lugging suitcases, no less, gave me plenty of time to curse myself. Why had I forgotten the Taser? And how in the world did I end up with a dog who was such a rotten judge of character?

Because I was pretty sure Charlie Marvin was a threat. I just wasn't sure how.

In the good-news department, I had fitness and youth on my side. By the time we hit the fifth-floor landing, Mr. Marvin was breathing hard and holding his side.

He stood back. I worked the first lock on my door. Second. Third.

"Cautious girl," he commented.

"You never know."

My door opened. Once again, I let him do the honors of going first. Then I propped open my door with the giant suitcase.

"In a building structured like this one," he commented, "seems like our every word might echo down the staircase."

"Oh, they will," I assured him. "Screams, too. And we know at least one of my neighbors is home."

He smiled more ruefully this time. "I spooked you that bad?"

"Why don't you tell me what you want to say, Mr. Marvin?"

"I'm not the real threat," he said quietly. I thought he looked a trifle grieved, even sad.

"Mr. Marvin—"

"He is," Charlie said, and pointed behind me.

Bobby was walking. Very fast. D.D. was talking. Very angrily.

"You didn't run a background check on Charlie Marvin?"

"We checked on him. Sinkus followed up on the

417

man just this morning. He does volunteer at the Pine Street Inn. He did have an alibi for last night."

"Oh yeah, and how do you know the Charlie Marvin volunteering at the Pine Street Inn is the same as our Charlie Marvin?"

"What?"

"You gotta go in person. You gotta show a picture. Of all the stupid, rookie mistakes!"

"I didn't make the call," Bobby protested again, then gave up the matter. D.D. was too pissed off to listen. She needed someone to grind up and he was the lucky body standing closest. That would teach him.

They'd put out an APB for a man matching Charlie Marvin's description. Since they had to start with what they knew, officers were converging upon the Pine Street Inn, as well as Columbus Park, Faneuil Hall, and the former site of Boston State Mental, all known Charlie Marvin destinations. With any luck, they'd pick up Marvin within the hour. Before he ever suspected a thing.

"It still doesn't make sense," Bobby grumbled as they hustled through the lobby. "Marvin can't be Uncle Tommy. Too old."

"My car," D.D. said, pushing through the heavy glass doors.

"Where's it parked?"

She told him, he shook his head. "Mine's closer. Plus, you drive like a girl."

"That would be Danica Patrick to you," D.D. muttered, but followed him swiftly toward his Crown Vic.

Then, as they were getting in: "Charlie Marvin lied. That's good enough for me."

"He doesn't fit," Bobby insisted, firing up the engine. "Uncle Tommy would be around fifty. Charlie Marvin looks to have jumped that hurdle at least a decade ago."

"Maybe he just appears old. That's what a life of crime will do to you."

Bobby didn't answer. Just swung his vehicle out, hit the lights, and headed full steam for the Pine Street Inn.

I whirled around toward my open door. Saw nothing. Jerked back around, hands out, feet spread for balance, expecting the counterattack.

Charlie Marvin still stood there, that beatific expression on his face. I thought I was starting to figure it out. Mr. Marvin heard voices when nobody was home. To give credit where credit was due, Bella also seemed to have figured it out. She sat down now, between us in the tiny kitchen, and whined nervously.

"Better late than never," I told her. Sarcasm is totally lost on dogs.

"You're very beautiful," Charlie said.

"Oh, I blush."

"Too old for my taste, though."

"And that quickly, the moment is lost."

"But you're the key. You're the one he really wants."

I stopped breathing again, feeling my mouth go

cotton dry. I should do something. Grab a phone. Yell for help. Run back downstairs. But I didn't move. I didn't want to move. I honestly, God help me, wanted to hear what Charlie Marvin had to say.

"You knew," I whispered.

"I found it. One night a few years back. When they first announced they were going to raze the buildings to the ground, I came back for a farewell tour. One last *adios* to a place to which I'd vowed never to return. But then I heard a rustling in the woods. Got curious. I'd swear to God there was someone out there, then *poof,* he'd simply vanished. It was almost enough to make you believe in ghosts. 'Course, I'm not that superstitious.

"Took me another four nights of scouting before I spotted the glow in the ground. I waited beneath the trees. Until I saw the man rise from the earth, bank the lantern, and disappear into the woods. I got a flashlight after that. Returned right before dawn. Found the opening, descended into the chamber. I never would've imagined. It took my breath away. The work of a master craftsman. I always knew it couldn't last."

"Who did it, Charlie? Who came out of the ground? Who killed those girls?"

He shook his head. "Six girls. Always six girls. No more, no less. I kept checking, kept waiting for something to change. But year after year. Two rows. Three bodies each. The perfect audience. And I never ran into the man again, though Lord knows I tried. I had so many questions for him."

"Did you kill them? Is it your work that was discovered on the grounds?"

He continued as if I'd never spoken: "Then, of course, I saw the story of the grave's discovery on the news. Another victim of urban growth. But that's when it came to me. This would force him into the open, make him want to check on his work one last time. So I started hanging out again, hoping to catch a glimpse. But all I saw was you. And you are a liar."

For the first time, his voice dropped, grew menacing. I took an instinctive step back.

"Who are you?" I asked him. "Because you're certainly no minister."

"Former patient, fellow aficionado of mass graves. Who are you?"

"I'm dead," I told him bluntly. "I'm the ghost that haunts the grounds. I'm waiting for that monster to return so I can kill him."

Charlie's blue eyes narrowed. "Annabelle. Annabelle Granger. Your name was in the paper. From the pit. You really are dead."

And then, a heartbeat later, his face broke into a smile. "You know, I had my heart set on your blonde sergeant friend," he said slyly. I saw the wink of the blade in his hand. "But come to think of it, Annabelle dear, you'll do just fine."

Bobby hastily described Charlie Marvin to the young Latino who greeted them at the Pine Street Inn. Juan Lopez agreed that BPD's Charlie Marvin was indeed the shelter's Charlie Marvin. Had been volunteering there for the past ten years, in fact. Score one for the good guys.

Except Mr. Marvin wasn't currently on the premises. Had taken off about an hour ago. No, Lopez didn't know where. Mr. Marvin was a volunteer after all. They didn't track the man. However, Mr. Marvin was known to work the streets, visiting with the homeless. The police might want to try some of the parks.

Bobby assured him they already had officers on the way. Marvin was wanted for immediate questioning.

Lopez seemed doubtful. "Our Charlie Marvin? Bushy white hair, bright blue eyes, always got a grin on his face, *Charlie* Marvin? What'd he do, man? Steal from the rich and give to the poor?"

"It's official police business. In regard to a murder."

"No way!"

"Yes way."

"Well, score one for AARP."

"Just give us a call if you see him, Mr. Lopez."

"Okay, but now that you got me thinkin', I'd head to Mattapan. Check out the grounds of that old mental institute. You know the one they've been digging up? Charlie's been hanging around there day and night ever since . . . Hey, you don't really think . . ."

"Thanks, Mr. Lopez. We'll be in touch."

Bobby and D.D. headed toward Mattapan, while Bobby got out his cell phone and dialed Annabelle.

anticipated Charlie's first reckless lunge, sidestep-ping on autopilot while my brain tried to sort out many things at once. Charlie Marvin was a former patient at Boston State Mental. Charlie Marvin had discovered the pit. Far from being horrified, Charlie Marvin had been impressed.

It would seem Mr. Marvin had a little violence in his past. He certainly knew how to move with a switch-blade.

After his first failed lunge, we neatly exchanged places within my tiny kitchenette. Before I got too far in congratulating myself, I realized Charlie's move had worked perfectly. He was now positioned between me and my open doorway.

He watched my gaze dart past his shoulder to my best hope at escape, and grinned broadly. "Not bad for an old guy," he offered. "I confess it's been years, but I think I got some magic left."

Bella backed into my legs. She had her hackles up, was regarding Charlie, a low growl in her throat.

Bark, I wanted to yell at my hyper dog. *This would be a good time to make some noise!* She, of course, continued to growl in the back of her throat. Which I couldn't really blame her for, because three minutes into my first confrontation with evil, I still couldn't manage a scream.

Fear sometimes paralyzes the vocal cords, my father had said. He really had done his homework.

Charlie stepped forward, I stepped back and bumped into my kitchen counter. The kitchenette allowed precious little room for maneuvering, but I already realized I couldn't let Charlie herd me deeper into my apartment. The open door, the exposed hallway were my best hope for escape.

I found my balance, prepared to take a stand. He was old, a switchblade wasn't as threatening as a gun. I stood a decent chance.

Charlie feinted low to the right.

I prepared to swing into an arcing kick.

Bella leapt up at the last minute.

And I heard my silly, heroic dog yelp as Charlie's blade buried itself in her chest.

Phone ringing.

Phone ringing.

Phone ringing.

The answering machine picked up. Bobby heard Annabelle's crisp voice announce, *"We are not home right now. Leave your name and number after the beep."*

"Annabelle," he said urgently. "Annabelle, pick up. We need to talk. Got some new information on Charlie Marvin. I'm running late, at least pick up the phone."

Still nothing. Had she grown tired of waiting for him, gone running off on her own? Anything was possible with this woman. Maybe that's why he felt so scared.

Screw it. He hit the brakes.

"What the hell—" D.D. exclaimed.

"He followed her."

"Who?"

"Marvin. He found her in the park last night. Twenty to one, Charlie Marvin knows where Annabelle lives."

36

BELLA WENT DOWN, the phone rang, and I heard my own voice ripped from my throat. "You son of a bitch!"

I launched myself at Charlie, knitting my fingers together and aiming for the soft spot at the base of his throat. He rolled, grabbing my forearm, slicing at me with his switchblade. I toppled, and we became lost in a tangle of limbs. In the detached part of my brain that preferred to watch rather than act, I thought this wasn't the kind of fight I'd been preparing for. There was no fancy footwork, no graceful dodging of well-considered blows. Instead, we grunted and heaved, pummeling each other frantically as we rolled across the floor.

I could taste sweaty salt beading down my face, feel stinging in my hands and arms. Charlie continued to slash madly. I continued to batter at his face, working with my right hand to hit his eyes, while defending with my left.

I was quicker. He was better armed. I was bleeding. He was short of breath. He sliced left, flaying open my cheek. I slammed the heel of my hand into his sternum and he fell back with a gasping cough.

I got my hands beneath me. Staggered to my feet. Lurched for the door.

I couldn't do it. Couldn't leave Bella. He'd kill her for sure.

Charlie was already up, weaving forward. I scuttled back toward the kitchen cabinets. He kept coming. I reached behind me, working the wooden edge of the cabinet with my fingers.

He came within range. I kicked for his chin. He ducked beneath and I finally showed a little skill, reversing my motion, catching the top of his head, and slamming it toward his knees. Not as much force as I wanted, but enough to get the job done.

I got the cabinet open, starting sifting through the disordered stacks of pots and pans.

Charlie was straightening up.

Come on, come on.

And then I found it. Edge of my cast-iron frying pan. The perfect weapon.

Charlie started advancing once more and I prepared to do something I never thought I'd do: kill another human being.

Suddenly, in the distance, the sweetest sound I've ever heard. Footsteps, pounding up the stairs. Charlie froze. I stilled.

Bobby, I thought, Bobby coming to rescue me.

A brown UPS uniform burst through my apartment door.

"Ben!" I gasped.

Just as Charlie said, "Benji?"

And Ben answered in a shocked voice, "Christopher?"

• • •

Bobby got caught in traffic. Of course he got caught in traffic. Because this was Boston, where driving was a blood sport, and just because the other vehicle had a siren and you didn't was no reason not to be an asshole.

He dialed Annabelle's number again. Got the answering machine, hung up. Punched the steering wheel.

"Temper, temper," D.D. drawled.

"Something's wrong."

"Because lover girl isn't waiting anxiously beside the phone?"

He shot her a look. "Seriously. She knew I was returning to take her to a hotel. She wouldn't just leave."

D.D. shrugged. "She has a dog. Maybe she needed to take her out or go for a run."

"Or maybe," Bobby said flatly, "Charlie Marvin beat us there."

His phone rang. He flipped it open without bothering to glance at the display. It wasn't Annabelle, but his buddy, Detective Jason Murphy from the Massachusetts State Police.

"Ran Roger Grayson, like you asked," Jason shot off rapid-fire. "Found record of a storage locker in a facility right off Route Two, north of Arlington. Grayson had been prepaying the fees in five-year chunks. Latest payment ran out a few years back, so the owner's filed a lien. In fact, if we want to come

427

down and clean out the whole thing, that works for the owner. He'd like to get the space back in circulation."

"Excellent."

"Criminal history was negligible. Nothing more than a traffic infraction, and that was twenty-five years ago. Grayson must be a regular choirboy."

"Traffic infraction?"

"Excessive speed. November fifteen, 1982. He was caught doing seventy-five in a sixty zone."

November 15, 1982. Three days after Dori Petracelli was never seen again.

"What else?" Bobby asked the state detective.

"What else? I just started an hour ago, Bobby—"

"What about Walter Petracelli?"

"Nothing yet."

"You'll let me know?"

"I live to serve. Not for nothing, Bobby, but don't let working for the city go to your head."

Jason clicked off. Bobby slid his phone back into his breast pocket. He whooped his sirens again. Nothing happened. The traffic was snarled too tight for any car to give way.

He glanced at his watch. They were on Atlantic Avenue now. One and a half, maybe two miles from Annabelle's apartment.

"I'm pulling over," he announced.

"What?"

"Forget the car, D.D. We're strong, we're fast. Let's run."

"Ben, Ben, thank God you're here. He's stabbed Bella. He's insane. You gotta help us. Bella, poor Bella, I'm here, girl, it's okay, it's gonna be okay."

I'd abandoned the cast-iron frying pan in favor of my dog, pulling her onto my lap. I could feel the warmth of her blood oozing all over her fine white fur. She whimpered. Tried to lick at my hands, tend her cut.

"Ben!" I shouted again.

But Ben wasn't moving. He was standing in my doorway, staring at Charlie Marvin.

"It was *you?* Oh my goodness, still waters do run deep!" Charlie said.

"She's mine," Ben said flatly. "You can't have her. She's *mine.*"

"Call the police," I was sobbing. "Call nine-one-one, demand Detective Bobby Dodge, ask for EMTs. I don't know who they send for dogs, but an ambulance should do the trick. Ben? Are you listening to me? *Ben?*"

Ben finally looked at me. As he stepped into my little apartment. As he closed the door and started working the locks, one by one, behind him.

"It's okay now," he told me solemnly. "Uncle Tommy's here now, Amy, and I'll take care of everything."

Charlie started laughing. The sound quickly turned into a wheezing rattle. The blow to his sternum had knocked something loose. Now that the buzzing was fading from my ears, I could feel my own aches and pains. My bruised ribs, sliced ankles, gashed cheek.

At least I gave as good as I got. Charlie's right eye was swelling shut. As he scooted across the floor, away from Ben, he favored his left side, gasping as if in pain.

My brain was not computing anymore. I didn't care about Charlie. I didn't understand Ben. I just wanted to get Bella out of here. I wanted my dog to be safe.

Which was the best thing to focus on, because the conversation going on around me was too terrible to believe.

"How'd you kill 'em?" Charlie wanted to know. "One at a time? In pairs? How'd you lure them in? I've always stuck to prostitutes myself. No one ever misses them."

"Did you hurt her?" Ben was still staring at Charlie.

"I've been looking for you, Benji. Ever since I first discovered the chamber. I thought *I* was clever. Working with the homeless so no one would question how I happened to be on such-and-such street corner at such-and-such night. Why I happened to know so many whores who disappeared. But then . . . I couldn't believe the ingeniousness of the chamber, the scope of your achievement. If only I'd thought of it first. Oh, the things I could've done."

"She's bleeding."

"How long did you keep them alive? Days, weeks, months? Again, the possibilities. My cover afforded me the perfect opportunity to relish the hunt. But after that . . . It's the lack of time, the need to rush, rush, rush that's always troubled me. You spend so much energy luring them in, binding them up, and then, just when you're starting to enjoy things, you have to be practical. Someone might hear a noise, someone might get curious. You have to end the romance and get the job done. Doesn't do any good to call attention to yourself, even for the special ones.

"Tell me the truth," Charlie wanted to know. "Weren't you the least bit inspired by my work? The nurse in '75. Totally an impulse job. I was out on the grounds. She was out on the grounds. One thing led to another. It was the biggest thing that ever happened to Boston State Mental, well, until your chamber was discovered. Benji? Benji, are you listening to me?"

Ben leaned over Charlie. The look on his face raised the fine hairs on the back of my neck. I dug my fingers into Bella's fur. I willed her not to make a sound.

I placed one hand on the floor and started silently easing myself and Bella toward the door.

"You hurt my Amy," Ben said. "Now I must hurt you."

At the last minute, Charlie seemed to realize he didn't have an ally. At the last minute, he raised the switchblade, realizing the danger he was in.

Ben caught Charlie's wrist in a single muscled hand. I heard the crunch of bones.

I hit the door, reaching up frantically, scrambling with the locks. Why, oh why did I have so many locks?

I couldn't look, but I also couldn't do a thing to block out the sound.

As my uncle tore the switchblade from Charlie Marvin's crushed hand. Then, very neatly, jammed the entire blade in Charlie Marvin's eye. A scream. A wet popping sound. A long, low wheezing groan, like air being let out of tires.

Then silence.

"Oh, Amy," Ben said.

I couldn't help myself. Huddled with Bella against the locked door, I started to cry.

37

"YOU'RE ALL I ever wanted, Amy," Ben was saying. "The other girls—they meant nothing to me. Mistakes. I saw the error of my ways years ago. And I waited for you. Until one day my patience was rewarded." He reached out with a bloody hand and stroked my cheek. I tried to shrink back; there was no place to go.

"Please unlock the door, Ben." I wanted to sound firm, but my voice came out shaky. "Bella, she's hurt. She needs immediate medical attention. Please, Ben."

He looked at me, sighed heavily. "You know I can't do that, Amy."

"I won't tell anyone about you. I'll say Charlie attacked me. Was crazy. I stabbed him myself. Look at the cuts all over my body. They'll believe me."

"It's not the same anymore. In the beginning, when

I found you again, it was okay. I realized immediately that no one else knew who you were. You were special, untouched. You belonged to me."

"I won't move. I'll stay right here. Everything can be just the way it was before. I'll order fabric, you can deliver it every day."

"But it's not. You know now. The police know. It's not the same."

I closed my eyes, fighting for control. Bella whimpered again. The sound gave me strength. "I don't understand. You made it twenty-five years without me. You took those other girls. Obviously I mean nothing to you."

"Oh no," he said immediately, earnestly. "I didn't stop because I wanted to. That's not how it was at all." Ben removed his brown cap. And for the first time I saw the furrow running along the top of his head, a twisted scar that bore no hair. "This is what stopped me. If it hadn't been for this, I would've pursued you forever. Twenty-five years ago, Amy, you would've been mine."

"Oh God," I moaned, because in that moment I finally heard it. Ben may not have looked like my father, but if I listened to his voice, his intense, earnest voice as he sought to make his very important point . . . He sounded exactly like my father. Same tone, same rhythm, same voice.

Had I realized it before, made the connection on some subconscious level? Then let him in, made him my sole connection to the outside world because blood was thicker than water and part of me had rejoiced in finding family again?

"All I've ever wanted was someone who wouldn't leave me," he was saying now, my father's earnest voice continuing to emit from a terribly scarred skull. "Someone who would have to stay. I thought your mom was the one, but she misunderstood. Then I got myself thrown into prison." His tone fell, then picked back up. "But when I got out, I saw you and I understood.

"The way you smiled at me, Amy. The way you gripped my finger in your pudgy little fist. You were my family. You were the one person who would always love me, who would never leave. And I was so happy. Until the day I showed up and you were gone. Your whole family. Vanished."

"Bella is hurt," I pleaded. "Please."

"It was a terrible time. I knew, of course, that you never would've left me by choice. Obviously your father had made you do it." Ben took my hand, stroked my wrist with his blood-splattered fingers. "So I started asking around. An entire family can't just disappear. Everyone leaves some kind of trace. But no one could tell me anything. Then it came to me. My brother would need a job to support his family. Who could help get him a job? His former employer, of course. So I broke into Dr. Badington's house. I found his wife."

"What?"

"I came by in the afternoon. Naturally, Mrs. Badington refused to speak at first, but by the time I was done with her cat, she told me plenty. About your father's new position at MIT. A house in Arlington. Better yet, she never related my visit to anyone. The kinds of things I did to her, after all, are not the things you mention in polite society. Plus I promised that if she ever said a word, I'd return and do the exact same things to her husband."

"Oh my God . . ."

"I set out for Massachusetts. I was going to see you that very night. But it was late, I got lost and the craziest thing happened. I got carjacked. Wrong place, wrong time, with four big brothers who beat the shit out of me. Then they took my clothes and they . . . And then there was darkness. For such a long time.

"Bit by bit, I came around. I relearned how to eat, dress myself, brush my teeth. I spoke to very nice doctors who told me my life had gotten off to the wrong start but now was my second chance. I could be whoever I wanted to be, they said. I could reinvent myself.

"And for a while, I tried. It seemed like a nice idea. I could be Benji, whose father was a CIA operative and not just some drunken asshole who one day murdered his own wife before blowing out his brains. I liked being Benji. I really did.

"But I was so lonely, Amy. You must understand what it's like. To have no family. To have no one ever call you by your real name. To have no one who knows the whole you, the real you, and not just the façade all of us must wear in public. It's no way to live."

"Stop it," I whispered, tugging at my hand again. "Stop it, stop it." But he wouldn't shut up. He wouldn't stop speaking, my father's voice, my own thoughts, wiggling like snakes into my brain.

"I found the culvert one day when I was walking the grounds. It intrigued me enough to make it my own little home away from home. I was doing well by then, still living in the institute but enrolled in a nearby school. The culvert became a chamber, the chamber my study hall, and then, one day . . .

"I saw her. Walking home from school. I saw her and I could tell from the look on her face that she saw me, too. She liked me, she wanted to be with me. She was the one who would never leave."

"Shhhhh," I tried again, "Shh, shh, shh. You're crazy. I hate you. My parents hated you. I wish you were dead."

"At the last minute, she changed her mind. She fought me. She screamed. So I had to . . . It was over very fast, and afterward I was sad. It wasn't how I wanted things to be. You must believe me, Amy. But then it occurred to me. I could keep her. I knew exactly the place. And she would never leave me then."

"You are sick!" I pulled hard at my hand one last time, finally got it away from him. He didn't seem concerned.

"I tried again," he said matter-of-factly. "And again and again and again. Each time the relationships started with such promise, then quickly soured. Until one day I understood. I didn't want any of those stupid, useless girls. I wanted *you*. And then I remembered what Mrs. Badington said. And I found you again.

"My Amy, my precious, precious Amy. We came so close that time. I took things slower, starting off with little gifts to gain your trust. The smile on your face as you opened each box, discovered each treasure. It was just how I'd imagined it to be. It was just what I wanted it to be. You were going to be mine."

He stopped, sighed, paused. I nearly wept in relief.

But he wasn't done yet. How could he be done, when we both knew the worst was yet to come?

"Roger saw me. I thought I was being clever, but, oh, big brothers. They have a way of knowing what little brothers are up to. And he knew. Of course he knew. I realized I'd have to move quickly. Except next thing I knew, cops had found my attic hidey-hole. And instead of sweeping you away, I was running from the law. By the time I regrouped, it was over. The house was there, but nobody was home.

"Roger," he said flatly, "had always been one smart son of a bitch. Naturally, I made him pay."

Ben's hand had come up. He was rubbing his scar almost thoughtlessly. A nervous habit meant to soothe? Or reminder of a memory that still burned?

"You kidnapped Dori," I murmured.

"Had to," he said with a shrug. "Needed someone. Didn't want to be alone. And she'd stolen your locket. I couldn't let her do that."

"She didn't take the locket, you bastard. I gave it to her. She was my friend, and I shared with her because that's what friends do. You're terrible, you're horrible, and I will never be with you. Your touch makes me sick!"

"Oh, Amy." He sighed again. "You don't need to be jealous. Dori wasn't who I really wanted. She was merely a means to an end. I took her and Roger came back to me."

I blinked wildly in shock. "You saw my father again? In Arlington?"

"Roger came home. Just like I knew he must. Once, a very long time ago, Roger loved me. He would hide with me in the closet and hold my hand while our parents yelled. 'It's okay,' he'd tell me. 'I won't let anything happen to you. I'll keep you safe.' Then one night, our father walked into the kitchen, found our mother standing there, and shot her three times in the chest. *Boom, boom, boom.* He turned, spotted me next. He raised the gun. I knew he was going to fire. Except Roger stopped him. Roger told him to put the gun down. Roger told him if he really wanted to kill someone, the least he could do was kill himself.

"And our father did exactly that. The dumbfuck pressed the muzzle against his temple and pulled the trigger. Bye-bye, Daddy. Hello, boarding school.

"Except in boarding school, Roger disappeared. He had his own classes, his own friends, his own life. He left me. Just like that.

"So I waited in the house in Arlington. Because I

knew then what I had always known. That Roger would come back. That it would be just him and me again. With a gun."

"You tried to kill my father!"

Ben looked at me. He shook his head sadly, touched his scar. "Oh no, Amy. Your father, my dear brother, tried to kill me."

Home stretch. Bobby and D.D. came jogging up Hanover, dodging pedestrians, ignoring honking taxis. Dusk was falling, the street growing crowded as eateries opened their doors for the night. Bobby and D.D. weaved around teenagers yakking on cell phones, mothers pushing strollers, locals walking dogs.

D.D. had an easy rhythm. Bobby was starting to flag. No doubt about it: Once this case was done, he was getting his sorry ass back to the gym.

Still no word from Annabelle.

He used his growing panic to power his stride.

And he ran.

I didn't believe him. My father with a gun? Even Mr. Petracelli had said my father couldn't stand firearms. Hearing about the night with his parents, I could certainly understand why.

But apparently, even for my liberal-minded father, Dori's abduction had been the final straw. Somehow, he'd gotten himself a gun. And then he'd caught a red-eye back to Boston to track down his brother.

"Roger, please don't go. Roger, I'm begging you, please don't do this. . . ."

According to Tommy/Ben, the two brothers had squared off in the darkened shadows of my former home. Tommy, bearing the crowbar he'd used to break in. My father, wielding a small handgun.

"I didn't take him seriously," Ben told me now. "Roger couldn't hurt me. He'd saved me. He loved me. He had told me he would always take care of me. But then . . .

"He looked so tired standing there. Asked me if I'd taken that girl. Asked me if I'd taken any others. What could I do? I told him the truth. That I'd kidnapped six girls. That I'd encased them in plastic and kept them as my own little family. And that it still wasn't enough. I wanted you, Amy. I needed you. I would never rest until you were mine.

" 'I used to believe,' Roger said quietly, 'that nature didn't really matter. Nurture could always overcome, whether it was parents nurturing a child or even a person such as me, learning to nurture myself. With enough time, attention, attitude, all of us could be anyone we wanted to be. I was wrong. DNA matters. Genetics live. Our father lives, inside of you.'

"I told my brother that was fascinating, given he was the one holding the gun. He accepted that. Even nodded as if that made sense to him.

" 'True,' he said, 'because on my own, I never thought I could do such a thing.'

"Then he shot me. Just like that. Raised the gun. Put

a bullet in my head." Ben's fingers brushed his scar.

"Shock is a funny thing. I heard the sound. I felt a burning sensation in my forehead. But I remained standing for a long time, at least I think I did. I stood and I looked at my brother.

" 'I love you,' " I said. Then I fell.

"He walked over to me.

" 'Promise me you'll never leave,' I said.

"And Roger walked out the door.

"I don't know how long I was there. I blacked out, went unconscious, something. But when I came to, I discovered I could move. So I left. I kept going until some guy stopped me and said, 'You know, man, I think you might need a doctor.'

"He called an ambulance. Six hours later, surgeons removed a twenty-two-caliber slug that had ricocheted around the front part of my brain. That was nearly twenty-five years ago, and I haven't felt much since. Not happy. Not sad. Not desperate, not angry. Not even alone.

"It is, dear Amy, no way to live."

Tommy's story seemed to be winding down. I was still frozen with shock. That my father had shot his own brother. That Tommy had managed to live. That two brothers' lives could be stuck in such a cycle of violence.

"You don't feel anything?" I asked tentatively. "Nothing at all?"

Tommy shook his head.

"You never stalked any more girls?"

"I can't fall in love."

"Then you don't need me."

"But of course I do. You're family. You always need family."

"Ben—"

"Tommy. I want to hear you say it. It's been so many years. Come on, Amy. For your uncle. Let me hear it from your lips."

Perhaps I should've humored him. But the instant he asked me to say his name, I couldn't do it. I was trapped in my own apartment, bleeding, exhausted, clutching my dying dog. Denying my uncle his name was the only power I had left.

I shook my head. And my dear emotionless Uncle Tommy bent and slapped me across the face. My lips split, I tasted blood. I drew it in and spat it back at him.

"I hate you, I hate you, I hate you!" I cried.

His fist slammed into my head, and my skull rebounded with a crack off the door.

"Say it!" he roared.

"Fuck you!"

He drew back his arm, but this time I was waiting for him.

"Hey, Ben," I yelled. "Catch!"

And I threw Bella at him, praying as I'd never prayed before, that even a homicidal maniac would have the instinct to grab.

Bobby heard the scream first. He was half a block

from Annabelle's apartment, twenty yards ahead of D.D. He was still trying to tell himself there was a logical explanation for Annabelle not to answer her phone, that of course she was all right.

Then he heard the yell. And kicked his pace into high gear.

The front door of her building slammed open. A young man dashed into the street. "Police, police, someone call the police. I think the UPS man is trying to kill her!"

Bobby hit the stairs as D.D. whipped out her phone and called for backup.

Ben staggered back under Bella's weight, and as he did so, I finally managed to scream, a shrill sound of pure frustration. I hated myself for sacrificing my best friend. I hated Ben for forcing me to do it.

I threw myself at the door, working frantically at the locks. I got the first two undone, just as Ben dropped Bella and grabbed at the back of my shirt. I whipped around and elbowed him in the side of the head, knocking off his glasses.

He fell back; I found the chain lock.

"Come on, come on, come on . . ."

My fingers were shaking too hard, they didn't want to cooperate. I was sobbing hysterically, losing control.

Then I heard it. Footsteps pounding up the stairs. A welcome, familiar voice. "Annabelle!"

"Bobby!" I managed to cry, then Ben tackled me from behind.

I went down hard, my nose thwacking against the door. Tears sprang to my eyes, another enraged scream bursting from my throat. The door shook, Bobby hurtling himself against it. But it held, of course it held. Because I had chosen this door for its strength, while accessorizing it with half a dozen locks. I had built a fortress to keep me safe, and now it would kill me.

"Annabelle, Annabelle, Annabelle!" Bobby roared in frustration from the other side.

Then Tommy's rasping voice, hot in my ear. "It's your fault, Amy, you made me do it. You've left me no other choice."

From far away, I heard my father. His endless lectures, his constant preaching:

"Sometimes, when frightened, it's difficult to make a sound. So break things. Bang your fist into the wall, throw furniture. Make noise, sweetheart, put up a fight. Always fight."

Tommy, grabbing my shoulders. Tommy, flipping me over. Tommy, holding up Charlie's bloody switchblade in his triumphant fist.

"You will never leave."

"I'm gonna shoot," Bobby yelled. "Get away from the door. One, two—"

Pinned to the floor, I tore the pendant from around my neck. Tommy raised his blade. I snapped the thin metal cap from my crystal pendant.

And I tossed my parents' ashes into Tommy's face.

Tommy reared up, wiping frantically at his eyes.

Just as Bobby opened fire.

I watched Tommy's body jerk, one, two, three, four times. Then Bobby kicked open my shattered door.

Instead of going down, Tommy twisted toward the sound, charging like a wounded beast.

I sprang to my feet. Bobby feinted left. Tommy went tearing through the shattered doorway, hit the railing of the fifth-floor landing, and flailed his arms wildly for balance.

I thought he might make it.

So I hit him low and solid from behind.

Then, my father's daughter, I watched my uncle fall to his death below.

38

THE TRUTH SHALL set you free. Another old saying. Not one I ever heard from my father's lips. Given what I now know about his past, I think I understand.

Six months have passed since that last bloody evening in my apartment. Six months of police questioning, storage-unit recovery, DNA results, and, yes, even a press conference. I have my own agent. She believes she can get me millions of dollars from a major Hollywood studio. And, of course, there will be a book deal.

I can't imagine myself talking to Larry King. Or profiting from my family's tragedy. Then again, a girl's gotta eat, and these days, the custom-window-treatment clients are hardly knocking at my door. I haven't decided yet.

At the moment, I'm in the shower, shaving my legs. I'm nervous. A little excited. I think now, more than ever, that there is much to learn about myself.

Here are the truths as I see them, thus far:

One, my dog is strong. Bella did not die on my kitchen floor. No, my incredibly brave canine companion held up better than I did, as Bobby hustled us into the back of an arriving patrol car and raced us to an emergency vet. Charlie had sliced Bella's shoulder all the way to the bone. Damaged some tendons. Cost her a great deal of blood. But two thousand dollars of the best medical care later, Bella came home. She is partial to sleeping on my bed now. I'm partial to giving her giant hugs. No jogging for us yet. But we're building up our strength with some very brisk walks.

Two, wounds heal. I spent twenty-four hours in the hospital, mostly because I wouldn't leave Bella's side until the vet forced me to go, and by that time I'd lost plenty of blood myself. My cheek required twelve stitches. My legs, twenty. My right arm, thirty-one. I guess my cover-girl days are over. I like my scars, however. Sometimes in the middle of the night, I trace the fine, puckered lines with my fingertips. War wounds. My father would be proud.

Three, some questions will never be answered. In my father's storage unit, I found my mother's prized sofa; my baby album, complete with my original birth certificate; miscellaneous family memorabilia; and finally, a note from my father. It was dated one week after we had returned to Boston, when I imagine his anxiety had been sky-high. It didn't provide an explanation. Instead, on June 18, 1993, my father wrote: *Whatever happens, know that I always loved you, and tried my best.*

Did he anticipate dying in Boston? Believe that returning to the scene of so much tragedy sealed his doom? I have no idea. I suspect he knew that his brother was still alive. No doubt my father had checked the papers for news of an unknown body found in an abandoned Arlington home, and when no such story appeared, realized his efforts hadn't been as final as he had wished. Then again, why not come back and try again? Why return to my mother and me in Florida?

I don't know. I will never know. Maybe killing isn't as easy as it looks. My father tried it once and that was enough for him. So after that, we ran. Every time a child disappeared, any time an Amber Alert hit the local papers, that was it. My father bought new identities, my mother packed our suitcases, and my family hit the road.

Ironically enough, the police believe Uncle Tommy never followed us. The bullet may not have killed him, but the brain damage it caused seemed to derail most of his psychotic impulses. He took a job with UPS. He became a model, if somewhat antisocial, citizen. He got on with his life.

Only my family remained rooted in the past, always running, always searching for a sense of safety my father didn't know how to find.

Four, some truths aren't meant to be told. For example, after much investigating, the police officially ruled Ben/Tommy's death an accident. In an armed confrontation with law enforcement, the suspect was shot four times through a locked door by an identified officer. The officer was then able to force open the door, at which time the wounded suspect raced from the apartment in a desperate attempt to escape. In his pain and confusion, he accidentally flipped over the fifth-story banister and fell to his death.

Needless to say, Bobby and I don't discuss this incident. Neither does D.D., who was in the downstairs lobby, and thus, according to the official report, was not in a position to see what happened before the giant splat.

Though, a few weeks ago, she gave me a T-shirt that reads: Accidents Happen.

Five, even psychopaths have community spirit. Charlie Marvin turned out to be former Boston State Mental patient Christopher Eola. The Boston PD now believe he murdered at least a dozen prostitutes while posing as a selfless advocate for the homeless. Taking a page from Ted Bundy's handbook—Bundy had volunteered at a suicide hotline—Charlie had cleverly used his position to ingratiate himself with potential victims while continuing to deflect the attention of the police.

He'd recently grown bold, however, with his latest

target being lead investigator D.D. Warren. A handwriting expert confirmed that the note left on D.D.'s car was most likely written by Charlie. The four dogs shot and killed the night of the rendezvous at Boston State Mental all bore identity chips that were traced to two different drug dealers/dog trainers, who confirmed a kindly older gentleman as the person who purchased their prized "pets."

Best guess—Charlie insinuated himself into the investigation in an attempt to identify and contact the original perpetrator of the mass grave. Along the way, however, he became infatuated with D.D. and started some head games of his own. The police found bomb-making materials in Charlie's Boston apartment. Apparently, he'd been plotting further misdeeds when Tommy had stabbed him to death in my kitchen.

Eola's parents refused to claim his body. Last I heard, his remains were dispatched to an unmarked grave.

Six, closure is harder to come by than people think. We buried Dori this morning. By we, I mean her parents, myself, and two hundred other well-wishers, most of whom had never met Dori when she was alive but were touched by the circumstances of her death. I watched retired Lawrence police officers cry, neighbors who twenty-five years ago searched in vain for her in the woods. The BPD task force attended the service, standing in the back. Afterward, Mr. and Mrs. Petracelli shook hands with every single officer. When Mrs. Petracelli came to D.D., she grabbed the sergeant in an enormous hug, then both women broke down crying.

Mrs. Petracelli had asked me if I would say a few words. Not the eulogy; their priest did that and he was okay, I guess. She was hoping I might tell people of the Dori I knew, because none of these people had ever gotten a chance to meet that child. It sounded like a good idea. I thought I would. But when the time came, I couldn't speak. The emotions I felt were too strong to share.

Mostly I think I should take that movie deal. Because I would like to donate the money to Mrs. Petracelli's foundation. I would like more Doris to be returned to their parents. I would like more childhood friends to have the opportunity to say "I love you, I'm sorry, good-bye."

The truth shall set you free.

No, the truth just tells you what was. It explains the nightmares I have three or four times a week. It explains the pile of vet bills and medical bills that I still face. It tells me why a UPS man I thought I knew only in passing listed one Amy Grayson as his sole beneficiary. It explains why that same UPS man spent the first fifteen years of his service constantly changing routes, apparently searching the entire state of Massachusetts for a family he was convinced couldn't have moved that far away. Until one day, quite by accident, all his searching was rewarded and he found me.

Truth tells me that my parents really did love me,

and it reminds me that love, alone, is not enough.

Really, what a girl needs is a sense of identity.

I'm as clean as I'm ever going to get. Legs and armpits shaved. Pulse points dabbed with oil scented with cinnamon. I should put on a dress. It's just not me. In the end I go with low-riding black slacks and a really cool gold-sequined camisole I picked up for next to nothing at Filene's Basement.

Definitely heels.

Bella starts to whine. She recognizes the signs of my impending departure. Bella doesn't like to be alone in the apartment anymore. For that matter, neither do I. I can still see Charlie Marvin's lifeless body sprawled in my kitchen. I'm sure Bella can still smell the blood soaked into the floor.

Next week, I decide. I will apartment hunt. Thirty-two years later, it's time for the past to be the past.

Doorbell rings.

Shit. My palms are sweating. I'm a wreck.

I cross briskly to my brand-new door, careful not to trip in my heels. I start working the locks—three, a slight improvement from five—while praying I don't have lipstick on my teeth.

I open the door, and I'm not disappointed. He is wearing khakis with a light blue shirt that complements his gray eyes, topped with a navy sports jacket. His hair is still damp from his shower; I can smell his aftershave.

Yesterday, at 2:00 p.m., with the last set of remains identified and no one alive to prosecute, the Boston police officially ended their investigation into the Mattapan crime scene and dissolved the task force.

Yesterday, at 2:01 p.m., we struck our deal.

Now he holds out a bouquet of flowers and, of course, a dog treat. It goes without saying that Bella won't be left behind.

"Hello," he says, a smile crinkling the corners of his eyes. "Bobby Dodge, pleased to meet you. Have I mentioned yet that I have a thing for barbecues, white picket fences, and barky white dogs?"

I take the flowers, hand Bella the chew bone. Keeping with the script, I stick out my hand.

He of course kisses the backs of my fingers and sends shivers up my spine.

"Nice to meet you, Bobby Dodge." I take a deep breath. "My name is Annabelle."

Author's Note and Acknowledgements

AS ALWAYS, I'M indebted to quite a few people who helped make this book possible. From the Boston Police Department: Deputy Daniel Coleman; Director of Communications Nicole St. Peter; Detective Juan Torres; Detective Wayne Rock; Lieutenant Detective Michael Galvin; and finally, my dear neighbor and fellow Kiwanian, Robert "Chuck" Kyle, BPD retired, who helped set all the wheels in motion (and has more stories than one author could ever hope to honor in a single novel). These people gave patiently of their time and expertise; naturally, I exploited all of them and took substantial fictional license.

My humble gratitude to Marv Milbury, former AN at the Boston State Mental Hospital. Marv is an exceptionally nice man whose stories are guaranteed to curl anyone's hair. During our lunch, even the waitress gave up working and started listening to him talk. Again, more stories than one book could hold, but I did my best. For people who are really into the history of mental institutes, I did have to fudge the time line of operations but tried to keep to the spirit of the mental institute experience.

Thanks also to forensic anthropologist Ann Marie Mires, who gave generously of her personal time to help me understand proper protocol for exhuming a thirty-year-old grave. For the record, the information on wet mummification came straight off the Internet, is probably totally incorrect, and shouldn't be held against Ann Marie. That's what fiction writers are for.

To Betsy Eliot, dear friend and fellow author, who came to my rescue once more. Not many people will still take your calls after you've asked them to set up a shooting in Boston. Betsy not only assisted invaluably with Bobby's first book, *Alone*, but when I called her up this time and told her I needed to tour an abandoned mental institute, she cheerfully drove me straight there. At dusk. In rush-hour traffic. Love you, Bets.

To the real-life D.D. Warren, neighbor, dear friend, and good sport, who never questioned me using her name for what we both assumed would be a fairly minor character in *Alone*. Leave it to D.D. to steal the show and end up in two novels. The real D.D. is as gorgeous as her fictional counterpart and, fortunately for all of us, equally dedicated to serving her community. She is also blessed with a handsome, funny, brilliant husband, John Bruni, who got to be a lieutenant in *Alone* but had to sit this book out. You're a good sport, John, and a wonderful poet.

To my brother Rob, who graciously volunteered his coworkers to populate and staff the Boston State Mental portrayed in my novel. See, I'm not the only member of the family who's devious and twisted.

To good friends and seamstresses extraordinaire Cathy Caruso and Marie Kurmin, who provided some basic information on custom window treatments. I didn't get to use as much as I would've liked—my fault, not yours. I swear I will do better next time.

And to the lucky Joan Barker, winner of the third annual Kill a Friend, Maim a Buddy sweepstakes at www.LisaGardner.com. Joan named her dear friend Inge Lovell to be the lucky stiff in my latest novel. This is what friendship will do to you. Hope both of you ladies enjoy, and for the rest of you, hey, come September the search for literary immortality will begin once again. . . .

Finally, under the care and feeding of authors: to Anthony, for all the reasons he knows best; to Grace, who is already at work on her first novel (she's partial to hot pink ink); to Donna Kenison and Susan Presby, who let me crash at the gorgeous Mt. Washington Hotel so I could make my deadline and preserve my sanity; and to our dear neighbors Pam and Glenda, for Monday ladies' night, cheese cookies, and leftover salmon. It's the little things that make a neighborhood feel like home.

Brooke County Library
945 Main Street
Wellsburg, WV 26070

Center Point Publishing
600 Brooks Road ● PO Box 1
Thorndike ME 04986-0001 USA

(207) 568-3717

US & Canada:
1 800 929-9108